ORAN-ROY

A NOVEL BY

KAYE SWAN

Author: KAYE SWAN

National Library of Australia Cataloguing-in-Publication entry

Creator: Swan, Kaye, author.

Title: Oran-Roy / Kaye Swan.

ISBN: 9780994286604 (paperback)

Target Audience: For young adults.

Subjects: Fantasy fiction.

Dewey Number: A823.4

Published with the assistance of www.bookpublishingaustralia.com

"On the 23rd of July, 2007, after completing Harry Potter and the Deathly Hallows, I started to become teary. What was I going to read now that my favourite book series had come to an end? But then, as corny as the expression is, a bolt of lightning shot through my brain and triggered an idea I had never even considered for myself! In that moment, I decided to begin this story.
The journey of writing has been beyond magical. Like the characters, I transcended to another world when writing."

Kaye Swan

"Dreaming cleansed the wounds of the past's painful memories.
Dreaming revealed what the future could bring.
Dreaming became a reliable friend, never leaving my side.
Dreaming made each word on these pages possible."

Kaye Swan

 *To those who supported me on this*
journey,
Thank you.

A special thank you goes to Robert Victor Stephenson and Elissa Jakymin for editing the manuscript, Lauren Stephenson for composing the carrier score, Barbara Dias for re-illustrating my original drawings, Thalia McMurray for the body paint art, and finally, to Perfect Skin Salon, for giving my nails a beautiful manicure for the book cover photo shoot.

"Whether you believe you can or whether you believe you can't, you're absolutely right."
Henry Ford

"I believe I can ... and I will."
Kaye Swan

Brianna's Symbols

The Carrier Device

Map of Oran-Roy

Chapter One

Happy Birthday

It had been three days since I had seen Ethan, Logan and Charlotte. I longed to see them. The faceless men cloaked in black, velvety robes had been ordered to find my whereabouts and imprison me. Their leader was my own flesh and blood.

Paying close attention to the water droplets falling from the ceiling and forming a puddle had occupied the empty hours in a chilling cell. I grew tired of seeing my reflection in the puddle of icy water. I tired of staring at that dark brown, thick, curly and uncontrollable hair, as well as a brown right eye, blue left eye and thick lashes and eyebrows. Handcuffs covered the markings on my wrists. On my left wrist was a circular marking containing a bow and arrow and on my right wrist, a circle filled by a cross. There was slight comfort in not seeing them. I felt normal; after all, what seventeen-year-old girl has tattoos on her wrists since her infancy?

The dungeon door thudded.

"Who's there?" My heart felt like it was beating in my ears. Was the guard here? Could it be my rescuers, my friends? I hoped that it was the latter. I started to shake on the cold dungeon floor and didn't dare blink. Another thud on the door followed. I let out an involuntary scream. The door opened. My friends were finally here. Relief overwhelmed me and my frayed nerves were somewhat calmed.

"It's about time!" I was still shaking. "Ethan, they took Charlotte! We have to hurry or we'll be too late!"

"Don't worry sis, we'll find her. Whatever it takes, Brianna, we will find her." I am so lucky to have someone as supportive and brave as Ethan in my life. Speaking of brave, Logan was also there. Those deep blue eyes and ebony-black hair dragged me in like a lifeline. Logan's light complexion was the perfect backdrop for his eyes.

"Here, let me help you with those." The closer he came, the faster my heart raced. But, did he feel the same about me? His rough and sturdy hands unlocked my handcuffs. As the pressure was released, a burning sensation gripped my wrists; red indentations remained.

"Are you okay?" His smooth fingers stroked the rough skin of my wrists.

"I will be."

"Come on you two, let's get a move on!" Ethan rolled his eyes and urged us along with a wave.

A cold chill ran down my spine as Logan's warm hands clenched my arms. Once I was steady, Logan placed his hands gently on my shoulders and met my eyes. "Brianna, do you have any idea where Charlotte is?" His cool touch almost distracted me from answering the question. I went scarlet.

"I overheard the guard. I think he said the north wing of the castle - near the King's Chambers."

Logan's eyes were still deeply focussed on mine. "Then that is where we will head!"

"*Come on!*" Ethan waved his hands again, ushering us along.

Logan's hands fell from my shoulders and held my waist to support me. "Let's go then." His voice was so smooth and hypnotic; he intoxicated me. It had to stop! There were more important things to deal with!

Logan guided me through the dark hallway, a collage of grey cobbled bricks and rustic chandeliers.

Ethan stretched his arm and stopped Logan. "*Wait!* I almost forgot. This belongs to you." My father's sword rested in Ethan's hands.

"Ethan, I'm … I'm speechless."

Logan covered my mouth and whispered, "Let's keep it that way, because I can hear a guard on his way down the hall."

The sound of footsteps echoed down the eerie hallway. Logan signalled for us to hide behind the dungeon door. The footsteps drew closer. I took long, slow breaths. The guard was now just outside the door. Was he checking on me, or just doing a routine patrol? Once again, I began to shake.

CLANG!

My sword! It slipped completely out of my hands! What had I done? The guard barged through the door. Ethan and Logan sprang forth, their swords drawn with intent. The clashing of metal resonated throughout the dungeon, the semi-darkness illuminated by the sparks that spat from the blades. Within seconds, the guard lay motionless on the floor. He was dead.

"I ... I'm sorry," I said, still in shock. *I could have cost us our lives. Why couldn't I control my nerves?*

Reassuringly, Logan held me. "It's alright Brianna! It's over!" For the moment, I was safe and secure and began to calm down.

Ethan had such a cheeky smirk across his face. "Just, try not to do it again." He returned my father's sword to my quivering hands.

As I walked beyond the door, my eyes met with Logan's. I could not let go. They were too perfect. The hypnotic nature of his eyes transfixed me, blinding me to my surroundings and causing me to trip over the dead guard's legs. Logan caught me. Once again I felt safe and secure. If only I could capture this moment and make it last. Our faces were quite close - so close I could feel his warm, sweet breath against my neck. My insides jolted. Our lips grew nearer. Finally, our lips met. His soft, smooth lips touched mine.

"Brianna?" Who was that? It wasn't Ethan. "Brianna Shield!"

Darn it! The sound of Mrs Smith ended my fantasy. I knew this moment with Logan was too good to be true - nothing more than a story fabricated in my mind - but certainly one to jot down in my growing journal of short stories at a later date.

"I'm sorry, Miss. I'm just tired."

"Brianna that is the third time this week I have caught you daydreaming in MY classroom!" It wasn't necessary for Mrs Smith to emphasise that this was *her* class. Mrs Smith's deep green eyes overlooked her oval glasses as her head tilted forward, giving me her signature death stare. Her hair was fluffy and fair. It may be silly of me to describe Mrs Smith this way, but her face always reminded me of a mouse - a mouse with a scrawny, tight face.

"It is unacceptable, Brianna!" Her glare was so intimidating - pity that I wasn't intimidated. "*Don't* let me catch you doing it again! Is that understood, Miss Shield?"

"Oh, yes. Precisely!" I said, which I inexplicably followed by saluting Mrs Smith. I don't know what came over me!

"I don't appreciate sarcasm in my classroom!" Mrs Smith turned around to continue writing on the board. The girls in the classroom looked horrified.

"What is wrong with me? No, there is nothing wrong with me - I have the right to be angry. I don't appreciate having a teacher who knows less about Jane Austen than I do. This is the third time this week we have discussed how social class acts as a barrier towards Mr Darcy and Elizabeth Bennett's relationship!"

"How dare you *backchat* me young lady?"

"What?" I didn't back chat, unless Mrs Smith can read minds. I was certain that I hadn't! Perhaps I was so angry that I did say it out loud! No, I was certain that I didn't speak! Mrs Smith just had it in for me; she must have planned the entire situation just to find a good excuse to remove me from her class. Beside me was Charlotte, my pale faced, petite friend with flowing brown hair. I turned to her for support. I knew she'd back me up. I doubted that the rest of the class would.

"Um ... Miss ... Brianna didn't say anything." Thank goodness I had Charlotte's support and friendship; after all, we had been friends since Kindergarten.

"Leave my class this instant! The both of you! I know what I heard! You can explain yourselves to Mr O'Hara."

"That's it!" I couldn't take this anymore. I kicked my chair, scrambled my books together and faced the entire class.

"Well, thanks for sticking up for me, you know. Thanks for the support. COWARDS!"

Charlotte followed me outside the classroom like a submissive puppy. I thought slamming the door would be the icing on the cake. So, what the heck?

BANG!

While storming down the corridor, I questioned what I had just done.

"How stupid, I could get suspended – no, wait, I could get expelled for this!" What came over me? I don't ever remember being that angry! *"What a mess I've made!"*

"Brianna! *Stop!* Just sit here and calm down a bit!"

"I ... I don't know what came over me, Charlotte. You know me. I ... I don't think I have *ever* reacted that way!"

"I'm kind of glad that you did, though. Maybe it will knock some sense into her." Charlotte and I laughed as we sat beside our lockers.

I buried my face in my hands. "What are my parents going to think?"

"They'll believe me. I'm a witness."

"Let's hope so. I'll need a great deal of evidence to get me out of this."

Charlotte placed a reassuring hand on my shoulder. "Hey, look on the bright side, Brianna; it is your eighteenth birthday tomorrow. Concentrate on that."

"Oh, great! Happy birthday to me!" Charlotte rolled her eyes in response to my sarcasm.

"Come on Brianna. Let's get some fresh air out in the quadrangle, before we face the music." She couldn't possibly be serious! Could she?

"You're kidding! It's bucketing down! Do you really think my hair needs to be any frizzier and out of control than it already is? Bloody Irish weather!" I questioned myself - was I being sarcastic or behaving like a precocious brat? My hair had always been towards the bottom of my priorities list. Something was wrong with me.

Charlotte rolled her eyes. "I've never seen you like this - so ... so ... restless and moody. Is everything all right?"

Charlotte was right. She could read me like a book. She placed her hand on my shoulder and turned towards me. Her pale face was concerned - worried. I could see it in her deep green eyes. I didn't like people to worry over me.

"I'm sorry, Charlotte. I ... I can't explain my reaction in class." Suddenly, my head felt light and numb. My breathing became rapid, as if a heavy object was plunging its way into my chest. My hands shook uncontrollably. My wrists burned. I let out a painful cry. I felt myself collapsing.

"Oh, my gosh! Brianna! Brianna! Help! Someone ... HELP!" The surrounding corridor turned into a foggy haze. I couldn't see Charlotte or the hallway. My body was quivering, but I wasn't cold. Charlotte's voice echoed through my ears, reassuring me that I wasn't dead. I was in an unusual state, like a coma, asleep - unable to communicate - yet, aware of what was going on around me. My body was lifted from the cold hallway floor and a floating sensation overwhelmed me.

*

BANG!

My heart jumped. My eyes opened.

"Oh, my gosh! Sorry, Brianna," Charlotte said, while carelessly closing the heavy door. As my eyes adjusted to the bright light, they revealed a white and sterile room. I attempted to lift myself up. Charlotte approached me in the bed and gently forced me down. "No. You have to relax. Doctor's orders!"

"*I'm in hospital? What happened? Did I hit my head?*" My vision was crystal clear. I felt fine. I brushed my left hand over my right wrist – recalling the burning sensation I experienced earlier. How strange. What caused it? Did I eat something that disagreed with me? Had part of my body shut down?

"So ... what happened?" I asked. It was difficult to speak. My throat was dry.

Charlotte sat beside me. "The doctor thinks that you had some kind of stress attack. Your blood pressure was quite high and the doctor mentioned something about breathing difficulties. Look, let me just go and get him. He expected you to be up about now."

"Wait, wait ... are you *trying* to say that I have a mental issue? *I'm fine*, Charlotte!"

Charlotte hesitated. "Well ... the exact words were ... an anxiety attack."

"*What!*" My life was fine! I wasn't stressed, distressed or mentally unstable! This was a joke! "Charlotte! I am *not* anxious about anything! Well, to tell you the truth, I'm a bit anxious now finding out about this! Is that *all* the doctor said?"

Charlotte looked away. She opened her mouth, and then paused. "Yeah, basically." I could tell she felt sorry for me. She looked uncomfortable. "Let me just get the doctor, Bee."

After a series of thorough, uncomfortable and *unnecessary* examinations, the doctors reassured me that my test results were normal. In other words, they had no *real* idea of what the hell happened to me.

Charlotte was eventually allowed back in.

"I am fine, Charlotte! You know ... you know that if I had any problems I would talk to you."

Charlotte nodded, but did not speak. She looked down into her lap. Her eyes welled with tears. I felt terrible. I put her under so much stress. "Charlotte? I'm sorry."

Gradually raising her arm, Charlotte wiped her tears with her loose sleeve. "It's not that. I - I thought I was going to lose you! I thought you were going to ..."

"Die? Well, I'm here! You'll have to put up with me for a bit longer!" I thought adding some humour would lighten the mood. I was so blessed to have a caring friend like Charlotte.

Finally, she began to laugh. "Well, since we're laughing now, here's something funny. Mrs Smith heard about what happened and I heard she thinks it's all *her* fault."

This couldn't be true! Mrs Smith actually felt responsible! "That woman doesn't have a guilty bone in her body!" Charlotte and I laughed. "Stop making me laugh, it hurts my throat!" I attempted to refrain from laughing. This, though, proved too hard.

"Have you told your mam and dad about this yet?" I asked Charlotte.

"It's night where they are Brianna, but when I Skype them next I'll let them know."

"Oh yeah! I forgot that they're on that Caribbean Cruise."

"I can't believe that they've already been gone for almost a week!"

"How long until they get back?"

"Over a month."

"That's ages, Charlotte!"

"Yeah it is, but it is their twentieth wedding anniversary. You know Mrs O'Sullivan, our neighbour? She doesn't mind checking up on me every evening. I told mam and dad to go and have a good time. They deserve it."

Speaking of Charlotte's parents reminded me of my own family.

"Oh! Where's my Mam, Dad and Ethan?"

"They were here all night. They're out for breakfast. I told them to go and get something to eat." It then occurred to me, if it was breakfast, I had been out for an entire day! Charlotte's face transformed. She appeared excited. "And, by the way, happy birthday!" Charlotte leaned across the bed and gave me a warm hug. She was right. It was my birthday! And what a way to spend it - in a hospital bed and recovering from a *supposed* anxiety attack.

The door opened. It was Mam, followed by Ethan and Dad; each of them holding a few balloons and Mam also holding a beautiful bunch of flowers. My face beamed.

"Happy birthday, Brianna," Mam, Dad and Ethan exclaimed in unison.

"And what a way to spend it, hey, sis?" Ethan said, teasing whenever the opportunity came.

Cue the hugs and kisses. Joy. Don't get me wrong! I love my family, but, the hugs and kisses I could live without.

Tara and Roy Shield were my adopted parents. My father Roy was a principal at our local school. If a complete stranger were to spend one hour with him, I'm sure they would say, "You should have become a comedian!" Looking beyond Dad's height, broad shoulders, solid build, beard and receding hairline, you would see a child.

Tara Shield was an accomplished horse rider and ran a successful horse riding business at our farm in Wicklow, Dublin, quite close to Blessington Lake. Mam also sold produce such as milk, butter, cheese, eggs, fruits and vegetables, which were all produced on our family farm. Mam's dark brown curly hair and ruby red cheeks epitomised her energy and passion for life.

Mam sat beside me and gently stroked my forehead. "Oh Brianna, do you know how much I worried about you? Thank God you're fine. Does your head still hurt? Are you hungry? I bet you're quite hungry after an ordeal like that; let me get you something from the cafeteria downstairs. How about a ...?"

"Mam, please! I'm fine, really. Don't fret!" I had to cut her off. She worried too much. "Mam, I know that you, Dad and Ethan heard what happened. Charlotte told me that according to the doctor I had an anxiety attack. I want you to know that I feel fine and if I had any problems whatsoever, I would come and tell you."

"Darling, it is okay to tell us what you have been through, or if something has upset you lately."

"*MAM!* I have *nothing* going on! *I'm fine.* Why don't you believe me?"

"It's not that I don't believe you, Brianna. I'm just worried. They said you had an anxiety attack. That means that you were and may still be anxious about something!"

Dad patted Mam's shoulder in support. "Your mother and I are just worried. We believe you, Brianna, but just try to understand that we are obliged to listen to the doctor's concerns and, in order for you to get better, we have to get to the bottom of what's causing the problem."

Ethan collapsed casually onto the base of my hospital bed. His hand supported his head while his elbow had sunk into the all too soft hospital mattress. "Anyhow, old chaps, let the older brother have a chat with his baby sis." I was grateful for this interruption. If only all of Ethan's intrusions came with such impeccable timing. I mouthed a quick *thank you* in his direction. Mam and Dad smiled.

"We'll go grab a coffee then," said Mam, as her warm hands brushed over my forehead, while Dad patted my hand. "Call us if you need anything."

"Yes, Mam," Ethan and I said in complete synchronization. Ethan, Charlotte and I were now alone. I gave Ethan's ribs a quick flick with my foot.

Ethan leaped in surprise *"Ouch!* What was that for?"

"I am only younger than you by a month, my *so-called older brother*!"

"Yes and that still makes me the oldest. Sorry, sis!" Ethan was such a tease; but I needed a laugh after this so called 'anxiety attack' ordeal.

Ethan defines the term 'individual'. His green eyes are concealed behind black horn rimmed glasses, framed by scruffy short brown hair. Ethan's thin build, lanky stature and quirky nature has convinced people that he is quiet and cowardly.

Ethan and I both share a passion for music, animals, superheroes and reading, but Ethan immerses himself in the boring and predictable drama of historical fiction, whereas I appreciate reading more *sophisticated* literary modes. Of course, I am referring to fantasy fiction.

Speaking of fantasy, my mind raced back to what I was imagining in English class yesterday. I remember a dungeon, a guard and being saved by Ethan and Logan. And I believe that my story ended with a kiss. I had to record this. Perhaps this could be priceless material for my future fantasy novel! I needed a pen and paper in a hurry.

"Is my school bag here?"

Ethan answered my question; even though it was directed at Charlotte. "It's in the car. Why? Do you need something?"

"Yeah, I do. A piece of paper and a pen would be great."

Charlotte grinned. "I just happen to have those very two things with me in *my* school bag." She shuffled through her bag and handed me a pen with her biology book. "Just use a page from the back."

I jotted down every intricate detail that I could recall from the daydream. After filling up one complete page, I was satisfied.

Charlotte looked puzzled. "What were you writing about?"

"That's for me to know and for you to find out in, let's say ... ten or fifteen years' time." I'd hoped that my dream of becoming a world-renowned fantasy author panned out; becoming a Broadway sensation required a voice, something I sadly didn't have.

Ethan's face beamed. "Charlotte, it's an idea for her *novel*." Ethan chuckled. Throwing a pillow seemed too kind. Perhaps another kick should do the trick. "*Ouch!* Cut it out, Brianna!"

"It serves you right! Brianna is allowed to have a goal or a dream to be a writer!" I appreciated this support from Charlotte. Every tiny amount of encouragement fuelled my ambitions of becoming a writer. People like Charlotte were catalysts; they made my dream seem possible.

Ethan appeared agitated. "That's it! Enough of the soppy goals and dreams, we have to throw this girl a party!"

I slipped back under the covers of the bed. I wasn't in the mood for celebrating. I felt like being alone for a few minutes, just to gather my thoughts and think over the events of yesterday.

"Ethan, I'm really happy that you'd love for me to celebrate and have fun. I'm just not in the mood for celebrating." Ethan's face began to drop. I felt terrible. "To be honest, I don't want a party. Just having dinner with the family and a day with you and Charlotte is fine."

"Okay, Brianna. I thought the least I could do for you after all this was to surprise you - make you laugh."

"I always laugh when I'm with you!"

"True - I have that effect on people." Ethan grinned. "I tell you what, how 'bout when you're back to normal and at home we give you a boring, typical, Shield family birthday celebration?"

I smiled. "That sounds perfect, as long as I am discharged from here as soon as possible."

Ethan's face lit up as a candle flame lightens a darkened room. "Well, from what I heard when eavesdropping, the word is you'll be out of this place by mid-afternoon. So," Ethan patted my leg and continued, "how does tonight sound?"

"Wonderful," I replied. "But, make sure you tell Mam I don't want to make a huge celebration out of this. *Okay?*"

"Will do," said Ethan, accompanied with a minor chuckle.

Charlotte began to shuffle through her bag. "Since it is your birthday, and I am too impatient to wait until we're at your house tonight, happy birthday!" As Charlotte spoke, she placed a large and delicately wrapped box, tied with a rainbow ribbon, on my lap.

"*Awww* Charlotte. Thank you! Should I open it now?"

"Go ahead!" Ethan encouraged.

I carefully untied the ribbon and attempted to avoid ripping the beautiful spotted wrapping paper. The paper fell away to reveal a mahogany box with an ornate key. I looked towards Charlotte in anticipation of what was inside. I turned the key and gently lifted the lid. The inside surface of the box was hidden behind a collage of photos. Ribbons, glitter and small ornaments decorated the photos. I recognised photos of Charlotte, Ethan, Mam and Dad, the farm, my celebrity idols and my two puppies - Lulu and Tess. My eyes were then drawn to a T-shirt folded in the box. As I lifted the shirt, Batman materialised.

"Charlotte! *I love it!*"

"There's more." Charlotte seemed so pleased by my reaction.

I was far too taken by the Batman t-shirt and the photos to even consider other presents. Looking back into the box, I found a leather-bound journal with a matching pen.

"Charlotte! This is wonderful! Thank you!"

"You're very welcome. But, I probably should have given it to you before, so you could have written down the idea for your novel."

"That's okay. This is deadly, Charlotte. I love it!"

Every day I was so grateful for Charlotte and Ethan's presence in my life. I cannot begin to comprehend what my life would have been like without them and the rest of my family. Despite being surrounded by love and happiness, I still questioned my origin.

Where was I from? Who were my biological parents? Did they ever love me?

My experience yesterday once again brought these questions to mind and made me reconsider who I was. The markings on my wrists were a constant daily reminder that I was different. I accepted that I was different and I was certainly not ashamed to admit it. I simply longed for answers. I felt like a hungry dog, chained to a wall just out of reach of its bowl of food. I needed the food; I needed the answers to my questions. Like the hungry dog, I would never be satisfied until I reached and devoured that meal.

Chapter Two

The Morrigan Book

"Brianna! For God's sake would you hurry up! Michael and Charlotte are going to be arriving any minute! The table needs to be sorted and drinks need to be ready for serving!"

Mam was in one of those *navy seal* moods. I had strictly told her not to make an incredible fuss over this birthday party. All I requested was for my family and close friends to attend. Let's see, that made six people, including myself, and Mam was treating this occasion as if it were my wedding reception!

"Mam, calm down! I am in my bedroom getting changed, unless you would like me to entertain our guests in incredibly baggy trousers and my painting shirt!" Not that Charlotte and Michael would mind. They were pretty much family, anyway. What was the point in wearing a brand new pair of *killer heel* shoes and an expensive dress that would most probably find a permanent residence in the deepest darkest facets of my wardrobe?

"Okay, okay, Brianna, just make it snappy please." After yesterday's ordeal, Mam just wanted to make me happy. I understood that and I loved her for it, but I believed her preparatory efforts for the party ran deeper than simply making me content. I had a suspicion that she was still worried about what occurred yesterday, following my English class. Occupying herself with multiple tasks for the party was taking her mind off considering the worst possible outcomes. Questioning my mother's thoughts made me contemplate my own.

"Is there an underlying condition I have that caused this reaction in my body? Did Mrs Smith really hear my thoughts or did she decide to act out of hatred towards me?"

I knew Charlotte would be analysing my reaction in class and waiting for the right moment to address it with me. The more I thought about it, the difficulty in finding an answer seemed to intensify.

Ding Dong.

"Brianna! Get the door, please." Boy, Mam's voice could carry!

"I'm on it, Mam!" After placing my last and very constricting *skyscraper* sized high-heeled shoe on, I took great care down the stairs and made a graceful dart for the door. First to arrive was Michael.

Michael was old and fragile in body, but certainly not in spirit. Despite his age, Michael's head held copious amounts of thick, savage white hair. He was not a large man, although hearing his deep and melodious voice from another room would have convinced you otherwise. Like me, Michael had two different coloured eyes. His right eye was brown and his left eye green.

Michael had told me that his left eye had changed colour after the accident. Sadly, he lost his son, daughter and wife in a car crash and had lived alone ever since. Ethan and I were never fortunate enough to meet our grandparents, we consider Michael as the grandparent we never had. Living down the road from Michael had its perks. Ethan, Charlotte and I would often stop at his house following school and indulge in his famous shortbread biscuits, accompanied by a cup of tea.

"Brianna, my dear! Happy, happy birthday," Michael bellowed in his usual enthusiastic manner. Before I had the chance to say hello myself, Michael placed a large and heavy cardboard package in my arms. "The old bookshop in town near the pub is closing. So, I had a decent rummage through the fantasy section and thought you would appreciate these." Michael signalled for me to open the box. Inside, there must have been at least twenty or more novels. My heart skipped a beat.

"Michael, this is fantastic! Thank you! Thank you so much! I can't wait to start them!" I gave him a warm hug.

Michael then held my hand and spun me around. "Look at you! You look beautiful my dear, just beautiful!"

"Well, I'm glad the final product you are seeing doesn't give away the discomfort I am feeling."

"Hush, hush, ya Mam will hear ya. Where is she anyway? Working away over that hot stove, no doubt."

"You guessed it. Here, let's..." my voice trailed off as I noticed Charlotte leaving her home through the still open door. She was about to make her way across the bridge. "Oh Michael, Charlotte is here. Mam is in the kitchen. I'll meet you there in a moment."

"Not to worry love, I'll see ya in a bit." Following a pat on my shoulder, Michael made his way towards the kitchen. Catching Charlotte there and then was flawless timing; it gave me an opportunity to ponder yesterday's incident. Hopefully I could make some sense of it all prior to Dad and Ethan returning with the present that I wasn't supposed to know about.

"Wow! Brianna! You look fabulous!" Charlotte appeared stunned; actually, stunned in reference to Charlotte's expression was an understatement.

"Thanks a million," my face started to blend in with my red dress. "Mam wanted to make an occasion; hence, the very expensive, and not to mention uncomfortable, dress that restricts my every breath. You know CPR, right?"

"Brianna, you are beautiful! And I am not just saying that because I am your friend! By the way, Happy Birthday - again!" Following her kind words, as well as a hug, Ethan and Dad pulled into the driveway in Mam's business van.

Dad mumbled something to Ethan that I'm sure had something to do with Ethan approaching Charlotte and I and added, "*Okay*, let's go round to the horse paddock, shall we?" Ethan placed his long and lanky arms around Charlotte and me, directing us toward the back of the house. "Look at me, surrounded by two beautiful women! And Charlotte - wow - purple is definitely your colour! But, Bee, I'm..."

"Not a word, Ethan!" Pinching Ethan was very tempting. I couldn't control the urge.

Ethan jerked. "Ouch! I don't have enough flesh for this kind of treatment!"

While attempting to refrain from chuckling, Charlotte said, "Well, eat then! Add some flesh to that skinny body of yours!"

I knew Ethan would have a comeback, he always did. "I have an extremely fast metabolism! And this is coming from the girl who weighs forty five kilos!"

"Okay, okay." This couldn't continue. I wanted to deal with the events of yesterday. "Moving on, I'm glad we're alone, as I would like to talk to you both about yesterday."

"Shoot," Ethan replied.

"Okay. Before you ask any questions, *please* hear me out and *please* don't laugh, because part of it sounds ridiculous!"

"Okay, Bee. Just get to it," said Ethan.

"Well, I will admit that I was daydreaming. I wasn't concentrating, because we were going over all that crap about social class and how it affected Elizabeth and Darcy's relationship..."

Ethan was growing impatient. "Get to the point, Bee."

"Okay, okay. Anyway, as I was daydreaming, Mrs Smith had a go at me - etcetera, etcetera. Then, as she was facing the board, I was kind of having a go at her in my head. I was thinking things like, *I don't appreciate having a teacher who knows less about Jane Austen than I do.* And following that thought, she acted as if she heard it! Charlotte was there! You saw her reaction!"

"Yeah, it was completely bizarre!"

I continued. "I was beside myself! I mean, was it a coincidence I was thinking that thought at the exact time she decided to get me into trouble?"

Ethan rolled his eyes. "Thank God this woman and I have never crossed paths! If she is having a go at you for doing nothing, I would not have survived her class!"

"Ethan, that's beside the point. Would Mrs Smith risk her reputation by falsely accusing a student? There were about twenty witnesses! That's why I keep pondering this possibility. My behaviour was also odd. I mean, for God sake, I saluted her! I slammed the door! I have never done that before! As I did these things, I felt hot and tense. As I left the class, my wrists were burning where my markings are! I'm sure the logical explanation is she just has it in for me, but I can't stop considering this option! Okay, now you can laugh and say I am being absolutely ridiculous."

Charlotte placed a supportive hand on my arm. "You're not being ridiculous. But, the question you haven't addressed yet is why did you collapse?"

"Perhaps I collapsed because I was so incredibly angry." I grabbed fistfuls of hair and allowed my head to droop. "I don't know any more. I just … I know I didn't have some sort of anxiety attack."

Ethan placed his hand on mine and reassuringly sighed, "I know, Bee. I know."

"Hey, you lot! Come on! Dinners ready," blared Dad, from the back door. On that note, arm-in-arm, Ethan, Charlotte and I headed to the dining room for the unforgettable splendour of Mrs Shield's famous cuisine.

Despite a gathering of six individuals, enough food remained for another sitting and Mam was still attempting to persuade us into an additional serving. "Charlotte, are you sure that you have had quite sufficient? You barely filled your plate, dear."

"Thank you Mrs Shield, but I am incredibly full. It was delicious, though."

Mam still hadn't given up. "Michael, would you like another spoonful of potato with stew?"

Michael patted his stomach and replied, "Oh, I'm fine my dear and my stomach, too, is quite content."

Perhaps now was a good time to speak to Mam alone and thank her for everything. "Here Mam, let me help you take the plates into the kitchen."

"No, no, it's your birthday, which means it is your day to get spoiled."

"Please, Mam. I'd like to."

"All right, if you insist." After collecting everyone's vacant plates, I followed Mam into the kitchen. Mam was already filling the sink with detergent and hot water for washing the pots and pans. With care, I positioned the plates beside the sink, then wrapped my arms around Mam's waist, allowing my head to rest on her back.

"Thank you, Mam - for today. It meant a lot. But, you didn't have to go to all this trouble just because of yesterday."

The tap stopped running, Mam turned around; her eyes could not contain her tears.

"Mam! What's wrong? What's wrong?!"

"I'm sorry; I didn't want you to see this." Mam raised her trembling hands, attempting to wipe away the tears. "It's just I ... I keep thinking that ... just ... I'm sorry. Don't worry."

"*Please*, Mam."

After quite a substantial pause, Mam replied, "I just ... I keep thinking that ... that you could have a condition that we, as your adopted parents, are unable to help you with."

"*Mam*. The doctors did a number of tests. Please don't worry yourself. What is the point in worrying when we really don't know anything yet for certain? *Okay*?"

Following a sigh, Mam held me and gently whispered, "You're right. You're right." She kissed my forehead, then, with her soapy right hand, raised my chin. "You know how much I love you, don't you?"

"Yes, Mam. Love you!"

Mam's smile relieved all prior sadness. "Ditto."

Following dinner, cake and the unwrapping of all but one present, Ethan, Charlotte and I browsed through the array of fantasy novels I had just received from Michael.

"This one looks particularly interesting," said Charlotte, while flicking through the pages of quite a thick book. "It's called *The Lost Keeper*. I have dibs on this - well, after you read it of course, Brianna."

Suddenly, Ethan leapt eagerly from the sofa on the far side of the lounge room, dodged the coffee table and came rushing towards me. "Hey! Hey, Bee! You have to check this out!" As Ethan spoke, he handed me the book he was just browsing. "Come on, Bee. Can you see it? Look closely at the cover!"

I stared intently at the front cover of the book, trying to understand what Ethan wanted me to see. The word *Morrigan* in bold, silver print overshadowed an illustration of a beautiful young woman. The woman held a sword in her left hand and had a crow resting upon her right hand. Her skin appeared incredibly pale against her wavy, ebony and shimmering hair. Her clothing was purple in colour and decorated in, what seemed to resemble, crow feathers. As I paid close attention to the woman's face, I realised her eyes were of different colours. Her right eye was brown and her left eye was blue. Just like mine.

"Is this what you wanted me to see, Ethan? The eyes are just like mine."

"Yes, but no, Bee." Ethan's tone indicated frustration from my inability to find what he so desperately wanted me to see. Impatiently, he produced a moaning sigh, positioned his finger on the woman's left wrist, tapped the book (just to make sure that I was paying attention) and directed me towards the woman's right wrist. Following another tap of enormous emphasis, Ethan said, "*Now* do you see?"

Once again, I stared closely at the front cover of the book, paying much greater attention to the areas Ethan had indicated. On the woman's right wrist was a small circular marking. Inside the circle, was a cross; identical to mine. On her left wrist, there was a circle surrounding a bow and arrow; again, just like mine.

"Ethan, this is incredibly bizarre!"

"What? What's bizarre? Show me," said Charlotte, while heading towards Ethan and me for a closer look at the book. "Let me see." I placed the book in Charlotte's hands and drew her attention to the woman's wrists, as well as her eyes.

Charlotte gasped. "Brianna. I'm ... wow! This is very, very strange." Charlotte's eyes could not escape the books hold. Her eyelids were gradually tightening and her left eyebrow was arched; Charlotte's signature for being deep in thought. "Either, this is pure coincidence, or, do you think...? No, I'm over thinking. Something that is this weird is probably a mere coincidence."

I looked in Charlotte's direction and attempted to refrain from moaning. "Charlotte, please! Just say what you're thinking. I don't care how stupid you think it is. I want to hear it!"

"Well, I was just considering - well pondering - the notion that perhaps your biological parents were somewhat connected to this book?" She paused.

"*And ...*" I urged her to continue.

"Perhaps they were the, or one of them was, the author. Well, there are a number of possibilities. They could have ..."

An idea sprang to my mind. " ... *Or*, they could have placed the tattoos on me after I was born, because they were obsessed fans of the book. It sounds stupid, but it could be true - *couldn't it?*" Charlotte, Ethan and I fell silent, lost in deep thoughts. We remained speechless for what seemed like minutes, individually contemplating a myriad of possibilities.

Ethan broke the silence. "You know, we still haven't addressed eye colour. Your parents do not have the power, let alone the capabilities to select your eye colour. So, I am thinking that this must have been written after you were born. Maybe," Ethan patted the book in Charlotte's hands and continued, "Just maybe, you were the inspiration for this book."

I snatched the book from Charlotte's hands and flicked through the first few pages.

"What are you looking for?" said Charlotte.

"The publishing date," I replied, while scanning the first page of the book. My eyes finally came to a year in quite miniscule print. "NINETEEN SEVENTY-FIVE!" I laughed. "Well, I don't think I was the inspiration for this book after all, Ethan."

"But, Brianna," said Charlotte, "Your guess may be right. Perhaps your parents were fans of the book and gave you the tattoos of this woman. We know they didn't write it, they would have had to be children or teenagers, and it is highly unlikely that a child or teenager would write a novel! *Wait!* Brianna, who is the author?"

In small silver print on the book's bind, there was a name. "It says, *Glynn Braeden*."

Perhaps I was right. Perhaps my parents were so heavily immersed in this book that, when they saw that my eyes matched those of the lead character, they decided to give me these tattoos. A feeling of anticipation rushed through me. This book came to me for a purpose. *Could it lead me towards my biological parents? Was it a sign?* I leapt from the lounge, kicked my all too uncomfortable high heels off and sprinted towards my bedroom.

"Hey! Bee! Where are you going?" cried Ethan.

"I'm going to Google this person's name. I'll be back in a sec!" I headed up the stairs, taking two at a time, in my haste to get an answer.

"Wait! Use my computer! Not yours!"

I stopped halfway up the stairs. "Why?"

"Um … well, um … Mam… Yes, Mam is checking something on yours. She told me to tell you she would be a while. Sorry, I should have mentioned it."

This was not true. I could tell when Ethan was lying. His voice was much higher in pitch when he lied.

"Dad and Michael are in my bedroom, putting together the antique desk from Madam & Miss Antique Shop that I am not supposed to be aware of just yet."

"And why would you say that, Bee?" said Ethan, with great volume.

"Say what, Ethan?" I replied.

"Don't be thick, Bee! You said ..." Ethan's words were cut off by Charlotte's interjection.

"Ethan, Brianna didn't say anything. *You* were the last person to say something." I hurried back down the stairs, stood in the lounge room archway, directly facing Ethan and Charlotte.

Ethan laughed and allowed his gangly body to collapse into the lounge chair. "What are you two playing at?! I know what I heard!"

"What did you hear? Ethan, I - I didn't say anything! Nothing at all!"

Ethan's face turned quizzical. "*You* said that Dad and Michael must be in your room putting together the antique desk you loved! The one in that Antique Shop you and Charlotte get all obsessed about!"

Ethan seemed more serious than ever before, but I didn't say anything, I know I didn't. Was this like the last time? Did this confirm my speculations about Mrs Smith in English class? As I did the last time, I faced Charlotte in hesitation and fear. "Charlotte, are you sure? Are you sure you didn't hear me?"

Just as in our English class, she silently confirmed, "Brianna, you didn't say *anything*."

This was beyond all comprehension. How could I, out of the billions of people on Earth, have a gift only possessed by characters in fictional books? What do you say after a moment like this? By the looks on Charlotte and Ethan's face, I was certain their thoughts were running in similar directions. Despite recent events, I wasn't entirely convinced that my thoughts could be sent to others. What I was certain about was where to begin looking if I was to make some sense of it all: *The Morrigan Book.*

"I ... I really have no idea what to say and ... and I'm sure you must be both thinking the same things as me, but let me say it out loud. I think I can project my thoughts." My throat was closing, constricting and losing all access to air. I had never before felt so uncomfortable speaking to the closest people in my life. I cleared my throat and attempted to carry on. "I don't know how I do it, I don't know why it happens, but I know the answer might be in this book and I'm finishing it tonight. I *must* get to the bottom of this and see if there is some reasonable explanation for all of this. If there isn't..." I paused, "...You can send me to the psych ward." Tears accompanied my final words. I was not one for crying. For me it was a rarity, a blue moon event. Charlotte interpreted these tears as an invitation to race across the lounge room; she held me more warmly than she had ever done before. Ethan and I were never known for being the *loving type* like Charlotte, which explained him placing one hesitant hand on my shoulder.

Ethan did the only thing he knew how to do in awkward situations such as this; he tried to make me laugh. "Well, I personally think that being able to communicate without opening your mouth is pretty impressive. I mean, just think, Bee! If you can make this a two way thing, you'll be able to get A's in all your exams with Charlotte in the room!"

"Ethan!" Charlotte said, in quite abrupt fashion. "Why do you have to say such stupid and idiotic things at times like this?"

In contrast with Charlotte's take on the situation, my tears turned into unrestrained laughter.

Ethan's emerald green eyes looked out over his horn-rimmed glasses and gleamed in Charlotte's direction. "See! Not so idiotic of me after all."

Charlotte ignored Ethan and directed all of her attention towards me. "So, are you ... well, what I mean is, do you *really* think you can do what you think you can?"

"Yes." I replied, as I wiped away the remaining tears. "It explains everything, doesn't it? English class and what happened just now."

"So, what will you do now?"

"The only thing I can do is read this book. It's too much of a coincidence for me to have the same eyes and the exact same markings on my wrists as this character. It could give me something to go from and, who knows, it could also explain what I am almost certain I can do."

"It's worth a try," said Ethan. Following Ethan's words, the sound of footsteps travelled from the stairs. Dad, Mam and Michael congregated around the three of us, beneath the archway of the lounge room.

After clearing his throat, Dad said, "Well, I hate to break up the party, but we have something to show the birthday girl. That is, of course, if she is willing to accompany us up to her bedroom."

"I would be delighted to," I said, linking arms with Mam and Dad, walking up the stairs like The Three Musketeers.

When we reached the top of the staircase, Mam, Dad and I, still arm in arm, processed towards my bedroom, accompanied by Michael, Ethan and Charlotte. I reached out for the golden knob of my bedroom door, which almost went unnoticed amongst a thick bed of posters proclaiming my love for Batman, clenched my fingers and twisted it.

Despite being fully aware of what awaited, anticipation overwhelmed me. Images of sitting at this desk and writing from dawn until dusk consumed my thoughts. It was incredibly easy to imagine Mam demanding that I leave my desk and come down to eat my supper as it was getting cold!

The open door revealed what I had so highly anticipated. The antique desk was directly opposite my bedroom door and placed alongside my bedside table. The caramel coloured wood was varnished to perfection and was supported by beautiful black coils of wrought iron. This was to be the desk where brilliant ideas would gather in my head, transcend from mind to paper and become the words of the stories that I knew I had to tell!

I approached the desk, caressed it with both hands and absorbed the rich smell of timber. "This is fantastic! Thank you! Thank you so much!" This was one of those rare occasions where I would initiate a hug.

"Well, we knew you would like it," said Mam, as I found my way into her arms. "Although," she continued, "your father and I can't take all the credit. Ethan was the one who found out that you were so interested in it in the first place."

I turned towards Ethan, who had made himself quite comfortable on my previously immaculate bed. "Ah, yes. I'm afraid I *do* deserve *all* of the credit," he said, while tilting his head downwards and fanning himself with the novel I was currently reading. "But, there is more, Bee. This one's just from me. Open the top right draw."

I immediately returned to the desk and opened the draw Ethan drew my attention to. A small box, wrapped in red paper and secured by a gold ribbon, lay in the middle of the draw. Carefully, I untied the ribbon and removed the red paper, attempting to keep it as intact as possible for future use. A silver box remained. I lifted the lid and inside the silver box was yet another silver box, but attached to a silver chain. I grasped onto part of the chain and allowed the small silver box to dangle at the end of the chain. The box had an intricate latch and, as I moved it, the box opened. It was empty.

"It's called a prayer box," Ethan said, as he leapt from my bed and moved to my side. "The reason it's empty is because you're supposed to place a piece of paper in it that has your goals or ambitions in life. I saw it at that shop you love and well, when she explained it to me, it reminded me of you, because ... because you like that sort of stuff." With these words, Ethan took hold of the chain from my hands and placed it ever so delicately around my neck. "The lady said that the box is kept near your heart, so ... so, it will help achieve what you desire most."

"Ethan, I'm..."

"...Speechless?" he said.

"Yes, speechless is the right word indeed!"

"But, speechless in a good way, right, Bee?"

"Yes, Ethan." Hugging Ethan confirmed my happiness. "Speechless, but in a good way. Thank you. And I know exactly what I am going to write to put in the box!"

In spite of the lack of enthusiasm I had for dressing up for the occasion, I did have a splendid birthday celebration, although all the happiness in the world could not relieve the pain of having to wear high heeled shoes and a face completely covered with unnecessary make-up for an entire evening.

Following a pot of tea, accompanied with Michael's renowned shortbread biscuits, and an evening concluded by Dad's traditional jokes, which I am ashamed to say still made me laugh, no matter how many times I had heard them, Charlotte and Michael returned home. The evening reminded me of the significant role that my family and friends play in my life; this gift was priceless and one that I would hold onto forever. But, when my birthday celebrations had come to a close, I grew anxious; I finally had a chance to start the Morrigan book and hopefully find some answers.

"Good night, everyone! And thanks again for a wonderful night!" I blared from upstairs, leaning over the staircase banister.

"Good night, love!" Mam and Dad replied from the kitchen.

"Night," said Ethan, who I discovered was standing in his bedroom doorway, directly opposite my own.

"Thanks again, Ethan. I'll wear it all the time!"

"I know you will," he replied, while making his way into his room. After Ethan's room became dark, he yelled, "And let me know how the book is! I know you'll have it finished by the morning, no doubt!"

I rolled my eyes, made my way into my bedroom, switched my main light off and yelled out, "Good night, Ethan!" Yes, Ethan was right. As long as my eyes could stay open, this book would most likely be completed before morning.

Chapter Three

The Change

After turning on my bedside table lamp and unmaking my bed, I nestled myself into a comfortable position. When satisfied, I removed the book from my bedside table, had a final scan of the front cover, then proceeded to chapter one. A strange new world unfolded before me.

*

Thousands of years ago, the Celtic people in the south of Ireland were enduring a terrible famine. It was a fearful and violent time.

On the eve of spring, villages were preparing to celebrate Imbolc, the spring festival. A young boy ventured away from the festivities into an open field to pray for his dying father. The boy surrendered to Daghdha, the God of all things good to the Celts, and prayed. He begged Daghdha to provide his family and fellow people with plentiful food at the time of Imbolc. He begged for his father to be healed, so that his mother and young infant sister would be provided for. The boy removed the tassel from his cloak and shaped it against the earth, forming a square shield knot - the symbol of Daghdha.

The boy lowered his head and waited, while praying incessantly, hoping for a miracle. No signs comforted the young boy and he reluctantly withdrew from the damp field, his shoulders slumped in disappointment.

As he reached the outskirts of his village, the boy heard a light chuckle from behind him. Surprised, he jumped and quickly turned around to trace the source of the mischievous laugh. There was no one there, not a person in sight. The boy decided to ignore the sound, quickly convincing himself that he must have been mistaken. Once again, that familiar, cheeky chuckle danced across the field. A cloud of mist descended on the field, consuming everything.

The mist's ever-firmer grip fuelled his anxiety. "Show yourself!" The boy's soft voice nervously pleaded with the source of the laugh.

"Hush! Hush, Darren Kael!" a rascally, yet warm voice replied. Two figures emerged from the mist, drawing closer to Darren. One appeared to be a beast of some kind - a wolf like creature, with smooth, but wavy grey matted hair, covering gangly limbs. The other almost resembled Darren - a small framed young boy, with long brown hair, dressed in regal green and brown garments. His emerald eyes were almost as rich as his green robes. "We have not yet met, but we know what awaits you," the longhaired youth explained. "We have been waiting for someone as selfless as you to come for a long time."

Darren's nervous heart was almost drumming out the surrounding sounds. "Why ... but ... how can you know what awaits me?" Darren stammered.

"It's not my role to tell you." The visitor's grin widened.

"But ... I .... I don't understand. What are ... why are you here?" Darren was still in disbelief, uncertain of what was happening.

"You don't know who I am?" The visitor laughed, mocking Darren.

Lost for words, Darren simply shook his head.

"Arawn," the visitor gestured down towards the large dog, "and I, Mabon, were sent by the very one you were seeking help from."

"Daghdha?" Darren breathed in awe. "He ... He answered my prayer?"

"In time he will. But, for now," a very jovial look swept over Mabon's young face, "Arawn and I would like to race you to the village."

"Race me?" Darren became even more perplexed.

"Yes!" Mabon laughed. "I never lose! And neither does Arawn."

Without warning, Arawn and Mabon began sprinting towards the village, their figures gradually becoming one with the mist.

"Wait!" Darren cried, as he ran after Arawn and Mabon. "When will Daghdha...?" Before finishing his burning question, Darren tripped over a small stone, landing head first on another sharp rock. His world became black.

*

Trapped in the darkness, Darren's mind became subjected to the wisdom of Daghdha. The unconscious realm his mind had slipped deeply into foreshadowed a future, a future Darren would bestow upon his people, providing them with freedom and comfort. Disparate and transparent visions seeped through Darren's mind; like an array of dyes sinking into water, gradually intertwining with one another to make a unified colour, an answer was being formed from the kaleidoscopic madness.

When Darren's visions came to an end, the gates of his mind opened, returning him to the present, urging him to share Daghdha's wisdom with his anguished people. As Darren stood up, warm blood ran down his cool face from the gash on his forehead, trickling over his fair lashes and falling from his cheek to the damp earth. Before even reaching his village to announce what awaited his people, Darren's visions were already coming to fruition.

Taking advantage of the villagers' participation in the rituals of Imbolc, hundreds of fierce men were thrusting stakes of fire into the air and quickly approaching Darren's village. But, before reaching the village, an enormous emerald green bird began slaying the army of bloodthirsty marauders. Like meat scraps tossed to a canine, men were effortlessly plucked from their horses and thrown aside by the creature of Daghdha.

Despite the decimation of the enemy, Darren's people were still going to struggle with little food to consume. But, after destroying the enemy, Daghdha's creature remained for the people, silently inviting them to ride upon its back and be taken to a new land, abundant in life that would sustain all. This land was Oran-Roy; ruled by the pure spirit of the Green King, Daghdha.

Daghdha's spirit was bound to Oran-Roy; a land hidden from mankind just below the southern tip of Ireland. The magic bound in Oran-Roy could only be released when an innocent, selfless and pure heart believed in its existence and yearned for its guidance. Darren was the key to Oran-Roy, unlocking its wonder with his noble qualities, opening a door to new beginnings for his people.

Daghdha's bird-like creature, Lleu, was amongst the spirits watching over the magic of Oran-Roy until the promised steward would arrive, whose selfless nature would allow him to shape Oran-Roy as a sanctuary for his suffering people. While serving

Daghdha and watching over Oran-Roy, some spirits turned against Daghdha's will. Lleu defended his leader, remaining loyal to him and his purpose for Oran-Roy at all costs. Refusing to side with the treacherous spirits, Lleu had to flee and surrender to another form; a form that would act as a refuge where he could no longer be threatened by the unworthy spirits. Under the protection of Daghdha, Lleu became the Oran-Roy bird, continuing to serve Daghdha in this form and, in turn, to serve the future human leaders of Oran-Roy.

*

Bewildered beyond belief, but having heard and received Darren's visions, the village accepted the bird's offer of freedom. Once arriving in Oran-Roy, families were asked to govern and protect particular regions of the land. From the woods of Daray, the plains of Cathal, the hills of Crag and Cargon, to the silvery coastline of Breena, Oran-Roy was now in the hands of Darren's people by the will of Daghdha.

*

Years passed and Darren was now old enough to not only lead his clan of Tarmon, but the other eight surrounding clans. With Daghdha's wisdom guiding his rule over Oran-Roy, Darren formed insignias to represent the clans of Oran-Roy. Clan's peoples embedded these symbols onto their right wrists, proud to acknowledge how they served their new home.

Darren's home clan was where the original people of Oran-Roy resided. At the heart of Oran-Roy, lay Tarmon, rich and lush in fertile crops and peaceful natural dwellings. The Tarmon symbol was a cross, depicting the unity of Oran-Roy's original people. After the forming of Tarmon, four other regions were formally decreed, each given to the stewardship of clan.

Daray neighboured Tarmon to the northwest, along the north-western coast of Oran-Roy. Mysterious and abundant in wild life, and home to the Arawn dog pack that served Daghdha, Daray's insignia was a paw print, symbolic of the many animals that called Daray home.

Cathal was south of Daray and to the west of Tarmon. Unlike its neighbouring clans, Cathal was copious in open green fields, stretching as far as the eye could see. The people of Cathal came to master the art of the sword. Their symbol was a cross-formed by two swords.

Kael creek and the swamps of Kerr separated Cathal from Crag, which lay to the south of Tarmon. Crag was a mountainous region and in the heart of winter the peaks became white with snow. In the spring the thaw poured cool fresh water into the Rona River. Rona streamed from Crag, skirting Tarmon's border, to Oran-Roy's eastern coastline to the shores of Breena. The people of Crag learned to endure the cold conditions and hunted by the bow, mastering archery. Their insignia was fittingly a bow and arrow.

Bryan was a rocky and rugged region, the original burial ground for the Oran-Roy people. The people who resided there were known as the guardians of the dead; they prepared those who were dying for their next journey and, with the Arawn pack from Daray, they helped them voyage from this life to the next. Over time, Daghdha's spirit gave the people of these clans wings and the gift of flight. The Lucians bore black wings and remained with the dying; the Prislens bore white wings and guided the spirits of the dead to the peace of Daghdha. Their insignia proudly adorned their chests; white feathers in a cross-like formation for the Prislens and similar markings in black for the Lucians.

*

While consulting his neighbouring clans beyond Tarmon, Darren fell in love with Glynn, a young woman from Cathal. Over time, the pair became inseparable and very quickly realised how much they needed one another above anything else. Their marriage was one of the first unions since their salvaged people had resided in Oran-Roy. Glynn left her duties in Cathal and helped Darren govern Tarmon, as well as the other clans. Shortly after their union, they began a family of their own with the birth of a daughter.

Oran-Roy was thriving under Darren's leadership. Clans were becoming prosperous, each specialising in certain fields and maintaining their land. The people of some clans were blessed and changed by Daghdha in their new home. After the Prislens and Lucians received the gift of flight, the people of the Daray clan were able to communicate with animals and transform into creatures themselves.

*

Darren's daughter, Donelle, had golden locks that fell effortlessly around her porcelain face. But, unlike her parents, Donelle did not have one insignia on her right wrist; she had her mother's symbol of the two swords of Cathal on her right and the Tarmon cross, Darren's symbol, on her left. It appeared that other children of couples who were not from the same clan were also born with an insignia of their parent's symbols on each wrist. In addition to the insignias, the children of these parents had different coloured eyes. Donelle's right eye was green and her left eye was brown.

While celebrating Donelle's seventeenth birthday, Darren was asked to attend to a matter of great urgency in Cathal. Once in Cathal, a troublesome mother confronted Darren; tears were streaming across her face as she clung to Darren's robes, begging for answers.

"My son! My son!" The mother sobbed at Darren's feet. "He ... he is not of Darian blood ... Something has ... has happened to him!"

Darren passed the distraught mother over to one of his servers to console, while the boy's father hurried Darren over to witness what was causing chaos.

At the base of a moss covered tree, curled up and clinging to the shadows, was a young man shielding his face with his arms. He was quivering from head to toe, his clothing drenched by sweat, not the dewy earth.

"It's alright, son," Darren assured the frightened young man. "Don't fear us. Please?" Darren offered the boy his arm. As the young man's arm reached out to Darren's, the light revealed the limb of an animal. After a few moments, the thick, black hair consuming the young man's arm began to fade, eventually revealing the pale skin of a human hand. "This is not to be feared," Darren commanded. "It is a gift from Daghdha and is to be embraced. Master your gift."

Over the next few months, Darren became aware of similar cases, where young adults were displaying rare and unique talents, physically manipulating their appearance, controlling the actions of others, foreseeing the time to come and exercising heightened human senses. Darren's daughter, Donelle, came to realise that her touch could heal an injury and that her dreams revealed the future.

Rather than frowning upon the rare gifts young mixed bloods were possessing, Darren valued them and wanted to ensure that others would not take advantage of their talents; he united *these people, by the shores of Breena, claiming it as their sanctuary. Under the spirit of Daghdha, Darren ensured that no harm would come to them, or anyone else true and pure of heart, while residing there.*

The Oran-Roy tree was the heart of this sanctuary. Despite the changing seasons, the tree's growth remained constant. Neither the cold harshness of winter, nor the intense summer heat, could alter the flourishing of the tree.

The first generation of mix-blooded children embraced the Oran-Roy tree and felt that the spirit of Daghdha was embodied within it. Over time, the mix-blooded adults became Druids. With Darren's guidance, and with his daughter, Donelle, guiding her fellow Druids by her visions, the Druids dedicated their lives to serving those who continued to suffer in Ireland. Lleu, the Oran-Roy bird, was the druid's means of reaching Ireland and returning home.

Like Darren's people years earlier, many Celtic people were still suffering gravely as a result of the feuding within Ireland. The Oran-Roy bird and the Druids saved those they believed to be pure of heart. More people were welcomed to Oran-Roy; Darren graciously harbouring many Celtic people, initiating them into Oran-Roy clans and providing them with a new purpose.

After many successful years assisting the suffering Celtics in Ireland, the people of Oran-Roy came to idolise the Druids; they insisted on honouring them, describing them as heroes, guardians, angels and Gods given to the people in human form. Respecting the wishes of his people, in the depths of his Tarmon castle, Darren erected the Hall of Heroes, a reverent, holy and dark sanctuary honouring the Druids with their statues erected in serene gardens.

In addition to the Druids, some children of couples from different clans were continuing to exhibit heightened human qualities throughout their youth. Families became very accepting of this and the Druids guided these children into becoming heroes of Oran-Roy to serve the people with their gifts.

One of these children was Cuchulainn; he was born to parents from Tarmon and Crag. Cuchulainn could withstand pain and speak in many different tongues. His ability to recite and understand countless languages made it possible to educate Donelle and the Druids in a language that they kept to themselves. The code of the Druids became: vos es fortis; dare vestry donum tamen usquequaque subsist versus, meaning: you are true; you are pure of heart; you are brave; share your gift, but always remain true.

*

Donelle, having led the druids and heroes of Oran-Roy for a number of years, consulted her ailing father, warning him of impending trouble. Despite the years, Darren's daughter, as well as the first generation of mix-blooded children, had not aged. It *appeared that their role for Oran-Roy would surpass a human lifetime.*

Sensing Donelle's pain as she awaited the death of her ailing father, Cuchulainn comforted her and they formed an inseparable bond. Cuchulainn and Donelle tried to ignore how they felt about one another, as Cuchulainn was promised to Delaney, daughter of Darren's nominated successor, Delano. With Donelle leading the Druid people and guiding upcoming heroes of Oran-Roy, Darren required a successor to lead Tarmon and the clans of Oran-Roy. He selected his younger cousin, Delano.

Delaney was a strange young woman; her effortless grace, serene ebony hair and pale complexion masked an inner struggle within her soul.

Delaney began to morph into a towering, black, snarling wolf-like beast. She left her home, prowling to find Enya, an annoying boisterous girl who made fun of her fascination of birds. Delaney was hoping to shock Enya beyond belief in her new form, but Delaney was not able to find her. In her anger, Delaney returned home, destroying everything around her.

Witnessing the destructive rage, Delaney's mother ran out and screamed, "Monster!" With a trembling hand, Delaney's mother raised a blade in the air against the beast, not realising that the beast was her own flesh and blood.

Hurt and disgusted by what she had been called by her own mother, Delaney allowed the beast to take over.

After the rage subsided, Delaney returned to her human form, covered with her mother's blood. She gave her soul to the beast within her.

Delaney lied to her father, Delano. He believed her story: that a mix-blooded man had lost control, attacked his wife and ran away, leaving her mutilated body behind.

Months passed and Delano grew fearful of Delaney, concerned that she, like the mixed blooded person he believed to have killed his wife, would develop a frightening ability. Aware of her father's feelings, Delaney remained patient, hoping that once her father assumed the throne after Darren's death, her dream of ruling with unmeasurable power and unleashing the beast within her, the beast she had named 'Morrigan', would come to fruition.

*

"Bee! Honestly! You're hopeless. Get up!" Ethan opened my blinds, hoping that the light would hasten my waking up routine.

"No! It's too cosy!" I mumbled, pulling the thick woollen sheets over my head. Not satisfied, Ethan ripped them out of my numb morning hands and plonked himself alongside my now scrunched up body.

"Did you finish it? What did you find out?"

Of course! The book! "Well I didn't finish it. My eyes couldn't stay open just after half way," I replied, finally finding enough energy to sit upright, to maintain a decent conversation without drifting back to sleep.

"Well," Ethan's eyes were practically bulging out of his head, dying to find out if I had discovered any links between the Morrigan Book, and myself. "Did you find out anything worth sharing?"

Without warning, an awful sensation consumed my gut. My stomach seemed to have a heartbeat of its own. I felt queasy and light headed.

"I feel awful!" I fell back into my bed once more, curling up into a ball. "Argh! The pain's brutal!" I grumbled, with my hands rubbing my aching abdomen.

"You look paler than usual," Ethan placed his palm across my perspired forehead. "You're burning up. Maybe something Mam made last night has upset your stomach. Want me to get Mam?"

"No," I quickly answered, just wanting to be left alone until my pain had past.

"Are you sure? I can get Mam if you …"

"I SAID NO!!!" I yelled.

The pain in my gut suddenly spread. Hot needles were poking in and out of my skin everywhere! I grew angry. Rage took control. My blood boiled. The heat made it feel as though my skin was stretching.

"BEE!" Ethan cried.

Hearing him only fuelled my rage.

"ARGH!" I roared.

I didn't sound like myself. I couldn't control my movement. My muscles were contracting, distorting and twisting as though I was a child's doll being pulled apart and destroyed! My body began to jolt backwards and forwards. The legs of the bed were scratching away the varnish of the timber floorboards. The pain barely allowed me to open my eyes, but when I did, I didn't see myself. Muscular limbs with rapidly growing black hair hid my pale skin.

The pain did not cease. Attempting to sit up and walk to the bathroom, I rolled off the bed, feeling like a tonne of bricks! My lamp and glass ornaments fell from the dressing table and shattered on the floor. The shattering glass echoed, piecing my ears.

As quickly as the pain had come, it suddenly vanished. I raised my body, looked down and saw two black bear-like paws. At first I wanted to leg it and hide, but my nose caught the scent of human flesh; the urge to satisfy my aching hunger drove my mind wild. In all the chaos Ethan had fled the room. I couldn't think. All I could do was find something fresh and warm to sink my teeth into. I leaped from the floor, charged out of my room and vaulted off the second floor down to the hallway below. The glass cabinets shattered and the staircase collapsed. The screaming coming out of the lounge room intensified the need to feed. I was the predator and my family in the next room were my prey.

Stop Brianna! Run away until it passes! They're your family! Your family! Control yourself!

The strong scent quickly supressed the last rational thought I had. The beast had consumed every ounce of me. No longer Brianna, I embodied the Morrigan beast. My hairy hind legs pushed me through the lounge room sliding door. The door split in two; a large piece of it hitting Tara in the leg. She fell and lay before me on the floor; an easy prey to supress the ravenous gut.

Our eyes interlocked. Despite her fearful gaze and painful wails, which were her last attempts to find her daughter within the beast, foam fell from my jaw, ready to consume and shred apart the woman who had raised me.

*

"You coming down for breakfast or not?"

My body jolted up beneath the warm, wet covers of my bed, tossing the Morrigan Book that was buried amongst the sheets onto the timber floor of my bedroom.

"Bee? You even up yet?" Ethan bellowed outside by bedroom door, reminding me to take a look at the time.

"Crap!" I had over slept by almost an hour! "Dammit! I didn't set my bloody alarm!" I grumbled, untangling myself from the python-like covers strangling my limbs. "Just have a piece of toast ready for me and I'll eat it on the way to the bus!"

"Fine," Ethan groaned, storming back down the stairs mumbling under his breath, most probably complaining about always doing things for me at the last minute.

My bedclothes were completely drenched in sweat.

"I'll have to hide them until they dry off," I whispered to myself, "Mam would freak."

Already behind my morning routine, I really should have been running around like a gimp for school. Instead, I leant down to retrieve the Morrigan book from my bedroom floor and sat on the edge of my bed to ponder my nightmare. I flicked through the book and navigated my way to the final page that I remembered reading.

"Hurt and disgusted by what she had been called by her own mother, Delaney allowed the beast to take over. After the rage subsided, Delaney returned to her human form, covered with her mother's blood. She gave her soul to the beast within her."

My mind replayed the events of my nightmare.

"Surely I can't be the same as the Morrigan beast just because I look similar!" I thought over and over. *"I won't allow myself to believe that!"*

But why did I doubt myself?

Chapter Four

History

Almost three hours into the school day people were still staring and whispering about the event that occurred two days ago. Despite the uncomfortable circumstance of people speculating behind my back, the day was kind enough to offer me some amusement in English class. Not only was Mrs Smith trying to avoid me at all costs, her nature and approach to the lesson was rather angelic and peaceful in comparison to her usual means of instruction. I guess that was one good thing that resulted from the apparent *anxiety attack* ordeal.

Recess went by in a flash and I still hadn't perked up the courage to confide in Charlotte about my nightmare.

Casually making our way to our separate History classes, Charlotte was going on and on about her science club experiment and, while pretending to listen, I was trying to find the right words to describe my nightmare to her. But how do you explain to your closest friend that you are worried about becoming a monster?

I found a seat at the very front of the class - a regular occurrence. Teachers would think of me as a *keen* student for being situated at the front, whereas my fellow students recognized me as a latecomer, with absolutely no interest in History. Still waiting for the teacher to arrive, I attempted to ease my concerns.

"Finish the whole book first before jumping to such a ridiculous conclusion!" I thought to myself. *"So far you have done nothing to give yourself a reason to think that you are capable of hurting people. Finish the book and then confide in Ethan and Charlotte."* I was almost beginning to think that the doctor's 'anxiety' prognosis wasn't so far off the mark.

After five minutes of waiting for Mrs Hansen, amid the staring and murmuring I knew that was taking place behind me, Mr O'Hara rushed through the classroom doorway and was followed in by another man.

The man was rather tall, muscular and professionally attired; his mahogany eyes were accentuated by his short, wavy brown hair. It would be fair to say that he was rather attractive. The diminished noise level and sudden whispering amongst the girls since he had entered the classroom supported the summation.

"Unfortunately, Mrs Hansen has been detained and will be for quite some time. Her son, as you know, has been recovering from a car accident and she is the only member of the family with the means to assist him during his rehabilitation. At this stage, most probably for the next month, Mr Lawson will be your teacher for History. Please make Mr Lawson feel welcome in our school community." Mr O'Hara clapped and encouraged us all to accompany him. Following the welcoming applause, Mr O'Hara concluded his speech. "I'll now hand them over to you, Mr Lawson, and get back to my meeting."

"Thank you, Mr O'Hara." Mr Lawson spoke with an air of confidence and refinement. "So, to History. It is indeed a great passion of mine and I am privileged to be sharing my passion for History with you." Stephanie Briggs was almost passing out in the back row. I had a suspicion that I wouldn't be sitting in the front row anymore. "I've been informed by your History teacher that you were concluding studies on World War II. Now, according to the requirements for this year, you are supposed to study the French Revolution and briefly address Napoleon." Prior to speaking again, Mr Lawson walked away from the board, removed his glasses and leant against the teacher's desk in an incredibly cavalier manner. "These areas are important to cover and we will cover them, but, just so we have an understanding, I was considering teaching our own history and aspects of this country that are relevant to who and what we are today. That way, I get to know you, you get to know me and I think that you'll find History quite an enjoyable subject."

I'd be surprised if Mr Lawson could alter the loathing I had for History. History and I just didn't go together, like mixing oil with water, it just wouldn't work!

*

The day had finally come to a close and Charlotte and I met up at the courtyard near the school exit, waiting for Ethan, to catch the bus home.

"And how was the rest of your day after recess?" Charlotte asked, while rummaging through her bag, attempting to retrieve her wallet.

"Mediocre. Oh, I've got a new History teacher. He seems okay. Stephanie seems to think he's *more* than okay if you get my drift."

"Oh, right." Charlotte chuckled.

"He seems to think that he can make us all enjoy History. So far, his attempts have not worked."

"Hey, it's been one day, for goodness sake! Give the man a break!"

"Anyhow," I said, trying to find a more interesting topic. "How was the science thing you had at lunch?"

"Oh, it was okay I guess. We're just trying to design a cool experiment for the local school competition. But, the people in it are a pain. I wanted to do it to be involved in something, but I regret it now. And before you say it, don't say I ..."

"... Told you so."

"Thanks a million, Bee," Charlotte replied, rolling her bright green eyes. Charlotte's expression transformed to bafflement. "Who's that with Ethan, Bee?"

I followed Charlotte's gaze, attempting to focus on the person walking directly beside Ethan. A few seconds passed by; the distance shortened and I identified Ethan's friend, Logan.

Logan was in our grade and attended the all boys' school across the street with Ethan, yet his tall, solid build made him appear too mature for high school. He was an acquaintance, someone whom I spoke to here and there, based on connections through people I knew, but I longed to be more than a mere acquaintance. I could not deny that since I met him, he found his way into my imaginings. I can get carried away - English class two days ago proved that. My immediate feelings for Logan were based on external qualities, but, I had hoped that, one day, my intense feelings for his exterior would resonate with a generous soul.

Love for a family member or a dear friend differed from the feelings I had for Logan. The anticipation that built up inside me when I saw his face was like a kettle coming to boil at intense pressure. My brain latched onto hypothetical visualisations of him and I spending time together and refused to let go! I set myself up to fall; I fast forwarded to what I wanted too quickly and, before my eyes, I could see what I wanted evaporating into pain, frustration and deep regret. I needed to step back, press the pause button and let things take their course. If only life was as easy as pressing a button, deleting all the crap that seemed to ruin chances for happiness.

"Oh, it's Logan, Bee. We haven't seen him around in a while," Charlotte said, as she swung her bag onto her right shoulder, readying to leave for the bus.

I went to speak, but struggled. I swallowed and that seemed to usher in the words. "No, he … he was at Church last Sunday." Don't ask me to tell you what the homily was about.

Ethan and Logan finally reached us. Their final steps were a cue for my heart to pick up the pace and for my pale Irish skin to turn beetroot red.

"Hey guys! Been a while! How've you been?" In person, Logan's voice was hypnotic, sending me into a trance.

"I'm okay, yeah … and how are you?" I couldn't believe that I managed to produce words of any kind!

"Not bad, but honestly, I'm over school. Just want to finish up and get on with things." Logan crossed his arms, leant against the brick wall, appearing incredibly casual. "So, Bee, Ethan tells me you ended up in hospital. Are you right now?"

Clearly, by my delayed response, I wasn't expecting to be asked a question; my focus was imprisoned by Logan's charm. Though, despite asking me a direct question, Logan's eyes were gazing beside my head at something in the distance. I decided I should still answer. "Oh, yeah. Thanks for asking, Logan. I'm fine now, nothing to worry about. The doctor just said..."

"Hey, Steph! How ya going?" Logan said, waving to Stephanie who was walking nearby, his focus now directed towards her *deliberately* shortened skirt. "I'll be with you in a sec! Sorry guys, I've got to dash. ...Got to ask Steph if she'll join me at the charity dance. Are you all going?"

Again, this was a moment when I wish life would offer me a remote and allow a rewind. I questioned what had just occurred. Logan had completely put aside what I was talking about. He didn't care! He had absolutely no desire to really find out how I was! Or, perhaps he simply forgot and was genuinely in a rush.

"Listen to yourself, Brianna! You're defending him for being rude! He brushed you aside!"

"I'm pretty sure that we're going. Aren't we, Charlotte?" Ethan asked.

"I guess. Well, you and Bee are in the Jazz bands. I was under the impression that both school's bands were playing for part of the evening, weren't you?" Charlotte replied.

"Oh, yeah!" Ethan said, gently slamming his palm into his forehead. "How could I forget?" I had an inkling that Ethan was not asking Charlotte about attending the dance; he questioned whether they would attend the dance *together*. For being one of the most perceptive people I knew, Charlotte was incredibly *unperceptive* about this.

Logan's attention was still directed towards Stephanie, now in closer proximity. "See ya!" he cried, hastening away.

No longer in earshot of Logan, Ethan's face demonstrated the need to release anger.

"What an absolute jerk! Can you believe him? He completely brushed you off, Bee! I can't believe I actually thought he was a decent fella! I thought he was asking me about you because he was genuinely concerned or wanted to take *you* to the dance! He must've wanted the gossip on what happened."

"Yeah, Bee! What a bowsie! He wasn't even looking at you when you were speaking! Well, at least Stephanie will keep him busy. I don't want to have a bar of him!" Charlotte passionately replied.

Ethan and Charlotte were not aware of the feelings I had developed for Logan. Their words of defence were bittersweet. Sweet for how deeply they cared about me, yet bitter, as they acknowledged what I was trying to deny. I replayed how Logan had behaved and longed to go back, edit the scene and profoundly yell, *'Cut!'* But life was not that kind.

I shrugged my shoulders and pretended not to care. "Yeah, he is a jerk. Honestly, I don't care, but thanks for thinking of me." As I said these words, my chest compressed, my eyes tightened, restraining my body from sighing. A tear of anger and extreme disappointment squeezed from the corner of one eye.

During the long ride home, my head rested upon the cool bus window, my breath fogging up the glass, every thought, excluding, *don't forget to record the Batman show tonight,* was mulling over Logan. I quickly discovered that I wasn't angry with Logan; I was angry with myself. I allowed myself to get caught up in an image of someone, rather than their true self. The Logan I had created was the person I wanted him to be. I know I didn't really know him; however, I was still saddened by the way in which I was treated. It hurt, but it's not very *'Brianna'* like to display emotions through tears. *Brianna is a tough girl and nothing gets to her,* my friends and family would say. I had to hold it together, supress what had happened and move on. I guess I could summarise this experience as my first form of heartache, first *crush* or first idea of what life offers with love. The anticipation associated with love is wonderful; the disappointment and regret in the aftermath of the blast is low. Life continues on, though, and the Morrigan book would now occupy my thoughts, once dedicated to Logan. I needed to confirm to myself that I wasn't going to wake up and find a werewolf staring back at me in the bathroom mirror.

*

To avoid his intended union with Delaney, Donelle and Cuchulainn fled to Ireland on the Oran-Roy bird. The pair united and in time they had a son, Keith. Concerned for the wellbeing of the Druids, the other young mix-blooded heroes and Donelle's dying father, Darren, Cuchulainn and Donelle returned to Oran-Roy with their son.

Once in Tarmon, Donelle urged her father to nominate Keith as his appointed heir, to assume the throne of Oran-Roy once he became of age. Darren agreed and before dying, Darren presented Donelle with a gift for Keith.

"The Druids and I designed this for you, knowing you would one day return," Darren struggled to explain, gently

grasping Donelle's ageless hand and placing a large locket into her palm. "You spoke of a war, a war where the Irish people would try to infiltrate the magic of Oran-Roy. For this reason, the Druids helped me design this. It plays a song," Darren explained, "a song that only the Oran-Roy bird will come to from now on. When opened, the song will summon the bird and the bird must respond to the will of the carrier of this device. This device is now the only means of entering and leaving Oran-Roy. Through Daghdha's wisdom, the Druids were able to keep Oran-Roy hidden, as it was when I was a boy. Whoever becomes the Carrier becomes the lifeline of Oran-Roy and bears the Tarmon cross on their hand. Protecting the Carrier protects Oran-Roy, but destroying the Carrier will destroy all of Oran-Roy, for, with its destruction, Oran-Roy will be visible to the outside world."

Donelle was by her father's side as he died peacefully in his sleep, Lucians at his side, with Prislens ready to carry his soul. Darren's enduring legacy was clear from the mourning he received from the Oran-Roy clans. But, following Darren's death, and without the fear of Ireland threatening Oran-Roy's existence, a new fear began to emerge. Festering its way throughout the clans, an unanswered doubt was gradually being transformed into a unanimous belief. This newly formed idea would erode the heart of what nourished the Oran-Roy people.

Despite the blossoming snowdrops of spring, the once unchanging Oran-Roy tree was in an autumn, fleeing from warmth and the joy of new life, preparing to endure a winter that would only welcome spring if its friend, Peace, decided to rekindle the eroding spirit of the people.

Like the tree, Cuchulainn was almost in the autumn of his life, but Donelle was forever trapped in spring. Their son, Keith, was not known to anyone; Donelle had foreseen that her son would come to rule Oran-Roy after the war. For this reason, Donelle asked the fellow Druids to remove Keith's ability and his insignia's, only leaving the symbol of Tarmon. Trusting her judgement, the Druids obeyed her orders and did not question her motives.

After years of festering, the rumours about the death of Delaney's mother had become a reality for the people. Delano, who had succeeded Darren, threatened to infiltrate the Druids and discover the mix-blooded person responsible for the death of his wife. Clans were associating random deaths and animal attacks with the mix-blooded people. Families were beginning to fear for the safety of their halfblooded children; some families even began to fear the power of their own children. The clans were demanding that Delano act and find the source of the killings, or denounce his rule over Oran-Roy. By way of compromise, Delano even exiled Delaney to the Darian forest, unknowingly giving her the freedom to formulate her plans.

Peace's enemy, Chaos, was consuming the heart of Oran-Roy. Mix-blooded people fled to the shores of Breena, where the Oran-Roy tree would provide them with sanctuary. Some were lucky; others did not make the journey. One by one, mix-blooded people were being exterminated in an irrational genocide fuelled by speculation and fear.

Chaos was merely a pawn in a game of chess; distracting the opponent from the dreaded Queen, Delaney, impatiently waiting for the opportune moment to offer herself to the people - when they had no choice but to surrender to her vision.

With little left to offer, Delano felt that he had to legitimise the wishes of the people. He ordered the clans to capture mix-blooded people and have them killed or confined, thinking that eventually wiping them out would relieve the problem. People defied Delano in attempts to save their mix-blooded children or friends, but these people were also killed or confined for defending the fallen heroes - the new name given to the guardians and heroes of Oran-Roy.

With nowhere left to turn and no one to protect them, the remaining mix-blooded people, in the refuge of the Druids, banded together to fight for a new King. Donelle was not sure what awaited the mix-blooded people, but she knew that, no matter what the outcome of the battle would be, one day her son would be King. The Oran-Roy people would serve a Tarmon King. They would believe Keith to be a pureblood, believing him to be the son of Darren's sister, born of Tarmon parents.

Caelan, one of the Druids, felt uneasy fighting a war for a King who did not solely belong to one clan. Donelle, Cuchulainn and other Druids urged her to look beyond the lie and realise that Oran-Roy would have peace again when ruled by a descendent of Darren. Despite their attempts, Caelan and other Druids could not bring themselves to fight a war built on a lie, no matter what it meant for the greater good. They left the Oran-Roy tree and sought refuge in lakes and rivers, scared to be harmed by those who feared them and ashamed by the state of Oran-Roy under their protection.

After leaving the Druids, Caelan's appearance was changing. No longer warm in complexion, Caelan's skin was pale and clammy, her ears became pointy and her eyes had widened, resembling the eyes of a cat. Leaving the Druids was taking its toll on Caelan and those who followed her.

Delaney and her army ruthlessly exterminated the mix-blooded people who had strayed from Breena. Donelle left the safe haven of the Oran-Roy clan by the Breena shores, seeking to heal the injured. Delaney, whose evil powers were now in the ascendancy, cursed Donelle's hands, turning her saving hands into hands of death.

Cuchulainn's army was depleted. Their goal of fighting for a new King was no longer the reason for battle; they were fighting *for survival. Fear of the mix-bloods' power drove Delano's purebreed army to battle. Keith fled on his father's horse, Epona. Cuchulainn ordered her to keep Keith safe at any cost.*

During the battle, Delaney revealed herself as the Morrigan beast, then dispersed into hundreds of crows, feasting on the injured heroes across the bloody field. Keith, compelled by his dying father's anguish, returned to the battleground. While being called to the next world, Cuchulainn muttered the creed of the heroes to his son and wife.

"Vos es versus, my son," Cuchulainn clung to Keith's arm, as Donelle sobbed against his chest, powerless.

"Always, father," Keith breathed. The Prislens escorted Cuchulainn's spirit to Daghdha's realm of peace.

The few remaining survivors were almost swallowed up by a black tunnel of wind; the crows were uniting together, forming the Morrigan monster. The snarling beast stood over the departed Cuchulainn. Epona knocked Keith out of the way, following her master's orders, compelling him to return to Donelle. Donelle felt helpless, unable to heal the injured and dying, including her beloved Cuchulainn.

Delano's army were forced to surrender to Morrigan. The waring ended when the beast killed Delano, leaving them with Morrigan as their Queen. Delaney had triumphed. Too powerful to be destroyed by the purebloods, they had no choice but to follow her rule, or meet their death.

Delaney consulted Caelan after claiming the throne, urging her to reveal the unwritten future. Caelan said that no matter what Delaney did, Keith would be King; Oran-Roy's allegiance would return to a descendent of Darren. Caelan warned Morrigan that a person who matched her strength would end her existence.

To overcome the prophesised future, the Morrigan beast tried to infiltrate the Druid's sanctuary where Keith was harbouring. She wanted to claim the carrier as her own, to leave Oran-Roy and force the Celts to surrender to her rule. But, not being pure of heart, the beast's foot burned as it crossed the threshold on Daghdha's holy ground.

Donelle and the other Druids could not kill Morrigan; they could not take a life on Daghdha's ground. The pure bloods were too weak to kill Morrigan, but Morrigan needed to be destroyed in order for peace to return to Oran-Roy. The Druids did the only thing they could; bind Morrigan to her crow form. While being bound, Morrigan's spirit dispersed into the nearest objects of value to her, vowing that if one drop of murderous blood hit Oran-Roy's earth, the beast would return and that the one who made way for her return would be rewarded. The Druids protected Morrigan's broken bow and arrow, claiming that if a murderous drop of blood was spilt on Oran-Roy's earth, the keeper of these possessions would be able to control the wrath of the returning beast and end her with her own weapon.

The Oran-Roy tree's bare branches were beginning to show signs of life. Peace was begging the small buds to open and leave the harsh battle of winter behind. With Morrigan now bound to the black crows of the barren trees of Daray, relying on Chaos to drive the people to murderous ways, the people called upon the Druids for answers.

Donelle and the Druids presented Keith, a descendent of Darren, to rule over the people. Keith was welcomed back into Tarmon, but like Delano before him, he prevented the unions of couples from different clans, in order to maintain peace and restore the order that had been forgotten by the people.

Chapter Five

A Sleepless Night

Knock. Knock. Knock.

The source of the heavy-handed knock didn't have to speak; I knew who it was.

"I'm sleeping soon, Dad," I whispered.

"You need your sleep, Brianna," Dad whispered, too. Very gently, he opened my door and peered through the small gap. "I don't care how exciting that book that Michael got you is, the doctor said you need rest and you know how your Mam will be if she knows you aren't sleeping right, okay?"

I groaned. *"I know, I know."* Before closing the book, I took a quick look at the page number. Dad still wasn't satisfied. I knew he wouldn't leave until the light was off and the book was out of my hands. *"Okay, okay!"* I plonked the book on my bedside table and switched off the lamp with a, *"Humph."*

"Better. 'Night."

"Good night," I grumbled. I wasn't going to settle for this. I was wide-awake and so close to finding out how I connected with the contents of this story. I had already discovered what the markings on my wrists meant, as well as why my eyes were each a different colour. There was no way I was going to stop now! Besides, it would be nice to know if I was going to turn into a bloodthirsty monster in the foreseeable future.

Impatiently, I bided my time and stared at the narrow gap between the foot of my door and the floor. As the beam of light vanished from beneath the door, I knew dad had switched the hallway lamp off downstairs, which was my cue to switch my lamp back on and continue reading. Nothing would stop me from completing this book now. Nothing!

*

Centuries later, the carrier device still remained within the royal family of Tarmon, who governed the clans of Oran-Roy. Kings would secretly use the device to call upon the bird and explore the world beyond Oran-Roy and understand how the world around them was changing. King Bowen Kael's daughter pursued the wonders of the outside world when taking secret trips on the Oran-Roy bird to Ireland. On her regular secretive visits, Glynn found love.

Too strong and genuine to ignore, Glynn committed herself to the Irish man, promising that one day she would explain to him where she was from and allow him to come too. Glynn returned to Oran-Roy and, before planning her next adventure, she discovered that she was with child. Knowing the law and knowing the potential consequences of having a mix-blooded child, Glynn took refuge in Daray amongst the Darian clan, who promised to care for the child once it was born.

Years later, Glynn's sister had a son, Zia, who would rule after the passing of Bowen. Zia, much like his aunt, was adventurous and hated nothing more than being confined to the walls of the Tarmon castle. Unable to use the carrier as often as he liked, Zia would often venture off into Daray, befriending the very trustworthy and loyal Darian people who had sworn to honour the word of any soul.

Leona, a very spirited Darian, befriended Zia and eventually, with the blessing of her clan, introduced Zia to his cousin, Dallas Conlan.

Zia visited Dallas whenever he could and, when possible, he reunited him with his mother, Glynn. When Dallas was seventeen, he started having dreams of the future. Once Zia became aware of this, he advised Dallas to leave Oran-Roy before his mix-blooded ability was discovered and traced back to Glynn, fearful that it would initiate war amongst the clans.

Dallas had a vision of himself residing in Ireland. He finally conceded that he needed to leave his home, in order to protect those dearest to him in Oran-Roy. When Zia and Glynn had access to the carrier locket, they helped Dallas arrive safely in Ireland, where he was introduced to his father for the first time.

Zia and Dallas' bond did not end there. Once he became King, Zia took adventurous trips to Ireland, visiting Dallas as often as he could, as well as collecting valuable information about the revolutionised world his people in Oran-Roy must never know. Zia summarised his research and interests in a small notebook. Zia's writings were safely locked away in the vaults of the Tarmon castle, fearful that, in the wrong hands, his secrets would become known and would jeopardize his people. Dallas had warned Zia to hide away the Morrigan possessions and separate the pieces. That way, those who would abuse its power would be unable access them upon Morrigan's return.

Zia had three children: Cillian, Sully and Keira Kael. His wife sadly passed away soon after the birth of his only daughter. Like her father and adventurous aunt before her, Keira befriended the people of Daray, thinking that her father was unaware. Zia and Dallas' loyal friend, ageless Leona, befriended yet another Kael, but to Keira's knowledge, she was the only Kael family member Leona had ever come to know.

The Darian clan grew close to those from Crag. Throughout history, the Crag people offered the Darian people refuge and protection in exchange for learning how to communicate with the creatures of Oran-Roy, the Arawn dog pack, especially. Craig, like Keira, secretly continued to remain in close ties with the Darian clan, despite the wishes of his people and family.

One evening, the fates aligned, crossing Keira Kael of Tarmon, and Craig Elsa of Crag, along the same path, both on their way to consult their Darian friend, Leona.

Over time, and across continuing visits to confide in Leona, Keira and Craig began to acknowledge a bond that was drawing them closer to one another. Despite the obvious obstacles in the way, forbidding two such people sharing a union, nothing could justify or convince Keira and Craig that their genuine feelings of love for each other were wrong. Socialising with people from other clans was unlawful and dangerous, given the volatile relations amongst clans and the law instigated by King Keith, centuries earlier, to maintain peace and prevent Morrigan's return, but how was the desire to love someone wrong?

*

One evening, when Keira and Craig were contemplating how to act, attempting to do what was right given their rigid circumstances, Cuchulainn's spirit, Keira's ancestor, consulted with the conflicted couple. Cuchulainn advised the pair to acknowledge their love, not to deny it. He explained that the will of Daghdha brought them together and it is that will that will restore Oran-Roy to the foundations Darren Kael envisioned for his people.

Cuchulainn assured Keira and Craig that their children, descendants of Darren, would help relieve Oran-Roy of Morrigan's constrictive curse. When Zia came to know of Cuchulainn's appearance, he offered Keira and Craig his blessing, but insisted that their union remain secret until it was safe enough for their mix-blooded children to end Morrigan's hidden, but constant threat.

Cillian, Keira's eldest brother, came to know of Keira's union and Zia's blessing. Rage consumed Cillian, knowing that his opportunity to rule would be overshadowed by his sister's children, whom were foretold to be Oran-Roy's long awaited answer of hope.

With the help of the Darian people, Craig and Keira took refuge in a cave well hidden within the forests of Daray. Keira and Craig welcomed a son into the world, Brogan.

*

Aware that Zia was no longer confiding in his sons, Cillian urged Sully to join with him and turn his sister and her mix-blooded child over to the people to decide their fate. Unable to locate their sister, Sully and Cillian decided to bide their time and orchestrate a means of coming to rule over Tarmon and subsequently, Oran-Roy.

Brogan was almost two years of age when Keira realised that she was once again expecting. Still weary and fearful of outsiders, Keira and Craig continued to be harboured by the Darian clan.

One rainy evening, when Craig was out hunting for food in the safe haven of the Daray woods, Cuchulainn appeared to him again, warning him of a monstrous betrayal that would jeopardise the lives of Brogan and of Keira and Craig's unborn child.

Cillian ventured into Daray, seeking out the cats of the woods. When he came in contact with their leader, he claimed that he would reward them if they could locate and divulge the whereabouts of his sister, Keira. Unlike the Arawn dog pack, led by Keelty and her mate Faolon, the cats of Daray did not associate with humans. But, with Cillian's offer too great to ignore, the cats prowled the woods, informing Cillian of his sister's secret location. Dougal, a cat of the Daray Woods, acted against the expectations of his station and confided in Leona and the Arawn pack, begging them to warn Keira of her impending arrest. When his treason became known, Dougal's tail was cut in half by the cat clan. He was exiled and left to fend for himself in the woods.

Keira was on the verge of giving birth to her child when Leona and Keelty warned them about Cillian. Only days before delivering her second child, Keira and Craig were taken to another cave on the outskirts of Daray, on the very border of Oran-Roy, in case they had no choice but to use the carrier device and leave on the Oran-Roy bird, fleeing for Ireland to protect their children.

On the eve of Keira's child being born, Zia died peacefully in his sleep, like his ancestor, Darren, before him. Craig kept the terrible news from Keira until after the birth of their daughter.

Devastated by the loss of her father, turmoil embroiled Keira's heart; she needed to serve her people, but also protect her children, even more so now that her brother would assume the throne. Keira and Craig decided to flee for Ireland to keep their children safe until it was right for them to return home.

As soon as Keira was physically able, Craig called upon the help of Keelty, to assist them in reaching Tarmon and Daray's border in order to ride the Oran-Roy bird to Ireland. Keelty, being a large wolfhound-like dog, was fast and extremely agile. For this reason, Craig strapped their newborn daughter to Keelty's back, in case an unplanned escape was required. Craig and Keira shared a horse and hid Brogan between them. Close to the early hours of the morning, Craig and his family made their way towards Tarmon's edge.

*

Knock. Knock.

My heart jumped.

"Bee?"

"*Ethan!*" I whispered harshly though gritted teeth. "You certainly know how to scare someone half to death!"

"Sorry!" he whispered back, while gently closing my bedroom door. "I went to the bathroom and saw your light on. You're lucky Dad and Mam are buggered."

"Yeah I'm almost done. But I *won't* be if you stay here!"

"Okay, I can take a hint!" He started making his way out of my room. "I just wanted to see if you had found out anything yet."

I folded the corner of the page I was on and let the book rest in my lap. "I wouldn't know where to start, Ethan." I ran my fingers through my hair trying to think of what to tell Ethan first. "I at least know what my markings mean and the history behind this place. It's *so* involved, though. It delves into war, family, love, lies and secrecy ... at the moment it feels like a recount of a medieval kingdom across a number of centuries and ..."

"What about your markings?" Ethan interrupted.

"The cross is the symbol or Tarmon and this one here ..." I stroked my left wrist but stopped speaking, "... Look, Ethan I could go into so much detail, but I literally have three chapters to go!"

Ethan was almost half way out the door. "*Alright! Alright!*" he hushed in annoyance. "But don't whine about being shattered when you can't keep your eyes open tomorrow!"

I rolled my eyes, not wanting to respond, in case that would lead to more conversation that could potentially lead to more time away from finding the answers that await me at the book's end.

*

Almost reaching the border of Tarmon and Daray, a large group of black horses, controlled by riders in deep purple cloaks, began to follow in an effort to prevent the Crag family from leaving

Oran-Roy. The band of horses had almost reached the escapees as they arrived on Tarmon's edge.

As quickly as possible, Keira used the carrier and summoned the Oran-Roy bird. The bird came almost immediately and Craig and Keira urged Keelty to go first with the children to ensure their safety. In Keira's attempts to place Brogan on Keelty, she was pulled back by one of the cloaked men. Craig drew his sword and attempted to protect his family. He was greatly outnumbered and was unsuccessful. Keira, Craig and Brogan were unable to reach the Oran-Roy bird.

Amongst the struggle, Keira urged Keelty to take her daughter. Keelty obeyed Keira and leapt onto the bird. As the Oran-Roy bird was leaving the cliff edge, beating its powerful emerald green wings, Sully Kael, one of the cloaked men, lunged towards the birds left foot and held on with incredible strength. While flying over the sea separating Ireland and Oran-Roy, Sully manoeuvred himself towards the back of the bird, and was almost in reaching distance of Keelty and the baby. He was not only after the child; he was after the carrier, the silver locket that Keira had placed around Keelty, to ensure its safety.

In only a few minutes, the bird reached Ireland. Before even planting its feet, Keelty leapt off the birds back and ran as fast as she could to protect the child and the carrier. Sully stumbled off the bird and pursued Keelty. After running for quite some distance,

Keelty had reached a small street with very few homes. Suddenly, bright lights came towards Keelty and she was forced to leap out of the way of an oncoming car. In her attempts to move, the strapping around Keelty's back had become loose and the baby was thrown from her back and lay crying on the road.

Sully, in search of Keelty, had finally caught up and was almost in reaching distance of the child. Keelty crouched down, arched her back, rolled her shoulders, pulled back her gums, displayed her razor-like teeth and growled ominously at Sully. The noise of the swerving car, as well as Keelty, caught the attention of a man and woman in the closest home.

The presence of the man and woman startled Sully. Fearful and confounded, he ran away.

"Wait! Sir! Don't go! You could be hurt!" screamed the woman. "Hey! Are you all right? Dear, call an ambulance or something! He's run off, but I think he was hurt," the woman cried out to her husband, just as she discovered the whimpering baby alongside the edge of road.

Thinking that she was doing the right thing by the baby, the woman shooed away Keelty. Keelty respected the wishes of the woman and ran in pursuit of Cillian's brother, to ensure that he would not return to harm Keira and Craig's child.

The woman's husband quickly joined her in comforting the abandoned child. While picking up the child from the road, the man found a small, silver bracelet beside where the baby had laid.

"Brianna," he said. "That must be her name."

"Hi, Brianna," said the woman. To ease the traumatised baby, the woman placed her fingers in the baby's palm, and discovered the Tarmon cross on the baby's right wrist. Thinking that this was rather peculiar, the woman quickly showed her husband and thought that she should also have a look at the baby's left wrist, which revealed the bow and arrow symbol of Crag.

*

"Wait, wait … I'm their daughter. How can I be?" I threw the book towards the base of my bed, brought my knees up to my chest, held my legs together and allowed my head to rest upon them.

"How can a book published in nine-teen seventy-five describe me? Could this be true? No, no. Don't be thick! As if any of that stuff is possible!"

Doubting my sanity, I ran to Ethan's room with the book in hand. I needed to share my speculations. I needed validation. I needed my brother.

Chapter Six

Speculation

"Ethan! Ethan! Wake up!" With these words of desperation, my trembling hands clenched Ethan's covers and pulled them totally off his bed. *"Come on! Get up!"* Ethan showed no sign of life - apart from breathing. I scurried over to the main light switch and, in the process, almost found myself amongst the sheets on the floor at the base of Ethan's bed.

Light loomed throughout the room, as a tide engulfs a shore. Ethan's eyes squinted tightly; his hands searched around the base of his bed, attempting to shield the light with the blankets now on the floor.

"Bee!" Ethan moaned, his hand on the bedside table in search of his glasses. "What the *hell* is the time?"

"Never mind the time, Ethan! This is *really* important!" Waking people up before sunrise was not a habit of mine, but this was a pressing issue that could not wait until the morning. "Ethan, I'm *so, so* sorry, but this really cannot wait!"

"Just get to the point, Bee," said Ethan, accompanied with a long, tiresome yawn, "so I can get back to sleep ASAP." Ethan had not yet made eye contact with me; his eyes still adjusting from the sudden exposure to light.

I sat beside Ethan at the base of his bed. "So, I gather you finished it, as I predicted," he said, followed by clearing the early morning frog in his throat. "What did you find out? Any leads?"

I proceeded to speak, but was unable to. The anxiety within me built up and bubbled like a pot of simmering water; I was restrained, words escaped me.

Ethan leaned towards me, attempting to make eye contact. "Bee?" he said, greatly concerned by my lack of response. "Bee? Bee, you're shaking! What the … *are you alright?*" His tone expressed great anxiety.

After a deep breath, I was able to find words. "Read the last few pages." My hands shuddered as I released the book into Ethan's lap. Without delay and at great speed, Ethan flicked the book's frayed pages and navigated his way to the final chapter. Sitting and waiting for Ethan's response was agonising. I needed someone to validate my sanity, to understand my position and hopefully provide me with counsel. Unconsciously, amid questionable thoughts, my right foot vigorously tapped the timbre floor.

"Bee! *Please!* I'm almost done! One sec," spat Ethan, without removing his gaze from the book. It was only when Ethan addressed the foot tapping that I realised what I was doing.

"Oh, sorry."

Finally, Ethan finished, but his gaze remained on the frayed book residing in his lap. "Wow!" he said, while running his hands through his untidy brown hair. "I'm … wow … just speechless!" Ethan slid his gangly legs back onto his bed, crossed them over and sat up to face me completely. "Bee, not only do those last few pages describe you - they mention Mam, Dad – our house! It's pretty darn close to the version Mam and Dad tell us about the night they found you! And you said this was published in *nineteen seventy-five*?"

I'm glad Ethan required only a one-word answer; I was still finding difficulty in conjuring up words. "Yeah."

"Do you think somehow, that Mam and Dad told this to someone, they wrote about it and there was a *typo* for the publishing date? I mean, perhaps it was published in *nineteen ninety-five*. You were born in ninety-one; it's a possibility, isn't it?"

Listening to Ethan's speculations gave me time to find words. "Ethan, how many books have incorrect publishing dates? Anyway, forget the date. The book explains so many things!" I told Ethan everything. While flicking through the book and pointing out crucial points, I found myself summarising almost every chapter. At the conclusion of my summary, beams of sunlight seeped through the parting of the emerald curtains. Sunrise.

"Don't you see, Ethan? These half-bloods or whatever they're called, some were gifted with abilities. If … *if* this is true, that could explain why I can project thoughts. But, *could* this be true? I mean, it is pretty way out. I'm speaking as if this is one hundred percent accurate, but I really don't know. I really do think this is beyond coincidence. I understand if you are a bit spectacle over it though. I am too!"

"What did you say?" Ethan said; confusion illustrated all over his face. "Did you say that you understand if I'm *spectacle*?"

"I … I did didn't I. I know that's not the word. Damn, what's the word? Anyway, don't worry." I waved my hand. I wanted to move on with the conversation despite my poor vocabulary; this though, was too much of an opportunity for Ethan to pass up. He began to chuckle. "You *know* what I mean, Ethan!"

"Yeah! But not telling! This is way too fun! I don't want to spoil the moment!" Ethan collapsed into his bed and was unable to restrain himself from laughing.

"Ethan! Damn it! Just say the *bloody* word then!" I demanded, while I thumped his left leg with the Morrigan book.

"*Alright, alright,* Bee. I think what you were *trying* to say was that you understand if I'm *sceptical*."

"Fine! SCEPTICAL! HAPPY NOW?" Under different circumstances or looking back at this moment, I'm sure that I would find humour in it. But, considering the predicament I was in, joining Ethan in laughter was impossible.

"Look, I think the only thing you can do now is to try and track down the author," said Ethan, as he returned to sitting in an upright position. "And, Bee," he whispered, "Don't tell Mam or Dad about this yet, *okay?*"

I nodded.

"They'll just worry and it won't help our investigative efforts."

"Don't worry, I won't tell them." I was revolted by the thought of keeping secrets from my parents. I was always keen on sharing as much as I could with them. When I had failed to share anything of significance with Mam or Dad, a part of my brain would trigger an overwhelming feeling of guilt whenever I was in their company, but this set of circumstances were different. Bringing up questions about my real parents and trying to explain that I was capable of projecting thoughts, would give them reason to fret. Ethan was right. Involving them now was too risky for our investigation.

"Well..." I said, inviting Ethan to provide me with some words of comfort.

"... You never did Google the author's name, did you?"

"No, I didn't."

"One sec." Ethan signalled me to sit alongside him at his computer desk. "Let's have a look." Within one minute, Ethan had navigated his way through almost ten hits on Google; all providing the same information. "He's anonymous, Bee. If ten sources are saying this, I'm pretty sure it's true."

"So, going to the bookshop where Michael bought it from would be pointless?"

"I'd say so. They'd tell you exactly what I'm telling you now. I guess we could look into the publishing company, but if the author used another alias, he obviously made sure that his publishing company wouldn't reveal his name because..."

"Ethan," I interrupted. "The name used for the author was *Glynn Braden. Glynn* is a female name, so..."

"So?" continued Ethan. "That really is irrelevant. The author is anonymous. For all we know, it could be a fella who used a female name. We really don't know!" Ethan closed his fist and thumped the desk in frustration. "This is fierce! There must be a way, Bee. There's *got* to be a way we can get to the bottom of this!" The passion Ethan showed towards something that most people would brush aside made me feel proud to have a brother who was willing to abandon everything to help me.

"Thanks, Ethan," I said softly, accompanied with a pat on his shoulder.

"For what?" He really had absolutely no idea.

"Caring. Most people would laugh in my face about this, but you are genuinely interested and willing to help me." There was a pause. I think Ethan was so chuffed he was unable to find words.

"Well ... err ... it's nothing, Bee. Really! You'd do the same for me. Anyway," Ethan would always minimise his worth in conversations like this. "I doubt that you or I will be able to go back to sleep. Let's get ready early and meet Charlotte and chat to her about the book. You know she'll be dying to find out about it."

"Sounds good," I replied. "And perhaps we could pop in over at Michael's and I could ask him about the book. You never know, he might know something." Ethan shrugged his shoulders. "It's worth a try, Ethan!"

Ethan nodded his head in agreement. "No, you're right. It's worth a try. Anyway," Ethan clasped his hands together, "Let's get ready and leave here in thirty minutes, meet Charlotte and make our way over to Michael's." Ethan took a quick glance at his clock. "We'll be pushing it, though. We'll miss the bus if Michael gets out the china, you know."

"We'll make it." I said, leaving the room with great haste, hastening to get ready.

After texting Charlotte to inform her of our departure time, I made my bed, put my navy blue school uniform on and raced downstairs for a quick breakfast. While devouring my buttered toast, Dad and Mam, still adjusting to the new day, slumped into the kitchen, only making a pot of tea on their minds.

"What's the hurry?" Dad managed to articulate, amongst an overbearing yawn.

"Ethan, Charlotte and I..." I swallowed, and then was capable of continuing, "...we have to check something out at school."

"Scoozy, Dad. Got to get ready," said Ethan, flying past Dad in attempts to reach the fridge. "Mam, where's the cheese? Don't worry, Bee's got it."

Within two minutes, Ethan and I had eaten breakfast and gathered up all the food we needed for the school day. Our bags were packed and ready to go.

"See ya!" Ethan and I blared, racing out the front door.

Mam delayed the slamming of the door. "Wait, don't forget your umbrellas! You'll be walking home in the rain by the looks of things."

Ethan and I raced back to the front door and collected the umbrellas.

"Are you *sure* you haven't forgotten anything else?" Mam asked.

Normally I'd brush off this question, but today it actually fulfilled its purpose. "Oh! Wait one sec, Ethan. I left the book on my bed!"

"Come on, Bee! *Hurry up*," grumbled Ethan, tapping his watch with annoyance.

Leaving for a second time, Charlotte was found waiting patiently at the gate.

"Morning all," she greeted. "So, what's the rush? Is there something you have to inquire about at school?" Charlotte's eyes found the Morrigan book in my hands and no longer required an answer. "Oh! You finished it! What did you find out? Did it give you anything to go on?"

"Plenty." I said.

"Plenty! Well then, fill me in! What are you waiting for?"

The ten-minute walk to Michael's home was devoted to filling in Charlotte on the Morrigan book. As we drew closer to the end of the lane, Ethan and I revealed all of the information we could possibly remember. Never could I recall such a time when Charlotte listened so intently to my words without contributing. Her mouth remained open in wonder at every new fact revealed and every speculation considered, reminding me of the rotating clowns at carnivals that capture balls with their wide-open mouth.

"Brianna, I have to read this for myself and get every ounce of detail! Can I borrow it and give it back to you tomorrow?"

"Ethan has beaten you to it. But, I'm sure that he'll finish it by tomorrow. Won't you, Ethan?"

"I'll do my best," Ethan replied with a mischievous grin, while opening Michael's rickety wooden gate. The creaky sound of the gate alerted Michael that we were paying a visit. Before reaching the doorbell, Michael was already standing in the doorway of his petite and in-need-of-a-paint-job cottage.

"Well, hello, hello! I didn't expect you to drop in till the afternoon! But come in. Do come in! I enjoy your company as always!" Michael's vibrant energy masked his loss and feelings of extreme loneliness. Apart from Charlotte and my family, Michael had no one to console or be consoled by. Whenever our visits came to a close, Michael insisted on another pot of tea; his way of begging us to stay.

Disregarding the poor paint job and ancient furnishings, Michael's home was incredibly well kept and made pleasant by a variety of vibrant paintings. The number of paintings compensated for the lack of, or rather, no family photos. Ethan, Charlotte and I never questioned Michael about his family, fearful that we might open a can of worms.

The three of us followed Michael into his small sitting room and took our favoured positions; Ethan on the sofa, Charlotte on the chair by the window and me in the rocking chair.

"Now," Michael said enthusiastically and clapping his hands together. "Would I be assuming correctly if I said tea for everyone?" Ethan, Charlotte and I gave each other subtle looks of guilt.

"Actually, Michael," I managed to say, after receiving looks from Charlotte and Ethan nominating me as designated speaker, "We can only be really quick. You see, we wanted to ask you something."

"Ask away, ask away!" As he did so regularly, Michael employed enthusiasm in his tone to hide his disappointment.

"Well," I continued, "can you remember this book you gave me?" I removed the Morrigan book from my bag and handed it to Michael.

"Yes, yes. The shop owner said that it was quite a good read, but unfortunately not well-received or known by the public."

"So, do you know anything at all about it? Did the shopkeeper give you any information on it?" After completing my sentence, Ethan met my gaze and widened his eyes, silently urging me to avoid revealing too much detail.

"I'm sorry love, but I really don't know much. All I know is that it is of a genre you would enjoy."

"That's okay," I replied.

"Well," said Ethan. "We really have got to make tracks, Bee, or we'll miss the bus."

"Yeah, you're right. Sorry, Michael. We really do have to go. But we'll call in sometime in the next few days. Would that be better?"

"That would be fine. It gives me something to look forward to. Off you go then and I might have a fresh batch of shortbread biscuits or muffins for your next visit."

*

"Well, that was a big help, Bee! I told you it would be a complete waste of time!" Ethan moaned, as the three of us were out of Michael's earshot and making our way down the lane.

"Cut it out, Ethan! It *was* worth a shot!" I blared.

The remaining minutes of walking to the bus station were in silence; each of us frustrated and all craving information that could point us in the right direction. Those minutes of silence were minutes of contemplation.

I was actually keen on school; ironically, it would distract me from thinking about who I *really* was, or, *what* I was, if I was indeed going to morph into a horrific monster and unleash havoc on my school and community.

"Boy that would make an interesting news headline," I thought sarcastically. *"Soon to be school leaver reveals that she is a werewolf and decapitates multiple students of her Dublin high school."*

*

"Well, Bee, I'll catch you at the end of the day. I've got that science thing on again at lunch," Charlotte said, heaving her locker door shut with great force - well, as much force as an individual of *forty-five kilos* was capable of exerting.

"No worries. Well, for lunch I was planning on doing some research on the Morrigan book anyway," I replied, as Charlotte and I walked down the corridor towards our History classes.

"Ethan has got to finish the book ASAP! I really want to start it on Friday." Charlotte's face lit up. "Oh, Friday!"

"What about Friday?" I queried.

"The charity dance for the two schools! For crying out loud, Brianna! You're playing in it! You'd think you would remember! It's in *two* days! I hope you're ready for it!"

"*Musically*, I am aware of the evening because I have been rehearsing for it for a few weeks now, but anything involving *glamming up* doesn't make its way onto my radar, Charlotte."

"What am I going to wear?! Wait, I know - the dress I wore on Tuesday night for your party! Cool, I'm all set then! What are you going to wear?" As close as Charlotte and I were, the subject matter of clothes was an area that I dreaded discussing with her.

"I guess the same goes for me. I'll just wear what I wore on Tuesday, too. Oh, and in regards to the book, I'm pretty sure Ethan had a few chapters to go this morning. So, I'm thinking that by this afternoon you can have a read of it."

"Great! Well, see you at the end of the day, then!" Charlotte bid farewell, waving, while continuing down the corridor, as I made my way into class.

The assumption I made yesterday was bang on; only one seat remained in the back left corner of the classroom. As I took my seat, Mr Lawson entered the classroom, with briefcase in hand.

"Well, good afternoon, ladies," Mr Lawson said, turning the teacher's chair around and sitting casually, resting his arms upon the chair's back. "Today, we are going to explore what you know about our Celtic history and we'll go from there!" He was incredibly excited about history - how *incredibly* sad. "Can anyone contribute a particular story, myth, legend, or any aspects of Celtic history to begin our discussion?"

Cue the substantial pause.

"Anyone at all?" Following another pause, Mr Lawson had another attempt. "*Anyone?*"

I hoped that this wasn't going to eventuate into a *Ferris Bueller* classroom situation. I had to end it! After all, this was one History discussion to which I actually had something valid and interesting to contribute - what a change. Perhaps Mr Lawson could be of use; perhaps, if I prevented myself from revealing too much detail, he might hold some key knowledge that related to Morrigan and be able to shed light on it, unconsciously contributing to my secretive investigation. It was worth a try.

I raised my hand.

"Yes! Thank you! Name please?" Mr Lawson asked eagerly.

"Uh, Brianna ... Brianna Shields, Sir."

"So, Brianna, what is it that you would like to share with the class?"

"Well, I am aware of a Celtic Goddess. Uh … Morrigan, Sir."

Mr Lawson's face lit up. "Yes, yes! Morrigan! Fantastic, Brianna! This is a great area of Celtic mythology that we can address! Is anyone else in the class aware of the myths in regards to Morrigan?" The class fell silent; the girls were far too preoccupied by Mr Lawson's *golden brown locks*, rather than his efforts to spark interest in the lesson.

Mr Lawson eventually caught on and continued. "In that case, Brianna, elaborate. What is it that you know about Morrigan?"

I knew I'd come to regret putting my hand up. "Well, I don't really know much, Sir." I didn't think now was the time for revealing my source of information. "*All* I know is that she was supposedly a shape shifter and her main form of being was the crow, which symbolised death."

"Very good, Miss Elsa! Is there anything else that you would like to add?" *Why did Mr Lawson call me Miss Elsa?* Elsa was the last name of Craig, my father in the Morrigan book. I pondered Mr Lawson's words, but quickly came to the conclusion that this was no mere coincidence; although, an additional coincidence in the course of the past few days of incredibly questionable experiences wouldn't drastically stir the pot. Would it? *Mental note to myself: be careful!*

"Uh - Sir. My last name is *Shield*."

"Oh, I'm terribly sorry! At my last school there was a girl in my class who displayed *very* similar traits to you with that name. I apologise. Sorry, *do* continue please," Mr Lawson urged, waving his hand as an invitation for me to continue. *Mental note: lame explanation. Be very careful!*

"Well, Morrigan was said to have caused a great war. From what I heard, she was of mixed blood and that is what made her incredibly powerful."

Mr Lawson's face was beaming. "*Please* do continue!"

"Okay. Well, because of Morrigan's actions, apparently people were too scared to have children of mixed blood, as they believed that they would end up turning into what Morrigan became."

"Brianna, *where* did you find this information?" Mr Lawson asked, as he rested his hands beneath his chin in a classic thinking pose. I was dreading this question and I knew that I had to work around it.

"I … I just … well, my family friend bought me a book on Celtic mythology and I have read certain sections of it." I was hoping Mr Lawson would take over soon and elaborate on the information I had shed, as I was afraid of accidently revealing too much information.

"I ask you for the source of this information, because some of the things you have mentioned are myths that I have never come across, myths that I haven't read in all my years of study and teaching."

"*Really?*" I attempted to display surprise, but I had always found it difficult to prevent my face from revealing my inner thoughts.

"*Damn! He didn't know anything, or wasn't revealing anything! Maybe he was better at this game than me. That was a complete waste of effort!*"

"We can continue this topic another time. Time is pressing and I did want to briefly address the end of the World War II topic. If we target it hard now, we should have it completed by the end of the week and might be able to delve deeper into our Celtic origins."

For the remainder of the lesson, Mr Lawson discussed the roles certain countries had during the war and he concluded the lesson by answering a few pressing questions.

Following my contribution to the lesson, I no longer felt the need to participate, which explained why my mind began contemplating the Morrigan book. Thoughts of me being a possible *half-blood* were inescapable. Thoughts of being born from another place, unheard of by humanity, was daunting and yet exciting, all at once. I had always felt that I was different for a reason and that I was intended for a unique purpose. Was this my opportunity to fulfil the purpose mapped out for me? During my reverie at the back of the class, I also pondered over the gift I believed myself to possess.

"Is it going to come and go when it pleases, or, will I develop the ability to control it, own it and use it at my own accord?"

The bell rang, abruptly ending my pattern of thoughts.

I was almost out the door when Mr Lawson said my name. "Brianna, before you go, can I ask the name of this book you referred to today? I would love to get my hands on it and have a read."

I was unsure whether to supply Mr Lawson with a fake name, or, reveal the name of the book, but then say that the book was no longer in my possession. "It's just called, *Morrigan*, Sir."

"Thank you, Brianna. Now, our final class for the week is on Friday. Would you be able to bring it in for me then, so I am able to have a quick read of it over the weekend? I am incredibly interested in it!" The passion Mr Lawson showed still seemed to amaze me.

"I'm actually not in class on Friday, Sir. I'm rehearsing for the charity dance, which is that evening."

"That's okay. Would tomorrow be too early then?"

"Will he ever give up!"

"My friend has actually borrowed it and I won't see him until the weekend. I'm sorry. Could I pass it onto you sometime next week? It all depends on whether my friend has finished it." My apparent *friend* would unfortunately be travelling overseas and intent on reading the book over his trip - what a shame! I was a terrible liar.

"Not to worry, Brianna. My keen historical mind will have to wait until next week then. Well, I'd best not keep you any longer - you'll be late for your next class!" Mr Lawson said, now scrambling his books and papers together.

"Okay. Bye, Sir." I said, with a forced smile.

"And thank you for contributing today. It can be hard to engage an unfamiliar group of students. Your contribution made my job much easier."

"No worries. Bye, Sir!"

I finally reached beyond the classroom door and I had never been so eager to attend Mrs Smith's class. Hastening away for English, I queried whether Mr Lawson felt that he had recognised me as a student to rely on for interesting discussions, or did he truly recognise me? Who was using whom, here? I pictured myself attempting to rush out of History, but always being stopped by Mr Lawson to crack on about an interesting historical chat. How long was Mr Lawson supposed to be filling in for Mrs Hansen? Once again, I reminded myself to be careful in his presence.

Chapter Seven

The Carrier

...Zia's frail hand released the silver carrier into his daughter's trembling hand. The black cross of Tarmon faded from Zia's wrinkled palm. Keira winced as Tarmon's cross imprinted itself on her right palm...

- Excerpt from 'The Morrigan Book'

"See ya tomorrow, Charlotte! I'll catch you at home, Bee. *Don't* be too long, you know what Mam's like when we're late for dinner," Ethan said, as Charlotte and I were about to enter the *Madam & Miss Antique Shop*.

The *Madam & Miss Antique Shop* was our second home. When school and other responsibilities permitted, a hot chocolate and a viewing of intricate, antique furnishings, jewellery and items of stationary beckoned us.

As we entered the store, Charlotte and I received the traditional greeting from the shop owner, Mrs Wilson. Mrs Wilson was a plump, middle-aged woman with great zeal and a contagiously uplifting presence. Her orange, vibrant, candy-coloured curly hair and luminous green eyes complemented her warm inner being.

"...Afternoon, my regulars! How are we doing today?" Mrs Wilson asked, with great eagerness.

"We're good, thank you, but how are you?" Charlotte enquired.

"Same old, same old, my dears. Brianna, were you satisfied with the desk? Ethan picked it out."

"I *was* indeed and it looks incredible in my room!"

"Well, I suspect the usual for you both," Mrs Wilson continued. "So, two hot chocolates, marshmallows for Brianna and none for Charlotte. Does that sound right?"

"How'd you know?" I responded rhetorically. Charlotte and I detoured through the shop and situated ourselves in our regular spot by the bay window, overlooking a sandstone fountain surrounded by an incredibly neat hedge and beds of roses. It was our favourite place to be.

"I'm so looking forward to reading this! I can't wait to start it!" Charlotte said, now holding the Morrigan book that Ethan had somehow managed to skim through across the school day - most probably in the back corner of classes.

"Well, we shouldn't be too long here then, I'll be keeping you from reading."

"True, true. Anyway, you have to go and get something from Michael's, don't you?" Charlotte questioned.

"I do. He has made *too* many muffins and needs me to take some home for us to eat. I know he just wants me to stop by again," I said, whilst fiddling with the salt and pepper on the table.

"Well, he's lonely, Bee. Anyway, how'd the research go at lunch?"

"I kept trying to find leads or connections to the author's name. No luck, though. But..." I refrained from speaking; Mrs Wilson had arrived with the steaming mugs of hot chocolate.

"Enjoy, ladies!" she said, returning towards the counter.

"Thanks!" replied Charlotte and me.

"Oh, you were saying, Bee..." Charlotte invited me to pick up from where I had left off.

"...Oh, yes." I sipped my soothing hot chocolate and then continued. "In History today, Mr Lawson started asking us if we knew anything about Celtic myths. No one put their hand up, so I thought it was worth a shot in querying..." Charlotte's eyes bulged and not as a result of the hot chocolate. "...*Don't worry!* I didn't reveal anything *really* important about the book! I just thought that it was worth a shot to see whether he could elaborate on the basis of information I gave him. He could have been of some assistance for our investigation."

"So then, he didn't know much about it?" Charlotte asked, with a slight hint of concern, as she hugged her mug tightly to absorb as much warmth as possible.

"Nope. Not really. But, the bad news is he wants to borrow the book. I lied and told him that a friend has borrowed it."

"Bee, don't you think it's a bit odd that he's teaching your class about Celtic mythology? I mean, I know he's new and all, but still, wouldn't he just continue with the work that your class was up to?"

Charlotte had a point and it resonated with my earlier concerns. I had never questioned Mr Lawson feeling the need to address Celtic mythology with us. I understood that he intended to 'break the ice' and establish a good relationship with the class; but, why not utilise the topic we were well into?

"I honestly don't know, Charlotte. Until you mentioned it, I hadn't really thought about it. I guess it is strange, though." I consumed the remainder of my hot chocolate and continued. "I mean, what kind of teacher asks his students to talk about something that he was unable to contribute to? And then, as *soon* as I finished what I had to say, he quickly pushed aside what we were talking about so we could get back to finishing the World War II topic. And that's not all..."

"Hmm," Charlotte's cogs were turning as she stirred the remaining contents of her drink.

"... He also called me *Miss Elsa*, after I spoke."

"*What?!*" Charlotte exclaimed. "*Miss Elsa* - wait, isn't that the last name of the family that you mentioned to me in the book?"

"Yep, that's the one."

"Wait, I'm still trying to adjust and let my head get around this. Have you told Ethan about this?"

"Yep, before we met up with you, while waiting for the bus."

"And what does he think?" Little time elapsed between my words and Charlotte's.

"He's pretty amazed. Well, shocked. Actually, he was almost speechless, which you and I know is a very rare thing for him."

Before responding, Charlotte scrunched up her napkin, released it into her now empty mug, pushed the mug aside and interlocked her fingers to rest her hands upon the table. "Out of *all* the names in the *entire* world, Mr Lawson *accidently* calls you that name, which links to the Morrigan story, yet he claims that the information you shared was information that he hadn't come across before?" Charlotte stared at me intensely, her eyes narrowed deep in thought.

"You know how I think you overanalyse things?" My question was rhetorical, but Charlotte still felt the need to rebut and argue her case.

"Yes, but..." I raised my right hand and ended her words of defence.

"...I agree with you, Charlotte," I said. "This is *too* way out to be a coincidence anymore." Suddenly, I felt tense and I became consumed by an extraordinary degree of unimaginable rage. "... And I am sick of that BLOODY WORD COINCIDENCE! MY WHOLE LIFE MUST BE A DAMN COINCIDENCE!"

With every angry word I released, my right fist tightened and repeatedly hit the flimsy table, the mugs and cutlery clanging in tune with every beat of my clenched fist. A tear of frustration seeped from my left eye. Silence fell throughout the cafe; the weight of dozens of judging eyes fell upon my shoulders. Charlotte's eyes and mouth simultaneously widened in utter shock at my outburst. Within seconds of my eruption, Mrs Wilson arrived at our table.

"Brianna. Perhaps you and Charlotte, should leave, love. Have a chat in the fresh air. *Outside.*" Mrs Wilson's voice revealed complete sincerity.

When attempting to stand, a tremor tingled its way throughout my body. My legs became weak and struggled to support my weight. My mind quickly considered my recent nightmare and assumed the worst.

Finally, my legs caved in. As I fell, my arms endeavoured to latch onto the flimsy table where I sat. The chair gave in and I drifted towards the floor; Charlotte's lunge was too late to prevent my fall. I was still conscious, my surroundings completely vivid, yet all sounds absent. My eyes found Charlotte. Her mouth was moving, but the words I heard did not correlate with her lips.

"Please, please be okay, Brianna. I can't lose you! Why is this happening again?"

I left Charlotte's gaze and scanned the many surrounding faces. A frenzy of whispers berated my ears, yet the shocked faces fixed on me neglected to move their lips.

"The poor, dear!"

"How embarrassing!"

"Is she faint? Perhaps I should suggest that we call an ambulance?"

"Why did she shout?"

"That girl is crazy! Is she on something she shouldn't be?"

As a car comes to a sudden stop, the whispers ended and a tide of sound channelled its way back into my ears, gradually returning, like a crescendo in a piece of music. Mrs Wilson and Charlotte assisted me back to my chair.

"Charlotte, I've got her, love. Use the phone in the back to call the ambulance," Mrs Wilson calmly demanded, her arm still supporting me, even though I was seated.

"No!" I managed to say. "No! I'm fine now, *really*, I'm fine!" I attempted to raise myself up from the chair and was successful. The anger that had engulfed me had vanished. Physically, I felt that the past few minutes had not happened. There were no signs of my most recent episode at all. I picked up my bag and headed straight for the door, Charlotte's feet echoing behind me. As we left the cafe, Mrs Wilson said something intended for

me to hear, but my mind was far too preoccupied with self-questioning to concentrate. I continued to walk and I didn't feel like stopping. I didn't want to stop.

"Bee! Bee! Just stop!" Charlotte cried, but she could see that I had no desire to talk. "*Okay!* If you won't stop, then at least slow down, *please!*" She pleaded again. I still had no intentions of stopping or slowing down. When Charlotte realised this, she ran until she was beside me and strived to match my walking pace. Charlotte did not speak; the expression on my face made it clear that I was deep in thought and not to be disturbed.

"Why is this happening to me? Has my sleepless night caught up with me?"

The only positive that I could draw from this was that I hadn't morphed into a black beast and torn a café apart.

First, I had experienced an apparent 'anxiety attack' that involved me projecting my thoughts to my English teacher. The following day, I received a book that described me, which was published sixteen years before my conception! My thoughts were projected into someone else's mind! I had the worst nightmare of my life and it made me consider that I was becoming a raging creature. Oh, but wait, there's more! Following these abstract events, I discovered that I had a new History teacher and he *accidently* called me *Miss Elsa*, the surname of the girl matching me in the Morrigan book! Finally, for the piece de resistance, I had an outburst in a public place that was followed by the hearing the surrounding people's thoughts!

I gained control over my feet again and stopped walking. My head drooped, my eyes staring blankly at my shoes. "I don't believe in coincidences anymore," I softly spoke to myself. "Everything … everything happens for a reason. And this is happening for a purpose. I *know* it is!" I blared, gritting my teeth to contain my anger.

Charlotte hesitated and then placed her hand on my shoulder. I was so immersed in my own thoughts that her light touch caused me to jump.

"Bee?" Charlotte asked, in a tone of sincere concern. "Bee … we really probably should go to the hospital. Just in case..."

"NO!" I shouted. "No! Promise me that the only other soul you will open your mouth to about this will be Ethan! Promise me, Charlotte!"

Charlotte fiddled with her hands, contemplating over what to do. "But, Bee, this could be serious! Can't we go just as a precaution?"

"Charlotte," I said with gritted teeth, "we know why this is happening. There is nothing that I have that the hospital can treat!"

"All right, all right!" Charlotte exclaimed, raising her hands up to signify defeat. "Well, since you *refuse* to go to the hospital, you have to tell me what happened back there. Exactly what did happen, Brianna?"

"I was planning to!" I exclaimed, a hint of annoyance in my voice. "I ... I think that I heard ..." I stammered; it was incredibly hard verbalising what I still had trouble making sense of in my mind. "I heard the thoughts of you and the people in the cafe."

Clearly shocked, Charlotte desired to find out more. "Whoa ... I mean ... whoa. Bee, this is ... is just so ... so..."

"...*Whoa* will do just fine, Charlotte."

"I just can't ... wow! Wait, okay then. What ... what was I thinking? Can you remember?" Charlotte continued to query with great keenness.

"What I remember is looking at your face and what I heard you say did not match your lips. You ... I think you said something like, *I can't lose you,* or ... yeah - something like that." By this stage of our rather unusual conversation, Charlotte and I had reached the cobbled bridge spanning the stream between our homes.

"Charlotte?" I asked with concern, as this was the largest pause within our discussion; an unusual thing when speaking with Charlotte.

Charlotte rested against the bridge and gazing into the distance, lost in a daze. "Bee..." her eyes still fixed on some far away place. "That is *exactly* what I was thinking." I situated myself next to her similarly lost for words. Well, what can you say after something so bizarre? After what seemed like many minutes pondering, Charlotte turned to face me.

"Brianna. I don't want you to feel isolated. Do you understand me? This is happening for a reason, as you said and, in time, we will discover why. It's easy for me to say, but try not to dwell on the *why* and try to focus on *what* you can do as a result of this. *Okay,* Bee?"

"Okay. You're right." I struggled to articulate. I was incredibly touched by Charlotte's words. Charlotte initiated a hug. Considering what had just happened and following her kind words, I accepted it warmly. Charlotte did not wish to leave me, but the day had passed us by. It was now too late for me to visit Michael. I would pop in tomorrow and find an alternative set of circumstances to explain why I had not been able to stop by.

That evening, I mustered up the last remaining strength I had left within me to conceal all my doubts and troubled thoughts over dinner. Ethan saw through my wall. His subtle looks of concern, as Mam and Dad were preoccupied with their well-endowed plates, confirmed my suspicion.

Following the normal routines of washing up and tidying the table after dinner, Ethan and I sat outside the barn for the chat he expected to have. Lulu found her way into Ethan's lap and Tess into mine, their black glossy coats hard to make out in the darkness of a moonless Irish night. After organising my jumbled thoughts into words for Ethan's ears, I realised that I was slowly becoming more accepting of the chaos that had surrounded me over the past week. Like Charlotte, Ethan, too, remained speechless for some time after my recount of the day's events.

"I've always known that you were meant to do something great, Bee. I mean, you can't possibly have tattoos on your wrists, two different coloured eyes and crazy curly hair for nothing, can you?" Ethan exclaimed.

"My hair is crazy now, is it?" I responded with an extremely hard-to-conceal smirk. "I happen to appreciate my curly locks *thank you very much*!" I needed these chats with Ethan; he brought me back to reality and showed me what was important.

"Anyway, forget this afternoon, for now. I believe that eventually you will be able to control this. But, moving on, I'm really interested in this History teacher of yours. *Surely* he has read the Morrigan book. It's *too* much of a coincidence for him to call you *Miss Elsa*, don't you think?"

Coincidence! That word refused to leave me alone. "I agree with you. It's weird."

"So, Bee, I can't help but ask you something." Ethan's tone turned serious.

"Shoot," I invited.

"Did you happen to make a *spectacle* of yourself today?" Ethan giggled; this was going to be a joke I would obviously never live down.

"You're hilarious, you know that?" I moaned sarcastically. "And so much for forget what happened this afternoon!"

Mam, demanding that we both needed to shower and get ready for bed, ended our light hearted conversation.

When I made my way to bed, I wrapped myself in the soft sheets and sheltered under the warm quilt. My thoughts turned to the Morrigan book. I mulled over Mr Lawson calling me *Miss Elsa*. I attempted to drag my mind elsewhere, but it was murder. I slipped from under my covers, with the idea of retrieving the Morrigan book, to confirm the surname by which I had been referred. I had almost left my bed when I realised that the book was not with me. Charlotte had it in her possession. In many ways, not having the book was a good thing. I needed my sleep and it was difficult to deny that the events of the day had demonstrated that need for sleep was great.

I resumed the comfortable position in my bed and allowed my mind to wander. I was too shattered to think any more. I felt my eyes grow heavy and I drifted into sleep.

It was night time in a damp and tree filled forest. I was riding a beautiful black stallion, but the ride was not for pleasure. A great deal of anxiety festered within me. I was riding out of fear - I was attempting to escape. My stallion was seized; cloaked men on steaming and snorting horses threw ropes around my stallion's neck and dragged it to the ground. My body was thrown off the horse's back. I heard a tremendous CRACK! A few of my ribs were broken and I struggled to breathe; the lack of air made me incredibly light-headed.

Two men, in cloaks that concealed their faces, held me and exerted an incredible amount of force on my arms, almost curtailing my circulation. Opposite me was a young man, an incredibly handsome man, even though a scar disfigured his wonderfully sculptured face. The scar stretched from over his right eye, across his nose and culminated at his left cheek. His knees were forced into the ground and two other cloaked men restricted his arms. His gaze was intended for me. It was intense and fearful of what was about to happen to us. Amongst all of the fear, I was still able to marvel at his solemn, yet remarkably beautiful, green eyes. His hair was short, flighty and almost black in colour. As my eyes remained locked in the power of his striking gaze, I felt as if this young man was significant to me; I sensed that we were inseparable - that we were far more than friends. We both feared a similar outcome, but what was that outcome?

A small ray of rare Irish sunlight seeped through the space between my blind and windowpane, ending my dream. When my heavy eyelids finally accepted the idea, I looked over at my bedside table clock. My alarm was to ring in thirty minutes, but I wasn't going to fall asleep again. I raised myself up from my cosy bed, sad to leave it, and placed my feet on the floor. I was satisfied and surprised that I had a night of complete sleep. As I thought over my sleep, I recalled my dream and was also thankful that in this one I wasn't transformed into a hideous beast.

I hurried across my bedroom straight for my school bag. I shoved my hand into it; searching for the notebook Charlotte had given me. I wanted to write down everything from the dream. I found the writing book's bind and heaved it from beneath my Mathematics and Religion textbook. As the notebook became free, something hit the timber flooring of my bedroom.

CLANG!

The sound continued to echo as my eyes attempted to search the surrounding floor surface. The room was still relatively dark, making it difficult to clearly identify any item on the floor. I walked around the base of my bed, proceeding to open the blind of my large bay window. As the window welcomed the new day's light, something shimmered beside the chest of draws near my door. I made my way towards the object with uncertainty.

"What is that?"

I bent down and grasped the shimmery locket-like object. The object was silver and circular, resembling a pocket watch despite its size. The circular part was almost large enough to overlap the palm of my hand. On one end was a latch, or knob, similar to the turning device of a musical box and on the direct opposite side of the circle, a long, silver chain was attached. I prevented myself from turning the latch, fearful that something bad would happen. The upright side of the circle's surface was decorated by an emerald green animal, which I recognised as a bird. The bird was within a circle and six bold words were equally distributed around the circle;

Bealach sin thugann mise chun baile.

"No," I said to myself. I tried to deny what I was thinking. I was trying to avoid having to deal with another dreaded *coincidence*. But, as I read the words over and over again, I could not deny them, I knew what they were. The words on the silvery locket were the words of the carrier, the musical device instituted by the Druids of Oran-Roy for summoning the Oran-Roy bird. This was the device described in the Morrigan book, the same book that described me.

"This cannot be possible!"

The only logical conclusion I was capable of making was that the large silver locket was from the *Madam and Miss Antique Shop*. Perhaps it fell into my bag by mistake as I rushed out of there.

"By what other means could it have found its way into my school bag? Did someone plant it there?"

My mind filtered through an array of questions, but was incapable of finding an answer that would distract me from the carrier.

"This can't be number six on my list of coincidences ...
Can it?"

Chapter Eight

More Questions

"…Morning, you two!" Charlotte greeted while making her way over the bridge. Ethan and I were about to return Charlotte's greeting, but no opportunity was provided; Charlotte's enthusiasm prevented us from getting a word in. "The book was *incredibly* fascinating! I just can't … I mean it's so interesting to consider that this *is* your story, that this is the *whole* story behind you being here!"

"Charlotte, you're talking as if we are *certain* that this is all totally true!" I was trying to be realistic; I was avoiding falling into the trap of thinking in just one way. I wanted the truth, not the *truth* that I wanted. The questions I had held onto for so long may have had an answer. But, what if it wasn't true? How could I bear coming to that realisation, after having accepted it so willingly? How could I deal with regret's pain?

Charlotte refrained from showing further excitement, to accommodate for my mood. Ethan, too, sensed my volatile state and refrained from making a comment that could potentially strike a raw nerve.

"Sorry, guys," I sighed, rubbing my head restlessly. I sensed they were walking on eggshells. "I'm just really tense and doubtful at the moment. I don't want to set myself up for a fall."

Charlotte gently leaned against me. "It's fine, Bee. I'd say I understand, but, the truth is, both Ethan and me have absolutely no idea what you are going through. So, the only thing we can do is listen and be supportive. Hey, Ethan?"

"I guess," Ethan quietly nodded in agreement.

"Here, there's something I should show you both." I quickly glanced around, ensuring that Ethan and Charlotte were the only witnesses of what I was about to reveal. The carrier shimmered when touched by daylight, as it left my right blazer pocket. Based on Ethan and Charlotte's gaze, there was no need of words to explain the silvery device that rested in my hands. Ethan and Charlotte met each other's eyes; both reflecting the same possibility.

"NO WAY!" Ethan blared, his eyes almost out of their sockets.

"*Shhhhhh*, Ethan!" cried Charlotte, taking a step towards me with her eyes unable to leave the carrier. "Bee, this is the *carrier* … right?"

I was about to respond *'yes'*, but, how could it possibly be what we assumed it to be? I mean, it's not every day you can say that you found the *apparent* device responsible for bringing you to

Ireland on a bird from a mythical place unknown by the rest of humanity. All of the self-questioning made me doubt my sanity!

"I ... I guess so," I eventually came to say. "Unless someone is seriously messing with me."

"*Why* do you do that? *Why* do you doubt what is *so* obvious? What else could it be? When you decide whether to believe that this is *actually* happening, Bee, let me know, will you?" Ethan exclaimed, incredibly annoyed by my state of denial.

"What is with that tone, Ethan Shield?" I blared defensively. Gosh! Throwing in the *Shield* made me sound like Mam!

"BEE! *When* are you going to accept that this is happening?! I would throw myself at this! All of your questions are being answered! WHO CARES about how these answers have come, just wake up and accept them!"

Ethan made complete sense, but I was afraid. I was afraid of hating myself, hating myself for convincing my mind of accepting something I deeply desired that was not yet in my grasp. If there was one thing I learnt from the 'Logan' saga, it was not to jump the gun.

"Ethan!" Charlotte yelled, as she slapped Ethan's right arm with as much might as she could muster. "Apologise! Apologise to Brianna NOW!"

"No, Charlotte he's right. You're right, Ethan." I took a deep breath; it was a breath of acceptance and it took Ethan to wake me up. Sure, what was happening gave me every right to doubt, but living in doubt is just as agonising as looking forward to something and being let down. In that moment, I decided to accept what was happening, like Charlotte and Ethan. "But," I continued, "There is one last thing I have to check that will help me become more accepting of this."

"Yeah..." Ethan queried.

"What is it, Bee?" Charlotte asked.

"I need to apologise to Mrs Wilson and, while I'm there, I want to make sure that the carrier didn't fall into my bag from her shop. You never know. If it did, she might know the slightest piece of information that could be of some help. What do you think?"

"I'm for it - just so you can *finally* accept this," Ethan muttered, running his fingers through his flighty brown hair.

"Why don't we go before school?" Charlotte keenly suggested. "We'd still be able catch the bus that would get us to school just before the bell! What do you say?"

Ethan and I looked at each other and nodded in agreement.

"It's a plan. Let's go!" Ethan said, clapping his hands together.

Within ten minutes, the three of us had reached the *Madam and Miss Antique Shop*. As we entered the shop, the bell rang and alerted Mrs Wilson of our presence.

"...Morning, you three!" Mrs Wilson announced; her enthusiasm hard to miss. It appeared that the events of yesterday had been completely wiped out of her mind. Either I would soon discover that Mrs Wilson had a terrible memory, or she was an incredibly forgiving and understanding person. "In for a morning drink or did you want to pick up something?"

"Uh," I barely managed to say. "I ... I actually came to apologise for... for what happened yesterday afternoon. I'm really, really sorry. I don't know what came over me and ..." My apology was cut short by Mrs Wilson shaking her head and waving her hands erratically.

"My dear, my dear," said Mrs Wilson as she walked towards me. "I have known you since your infancy. Whatever *happened* happened and I believe that you had a *human* moment. No hard feelings, love. *Okay?*" Mrs Wilson patted my left shoulder and continued. "I know you wouldn't deliberately act out as you did. All is forgiven and in the past. Are you feeling all right, though? You were a bit unsteady on your feet afterwards."

"Uh ... low blood pressure," I pulled out of thin air. I didn't sound very convincing. Once I realised where Mrs Wilson and I stood following yesterday's events, I released a contented sigh of relief. I urged my heart to recline back in an armchair after its intense workout. I felt confident enough to enquire about the carrier.

"Well, thank you for understanding."

Mrs Wilson responded with a nod and smile. Her reaction was a cue for Ethan to nudge my side and urge me to query about the carrier. I responded with a glare of, *"I'm getting to it!"*

"One last thing, Mrs Wilson." I removed the carrier from my blazer pocket and rested it in my hands before continuing. "Has this come from your shop? Were you selling something like this?" I invited Mrs Wilson to hold the carrier and analyse it. Her eyes tightened and her left hand stroked the side decorated with the emerald bird. It appeared that she was quite taken by the carrier, her reaction not the one I had hoped for.

"I'm sorry, love. I haven't sold anything like this or seen anything like it." Mrs Wilson handed the carrier back to me. "Where did you get it?"

I laughed and said cryptically, "That's what we trying to figure out," leaving Mrs Wilson somewhat bemused.

"Well, thank you, Mrs Wilson, but we really better get going … got to get the bus or we'll be late," Charlotte said, feeling the need to remind me of the time.

"Yeah, we best be off," Ethan added.

"Well, no doubt I'll see you all soon. Take care and I'm sorry I couldn't be of more help," Mrs Wilson said and made her way behind the cafe counter to attend to a customer.

Despite the hastened walk to make the final school bus, Ethan, Charlotte and I still managed to discuss our new insights in regards to the carrier.

Ethan, now holding the carrier, decided to put forward his theories first. "Okay. So Mrs Wilson claims she doesn't know anything, that doesn't mean that's the truth!" He continued to analyse the carrier in his hands, hoping that it would help him come to an answer. The more Ethan fiddled with it, the more frustrated he became. Like me, he was a rather impatient person and he desperately longed for answers just as much as I did. "And the book! *Surely* Michael knows something! Or ..." Ethan's new thought provoking idea made him stop dead.

"...Or *what*, Ethan?" I queried.

Once he had processed his new theory, Ethan continued to walk, which seemed to usher in the words. "Okay. What we have to look for is a connection; something that connects the book with the carrier." As Ethan spoke, his hands became incredibly vocal. I snatched the carrier from his hands, fearful that his passion, now responsible for his erratic hand movements, would result in a broken carrier. Removing the carrier from his hands didn't seem to faze him. He continued to pour out his theories, despite being interrupted. "There is either an event, or one person that connects the two things."

Charlotte was becoming frazzled and slightly agitated after hearing Ethan's theories. "Yes, Ethan, they are *great* theories, but, how the *hell* are we going to find the answers?"

"I *don't* know!" Ethan rebutted. "Don't have a go at me! At least I'm formulating *some* theories!"

The three of us hopped onto the bus feeling frustrated, uncertain and anxious. Our questions still remained unanswered and they continued to keep mounting up, like unanswered questions on the eve of an exam.

"When are we going to be able to remove some questions from our pile? Will we ever reach explanations for all of the events of the past week?"

Sitting on the bus, questions poured in and out of my mind like paper going into a shredder. I'd consider a possible theory, but then come to realise that it was a stupid, irrelevant idea and I'd shred it. The three of us spent the entire bus trip in silence, with iPod's at full volume, attempting to block out the noise. I fiddled with the cool carrier in my blazer pocket and Annie Lennox's song titled, 'Why', appeared on my shuffle. How ironic, because that was *all* I was thinking.

"Why? Why me and why all of this?"

*

"Bee, can I have one last look at it before we go to English?" Charlotte begged.

"Alright, but make it quick." I removed the carrier from my blazer pocket and quickly placed it in Charlotte's hands. I scavenged my locker in search of books for the next two classes, while Charlotte's attention did not leave the carrier. The hallway was almost completely vacant by this time, an indication that we were cutting our timing rather fine to get to English. But, then again, Mrs Smith was playing nice, so Charlotte and I didn't make much of an effort to arrive on time. One *could* assume that we were taking advantage of the incident that occurred a few days ago. I finally found the books required for my classes and, as my shoulder heaved my faulty locker door shut, Charlotte and I recognised Mr O'Hara's overbearing voice from a nearby corridor.

"Charlotte! Quick! Drop it in my pocket!"

As Charlotte attempted to release the carrier into my right blazer pocket, the chain latched onto one of her blazer buttons.

"Here! Let me!" I whispered harshly and placed my books on the nearby bench to free my hands in order to help Charlotte.

"*Quick, Bee!*" Charlotte hushed at me desperately. "*Damn!*"

"What?" I exclaimed when attempting to untangle the carrier chain still attached to Charlotte's blazer button.

"He's seen us."

The chain finally became free. I turned around and saw that Charlotte's observations proved to be bang on; Mr O'Hara's eyes seemed to light up when he spotted late students.

"Ladies, are you aware of the time?" Mr O'Hara asked rhetorically. "Why are you not in class yet?"

I was too preoccupied with masking the carrier to produce a valid excuse. Charlotte realised this and was spontaneous in her response. "Brianna has had some … uh … locker problems, Sir."

"*Really?*" It was clear that Mr O'Hara doubted our story. "And what is that in your hands that you are hiding away, Miss Shield?"

"*Damn!*"

Part of the carrier's chain was visible despite my efforts to hide it away in my clenched hands. I had to come up with a guff that sounded convincing!

"Uh … you see …" *Bee, spit something out or it's obvious what you are trying to do!* "…Well … I'm sorry, Sir, I … I should have spoken to you about this as soon as I returned to school after … after not being well the other day, but, I … I was too … well … mortified." *I think he is buying it! Keep it up!* Mr O'Hara's facial expression of, '*I don't believe you*', began to fade. It gave me confidence, spurring me on to continue. "It's a..." I thought that hesitating earn some sympathy. It seemed to work.

"Yes, Brianna, *do* go on please," Mr O'Hara invited.

"It's a … a medical necklace, Sir."

"Well, that's fine, but it still doesn't explain you being late to class." Mr O'Hara sighed, and then continued his lecture. "Well, I do have to admit, I very rarely find you two doing the wrong thing. Off you go then!" With these marching orders, Mr O'Hara turned around, making his way back to his office, when a final thought occurred to him. "And, Brianna, before you go, if that is indeed a medical necklace, school health regulation instructs that it must be worn at all times by the student." To satisfy Mr O'Hara, I placed the chain around my neck so he could see, but carefully masked the carrier with my hand until I was able to let it hide behind my school blouse. "Good. Run along then!"

On that note, Charlotte and I scooped up our books and hastened to English.

"Well done, Bee!"

"Thanks."

During our walk, or, rather, slow jog, I felt the coolness of the carrier gently bounce up and down against my chest. The classroom door was already shut, which would normally imply a possible lunch time detention; however, in light of recent events, Mrs Smith, acting like a lady in waiting, opened the door for both Charlotte and I and kindly ushered us to two empty seats in the front row.

"I could get used to this!"

Once seated, Mrs Smith returned to the lesson's content, without displaying any signs of being disrupted. This particular lesson was devoted to contrasting Austen's Victorian context with our own. We deliberated over whether values have remained universal over time, or have changed and developed throughout the ages. I felt that my suggestion a few days ago might have caused Mrs Smith to question her approach.

Halfway into the lesson, Mrs Smith asked us to contribute our thoughts in regards to context and its effect on the human condition. A girl to my left (whom I was ashamed to admit I didn't know by name, so I identified her as 'Popular Teacher Suck-up') spoke for what felt like an eternity. I was attempting to listen, but lost focus once she mentioned something along the lines of, *"it would be strange if we spoke as Austen's characters did in our context"*; completely missing the point of the discussion.

Now blocking out what anyone was saying, I picked up my pencil and began to sketch the man from my dream onto the next blank page of my book. Once satisfied with his eyes and other facial features, I worked on his flighty hair. When content with his hair, I decided to conclude drawing once the man's scar was complete. My pencil tip just reached the nose, when strangely and rather suddenly, with no hint of a warning, a burning sensation consumed my right hand. My hand released the pencil. It clattered against the table and then fell to the floor. No one seemed to notice. The sensation in my hand went beyond my palm and prickled on up to my fingertips. It took all the energy within me to restrain myself from releasing a painful scream! My left hand clenched the edge of the desk. I bit my bottom lip, still attempting to refrain from screaming. I had to leave class. *What the hell was going on with me this time?*

"Miss! Miss!" I pleaded painfully. "I … I think I'm going to be sick! Can I leave? PLEASE!"

Mrs Smith did not hesitate. "Of course! Go, dear!"

As Mrs Smith released her first syllable, I rushed from the classroom and was just beyond the door before she spoke her final syllable. I had almost reached the girl's bathroom when the skin of my right palm felt as though it was being ripped apart; it was as though a knife was carving its way into my skin! I didn't want to look at my hand; I didn't want to see what felt too painful to express in words! I reached the toilets, fell to the floor and curled up in a ball, with my left hand constricting my right wrist. The floor was cold and covered by small puddles of excess water. In my moment of agony, I was thankful for the water seeping into my stockings; it temporarily removed my focus away from my throbbing hand.

Just as quickly as it had come, the pain suddenly dispersed. I raised my body up from the cold, damp floor and leaned against the tiled wall. Pain no longer present, I turned my right palm upwards and was beyond bewildered by what my eyes came to see.

A circular black marking, resembling the ones already on my wrists covered my entire right palm. The circle was outlined by a bold arch. The patterned border enclosed a large compass-like cross; two words lay at the heart of the cross, and each cross strand held a word towards the outer edges. I turned my hand to make out the words and gasped.

Bealach sin thugann mise chun baile.

I read the words printed around my palm over and over again, trying to convince myself that I now bared the carrier symbol like the Tarmon ancestors within the book.

"How did I not realise that by wearing the carrier this would happen? This is exactly what happened in the Morrigan book! The person who bore the carrier wore the symbol of Tarmon on their right palm! The cross! Of course! The cross was the mark of Tarmon. My mother's clan!"

Still in shock, I rushed over to the bathroom sink, pumped out an overbearing amount of soap and rubbed my hand profusely.

Nothing.

The symbol did not fade away.

"How can I possibly hide this?"

I clenched the edge of the sink and looked intensely at my reflection. I stared at myself for minutes. Tears of frustration and bewilderment seeped from my eyes.

"STOP!" I yelled at my reflection. "STOP IT! ACCEPT THIS DAMMIT!" After a few deep breaths, the tears ceased. The sleeve of my blazer smeared away the remaining tears over my flushed cheeks. Now in a better state, I had enough courage to look at the carrier's symbol. My left hand stroked over my right palm in awe. As I remained at the sink in a state of silent wonder, I recognised Charlotte's 'lightness of foot' from the corridor.

"Bee! You're *wet*!" Charlotte ran towards me and clenched my shoulders with concern. "What happened? Did it happen again like the last time?" My delayed response worried Charlotte. "Bee! Answer me!"

My answer was silent. I raised my right hand and turned my palm towards Charlotte.

"OH MY GOD!" Charlotte's hands released my shoulders, seized my right wrist and pulled it towards her. "It's … it's … it's the carrier symbol! Of course! You put it on! How could I forget that? It's just like the book said!" Charlotte directed her attention away from my palm and met my eyes. "You *have* to believe this now, Brianna. You *cannot* deny this!"

After withstanding the pain I had just felt, I could not deny who I was. What kind of person would I be if I chose to ignore this? The bell rang for the next class, giving me no time to calmly process events with Charlotte.

"Brianna, Ethan and I have a free period next and I think I know how we can hide the symbol." Charlotte supported my right arm and guided me back to the English classroom. "Bear with me and do what you can to keep your hand hidden until we see you at the end of the day. Okay?"

"Okay."

We collected our books and Charlotte was off in a flash. I had absolutely no idea what she was planning to do, but I didn't doubt her intentions for one second. My main priority was to keep my right hand out of Mr Fletcher's sight during Religion.

As I took my seat at the back corner of the classroom, Mr Fletcher dropped a crate full of well-used Bibles on his desk. A cloud of dust rose from the crate as it made contact with the table.

"All right, ladies! Hush now! Today we will be using the Bibles rather than the prescribed textbook." Mr Fletcher walked down the aisles and handed each girl a dusty Bible. When Mr Fletcher reached the front of my aisle, I pulled my right blazer sleeve down and held it tightly to shield the symbol.

"Here," Mr Fletcher said as he held a Bible quite close to my face. Mr Fletcher turned around proceeding to return to his desk, but something made him reconsider. "Uh … Brianna, you're wet! You're blazer is completely wet!" Mr Fletcher's face was *completely* baffled as to why my blazer was wet. "Do you have an explanation for this?"

I did have a very good reason as to why my blazer was wet, but, obviously, I would once again have to rely on my poor storytelling skills. "Yes … well, you see, I happened to slip into a puddle on the playground, Sir."

"It hasn't rained all day, Brianna."

That was pretty pathetic, Brianna! "Um … it's well … I..."

"Remove your blazer, this instant. I've never known you to be the lying kind."

"But, I..."

"NOW!" the class was now entirely silent. This was definitely one of those occasions where you could hear a pin drop.

"When is a teacher going to give me a break?"

It turns out that discovering who you are can pay a pretty hefty price on your schooling.

I hesitated to remove my blazer, but a change of expression from Mr Fletcher convinced me to act fast. I didn't need this! Once my arms were free, I rested the blazer over my right hand.

"HANG-IT-ON-YOUR-CHAIR!" Mr Fletcher demanded through gritted teeth.

"WHY?" I exclaimed back. How dare he belittle me like that? "It's just fine here!" The rest of the class looked on in utter astonishment!

"You're hiding something, aren't you, *Miss Shield?!*"

"And why would you assume something like that, *Sir?*"

"Something is in your hand. Show me!"

"Nothing is in my..."

"SHOW ME!" This was an absolute mess! I had no choice now; I had to show Mr Fletcher my hand. Why did my darn blazer have to be wet? I rested my blazer over the desk and allowed Mr Fletcher to see my hands.

"*Tattoos* are *NOT PERMITTED AT SCHOOL!* Go and wash it off NOW!" Mr Fletcher clearly assumed that it was temporary; boy was he wrong.

"Believe me, Sir. I've tried it," I said with a chuckle that was difficult to hold back. "It doesn't wash..." I was unable to finish my sentence, yet again.

"GO NOW!"

"I've told you! It doesn't come off!" I cried defensively. "It's one that wears away after a week!"

"Very well, then. I'll be informing Mr O'Hara of your wrongdoing and you will attend detention tomorrow at lunchtime. Understood?" I wasn't going to argue my way out of this one. At least a detention meant that Mam and Dad wouldn't be informed of anything. "Understood, Brianna?" I still hadn't responded.

"Yes, Sir," I replied, refraining from yelling with all my might.

I remained silent for the remainder of the lesson. Occasionally my eyes would meet a girl's wandering gawk. I'd be the talk of the school now. When the bell rang, I leapt from my desk and rushed in anticipation of meeting Charlotte and Ethan.

"What could Charlotte possibly have up her sleeve?"

"Bee!" Ethan cried from the bus area as he saw me exit the school gates. Charlotte looked nervous and flushed in the face, whereas Ethan had a grin from ear to ear and seemed incredibly proud of himself.

"What did they do?"

"Quickly! Before anyone sees!" There was a great deal of anxiety in Charlotte's voice.

"What's got you so anxious?" I asked.

"Wait till you hear what we did! Charlotte was great! Weren't you, Charlotte?" Ethan waited for Charlotte's response, but she was too frazzled unwrapping whatever was in her hands to take notice. "Okay, well, I can't take *all* the credit, Charlotte formulated the whole plan!"

"So, I assume that Charlotte filled you in on my hand."

"She sure did! I can't believe it! Let's have a look!" I showed Ethan my hand and he appeared speechless.

"Anyway," I said, as I removed my hand from Ethan's. "So, *what* happened? What did you end up doing?" I queried rather impatiently.

Charlotte finally removed what she was attempting to remove from the plastic covering; it revealed a large bandage. "Give me your hand."

"See, Bee!" Ethan cried. "We stole a bandage for you! So, what we thought we should do was..."

"SHUSH!" Charlotte whispered.

"Why are you ashamed? We did it to help Brianna!"

"I'm not ashamed, Ethan. I just don't want to get caught!"

"Wait, wait … you both stole this bandage for me?"

"Yeah!" Ethan was beaming. "You see, what happened was - Charlotte went to your office lady who she claimed needs to a see a dead corpse before providing a student with a bandage of any kind! So, I hid beneath the desk and Charlotte ran through the sick bay door as if she was about to throw up! She faked the gag and everything! Absolutely brilliant!"

"Yeah and…" I hurried Ethan along.

"So, while she ran through and faked being sick, the office lady rushed in after her shouting at her saying, "You cannot just burst through like that!" So, while the office lady was preoccupied with Charlotte, I scabbed the key to the draw beneath the desk and took the bandage!"

"And she didn't see you? How did Charlotte get out of there?"

"To signal Charlotte that I had retrieved the bandage, I slammed the door. But, Charlotte took her time. She thought that if she was miraculously better after a glass of water that that would be a bit suspicious. So, after five minutes of pretending she felt like she was going to be sick, she said that she would go to the toilet and come back if she still needed to. She was brilliant, Bee! I wish you could have seen her!"

"Wow! I'm impressed!"

"There!" Charlotte announced. I looked down at my right hand and was unable to identify the carrier symbol now beneath the thick white bandage. "We thought that you could explain to your Mam and Dad that the hot water from the kettle in the senior kitchen spurted onto your hand. What do you think?"

"I like it! Good thinking ... but, there is a slight problem," I said.

"What?" Ethan and Charlotte replied together. The next few minutes waiting for the bus were devoted to explaining the events of the past hour.

"Don't worry, Bee," Ethan said quite sympathetically. "Mam and Dad shouldn't find out. This is your first detention ever! And that Mr Fletcher is a jerk!"

"I was pretty rude, though," I admitted. "And your efforts to get me a bandage were practically for nothing. Word of mouth travels fast around this place."

"You were angry! I would have reacted the same way!" Charlotte reassured me.

"Thanks, Charlotte but I cannot imagine you *ever* behaving like that!"

"Well, I did just do something pretty outrageous today. Didn't I?" She had a point and we all had a chuckle thinking over Charlotte's performance.

The bus finally arrived and we hopped on in good spirits in contrast to the morning.

"So," Ethan said once we got settled into our seats. "When are we going to give it a go?"

"Give what a go? What are you talking about?" I was baffled.

"Bee! The *carrier*," Ethan hushed secretively. This had never crossed my mind until that moment. Well, it was obviously real now. I most definitely didn't imagine all that unbearable pain! The carrier was in my possession. I could potentially journey towards my place of birth. This was incomprehensible, yet too exciting to disregard. I had to try. I had too! This could answer everything and put my questions to rest! My heart leapt at the possibility of venturing away on a journey as my favourite fictitious characters had done in the books that I read.

"How's tomorrow night, then? After the dance?" I announced, with little thought. I was too excited to delay this any longer. "We'd be pushing it if we went tonight, but, at least tomorrow night, we'll get home late and when it's *assumed* that we are in bed, we'll give it a go! What do you say?"

"I'm in!" Ethan agreed.

"Me too," Charlotte answered with a smile.

"Great!"

Once home, I informed Mam and Dad of the *apparent* accident I had suffered at school. They bought it! I was pleased by their reaction, but, I do have to admit, a heavy feeling consumed the pit of my stomach, which I knew was guilt.

Initially, I struggled to sleep that night, too excited at what awaited me the following evening. I wasn't referring to the dance. I lay in bed and ventured through all the possibilities the carrier could bring. I had hoped that the physical pain and teacher trashing I endured would be worth it. Perhaps I would meet my parents and finally learn whether I did indeed possess a gift of some kind! I could not deny that tomorrow evening would most definitely be a night to remember. Once I reached this conclusion, I fell asleep. In that moment, my mind was at peace and content with the possibilities that tomorrow night could potentially bring. I was certain that tomorrow night was going to change my life as I knew it.

Chapter Nine

A Night to Remember

...Keelty was unable to reach Sully in time. He had climbed over the fence of a nearby home. She remained patiently by the fence, hoping for him to retreat quickly. As the night drew on, Keelty's adventurous day caught up with her. When she awoke the next morning, she followed Sully's scent heading towards Dublin...

- Excerpt from 'The Morrigan Book'

The lunchtime bell was normally the highlight of the school day, an entire hour with Charlotte, where we had the opportunity to discuss the events of the school day, our plans for the future and even share some candid jokes about one another. I couldn't say that that applied this particular Friday. Lunchtime came in the blink of an eye, the dreaded detention was on me before I knew it. Charlotte did not bid me farewell with words, but gave me a sympathetic expression that implied, *"Hang in there, Bee"*.

As I ventured towards the designated detention room, the sound of girls laughing and conversing with their friends echoed into the abandoned corridor from the nearby courtyard. A queasy feeling filled the pit of my stomach, fearful of what I was about to endure. I attempted to ignore the nerves through positive self-talk.

"Come on, Bee. What could possibly be so daunting about detention," I whispered to myself. "You'll probably just have to write some lines or ..." I stopped talking when I realised that I was not alone. Feeling like an idiot, and a little mortified, my face turned scarlet; Megan, a girl from my English class, had heard my entire *pep talk*.

In contrast with Megan, I did not embody traits typical of a girl who spent most of her lunchtimes in detention. Megan's black hair was straightened with blonde streaks and tied up in a rather untidy ponytail, which was quite difficult to find amongst the 'bird nest' style she was attempting to model. Her soft, calm blue eyes appeared incredibly harsh surrounded by heavy black eyeliner. Her school shoes were extremely worn - she might as well have walked around in bare feet. I couldn't say that I knew Megan. All my ideas of her were based on rebellious rumours.

"What are you here for? I don't normally see you here," Megan queried.

"I'm never here!" I blurted out. I sounded so defensive. My reaction gave away my nerves. "Uh ... I mean ... this is my first one."

"First one ever?" Megan's response clearly indicated that my clean record astonished her. Why was it so hard to believe that this was my first detention ever?

"Yes, like I said ... this is my first one ... *ever*." My tone reflected my annoyance; I was never good at masking my feelings in my voice or facial expressions.

"What you in for then? You didn't answer my question."

"I was caught with a fake tattoo. You?"

"I was smoking in the girls' toilet." Megan was intimidatingly upfront. Detention didn't seem to faze her. She shrugged her shoulders, placed her hands in her pockets and slumped against the wall. "I normally get away with it, but, some loser first-year dobbed me in."

"I see," I quietly replied. "So ... uh..." I hesitated. "What happens? What ... what do they make you do?"

"It depends on the teacher, really. If you have Fletcher, Mills or Adams, you cop a lot."

"Like...?"

"...Like scrubbing graffiti off class desks, the toilet doors or worse."

"...And if we're lucky and get a nice teacher, what do we normally do?"

"Oh. Just lines, or a letter of apology to Mr O'Hara." That seemed reasonable. *Fingers crossed a nice teacher was allocated for today!*

I leant against the wall opposite Megan, waiting for the teacher's arrival. It appeared that Megan and I were the only students on detention. After a few minutes of silence and avoiding direct eye contact with Megan, the sound of brisk footsteps entered the corridor. I turned my head and recognised Mr Lawson hastening down the long empty corridor. I hoped that Mr Lawson would still remember our last conversation. Perhaps he would go easy on me in light of what I contributed to the lesson.

"Sorry for my timing, ladies," he said quite out of breath. "I was held up by Mr Adams. We were having a long discussion about politics." Mr Lawson fiddled with his keys and eventually found the right one to unlock the door. "Right, in you come ladies!"

The detention room smelt of dust and old school books. With only two tiny windows in the back corner, little light made its way into the room, adding to the dismal décor. The staff was aiming to channel dismay, I'm sure. Megan did not wait for Mr Lawson; she knew exactly what to do and proceeded to the isolated desk in the far back corner, which I assumed was her regular seat.

Mr Lawson sat at the front desk and removed a folder from his briefcase. "Have a seat, Brianna."

I seated myself near the front and awaited Mr Lawson's instruction. "Megan, I presume?" Mr Lawson asked Megan, looking over his glasses.

"Yep," she replied.

"And Brianna is also here. Good! Everyone is present and accounted for." Before speaking again, Mr Lawson retrieved a piece of paper from his case. "Now, I don't know what goes on here, I was asked to monitor you both at the last minute. Mr Fletcher was supposed to take this detention, but he informed me that a meeting was scheduled at the same time."

"We just write a letter of apology," Megan said. I turned around to face her; she was slumped so low in her chair that I could only just make out her face over the desk's surface.

"Very well, that's fine. But, before you attend to that, I need to record why you are both here. Megan?"

"Smoking."

"Brianna?"

"Uh ... having a fake tattoo."

"I see," Mr Lawson's eyes remained focussed on the paper in front of him. Once he finished writing, Mr Lawson gazed in my direction; his face rather quizzical. "I can't help but notice the bandage, Brianna. Is that attempting to *conceal* the tattoo?"

"It is, Sir, but I..."

"No, no. I don't have a problem with that. At least you are trying to make amends," Mr Lawson replied, as he removed his glasses and returned the papers to his briefcase. "Well, gather some paper and you may begin your letter of apology. I will collect them at the end."

And you were worried, Brianna! It appeared that my nerves failed to serve their purpose. Sure, writing a letter during one of my favourite parts of the day was not the most enjoyable thing to do, but at least that was *all* I had to withstand; apart from Mr Lawson's constant questions.

"Brianna, History is the final class of the day, but I remember you mentioning to me that you have rehearsal. Is that correct?"

I stopped writing to answer. "Yes, Sir. I'm rehearsing for the dance that's tonight."

"Well, you're in luck, because I happen to have the work I was intending to give the class! Lucky for you, otherwise you would have been behind!" Oh yes, *lucky* indeed. Mr Lawson removed some worksheets from his case and placed them on my desk.

"Thanks." I tried to sound grateful; hopefully Mr Lawson interpreted my response that way.

"You're very welcome!" I returned my attention back to the letter of apology and only managed to complete one sentence before being interrupted again. "We were going to continue discussing World War II and conclude by addressing how it affected people on a global spectrum. It's a shame you'll miss it!"

Yes, what a shame...

"Well, thank you for letting me know in advance."

"...My pleasure, Brianna."

The next fifteen minutes were surprisingly silent. I expected to be interrupted by Mr Lawson a few times, but this wasn't the case, much to my surprise. I peered towards him at the front desk every couple of minutes and each time he seemed extremely focussed; his eyes hadn't left the piece of paper in front of him. With five minutes to go, both Megan and I had completed our letters. We sat in silence, waiting for Mr Lawson to take notice, but he was far too preoccupied with whatever he was writing down.

DONG! DONG! DONG!

The bell broke Mr Lawson's concentration, surprising him so much that he almost fell off his chair. "Goodness, I can't believe the time! Please leave your apologies with me and I will pass them onto Mr O'Hara. You may leave now."

Megan slumped towards the door and gave me a casual wave as she left. I subtly waved back, feeling sorry for her. After handing the letter to Mr Lawson, I made every effort to leave the room before he could initiate another boring conversation or ask of matters that I thought best to avoid. *Yes! I'm in the clear!* I had successfully left the room without Mr Lawson muttering one syllable! Making my way to the music room for rehearsal, I felt relieved and couldn't make sense of how I had stressed about detention. Looking back, I was embarrassed with myself; I worried about nothing! I always seem to assume things far too quickly and blow things completely out of proportion. It was behind me now, although, now I had to endure a night of glitter and glam. I think I would rather have taken the detention again, but, the adventure awaiting Ethan, Charlotte and I that very evening would help me tolerate an evening of make-up and uncoordinated dancing.

"Bee, can I come in or are you still changing?" Ethan asked, just beyond my bedroom door.

"I'm good, you can come in ... just trying to do something with all this fuzz!"

Ethan hesitantly opened the door as my eyes were still glued to the mirror, trying to make something of my obstinate hair.

"How is this? Or is it *too much*?" There was a great deal of uncertainty in Ethan's voice, which caused me to turn towards him immediately. Ethan was wearing his black suit pants, Armani shoes (that he only wore when he really wanted to make a good impression), white collared shirt and a black vest. Combining his clothing choice with his incessant questioning about his appearance, I knew Ethan hadn't gone to this much effort simply because he was performing in front of people. Ethan wanted to impress Charlotte. I'd had some suspicions before, but this confirmed them. Should I be honest with him and say that he looked amazing and get his hopes up, thinking that Charlotte would mimic my reaction? Or, should I come across very casual, preparing him for Charlotte's reaction that could potentially be the one he was *not* hoping for? *What to do?*

"Ethan, you look great, but I know why you went to all this effort." I decided to adopt the honest, yet caring approach. The last thing I wanted was for Ethan to experience what I did with Logan.

"Is it *that* obvious?" Ethan realised I was referring to Charlotte.

"Well, I think so, but, I don't think Charlotte has a clue."

Ethan slumped onto my bed and sat there looking most doubtful.

"Look," I said as I slumped beside him, "if you know this is how you feel, maybe the best thing is to show it and see how she reacts. If she doesn't react in that way, then you know where you both stand. But, I ... I just don't want you to get hurt, okay?" Ethan was not in the mood for speaking after my honesty, so I tried to reassure him. "It's just ... I ... I know what is feels like to want someone and then find out that they have no interest. It hurts and I don't want that for you."

Ethan turned to face me, his face rather stunned by what I had just shared. "How would you know what it feels like? You haven't had a boyfriend!"

"I know that! But, I ... In my mind I thought that something could eventuate with this person. I got myself all worked up about it and anticipated too much too soon." I returned to preparing my hair, hoping the conversation would return back to Charlotte and Ethan.

"Well, now that you've spilled the beans, you've got to tell me who!"

I placed the hairpiece that I was attempting to rest in my hair on my dresser and turned to face Ethan. In that moment I questioned whether I should express my heartache, or continue to keep it bottled up inside. I decided to share, opening up to Ethan. He was my brother and at least he would be able to learn from my experience.

"It was Logan, Ethan."

"*Seriously?*" Ethan stood up, shocked by what I revealed.

"*Yes!* Happy now, Ethan?" I returned to fixing my hair, attempting to avoid further embarrassment.

"Well, I didn't see that coming."

"Neither did I until it did! Don't judge me!"

"Whoa!" Ethan waved his hands and looked taken aback by my accusation. "I'm not judging you! I'm just surprised that I didn't pick it up. I'm normally quite good at picking up things."

"Apparently not." I threw the hairpiece on the floor in frustration; my curly locks would remain as they were.

"Bee?" Ethan asked in a sympathetic tone.

"What?" I exclaimed, rummaging through my draws trying to find the prayer box necklace Ethan had given me.

"Come and sit here." Ethan patted my bed, inviting me to receive some counsel. I found the prayer box and left it in my hands as I joined him. "Are you okay? Be honest with me."

For the past week I hadn't been *okay*, but at least I had this off my chest now. It was almost therapeutic opening up to Ethan. I was surprised by his willingness to sit and listen to me express my feelings of sadness and frustration for a good few minutes.

"Well," Ethan said, "I know you'll be okay, Bee. Logan's a gobshite for not being interested in you!" He placed his arm around my shoulder and continued to send words of confidence my way. "One day, you will meet a fella who won't be able to take his hands off you!"

"*Ethan!*" I exclaimed. "Let's not go down that road just yet!" This was my moment, my moment to beat Ethan at his own game. "Now *you* are making a *sceptical* of yourself!"

He laughed and replied, "I am, aren't I?"

"So, back to you and Charlotte," I redirected the conversation. "At least you can learn from my experience. If she is willing to show the feelings you have for her in return, then go for it, but, if she hasn't picked up on anything by now, I doubt she sees you in that way. I just don't want you to feel like I have. Don't anticipate things too soon!"

Ethan patted my back rather than saying *thank you*. He looked at his watch and when he realised the time he almost deafened me. "WHOA! That can't be the time! Hurry up, Bee! We're going to be late for the final rehearsal!" Ethan raced out my room.

"Hey! You wanted to chat!" The only positive thing that came out of rushing was not being able to do my hair. I quickly put my prayer box necklace on, which reminded me of the carrier in my bedside table draw. I couldn't leave it where it could potentially be found. I retrieved it from the draw, moved my bed aside and lifted up the loose timbre plank of my bedroom floor. I dropped the carrier into the tight gap, knowing it would be safe.

*

The dance went by in a blink of an eye! Ethan played the drums to perfection and my saxophone solo went as well as it could have. A few people questioned me about why I had a bandage on my right hand; word had not yet spread of my outburst in Religion, so I decided to tell the set of circumstances Charlotte and Ethan had prepared for me. Thankfully, Charlotte only dragged me onto the dance floor for no more than ten minutes. Apart from performing and being on the dance floor, Charlotte, Ethan and I spent the majority of the night by the food table. Ethan attended to

Charlotte for most of the evening, bringing her food and drink, hoping that she would show some signs of interest. But, by the evening's close, when Charlotte was conversing with a group of girls in our grade, Ethan gave me a look of, *"I tried, Bee."* I replied with a sympathetic expression. Whilst making the most of the free food, I couldn't help but let my eyes wander and I found Logan in the crowd of people. I felt queasy, but not just when I found him with Stephanie. Seeing him reminded me of everything I was trying to put behind me. Ethan sensed this and tried to take my mind away from Logan.

"Come on, Bee, let's go and put away the instruments and equipment." I signalled Charlotte, pointing towards the music room to inform her of where Ethan and I were going. She nodded and remained with the group of girls to continue the discussion of what they would be wearing at the next school dance.

By the time Ethan and I had dismantled the school drum kit, all of our fellow musicians had left. The only remaining task was returning my saxophone to the instrument store room.

"Ethan, while you're finishing up with the microphones and speakers, I'm just going to take my saxophone back to the store room. Okay?"

"Yeah, that's cool. Don't be too long though. Have you forgotten about our plans for tonight?"

"Of course not! Don't worry, I'll be quick."

"I'll meet you there in a bit, anyway. Then we'll meet Charlotte at the school gate. Dad said he'd be waiting there after ten-thirty."

"All right."

Carrying my tenor saxophone case was hard enough on its own, but doing it in heels was just ridiculous. I finally made it to the store room and, once I stopped, I realised that my feet were starting to show signs of wearing heels for an entire evening.

Typical! The highest shelf was the only available space for my saxophone. "There's no way I can get it up there on my own," I said to myself. After a few attempts, I realised that my original expectation was right, so, I decided to wait for Ethan. *Perfect timing!* Less than a minute later, I heard Ethan's footsteps coming from the outside corridor.

"Good timing, Ethan! I need you to help me with my..."
The lights turned off.
"Ethan? Ha, ha! Very funny! Turn the lights back on!"
Silence.
"Ethan?"
Nothing.
"Ethan!" I exclaimed. "Stop being thick and turn the lights on! Come on!"
Still nothing.
"ETHAN! THAT'S IT! You're so..." A firm hand clasped my mouth shut. I tried to scream, but it was useless. A solid

arm wrapped itself below my rib cage. I struggled to breathe. I was being dragged back into darkness, into nothingness. I couldn't see anything. The arm's grip tightened beneath my ribs. My body quivered uncontrollably. My hands, shaking in fear, did their best to drive my fingernails into the hand covering my mouth ... useless. The vine-like arms pulled me up; there was no ground beneath my feet. I shuffled my limbs back and forth, desperately attempting to squirm free from the stranger's hold. I had nothing and no one to help me - I was alone. I tried to formulate a plan, but all my entire mind let me hear were thoughts of family, friends and my life. *Is this it? Is my life going to end?* Scared beyond reason, my mind was no longer behaving rationally. The being was still pulling me backwards. My feet were still scuffling and one of my shoes hit the ground. The sound ignited a spark in my mind. I brought my left foot up towards the back of my thigh. My left hand, trembling beyond fear, removed the high-heeled shoe. I let the shoe slip into my palm, but had the heel free from my grasp. Adrenalin and anything else fuelling within me, drove the heel of the shoe into the being's face.

"ARGHH!" The vines released me. I ran. My feet burned against the cold concrete floor. *Where do I hide? Where do I run?* My mind couldn't reason. I was lost in a school building I had known for almost six years. Disorientated and panic-stricken, I darted to the closest door along the outside corridor. The door revealed a staircase. I had almost reached the second floor, when harsh, fast steps were beginning to make their way up the stairs. I found the second floor door and darted through. Just beyond the doorway, were the tall standing lockers. I hid behind them, praying that the being would turn left. It did. When I could no longer hear the footsteps, my shaky knees sprang my body up to hustle back down the staircase.

"Bee?" I was never so relieved to hear Ethan's voice. I tried to scream his name, but fear restrained me. All I could do was run to Ethan. "Bee? ...You still here?"

"Ethan!" I barely managed to say, "I'm here! I'm..."

*

My eyes flickered open, revealing only complete darkness. I attempted to raise my head and, as I did, it throbbed terribly. Once upright, I tried to raise my body, but was unable to do so. Ropes against a chair, the ropes so tight, they imprinted into my arms and legs, had restrained me, acting like a python, constricting its prey. With the little energy I had, I flexed my arms and legs, trying to slacken the ropes, but it was useless. The ropes were far too tight for my movement to have any effect. I accepted that I was stuck. My only way out of this was through someone else's intervention. When I came to this realisation, I replayed what I last remembered in my mind. *There was someone ... probably a man, based on how they managed to hold me ... and they were trying to restrain me. I managed to get away. I heard Ethan.*

ETHAN! Where is he now? Then ... there was nothing. I must have been knocked out.

My chair jolted.

"*Ouch!*" Something hard hit the back of my *already* sore head.

"Bee? That you?" The voice cautiously whispered. It was Ethan.

"Ethan!" *Thank God!* I thought I was alone! "What the *hell* happened?" I whispered anxiously.

"*I don't know!* One second, I was trying to find you and the next, I heard you running towards me! Then, I saw a fella in black standing over you! He had just knocked you out! So, despite being scared shitless, I charged at the bastard and before I knew it, I was out cold too!"

Screech.

"Ethan!"

"Brianna! We've been locked up for no reason! I'm allowed to swear at a time like this!" He did have a point, but that wasn't what I meant.

"No! The noise ... the screechy noise ... did you hear it?"

"No."

Screech.

"There it is again!" I announced.

"I heard it that time!" Ethan replied. "I think someone's coming, Bee!"

After hearing the second *screech*, footsteps gradually came into earshot. The footsteps stopped and I recognised the sound of a door opening. The door was slammed shut and the footsteps made their way towards us. We were in a helpless position, unable to run, unable to see and with no knowledge as to where we were. It was hopeless.

"Where is the carrier, Brianna Elsa?" The deep voice asked from the darkness - a murky, shapeless and sinister figure.

Do I lie? Or, do I say I have it but it's not with me? What the hell do I do?

So scared and uncertain of what to do, my heart leapt in a way I had never felt it move before. I was almost certain that Ethan could hear it beat from my fear.

"Uh ... I don't know what you're..."

"ANSWER ME!" My body shook as the voice intensified. "ANSWER ME NOW OR SUFFER THE CONSEQUENCES!"

"I ... I honestly don't know what you..." The man slapped my face. The harsh sound caused Ethan's body to jump, as well as my own.

"DON'T YOU DARE LAY A HAND ON HER YOU SON OF A..." Ethan's words were blocked by a slap to his own face. Ethan's glasses cracked as they made contact with the floor.

In my state of shock, my breathing became incredibly rapid and tears of fear fell against my already swelling face. It was difficult to hold back a wail. Ethan's body shook against my back. His breathing was much louder now too. My fear and pain was too difficult to hold back and my body released a wail.

"SHUT UP!" The monstrous voice echoed against the chamber walls by which we seemed to be surrounded. "THE SYMBOL LIES ON YOUR HAND! I KNOW YOU HAVE IT! ANSWER MY QUESTION!"

The bandage was still on my hand. *Had he taken it off and put it back on?* My wail brought me back to focus. Fear and pain now released, I knew that I had to hold my ground. I didn't know who this man was or how he knew about the carrier, but one thing that I was certain of was that he needed the information I had. I would be safe until he found the carrier, because he needed me to reveal its location. My only option was to put up a defensive front and frustrate the man to buy us some time.

"How do you know my name?"

"ANSWER ME! WHERE IS THE..."

"HOW DO YOU KNOW MY NAME?" I screamed so harshly that my voice became raspy. Satisfied with my response, I decided to attempt to spark fear. "Once we're found, you will be locked up yourself! Then, you definitely won't be able to have the carrier!"

"You fool! You don't even know where you are! You won't see the light of day until you tell me where the carrier is!"

"Fine," Ethan said, picking up on my attempts to create fear and delay the man's actions. "We'll just sit back and relax, because you'll need us until we tell you where the carrier is, but we all know that isn't going to happen, right Bee?"

"Right," I added.

The man threw something against the stone wall. Our plan was working; we were frustrating him and getting under his skin.

"You do have a point," the man said calmly in contrast to his previous responses. His change of tone worried me. "I do need you alive to find the carrier, but I only need *one* of you alive. And what do you know; there are *two* of you here. So, who's it going to be? Eeny, meeny, miny, moe..."

Screech.

Ethan and I remained silent, trying to listen intently to the familiar screech. Is there an accomplice? Or are we being saved?

"Who's there?" The man's tone was insecure. His reaction gave me hope. "Who is there?"

Silence.

As the man ventured towards the sound, Ethan turned as best as he could to whisper in my ear. "You okay, Bee?"

"Not really," I whispered back. "Well, actually my wrists feel like they are on fire. And you?"

"The same, but I think my jaw is about to fall off. Although," Ethan's tone became excited, "I think we might be in the clear soon. He's scared. Based on that reaction we know he's on his own. Someone could be coming for us."

"I hope you're right, I really hope you're..."

"ARGH!" The man screamed. It sounded like he had been pinned to the stone floor. Growling noises found their way into the chamber. Ethan and I sat in silence, attempting to focus on the scuffle occurring just beyond the nearby door. "ARGH! GET OFF!" The growls continued. It sounded like a dog was mauling the man!

SLAM!

"Hurry!" A female voice urged. Suddenly, the ropes fell from Ethan and me. We were free. She placed Ethan's glasses in my unstable hands. "Hold your brother's hand and feel your way to a door just a few steps in front of you! Go!" I followed the lady's instructions, clamped onto Ethan's hand and pulled him. I finally found a doorknob and I turned it. As I released it, the door revealed a narrow cement staircase.

"Bee! How'd we ... what happened?" I didn't answer Ethan. I concentrated on finding a way out. We scurried up the narrow staircase for a few minutes until we discovered light seeping through a metal drain-like covering. "Let me!" Ethan urged. He pushed passed me and heaved the drain open. It flew up and made a terrible *CLANG*. Ethan hoisted himself up and then reached back down to help me through.

We found ourselves on a quiet city street, dimly lit by street lamps. I recognised a clothing store Mam had tried to convince me to enter only a few weeks ago when she tried to get me to try on some dresses. We were on one of the main streets of Dublin, quite close to school.

Ethan looked at his watch. "THREE-FIFTEEN! We've been here for hours!"

"Is your phone still on you?" I asked, still rather out of breath and shaky.

"One sec," Ethan searched his pockets. "Damn! It was in my jacket!"

"Wait, calling the police or emergency services is free! Where's the nearest pay phone?"

Ethan and I ran up the abandoned street until we eventually found one. I returned Ethan's glasses and he called the police.

"They'll be here soon." Ethan sat on the cold curb and invited me to join him. We held each other, as we waited for the police and quietly shivered - not just from the cold. Under the light of the street lamp, I realised just how hard Ethan's face had been hit. His right cheek and jaw-line were swollen and bruised. His lip had also been cut and a trickle of blood remained on his chin.

"Thanks for sticking up for me," I said, while holding Ethan's arm. "Do you think we'll be safe here until the police come, or should we keep moving in case?" I asked. After the ordeal we just endured I was astonished as to how I could put a complete sentence together.

"We are already reasonably far away, besides, I think that dog took care of him. But, Bee," Ethan questioned, "How were our ropes untied? Did you manage to do it? How'd you know there was a way out?"

"The lady, Ethan." *How did he not hear her?* "She handed me your glasses. She told me about the door."

"Bee, all I heard was a dog attacking that man. There was no lady. I didn't hear a lady's voice at all."

Chapter Ten

The Oran-Roy Bird

...Zia finally reached the cliff's edge. It was time to return to Tarmon. He stroked the carrier, turned around and looked at the setting sun allowing the night sky to cover the nearby town in a blanket of black. He wondered whether this would be his last adventure in Ireland...

- Excerpt from 'The Morrigan Book'

Before the police car had even made its way onto the driveway, Mam, Dad and Charlotte were already legging it to see us. Not yet standing upright and making my way out of the police car, Mam pulled me into her arms. All I could see was her frizzy red hair. Unable to find the right words, Mam stroked my head and back repeatedly. Her hands were shaking so profusely, it seemed as though she had ventured out into Arctic conditions. In that moment, I put aside our ordeal. Mam, Dad and Charlotte must have gone through hell waiting for news of us. Mam refused to let me go as Dad attempted to greet me.

"Let the old man in, love!" Dad blared, as he pulled me against his torso, my feet struggling to maintain contact with the ground.

After Ethan and I received warm welcomes from my parents, Charlotte politely pushed passed the police officers and delicately flung her arms around me.

"You...have put me … under a ... a lot of stress this week, Brianna," she said in laboured gasps, trying not to cry.

"Sorry, I'll try not to make a habit out of it," I barely managed to say, as Charlotte's arms began to squeeze the life out of me now.

Charlotte breathed a peaceful sigh and then freed me from her bear hug to welcome Ethan. For the first time, Charlotte hesitated when approaching Ethan. Ethan realised this and waited on Charlotte's response to indicate how he should reply. But, strangely, Charlotte and Ethan simultaneously stepped towards one another, hugged *very* briefly and then, *very* quickly, and stepped away from each other, avoiding eye contact. Ethan's behaviour didn't surprise me in the slightest, but Charlotte's reaction caused me to question all of my prior judgments. *Perhaps I was wrong. Perhaps Charlotte does have feelings for Ethan.*

The police officers suggested that Ethan and I make our way into the house. Mam ushered us in and Charlotte decided it was best if she joined us. Mam went back out so that she and Dad could have a word with the officers.

The three of us sat on the large sofa by the fireplace in complete silence, until the absence of noise clearly began to bother Charlotte. She left the sofa and proceeded to turn on all of the lights in the lounge room, hoping that it might *switch* Ethan and me into a talking frenzy. She was dying to know what happened. I wanted to say everything, but I just had no idea where to begin!

With the room now drowned in light, the injuries we had incurred over the course of the night became rather more obvious.

"Oh, my God!" Charlotte's hands covered her mouth in shock. "What did they do to you? Are you alright?"

"They knew about the carrier, Charlotte," Ethan answered. "We didn't let anything slip and he ... well ... our bruised faces reflect how he responded."

"So ... how did you ... wait ... did someone save you? How'd you escape?" Charlotte was now sitting opposite us, holding her knees up to her chest in anticipation of what we were about to share.

Ethan continued. "Well, we were ... actually ... I don't know. Brianna never did tell me how we became untied. But, she said there was a lady, didn't you, Bee? But, I never heard a lady's voice." Ethan looked at me, inviting me to explain.

"The voice was as clear to me as how you are both speaking to me right now. I *know* it wasn't in my..."

"Brianna," Charlotte interrupted, "perhaps the person who saved you knows about the book. What did you hear her say?"

"I guess that's a possibility," I replied. "All the lady said was for me to take Ethan and search for a door that was in front of me."

Ethan removed his crooked glasses from his face and fiddled with them, perplexed by the voice I described. "The only thing I heard, other than the man, was a dog, Bee."

Something ignited in my brain, triggered by Ethan's words. "A DOG!" I exclaimed. Ethan and Charlotte jumped, quite stunned by my reaction. "...Guys! The Morrigan book told of Keelty! Remember? Keelty was in the Arawn pack from Daray and she was close with my father, Craig, from the book! Do you think it was her? Do you think she was the dog who attacked him?" I paused, waiting for some confirmation. "It fits, doesn't it? Keelty would have been in Ireland for eighteen years since she helped me get here!"

Ethan and Charlotte's facial expressions transformed, proving to me that they had welcomed my recent theory. Their reactions were the ones I was hoping for.

"Yes, Bee!" Ethan leaped from the sofa. "That has to be right! It explains everything! Because..."

"... Because," Charlotte interrupted again, "Brianna is half Crag! People from Crag can communicate with animals from Daray!"

"Yeah!" I cried enthusiastically. "That explains why I heard Keelty speak and Ethan didn't! Although..." I left the sofa and paced up and down the room, trying to decipher the missing piece of the puzzle.

"What, Bee?" Ethan queried.

"It's just ... Keelty fits, but, that doesn't answer who kidnapped us, Ethan." The halt in my thinking translated into my pacing around the room. *Who could the man be? Other than Ethan, Charlotte and I, no one else is aware of the carrier.* "I mean, you are the only people who know about the carrier. Can ... can you think of anyone who could possibly know of the carrier besides us?"

"Well, let's try and go back to the book," Charlotte keenly suggested. "Other than Keelty, only two people have left Oran-Roy and come to Ireland." She paused before continuing. "Sully Kael, your uncle, and Dallas Conlan, the friend of your grandfather." Before Charlotte had time to elaborate, Ethan cut in.

"It's Sully ... Sully is the man who caught us tonight. It makes sense. After all, he was working with Cillian." Charlotte and I glanced at each other, checking whether we were on the same page as Ethan. "It fits!" he blared, thinking that we were both doubting him.

"No," I stressed to Ethan, "Charlotte and I agree with you! It must be Sully! I just can't understand - why now? Why, after eighteen years, would Sully decide to see if I had the carrier?"

"That's a good point," commented Charlotte. "But then, that also begs the question of why Keelty would wait eighteen years to approach you?"

"That is a good point," Ethan said, hoping that supporting Charlotte would earn him some brownie points. "And what about the Dallas fella. He is technically your third cousin … I think. Do you think he could have anything to do with this?"

I returned to the sofa and sat beside Ethan before commenting. "Well, Zia helped him escape Oran-Roy when he was seventeen because he didn't want to chance him being discovered as a half-blood. He'd be really old now. He might not even be alive. We just don't know."

Ethan slumped further into the sofa, demonstrating signs of annoyance at not knowing the answers to the millions of questions we had. "This sucks! How the *hell* are we supposed to find this out! There are too many bloody questions to be answered!"

I felt Ethan's annoyance. I craved answers so desperately that I was almost certain I would go to drastic lengths, like enduring twenty school dances to achieve them! My thoughts swirled: *Are the questions ever going to end? Will I ever reach a state of contentment, knowing that all my questions have been answered? I am sick of asking questions about questions!*

The evening's ordeal put a stop to our plans of testing the carrier and once again, removed the chance of receiving any answers. Or, did it?

"That's it!" I announced. "We're testing it tonight, or rather, *this morning*. It's still dark and when Mam and Dad send us off to try and get some sleep, we'll go then." I waited for a response from Ethan and Charlotte, but it didn't come. I decided to be more persuasive. "Look, we're in danger. Whether the man who took us is Sully or not, someone is after the carrier and us, so we should leave. We'll be safer away from whoever they are and, if we leave with the carrier, at least they won't have any chance of making it back to Oran-Roy and following us. So, do you agree?" Still no answer; they were testing my patience. This was the most drastic decision of my life and I wasn't receiving any input! It was difficult to hide my frustration. "Come on!" I cried angrily. "When we decided on this yesterday you were both up for it! What's the problem now?!"

"Well," Charlotte said subduedly, "we never did really consider the implications this plan would have on your parents, as well as mine." Charlotte glanced over at Ethan, hinting for some support, and in light of Ethan's feelings, he didn't hesitate.

"I think Charlotte's got a point, Bee. What are Mam and Dad going to think when they wake up and we're gone? We could be gone for quite some time, gathering up some answers."

I released a stressful sigh and ran my fingers through my hair, clearly irritated by Ethan and Charlotte's indecisiveness. "We'll leave a note!" I forcefully suggested. "We'll tell Mam and Dad the truth in the note, but instruct them to tell the police that we're missing again. They'll just assume it's the same person from tonight, or yesterday evening ... *whatever*!"

"They aren't going to believe it, Bee. They won't believe any of it, no matter what we write in a letter," Ethan admitted.

"You're right, I know you're right."

"Although," Charlotte said, "you could leave the book behind for them to read with the letter. That way, they can at least ... well ... *hopefully* understand why we had to leave."

"I hear you, but having the book with us is probably best. If we need to recall some details it'll be handy." Before speaking again, I ran my fingers through my hair again, really frustrated thinking about how Mam and Dad would react. "They're going to think we're insane!"

"Yeah, they probably are." Ethan laughed. At least he found the prospect of our parents denying our sanity a funny idea. I certainly didn't. "Okay," he said, when he felt the need to laugh no more, "As soon as Mam and Dad have a chat with us and let us go up to have a rest, Charlotte, you should ask them if you can stay over, just to make sure Brianna is alright, okay?"

"Yep, that's a good idea."

"Good, and Bee, when they think we're all asleep, I'll meet you both in your room. We'll write the letter, leave it by Mam's bedside table and then we'll go. How does that sound?"

"Good," I answered. "Charlotte?"

Charlotte was rather hesitant.

"Charlotte?" I asked again. "Are you okay about all of this?"

Charlotte was squirming in her chair, clearly doubtful about what this decision would involve. "Well, it's just, what are my parents going to think? Will ... will they be able to read the letter and be on the same page as your parents when they come back home, or will they be in the dark? It's just ... I ... I know what it's like to feel like you've lost someone ... tonight for instance. I don't want my parents feeling that way."

Ethan and I looked at each other and nodded in agreement.

"How about in the letter, we ask Mam and Dad to let your parents know everything that we have told them when they come back?" Ethan asked sympathetically. "Although," he continued, "You could let your neighbour, Mrs who again?"

"O'Sullivan," Charlotte and I voiced together.

"Yeah, her! You could tell her that you just got selected for the school's USA yearly trip. You can tell her that it was a few months ago that you applied and you missed out, which happens to be true, but someone dropped out last minute and they needed to fill in a spot urgently! Ignorance is bliss!"

"I like that!" Charlotte's face beamed. "That's a better idea. Until your parents speak to my parents, let's not make them worry and I'll Skype them when I get back home and tell them that I'm going on the school trip. I'll explain that I got offered it last minute. They'd already signed all the paperwork when I applied, so it should work."

The engine of one of the police cars roared outside in the silence of the early hours of the morning, giving us the heads up that Mam and Dad were on their way back inside. Mam and Dad walked straight towards the sofa where Ethan and I were sitting and just managed to squeeze beside the both of us.

Dad placed his left arm around me and rested his right hand on Ethan's knee. "Before we get into details, we have to know, are you okay?"

I looked over at Ethan and we both nodded.

"Are you sure?" Dad asked again, not satisfied that we *were* fine by our lack of response.

My eyes widened, intending for Ethan to infer that I had nominated him as speaker. He knew I'd find it difficult to hide away my feelings in my voice. "Yeah, Dad ... Bee and I are okay. What we went through was strange and scary, but we're good now."

"Alright," Dad said through a sigh. "Is there any reason you think this happened?"

"I know you've been through a lot, but we *really* need to know what you know so we can keep you safe," Mam felt the need to add.

My eyes flickered at Ethan, again nominating him as speaker. "We really haven't got a clue. We're not involved in anything bad in or out of school ... perhaps we were mistaken for someone else. We are just as baffled as to why this happened as you are." That was a much better description than what I was planning on putting together.

Mam glanced over at Dad, hinting that she wanted to have a word in private and allow us to go up to bed. "Okay," Dad said based on Mam's not very subtle hint. "The police are leaving a patrol car outside the house for the next few days, just to make sure you're all safe until they find anything."

Mam raised herself from the sofa and pulled Ethan and me towards her. "I was worried beyond belief! I can't imagine ever losing either of you, let alone both of you!" Tears fell from Mam's gleaming blue eyes. "We love you both and want you to feel that you can tell us anything, alright?" Mam said in a shaky voice.

Ethan and I responded with a nod. I wiped away her tears and she hugged us both. Her reaction was beginning to make me doubt the power of the letter that we were intending on leaving behind. I wondered whether Ethan felt the same.

"Well, go and get as much rest as you can," Mam said, as she let us go. "Charlotte, I think it would be best if you stay here with Brianna. When we spoke to Mrs O'Sullivan earlier she said that would be fine. Would you like that, Brianna?"

"Yeah. Thanks, Mam."

Well, that was unexpected. Maybe this plan will work after all!

"And the two of you need ice. I'll go get a pack of peas from the freezer." Mam was trying to be strong, but I knew she was just as scared and confused about this as we were.

The three of us left Mam and Dad to speak privately in the lounge room and made our way upstairs, with Ethan and me holding packs of peas on our purple faces. Within half an hour, we had each showered and were in our pyjamas ready for bed; Charlotte wore an old night dress of mine that was far too small for me now, yet hung on Charlotte's tiny limbs.

"Goodnight!" Ethan yelled from over the staircase banister for Mam and Dad to hear from downstairs. "Well, it's actually morning," he hushed to himself.

"Are Brianna and Charlotte already in bed, Ethan?" Mam asked from the bottom of the stairs.

"Uh ... not sure," Ethan replied.

"Night!" Charlotte and I both yelled from my room, confirming that we were not asleep.

"Alright then, night! Your Dad and I are off to bed too. Come to us straight away if you need anything, all right?" Mam asked with great concern in her voice.

"We will," the three of us answered simultaneously.

Quietly, Charlotte raced over to my computer ready to Skype her parents. While it loaded, she rehearsed what she would say and made sure that it sounded believable. Like me, she wasn't a good liar, but as Ethan and I had realised, Charlotte too knew the importance behind what we were about to embark on.

*

It was now almost six o'clock and we hadn't heard any noise from Mam and Dad for quite some time. I wanted to ask Charlotte about whether she felt anything for Ethan, but, given the circumstances we were in (and the chance that Ethan could potentially walk in on us), I decided to leave it for another time.

There was a gentle knock at my bedroom door, which indicated to Charlotte and I that Ethan felt that this was the appropriate time to act.

"Can I come in?" Ethan whispered from behind the door.

"Yep," I whispered back.

Ethan was wearing his typical 'nerd' ensemble, but Charlotte and I were still in pyjamas.

"You're not ready yet?" Ethan said surprisingly.

"We wanted to wait until you gave us the heads up!" I insisted.

"All right, all right. Well, how about I write the letter in my room while you both get ready. Okay?"

"Yeah," I agreed, "Plus, your writing is hard to miss. Mam and Dad will know you wrote it."

"Thanks, Bee," Ethan said sarcastically as he left my room.

Once again, Charlotte had to rely on items from my wardrobe to wear, which proved to be a *very* difficult task.

Eventually, I managed to find a rainbow jumper (which I last wore three years ago that was far too small for me now, but far too nice to give away) and an old pair of jeans that my fourteen-year-old self was able to share with the eighteen-year-old Charlotte. Luckily, shoes weren't a problem; Charlotte's feet were only slightly smaller than my own, so she was content in wearing my previous pair of white sneakers. Once Charlotte was ready, she decided to help Ethan with the letter, which gave me a chance to collect a few things for the trip.

Since Charlotte and Ethan had adopted casual attire, I decided to do the same. I pulled out the first pair of jeans in my pants draw and scurried through my wardrobe to find my warm Batman jumper and converse sneakers.

I had already taken too long getting dressed and I still hadn't packed some things in my bag! In my moment of rushing, all I could think to pack was the Morrigan book, a cardigan, some chocolate I had secretly stashed in my room, a water bottle, my wallet, iPod and mobile phone. I knew there was something that I was forgetting. In the mad rush, I realised that my right hand was still bandaged; I decided to leave it that way, just in case, but that wasn't what I had forgotten about.

As I proceeded to leave my room, I took one last look at myself in the mirror of my dressing table. I was still wearing the prayer box from Ethan. Seeing it reminded me that I still hadn't written anything to put in it. I adjusted the necklace, so that the opening was now behind my neck, which reminded me of the object I had failed to pack - the carrier. As I moved my bed aside to collect the carrier beneath the loose floorboard, Charlotte and Ethan quietly re-entered my room.

"Ready, now?" Ethan asked.

I got up from the floor, pushed my bed back into place, flung my bag over my shoulder and hid the carrier beneath my shirt. "Ready as I'll ever be."

"Ethan and I have already put the letter beside your Mam's bedside table. We also thought that we should pack as much food and tools as possible, just in case," Charlotte said, as she opened her bag to reveal a large portion of food and extra supplies, including bandages, toiletries and a rope.

"Cool," I said in a pressing tone, trying to hint that we should leave immediately. "We can't go out the front door; the police will see us ... our only way of leaving here without being seen is through the back."

"But, Mam and Dad will hear us from the back!" Ethan said nervously.

"Don't panic!" I insisted. "I thought we could climb down the trellis from just beneath my window, just like in those teen movies."

Charlotte's expression made it clear that she wasn't in favour of *my* idea of a way out.

"Well!" I directed at Charlotte. "Do you have any better suggestions?"

Charlotte shook her head. Ethan appeared rather game; I sensed that climbing down a trellis was an adventurous and exciting feat that he had always wanted to do. I was rather excited, too.

Ethan assisted Charlotte out of my window first and made sure that she had a firm grip of the trellis before letting go. Surprisingly, Charlotte *very* quickly and *rather* impressively, reached the bottom with little trouble. Ethan then helped me out of the window and, when satisfied that I was secure, he climbed through the frame and shut the window as he rested on the top of the trellis.

Before we set off, I felt a pang of guilt. *What are Mam and Dad going to endure while we're gone? What are they going to think?* I didn't know how long we would be and I didn't know what we would face. In that moment, I looked towards the only home that I had ever known and thought that this could possibly be the last time I would look at it if things were to go horribly wrong.

"We'll be back, Bee," Ethan said and gently patted my back. His tone revealed that he was also feeling a little uneasy about leaving home. "This is something that we have to do and when the time is right, Mam and Dad will realise that and we'll be able to come back and explain everything."

Ethan was right. Sure, leaving home and going out on a limb like this was incredibly risky, but I faced the same level of danger in staying at home. A queasy feeling engulfed the pit of my stomach. Words could not disguise the guilt I felt. Rather than expressing these feelings through words that would expose my guilty feelings, I turned around and began to walk. I feared that if I opened my mouth to speak, it might have caused me to cry and I was *too* stubborn to allow that to happen.

We had almost walked past the barn, when Tess and Lulu began to bark after us. I rushed over to their kennels and urged them to be quiet. It was almost as if they knew that the three of us would be gone for some time.

"Shhhh, shhhh. Don't worry; we'll be back before you know it!" I said, as I stroked their heads.

"Come on," Ethan urged, "we've got to get near the cliff before the sun comes out or we'll be seen!"

Ethan was right. We had to press on. We couldn't chance anyone seeing us leave. But as we walked further on, almost completely off our land, the dogs continued to bark!

"Shut up!" Ethan hushed harshly. But it was no use. Mam and Dad would come out soon and try to quieten them down if they continued to bark.

The barking didn't cease.

"We've got to take them!" I cried.

"No!" Ethan cried back.

"What else can we do?"

"Quickly, though!" Charlotte informed us.

As quickly and as quietly as we could, Ethan and I let Lulu and Tess out from their kennels and let them walk with us.

Charlotte was the only one who seemed to be thinking clearly at this point in time. "If the bird does come, how are we going to get the dogs on it?"

"I don't know!" I blared, quite annoyed with myself for not considering the dogs in our master plan. "We couldn't just leave them there, could we? They were barking up a storm and would have blown our cover!"

As a result of being delayed by the dogs, the intended walk to the cliff's edge turned into a brisk jog, but the dogs were completely unfazed by all of the fuss they had just caused. Tess and Lulu had their heads held high and were quite content running on ahead. The sky was gradually becoming lighter, but seeing wasn't becoming any easier, with the early morning mist descending. With roughly two hundred metres to go, I pulled the carrier out from beneath my blouse, to have it ready in case we needed to leave in a hurry. Our pace seemed to pick up during the last hundred metres, probably fuelled by the anticipation we were feeling.

We had almost reached the cliff's edge, when a noise in the far distance caught our attention. The dogs turned around immediately and darted straight past us towards the sound. I turned around, trying to make sense of where the sound had come from.

Tess and Lulu were no longer in my sight; they were hidden in the mist.

"Tess! Lulu!" I cried, but the dogs didn't come.

"What was that sound?" Charlotte asked, looking rather puzzled.

"I don't know," I replied, "but we've got to get a move on! Where the hell have they run off to?" I turned around and jogged back the way I had come, trying to find the dogs. I heard a deep, mellow bark. It didn't sound like Tess or Lulu.

"Brianna!" A female voice said from a fair distance away. "Brianna! You must leave, now!" The voice was incredibly familiar to me. Could it be Keelty? I needed to confirm that it was indeed Keelty.

"Guys, did you hear that? Did you hear someone calling my name?"

Their puzzled expressions answered my question. I didn't give either of them the opportunity to query. I ran directly into the cloud of mist, trying to get closer to where the voice had come from.

"Bee! Where are you going?" Ethan cried.

"Just stay where you are. Trust me!" I was trying to concentrate on tracking down the voice.

"Brianna!" It said again. "Go back! Go back near the cliff and have the carrier ready!" The voice was scared. It was getting closer. "Go!" it said again and this time, it sounded like it was only metres away from me. The mist was beginning to lift. I could just make out the house, but I still couldn't see anyone near me! Something brushed past me, causing me to turn back towards the cliff. A large four-legged creature was facing me. It was difficult to decide what it was.

"A horse," I thought, because it was far too big to be Tess or Lulu; it was at least double them in size. Fearful of what the creature was, my steps towards it were gradual and steady. Drawing closer, I began to make out thin, flighty hair outlining the animal. The head was enormous with small, floppy ears towards the back. The animal's legs were significantly thin in contrast with the solid, upper body that they were supporting. Even when I was almost directly in front of the creature, I struggled to find its eyes; they were partially covered by thin, grey straw-like pieces of hair. The tail was long and had a curly end, with wisps of grey hair along its length. The animal's head was level with my waist. It had every resemblance to Keelty, the Irish wolfhound and head of the Arawn pack of Oran-Roy. It was her - just as the Morrigan book had described. I just knew it.

"Keelty ... is that you?" I asked cautiously.

"Yes ... it is me, Brianna Elsa." Her lips were moving and I was communicating with her just as I would with anyone. *Wow! I'm talking to a dog! I AM TALKING TO A DOG! This is insane!*

"Yes, it can be a little shocking, can't it?" Keelty said, responding to my thoughts.

"Of course!" I said, quite astounded by what had just happened. "You can also hear my thoughts, and I can hear yours! Because ... because I'm half Crag!"

"Indeed," Keelty replied, but this time, her lips did not move. *"But how do you know this? How do you even know of me? You have not lived in Oran-Roy to be aware of this knowledge?"*

"It's a long story," I said out loud. It still didn't feel natural using my thoughts to communicate, but, in saying that, I was talking to a dog!

"There's no time!" Keelty urged and she motioned with her head, suggesting that we make our way towards the cliff. "We must hurry! Have you summoned the bird with the carrier yet?"

"No, but," I paused. It just occurred to me ... the dogs! *Where are the dogs?*

"Don't worry!" Keelty affirmed, "They're back at your home. I led them back there so we wouldn't have difficulties leaving." It was still a little unsettling having my thoughts answered by a dog, but I didn't have time to address that! I had to press on!

"Ah ... thanks, I guess."

"Quick, follow me!" Keelty proceeded forward. Her stride was long and she bounced up and down like a horse trotting. I jogged behind her and, within a few moments, we arrived at the cliff's edge to join Ethan and Charlotte.

"Where the hell did you run off to?" Ethan exclaimed, but then, his eyes found Keelty and he no longer needed an answer. "So ... so that's ..."

"Keelty!" Charlotte announced. "That explains why Brianna could hear the voice!"

"The carrier, Brianna! You must use it now! I sense that we're not alone!" Keelty was anxious. I sensed this not only by her tone, but also by the way that her eyes feverishly scanned the surrounding land. She lowered her head and her nostrils flared.

"So, I just turn this latch, Keelty?"

"Yes, a few turns should be enough to begin the song."

Ethan and Charlotte's eyes had widened, clearly astonished by what they had just witnessed.

"This is too weird!" Ethan seemed spooked. He tugged on Charlotte's sleeve and tried to keep his voice to a whisper, but I was still able to hear him. "Brianna is speaking to a dog! And it's talking back to her in a weird dog mumble!"

"You're about to put a hole through this jumper, Ethan," Charlotte said, while she was attempting to loosen Ethan's grip on her sleeve. "Yes, I know Brianna is talking to a dog, but we can deal with that later, all right?"

Ethan replied by silently nodding.

"Tell them to stand as close as they can to the edge of the cliff!" Keelty instructed.

"Guys, stand as close as you can to the edge, just in case we need to leave fast. Keelty thinks someone is coming."

Still spooked, but trying to hide that from Charlotte through candid humour, Ethan whispered to her, "We're taking advice from a dog! ...A dog, for crying out loud!"

My hand was shaking terribly. I pulled out the carrier from beneath my jumper and rested it in my left hand, allowing my right hand to turn the latch. After turning the latch three times, the carrier opened and revealed cogs and wheels like the inside of a music box. The sound it played was peaceful, as serene as a lullaby. It was beautiful; simple and gentle, but ironically powerful to hear. The notes were enchanting and sent goosebumps up my spine. The sound was so moving that my eyes began to water. As the music slowed down, the hair on Keelty's neck stood up.

"STAND AS CLOSE AS YOU CAN TO THE EDGE!" Keelty screamed, but for Ethan and Charlotte, it must have just been a fearful bark. Keelty was right, we were not alone, and someone was coming. A dark figure was emerging towards us from the mist. It was not close enough for us to identify any clear features. All that we could deduce from the large, black and haunting silhouette was that the figure was indeed a man.

"Sully," Keelty hushed angrily under her breath and bared her teeth. "I'd smell his fowl stench from miles away." She began to growl and arched her back, ready to strike if she had to. She had saved my life once before and I could sense that she was willing to save it again.

The haunting figure was getting closer; Keelty grew tense with every step he took towards us. The mist revealed a tall man with short, brown, wavy hair. He was limping and favouring his right side. Blood was smeared across his face and it appeared to have trickled down his neck, staining his white collar. The blood distracted me from looking at the man's face directly. As I saw past the blood, I looked into the man's hollow, golden brown eyes. *It can't be ... it can't be him!*

"MR LAWSON!" I cried. "You're Sully! My ... my uncle?"

Mr Lawson, well, Sully Kael, reached for his coat pocket and revealed a gun. "Where is it? I know you have it! Hand it over! NOW! Or I'll shoot! I will!" His voice was shaky, but desperate; Keelty's attack appeared to have traumatized him. The gun shook in Sully's hand, as he waved it from left to right, ready to fire if any of us made a run for it. It's murder to describe how unsettling it is having a gun pointed at you. My mind was racing! I thought of delaying him and giving him reason to fret.

"So, that's why you asked me about my bandage in detention! That's why you also called me Miss Elsa in class!"

Sully disregarded my remarks completely. The carrier was the only thing occupying his thoughts. "HAND IT OVER NOW! I WILL SHOOT! I WILL!"

My heart was racing, my breathing was rapid, and I didn't know what to do! I didn't want to look over at Charlotte and Ethan, fearful that the slightest flinch from me would cause Sully to shoot.

"The bird is coming, I can hear it," Keelty whispered to me, even though she was communicating to me through thoughts. *"Brianna, I will command it to stay beneath the cliff. Keep talking to Sully until then ... distract him!"*

"Okay, I'll do my best," I thought back.

After answering Keelty, the surrounding sounds of the early morning were amplifying in my ears; similar to the sensation I had felt at Madam and Miss Antique Shop, but this time, it was not painful and it ended very quickly.

"Why doesn't Brianna get the dog to attack him? That could give us a chance to run! But how the hell do I tell her that?" I resisted turning towards Ethan, I knew that I had just heard his thoughts, just like I had heard the thoughts of people in the cafe, but moving, at this point, could be fatal. I questioned whether being able to hear his thoughts would allow me to speak to him through thoughts. What other choice did I have? I had to try.

"Ethan," I said to him in my mind, *"Don't look at me. Can you please try to distract Sully, just until Keelty and I have formulated a plan?"*

"Why do you need the carrier, anyway?" Ethan said, confirming that we had successfully communicated through thought. "You've been stuck here for years! Why would Cillian need you after so long?!" Sully turned his focus to Ethan. It was working!

I stared intently at Sully, so that he would assume I was concentrating on him, but my mind was far too occupied with formulating a plan with Keelty to take notice of his words.

"Keelty," I thought. *"Do you think you could lunge at Sully once the bird is in place and once we've got him distracted? Then we can jump onto the bird and you can join us. That's all I've got at this point ... unless you have any better ideas..."*

"No," she replied. *"Your ideas are sound, Brianna. In a few moments the bird will be just beneath the cliff's edge. As soon as it's there, I will attack Sully, which is the cue for you to jump down onto the bird without delay."*

"But why now, Sully?" Charlotte asked, picking up on Ethan's tactics. "Why, after eighteen years, do you decide to come after Brianna now?"

"Because ... because of that damn dog!" Sully blared, pointing the rattling gun down at Keelty. "She ruined everything! She drove me away! Every chance I had! And then, she lost the carrier! It took me all this time to find it! The trail went cold!"

"The bird is here. Get ready, Brianna," Keelty announced, absent of fear. *"NOW!"* she cried only for me to hear. Keelty crouched down and her hind legs drove herself up from the ground, aiming straight for the gun in Sully's quivering hand. The gun fell

to the floor and landed a few feet away from Keelty and Sully's scuffle.

"*Quick! Jump!* The bird is here! *TRUST ME!*" I assured Ethan and Charlotte, but their expressions were doubtful. Yeah, taking a leap off a cliff to land on a bird was risky, but we didn't have any other choice! We had to take the chance; we had to take the leap ... and we did.

I closed my eyes and leaped. As my feet made contact with the back of the bird, my knees gave in. The feathers so smooth, I was slipping off the birds back! I dug my fingers into the bird's feathers and hung on for dear life! The Oran-Roy Bird cried a deafening squawk when I tugged its feathers. I glanced over the bird's back to discover that I was in arm's length of the cold waves crashing against the harsh rocks below.

"Here goes!" I heard Charlotte call out from above me. "AHHH!" she screamed, until she made contact with the bird's back.

"SHIT!" Ethan exclaimed from above, before jumping. Ethan swore again, but this time, the word lingered until he successfully grabbed hold of some feathers.

The Oran-Roy bird's wings pressed down against the air, propelling itself up above the cliff. Keelty leapt onto its back and the bird's wings began to flap ferociously; every flap sounding like a small cyclone.

The Oran-Roy bird's head was eagle-like; it bore a striking resemblance to the griffins I had read about in books. The early morning rays of sunlight reflected against its large, emerald green feathers, almost blinding us. The tail was long and delicate, and moved like a ribbon in a breeze. Each wing was at least twenty feet in length.

Gradually, we were being raised higher and higher into the early morning sky. Sully, still standing on the edge of the cliff, was becoming smaller with every flap of the bird's colossal wings. The harsh cold air whipped across our faces as the Oran-Roy bird made its way to the place I hadn't been able to call home for eighteen years.

Chapter Eleven

Daray

Ethan cried out loudly, but the sound of flapping wings drowned out his words completely. Hesitantly, I twisted my head around, attempting to look at Ethan and hopefully understand what he was saying by lip-reading. Before finding him though, my eyes came across Keelty, doing her best to stay on the bird without any fingers for assistance. Her back was arched, because her paws were so deeply immersed in the feathers of the bird's back; she was struggling to maintain a safe and secure hold. *How on earth did she manage to do this with me on her back those eighteen years ago?* I tightened the grip of my left hand around the feathers to keep me secure, then, stretched my unsteady right arm around Keelty's back for support. It was the least I could do to make the trip a little easier for her. Keelty made a gentle nodding gesture to show me her gratitude.

"You're welcome," I replied through thought.

I glanced at my watch and saw that it was close to seven o'clock; the sun was now completely visible in the distant horizon. Suddenly, the bird began to drop. I applied extra pressure on Keelty, preventing her from flying off.

"We're close now, Brianna," Keelty communicated through her thoughts.

In between the movement of the bird's wings, I was able to make out a distant, green mass of land through the clouds. The land grew with every beat of the Oran-Roy bird's wings. Drawing closer and closer, the flapping slowed and the bird gently glided towards a cliff's edge that was abundantly blessed with tall, green, flourishing trees.

The Oran-Roy bird's eagle-like feet ripped through the top layer of trees. Branches cracked, snapped in two and flew in all directions.

"AH!" Charlotte cried painfully.

"Ouch!" Ethan also cried.

"Ah!" A rough-edged stick had scraped my forehead and just missed my left eye. *"Ouch!"* Another stick scraped the surface of my skin, this time finding its way beyond my hair and scraping the back of my neck.

THUMP!

My body almost flew off the birds back as it made contact with the ground. After the intense impact, I raised my head out from the bird's feathers.

We were completely surrounded by tall, thin tree trunks coated with moss. The early morning light seeped through the gaps in the leaves of the trees, dappling the ground, the patterns dancing as the wind above stirred the leaves. Keelty leapt off the bird rather gracefully, whereas I found the exit a struggle. I stretched my body towards the bird's side and slid down, letting gravity work its magic. The considerable amount of time between leaving the bird and making contact with the ground made my heart skip a beat. Charlotte then slid off and was closely followed by Ethan. When Ethan's feet became firmly planted on the ground, the Oran-Roy bird left without delay. As it took for the sky, its enormous wings shook the nearby trees, breaking branches and scattering leaves down towards the forest floor. Within seconds, the bird was out of sight and the sound of its powerful wings faded away.

"If that's the way we have to get back, I'm swimming!" Ethan slid down the base of the closest tree and sat up against it, trying to recover from the terrifying trip.

"I'd forgotten how much you hated flying," I said.

"I think I'm going to be sick!" he exclaimed.

"You'll be all right," I insisted. "Take a few deep breaths and just sit there for a bit."

Crack.

"Did you hear that?" Charlotte whispered.

"Yeah," I whispered back. "Keelty, is someone there?"

Keelty lowered her head to the ground and flared her nostrils. The grey wispy hair on her neck remained flat, so I assumed that we were not in danger. "People are approaching us, but I don't think they mean us harm."

Gradually coming around, Ethan stood up and made his way to stand beside me. "What did the dog say, Bee?" he asked curiously.

I had forgotten that I was the only one able to hear Keelty. I would have to get use to translating. "She sees people coming, but believes that they are harmless."

At the conclusion of my words, figures jumped through the bushes and surrounded us. Arrows were only inches away from our faces and in position for release.

"Yeah! They definitely don't mean us any harm at all, Bee! Are you *sure* you translated the dog correctly?" Ethan whispered, panic-stricken.

With only a limited amount of light, we were unable to identify the figures' faces. But then, the beings lowered their arrows and someone spoke directly in front of me; a gentle voice came from the darkness.

"Brianna Elsa?" the soft, young female voice asked. "...Granddaughter of Zia Kael and daughter to Crag and Keira Elsa?"

I hesitated before responding. I almost answered, *"No!"* But, remembering the Morrigan book, which made me reply, "Yes. I'm Brianna Elsa ... but ... but please don't hurt us ... we're only just..."

"We are not intending to harm you; rather, we intend to help you." After these words, a female figure emerged into the dim light. She was rather young and appeared to be around my age, with skin as white as a porcelain doll. Her eyes were yellow and cat-like. She was slim and incredibly lean, with short, but flighty hair, with wisps of orange, red and brown streaks running through it. Her knee length leather boots, corset and the rest of her attire reminded me of the medieval dress-up days we endured in History class. I attempted to make a connection between her and the Morrigan book, but I couldn't put my finger on it.

"Uh ... how do you know of me? How do you know my name?" I asked nervously.

Following my response, the other surrounding figures came into the light. The darkness revealed two relatively young men, who moved forward to stand on either side of the unknown girl. The young man on the girl's left was tall and lean with thin, straight brown hair that fell just above his broad shoulders. He had very distinct cheekbones and a strong jaw line. The young man's eyes were an amber brown colour. I also struggled to associate this man's appearance with a character from the Morrigan book.

The other young man was tall and lean in stature as well, with hair that was short and flighty and almost jet-black. His eyes were an emerald green colour and stood out against his pale skin. This man also had a very pronounced jaw line and prominent cheekbones. A long black cloak hung from his broad shoulders. There was something that was not quite new about this man, something that I felt I had either read in the Morrigan book or had seen somewhere before. The young man's beautifully sculpted face was disfigured by a scar, which stretched from over his right eye, across his nose and culminated at his left cheek. *Where have I seen him? I know I have seen his face before! But, where was it?*

Then, it dawned on me. I had seen the man in the dream I had just before finding the carrier. *Does that mean I am able to see things before they happen too? Am I a psychic? Will what I saw in my dream eventuate?*

While pondering my dream, I stared in awe at the man and, based on the bemused look he offered in return, I was certain that my face looked odd. He quickly drew his eyes away. *How embarrassing!* Despite averting his gaze, I struggled to refrain from staring most intently at him. Apart from the shock of realising that I had seen this man in a dream before knowing of him, I will admit, he was interesting, which made turning my eyes elsewhere a very hard task indeed.

"We know of you, Brianna, because of Zia ... your Grandfather. Your eyes also tell me who you are. You see, these days, it's rather rare, or, almost non-existent to meet a person of mixed blood," the girl explained. "Twenty years ago, to this day, your Grandfather instructed me to hand this to you." The girl handed me a small rolled up piece of sandy coloured parchment. "He instructed me to tell you to slot it into a small, thin compartment of the carrier. Apparently, only the person who bears the carrier can retrieve it once placed there. Before you ask me its purpose, I must tell you that I do not know. I sense its importance. Zia said that in time it will serve you well. Trust Zia. He was a wise man."

"*Wait!*" I cried out. "He gave this to *you twenty years ago*! How old are you?"

The girl chuckled before responding. "*...How silly of me!* I didn't even introduce us! Although, I did think Keelty would have explained everything to you by now. By the way, it's been quite some time Keelty, how have you been?"

"Things were far more difficult than I expected them to be," Keelty hinted. "Although, considering the circumstances, I am well and very happy to be home." It appeared that this lady could also communicate with Keelty.

"In that case then, I'm Leona. I'm a Darian. You are in Daray, the home of my clan." Leona pulled up her right sleeve to reveal a small circular marking similar to my own. Leona's, however, had a paw print over a cross, which appeared to be the cross of Tarmon. "Darian people communicate with the animals of Daray, as your father's people can and as you can, I suspect. Darian people can morph into any animal we desire and we live for hundreds of years, you see. I'm really ninety-eight years old." Charlotte, Ethan and I still gasped, even though we were vaguely aware of the Darian people from the Morrigan book. Although forewarned, the book couldn't prepare us for seeing in person a ninety-eight year old with the appearance of an eighteen year old!

The shocked expressions on our faces made Leona reinforce, "We age, but very slowly though ... anyway, this is Ewan, Ewan Kael." Leona patted the shoulder of the man with the long hair to her left.

"Leona - Zia's friend! You were in the book!" Our new acquaintances appeared puzzled and didn't seem to take any notice of my epiphany.

Ewan stepped forward and pulled his right sleeve up to reveal the Tarmon cross. "Hello, Brianna. I'm your cousin. Your mother and my father are siblings ... *although*, my father and I haven't seen eye-to-eye for quite some time. You see, my father is Cillian..."

"...Kael. Cillian Kael," I interrupted.

"Yes," Ewan replied. "But, how do you know of him?"

"... Long story, but I learnt about my family and this place from a book."

"A book!" Leona said with a great deal of surprise. "You know of such matters because of a book?"

"Yes." I answered. I knelt down and removed my small back pack, rummaged through it and pulled out the Morrigan book. "See!" I handed it to Leona. "That's why I just realised who you were, that you were Zia's friend. But, based on your response, I assume you were unaware of this book."

"You assume correctly," Ewan answered.

"Let's talk about that when we get back," Leona suggested, as she returned the book back to me. Leona then patted the shoulder of the man with the scar across his face. "This is Quinn by the way, Quinn Logan ... or, *Quiet Quinn* as I like to call him," she said, accompanied with a slight chuckle.

Logan. Of course the name of the person I was trying to get over would crop up! You'd think escaping to a distant land would reduce that chance!

Spending only a few short moments with Quinn Logan, I had already developed deep sympathy for him. I suspected that there was a story behind his scar; an incident that did far more than disfigure his face. Quinn's exterior masked his disfigured soul. Perhaps his scar destroyed a part of him and tarnished a confident young man.

Insecurely, Quinn stepped forward and pulled his right sleeve up to reveal his circular marking; inside the circle was a sword. "I am from Cathal, Brianna."

"It's ... it's nice to meet you." I replied, trying to avoid staring at the scar; I didn't want to give him another reason for finding me odd. To try and mask this, I decided to introduce the others. Not only would it stop me from staring, but perhaps it would distract Quinn from my flushed cheeks. "...Uh, and this is Ethan and this is Charlotte."

"Hi," Charlotte said rather quietly, with a hesitant wave.

"Hey," Ethan said, also rather quietly. "We're not from here."

"Yes, we gathered that. Well," Leona cried enthusiastically, "let's make our way back quickly. We can't risk staying out here any longer than we already have. We can talk about everything when we return to the cavern. The others will be excited to meet you, so we really should press on." At the conclusion of her words, Leona turned around and began walking into the dark forest.

"You go on," Ewan insisted to the three of us. "Quinn and I will be just behind you, keeping watch."

Keelty followed on closely behind Leona and the three of us pressed on forward; Ewan and Quinn were close behind with their arrows at the ready. Before following Leona and Keelty though, I contemplated whether I was making the right decision. I quickly came to realise that there was no other option. Despite having just met Leona, Ewan and Quinn, Keelty's trust in them gave me confidence that they had the best intentions of keeping the others and me safe.

As the distance grew between us and Ewan and Quinn, I thought now was a good time to tell Charlotte and Ethan about Quinn and my dream.

"Hey, guys," I whispered cautiously, causing Ethan and Charlotte to come closer towards me. "You know Quinn? This is going to sound *so* strange, but I've seen him before! I saw him in a dream just before I found the carrier!"

"Really?" Charlotte hushed in astonishment.

"Yeah!" I insisted. "I even have proof. I wrote about the dream in the journal you gave me for my birthday."

"Wow," Ethan said, also astonished by what I had just revealed. "Just when we think we know everything, more things crop up. Do you think... nah ... it couldn't..."

"What?" My tone urged Ethan to reveal whatever he was hiding.

"Do you think you can also predict the future?"

"I thought the exact same thing, Ethan, but I just don't know."

Ethan's face suddenly lit up. "How cool was before, Bee? You communicated with me telepathically!"

"You communicated through thoughts again, Brianna?" Charlotte asked quickly, not wanting to delay receiving my answer.

"Yeah, we did. It was different this time though. When I heard Ethan's thoughts, it didn't hurt as it did in the cafe."

"Not long now! Let's try and be quick!" Leona urged.

The urgency in Leona's tone caused the three of us to unconsciously pick up the pace. Quinn and Ewan were now right behind us, still alert to any potential dangers surrounding us.

While we were walking, I realised that the parchment Leona had given me was still in my hand. Despite the concentration required for hastening through an unknown forest, I couldn't wait to lay my eyes on this piece of parchment and there was just enough light for me to have a good look at it. So, being my usual impatient self, I unrolled parchment, revealing a small map of Oran-Roy. The map was illustrated with black ink. All of the major clans of Oran-Roy were labelled and drawn to represent the characteristics of their province. Towards the bottom left of the parchment, there was a knight on a horse beside the cross of Tarmon. The knight was named Cuchulainn; the name of the hero I had encountered in the Morrigan book who came to my parents to warn them of the dangers they would face. The map seemed to illustrate Cuchulainn's battles across Oran-Roy.

After a substantial look, I pulled the carrier out from beneath my blouse. My hands stroked the back of it and tried to find the thin compartment Leona was referring to. As my right hand was feeling along the edge beside the latch, my nail made contact with a small groove. I applied some pressure and sure enough, a small compartment revealed itself. I had almost fit the piece of parchment in when a hand pressed hard against my left shoulder. It made me jump.

"What are you doing? Put that away! Quickly!" Quinn hushed angrily. "This is not the time or place! Do you understand?"

"All right!" I cried. *Did he really have to be so condescending?* I finished stashing the parchment into the compartment.

Following his outburst, Quinn pressed on forward, leaving Ewan to monitor us.

"Don't mind him, Brianna," Ewan insisted, as he met my pace and began walking beside me. "I've been his friend for years and he hasn't always been like that."

"What made him so grumpy then?" I queried.

"It's a long story, but I don't think I should be the one to tell you. He should tell you - when he's ready. He became a changed person the day he got that scar. I've learnt not to be so harsh on him. He really has been through a great deal."

"But still," I affirmed, "He didn't have to speak to me like I'm an idiot!"

"An *idiot*? What's an idiot?" Ewan asked.

"Oh. You don't use that word here?"

"... Can't say we do."

"It means dumb or not very smart ... not intelligent."

"I see."

"Hey, how do you speak English here in Oran-Roy anyway? The book only mentioned something like one of the Kings of Tarmon learning it through his travels. It said that it was only spoken by Kings and those closest to them when they were discussing really important matters."

"Yes, well, it was only until just before your birth that this information was revealed. We have spoken English for decades now. Eventually, it spread from the King, through to his family and was then gradually adopted by everyone."

"So, before that, only Gaelic was spoken?"

"Yes, Gaelic and Latin. Prior Kings before Zia also learnt Latin through their secret travels on the Oran-Roy bird. Cuchulainn before them also made it possible for us to become aware of several languages."

As Ewan and I continued our discussion, Charlotte and Ethan walked on only metres ahead. I think they realised I had a lot of catching up to do.

"So, tell me, Ewan, I ... I don't want to come across as too nosey, but, why did you and your father go separate ways? Based on the book, he is the reason why my parents sent me away - to protect me from him."

Ewan sighed before answering. I sensed that his father was a touchy subject. "I was eight when you left, Brianna. But, I can still vividly remember overhearing my father's plotting and scheming behind your parents', as well as our Grandfather Zia's back. It was only when I was eleven that I realised how dreadful my father *really* was. His envy and scheming consumed him and turned him into someone I didn't want to be!"

"I can't imagine how hard it must have been ... coming to accept that ... that your father was..."

"Lost! ... So severely lost in his own agenda that he completely discarded his family's needs."

"...And your mother, Ewan?" I asked cautiously.

"She became extremely ill amid all of my father's plotting. I think the change in him put a great deal of strain on her - that's what made her ill."

"Is she ... is she all right now?"

There was a large pause, which made me feel that I had crossed the line.

"Sorry, Ewan," I quickly apologised. "I didn't mean to pry."

"No. Don't be sorry, Brianna," Ewan advised me. "My mother has been dead for fifteen years. Her death made me realise that I had to be free of my father. That's when I left Tarmon, when the Darian people and your father took me in."

"My father took you in!" I said, quite astonished. "So, you know him well?"

"He has been more of a father to me than my own."

"And my mother ... you must obviously know her too?"

Ewan released a sigh before responding. It made me dread the upcoming answer. "I'm afraid I don't."

My heart sunk and I immediately thought the worst. Ewan glanced at my face and read my shocked expression.

"She's alive, Brianna!" He insisted, "But she hasn't been in contact with your father since the night you left."

How do you respond to news like that? "I don't ... I'm ... I'm sorry for asking so many questions, Ewan. I know I haven't been here for eighteen years, but, I ... I think I have the right to know..."

"Don't apologise, Brianna," Ewan affirmed as he placed a reassuring hand on my shoulder. "I will answer all the questions you desire to be answered." Ewan temporarily drew his attention away. "But not yet, for we have arrived."

Sure enough, we had arrived at the cavern Leona had mentioned earlier, but it was well hidden. Keelty quickly scanned the nearby area and nodded at Leona, indicating that we were safe. Following Keelty's cue, Leona ran her hands over a mossy, stone wall imbedded between large trees with enormous, protruding roots. When her hands stopped, Leona dug her fingers into a groove of the stone wall and began removing a camouflaged covering. Quinn and Ewan rushed over to assist Leona in sliding the stone door. When they had formed a slit large enough for us to fit through, Ewan raised his arm and invited Charlotte, Ethan and myself to enter first.

I lowered my head to make my way through the small gap. Beyond the door was a mass of black, apart from the thin ray of light coming through the stone wall opening. Once we were all in the cavern, the stone wall was slid shut. We were in complete darkness. But, suddenly, flames deep within the cavern vanquished the darkness.

"I see you have found what you were looking for then," a rather eloquent, young male voice said from the darkness.

"We did indeed. Dougal, are the others here?" Leona asked.

"We are," another young male voice announced. After his words, more light radiated from deep within the cavern. The light revealed three creatures. The middle figure was angelic, not only because of his large, white wings that sheltered the entire back of his body, but also due to his radiant blue eyes, which were accentuated by his long, blonde hair. The man's face was sculpted to perfection and his torso was muscular. Unlike the other Oran-Roy people I had just encountered, the man's marking rested in the middle of his chest and was much larger than my own. The bold circle enclosed two white feathers crossed over one another. My mind quickly drew back to the book and realised that the white winged man was a Prislen; a member of the white winged clan found on the outskirts of Daray.

The Prislen stepped forward and offered his arm. "Brianna Elsa and friends, my name is Zephan." I shook his hand as he introduced himself. "Seeing you again gives me hope. Welcome home."

"Uh ... thanks, I guess." *That was a nice compliment!*

The second creature bared every resemblance to Keelty, despite being of larger size and having long, white hair.

"*Faolon!*" Keelty cried joyously as she ran towards the white Arawn. Keelty and Faolon rubbed their heads, which I inferred was equivalent to a long awaited hug.

"Brianna, this is my companion, Faolon," Keelty announced, as she and Faolon came forward.

"It's very nice to meet you," I replied. Charlotte and Ethan's expressions were again rather puzzled. "Oh, guys, this is Faolon, he's Keelty's mate."

"Ah ... I see," Ethan said. "I'd say *hello*, but will they understand me, Bee?" Immediately following Ethan's question, Keelty and Faolon barked. "I'll take that as a yes, then."

"Uh ... hello," Charlotte also received a greeting bark from Keelty and Faolon.

"So the dogs have set in, have they?" A sophisticated young male voice came from below. Then, my eyes came across the third creature. It was a cat. As it moved into the fullness of light, the cat sat upright and his smoky green eyes scanned my body up and down. It was a little unsettling and I couldn't call myself a *cat* person. The cat was predominantly brown with thin, black stripes spread across its back. Strangely, the cat appeared to be missing half of its tail.

The cat noticed me staring at its tail, which gave him reason to say, "Yes, not a pretty sight at all."

"This is Dougal, by the way Brianna," Leona announced. "He's an acquired taste."

"A delicacy, I prefer to say," Dougal responded smugly.

"That's okay, Leona, I can't say I'm that fond of cats anyway," I said with a cheeky smirk.

"Moving on," Ewan felt the need to hurry things along, "The three of you and Keelty must be hungry. Why don't you all sit by the fire, have something to eat and then we can answer any of your questions, before Rona joins us."

"*Rona* ... who ... who is Rona?" I queried.

"She is a Lucian, Brianna." Zephan answered. "She is my companion now ... so to speak. We are close."

"But, based on what I already know, I thought that Lucians and Prislens were forbidden from interacting with one another, as well as seeing humans."

"That is why myself, Rona and Dougal are here." Zephan invited us to sit beside the fire before continuing. "By helping you and your family on the night of your escape, we were all exiled from our clans. Rona assisted me not too long after the night you left. I was badly hurt by my old clan members. She was seen helping me and she was then exiled by the Lucians."

"It cost me my tail." Dougal felt the need to remind everyone.

The lengths everyone went to keep me safe astounded me. I am alive because of their selflessness. They sacrificed so much for me. How would I ever return the favour? I felt terribly guilty.

"I'm so sorry," I cried sympathetically. "You've done so much for me and it has cost you everything!"

"It's much bigger than that," Quinn urged, leaning against the stone near the cavern's opening. Before speaking again, he walked towards our gathering and crouched by the fire. "You speak of this book, Brianna. Surely it must have revealed the wrath of Morrigan."

"It did," I replied.

"Well, Morrigan's legacy has almost been parasitic to Oran-Roy and its people since she vanished. But now, your uncle might expose her wrath again." Quinn's expression turned cold. "And you returning is putting more people at risk than ever before!"

"Quinn!" Leona cried. "This is not Brianna's fault! What has gotten into you?"

"If Cillian finds out of her return, he will release Morrigan! And then we'll all be..."

"Quinn!" Ewan stood up and cried out harshly. "We've spoken about this! There has always been the possibility that things could get worse before they got better! We need Brianna here and you know it! One day, Morrigan will have to return so she can be put in her rightful place! Until that day, no one can truly be at peace!"

Quinn raised himself up from beside the fire and stormed towards the cavern's opening. "I'm getting food," he said through gritted teeth. Then, he was gone. The last thing I intended on doing was making things awkward upon my arrival. *What does Quinn have against me anyway? I've been in Oran-Roy for almost an hour and already I've got on someone's bad side!*

"I'm sorry, Ewan."

"Don't apologise, Brianna." Ewan joined me by the fire. "Quinn's scared and he is holding onto a lot of anger and he tends to take it out on people who don't deserve it."

"That has definitely got a Bee in his bonnet! Get it!" Ethan chuckled, being his predicable, humorous self in an awkward situation.

"Hilarious," Charlotte sarcastically replied, while rolling her eyes. The others had puzzled faces on account of Ethan's odd sense of humour.

"Brianna, did you and your friends have any questions? We have time until Rona arrives." Ewan offered.

"Well, yes, I do. Before, Ewan, you didn't really answer my question about my mother."

"The night you left, Brianna, was the last night I saw her too. We know that Cillian," Ewan became tense and uneasy as he spoke his father's name, "Has imprisoned your mother these past eighteen years. Your mother is Tarmon's true Queen, but ... but we fear that Cillian has only kept her alive in an effort to extract information of Zia's hidden writings."

I didn't know how to respond. Again, someone who did so much to keep me safe was paying the price. My own mother was being held prisoner for my entire lifespan! I know I hadn't met her yet, but the Morrigan book almost made me feel as though I had.

"...And my father, Ewan ... could ... could you tell me about him? You mentioned he was more of a father to you than your own."

"Yes, Craig is currently in Crag and that is where Rona is as we speak."

"Is she bringing him here?" It was hard to hide my excitement.

"It would be pointless bringing him to Daray, Brianna. We intend on taking you to the Oran-Roy clan itself, to see Donelle, the Druid."

"Like in the book, Bee," Charlotte advised. "Because you are of mixed blood, you need to consult Donelle at the Oran-Roy clan as the past heroes did."

"Of course!" I cried. "And I guess you could say that I am distantly related to her ... very distant."

"So, is Brianna's father meeting us in Oran-Roy, the clan?" Ethan asked Ewan.

"No. We intend on resting in Crag before we journey to the Oran-Roy clan; it can be a difficult task."

"Then why is Rona in Crag?" I quickly asked.

"All those working for our cause were aware of your journey here this morning, Brianna, your father included. You can imagine how long he has looked forward to this moment - well, we all have."

"You have brought back hope," Zephan insisted.

"Thank you, but ... but why is Rona...?"

"Ah ... Rona is in Crag helping your father prepare for your coming. She is advising your father to meet us at Kael, between Daray and Crag. Before arriving in Kael though, we have to make our way through the part of Daray directly between Cathal and Tarmon, which is a risky journey. We are certain that Cillian and his followers have infiltrated Cathal now, so passing through there will be a struggle." Ewan explained.

"So that's why that Quinn bowsie is a bit moody. His clan has been infiltrated," Ethan speculated.

"I guess one could say that," Ewan answered. "But, back to the plan. Once past Daray, Kael will be a safe haven. Meeting at Kael will reduce the time that we are in danger of being seen with you, rather than continuing to trek on to Crag in one trip."

"...And Kael is the friendliest of places." Dougal said cunningly, as he gracefully leapt onto a large rock protruding from the cavern's stone wall. "The Kaelin people have control over the marshlands of Kerr and the Kael Lake. They do not like to be disturbed."

"Yeah, we figured that out from the book," I said. "They're sort of like, mermaids, aren't they?"

"One could say that," Dougal replied. "The Kaelins are a water-dwelling people and have a gift that many here in Oran-Roy envy. Like my own cat clan in Daray, they possess the ability to see things before they happen. But, unfortunately, with my current status as an outcast from my clan, I no longer possess the ability to see the future."

"Why is that?" I asked.

"I am not certain as to why, but I suspect I need to be surrounded by fellow members of my clan to utilise my gift. Yes, apart from my tail, that was another sacrifice, one of the many I had to make, after choosing to take part in your escape."

"Would you stop bragging about all of the sacrifices you had to make?" Leona yelled at Dougal, clearly annoyed by his manner of words. "Just ignore him," Leona affirmed. "I've learnt to over the past eighteen years."

"So, tell me, Leona, what have you been doing the past eighteen years, then?" I asked.

"Well, we don't know how Zia would know of your return, but, based on what he told us, we prepared for this likelihood by trying to bring as many clans within our cause together as we could, to destroy whatever is left of Morrigan. Apart from that, I and everyone else you have met today have been trying to infiltrate Cillian's plot, to try and unravel the corruption he has brought to Tarmon and now Cathal, we suspect."

"So, you've been busy," Ethan said, trying to add to the discussion.

"Yes," Leona said with an unusual smirk.

"Leona," I said, drawing her attention back to me, "I am aware of why the trip to Oran-Roy is required, but I don't think we should make that trip if it is going to be so dangerous."

"We have to, Brianna!" Leona cried. "You are of mixed blood and you possess a gift! You must consult Donelle to find out what you possess!"

"But I know, already!" I insisted. "Wouldn't I just be putting more people at risk by making this trip?"

"Don't let what Quinn has said affect you, Brianna," Leona declared.

Charlotte tugged my sleeve and whispered, "Don't you think we should ask them about Dallas Conlan? If he is the man we suspect is behind the book, perhaps they might know him."

"Good idea," I whispered back. "Have you ever heard or known of anyone by the name of Dallas Conlan?" I openly asked of everyone present, but their faces were blank. "I suppose not."

"Why do you ask about him?" Keelty queried. "Is he from this book you speak of?" The opening of the cavern's entrance interrupted Keelty's question. Quinn came in and was closely followed by a beautiful young woman whom I assumed to be Rona. Just as Zephan had described her, Rona bore the large black wings of her Lucian clan. She, too, had a large circular marking on her chest, but instead of white feathers, hers were black. Rona's hair was long and wavy and mahogany brown in colour. A white feather (which I suspected was from Zephan's wing), rested in her hair beside her right ear. Rona's red eyes matched her hair rather well. She was tall and lean and her attire was incredibly similar to Leona's.

"Brianna Elsa," Rona said as she walked closer towards me within the cavern. "I come with good news. Your father is on his way to Kael as we speak. He is preparing for your arrival and he is most looking forward to seeing you again."

Chapter Twelve

Temptation

..."*Come into the water Craig. We will show you whether you and Keira will have the future that you dream of.*" *On his many journeys through Kale Creek, on his way to see Keira, the Kaelens repeated these very same words to Craig...*

- Excerpt from 'The Morrigan Book'

"He ... he knows I'm here?" I needed someone to pinch me! I couldn't come to terms with the idea that I was about to meet my father - my father who I had never seen, but merely read about in a book! It almost felt like meeting an admired character from a beloved story or film! *What will I say when I meet him? How should I greet him?* Questions poured in and out of my mind.

"Yes, he knows of your arrival, Brianna," Rona reinforced. "He and a few of his men are on their way, as we speak, to Kael. At dusk, your father and his men will aim to be on Kael's border, to meet us and protect you."

"Do you think Cillian knows that I'm here?" I inquired impatiently.

"No, I do not think so. He has no way of knowing; however," Rona hesitated before continuing, her ruby red eyes flickered towards Zephan, hoping that he would provide some input soon. "Cillian has had his men patrolling that area rather frequently of late. Zephan and I have been watching them for some time and it appears that they have increased their guard over the past few months. So..."

"So," Zephan continued, finally picking up on Rona's hint, "we must consider that Cillian suspects you have arrived. That is why we are taking great caution in making our way beyond Tarmon."

"... But, how could Cillian have any idea of our whereabouts?" Charlotte queried.

"Cillian's spies lurk throughout Oran-Roy," Quinn insisted. "There's no telling how much they know."

"... Or who is helping their cause," Ewan added. "You aren't the only mixed-blood in Oran-Roy, Brianna."

Ewan's words ignited fear in my mind. Was he suggesting that there are others like me, but they are assisting Cillian's cause?

"Who else do you know of, then?" I questioned.

Ewan quickly glanced at Quinn before answering my question; again making me suspect that there would be more fearful news. "It's your brother, Brianna ... Brogan."

Of course! The book said that I had an older brother! But, he was unable to reach the bird in time!

"What became of him after I left?" I asked urgently, but everyone remained quiet, which made me uneasy. "What became of him?" I asked, this time with more force. "Is he with my mother?"

"No," Ewan answered. "Brogan was two when you left, Brianna. My father took him in. He was hoping to raise him and have him support his cause when he was mature enough to be of some use to him. With his mixed blood and the possibilities that it may confer, Brogan was seen as a prize for my father."

"But, how could you leave your father and leave him behind?" I cried.

"Believe me, Brianna, I did what I could!" Ewan urged. "But, your brother was too young at the time to put faith in me over a man he believed to be his father!" Ewan could see how this news was bothering me, which explained why he felt the need to further explain. "Brianna, he was only five years old! What five-year-old child puts their trust in an eleven-year-old?"

Ewan was completely right in justifying himself. I was just so mad that I needed to put the blame on someone else, to try and put myself at ease. "I'm sorry, Ewan. I know you would've done everything in your power to help my brother." I was about to go on when Ethan placed his hand on my shoulder, signalling that he would ask on behalf of me.

"So, do you believe Brogan is working alongside Cillian?" Ethan directed his question at Ewan, but Quinn answered.

"That is the only logical conclusion we can come to, as Brogan has made no attempt to contact Ewan or leave Cillian when the opportunity had arisen."

"Do you have any idea of what Brogan can do yet?" Charlotte asked openly to everyone present.

"We have merely theories," Dougal answered, as he gracefully leapt from one protruding stone of the cavern to another. "In our attempts to spy on Cillian, we have been discovered rather quickly and we have almost been captured."

"What did he say?" Ethan asked. I quickly translated and then signalled Dougal to continue.

"It's appears that..."

"Wait! Someone expected you to be there," Ethan interrupted.

"Yes, boy, but, I do not appreciate being cut off from speaking, if you please," Dougal grudgingly cried, but I knew that Ethan would have been unable to hear Dougal's catty comment.

"Just because he can't understand you, that doesn't give you the right to be so rude!" Leona said.

"I was merely returning the favour," Dougal replied proudly.

"So, the cat was rude to me, was he?" Ethan said, amongst much chuckling. "That's okay," he quickly brushed aside, "Like Brianna, I can't say I'm much of a cat person, anyway."

Dougal hissed, clearly intending Ethan to receive an answer he could understand, but it didn't bother Ethan in the slightest, which explained why Dougal returned to a high perch within the cavern's wall to sulk.

"As I was saying," Ethan announced, directing a sneaky look up at Dougal, "someone was expecting you to be there and Brogan is the only mixed-blood you know of in Cillian's group. Do you think his ability could be of a similar nature to Brianna's? Do you think he can hear thoughts? That would explain why he knew where you would be."

"Yes," Quinn answered, "We believe his ability to be something to that effect ... but we're merely guessing. He could be like the Kaelin people and witness things before they happen, or he could indeed be capable of looking into the minds of others." Quinn scrunched his eyebrows and appeared to be deep in thought. Before speaking again, Quinn approached the fire, crouching down in front of me, so that his green eyes were gazing right into my own. "Brianna, what do you possess? What are you able to do?" Quinn's tone was condescending. He was doubtful about what I was going to reveal. Was he trying to embarrass me even further than he did earlier? Why was he so hard on me?

I opened my mouth to answer him. I wanted to show him that I didn't feel intimidated by his need to make me feel inferior, for whatever reason he had, but all of the surrounding faces in the small cavern turned to face me and the pressure made me hesitate.

"Well," I finally managed to say, "based on some things that happened to me back home, it ... it seems like I can send my own thoughts to another's head, as well as hear another's thoughts."

"Show him, Brianna," Ethan encouraged, making me sense that Ethan too, had picked up on Quinn's intentions. "Just like before we got on the bird, Bee! Tell Quinn what he's thinking, and then he'll believe you!"

Instantly, Quinn raised himself up from his crouched position. "No, no," Quinn cried, shaking his head and looking down to the ground. "There is no need for her to read my thoughts." His cheeks became flushed.

"Scared ... are you, Quinn?" Ethan's 'older brother' protective instincts took control. After trying to make a mockery of me, Ethan wasn't going to rest until Quinn was put in his rightful place.

"Ethan!" Charlotte blared. "Don't be an idiot!"

"You needn't worry, Quinn," I said, deciding to end Quinn's humiliation. I stood on the stone I was sitting on to meet his gaze. "At this stage, I can't do what I do whenever I like. It comes and goes."

"Very well," Quinn said dismissively, while averting his gaze from mine.

The fear Quinn exhibited made me find him even more peculiar than I did before. He puzzled me. One moment he came across as confident and intimidating and the next, shy and insecure.

I knew that he had a story that would shed light on his behaviour. *What was he hiding? What was he scared of revealing?* Quinn returned to the corner of the cavern, seeking solitude, obviously uncomfortable with any company. In that moment, I felt sorry for him. I quickly glanced over to Charlotte and she showed a sympathetic expression; she was also feeling sorry for Quinn.

"So, Brianna," Charlotte quickly said, trying to draw everyone's attention away from Quinn, "How did you speak to Ethan before we were on the Oran-Roy bird?"

"I ... I can't explain it really," I answered. "It wasn't painful like last time. I'm not sure what really brought it on."

"How were you feeling when you heard Ethan's thoughts, Brianna?" Zephan enquired.

"Uh ... well, at the time a gun was being pointed at me ... so, I ... I guess I was pretty scared."

"...Gun? What's a gun?" Rona asked.

"Oh, it's ... uh..." Whoever would have thought that I'd ever find myself in a situation where I would be describing a gun, "It's a small, metal weapon. It does what a bow and arrow does, I guess, but it's much smaller and its bullets get shot through..."

"Never mind that," Zephan insisted. "How were you feeling the other occasions when you were able to hear thoughts?"

"I guess I was angry or really frustrated. Why? Do you think how I feel somehow contributes to whether I can hear or send thoughts?"

"I do," Zephan answered. "You see, Brianna, as I suspect you have learned from this book that you have mentioned, I assume that you are well aware of what is expected to be carried out by mixed-blooded children when they come of age."

"Yes," I responded. "They go on a pilgrimage, so to speak, to reach the Oran-Roy clan and consult with Donelle."

"By consulting Donelle, one becomes aware of their potential. You have never had that opportunity. As you were unaware of what you possessed, until recently, I believe that it might take some time until you can master your gift."

Ethan gave me a slight nudge before saying, "You know, Bee, this is pretty cool! This whole idea about mastering your gift is just like learning to use the force! Like in Star Wars! I'm so jealous!"

"Trust you to make a Star Wars reference!" Charlotte exclaimed. "Typical, Ethan," she mumbled under her breath.

"Well! It is like Star Wars!"

"What's Star Wars?" Leona asked, with the most unusual look on her face.

"Uh ... perhaps another time," Ethan suggested. "I could go on for days if Bee would let me, but the look on her face is telling me to resist, I'm afraid."

"Well," Leona cried out enthusiastically, "We've spoken enough about Oran-Roy. Why don't you three tell us about Ireland?"

The next few hours involved Charlotte, Ethan and me describing our life in Ireland. Mere aspects of our average way of life were far beyond the imaginations of our new acquaintances. Our forms of keeping in touch seemed to intrigue them the most, especially when we were trying to explain the purpose of a computer and the various modes of communication it allowed. Describing an iPod also proved to be an entertaining discussion, mainly from Ewan's astonishment and him saying, "You can carry music around with you in a tiny box!"

*

"This food is amazing!" Charlotte cried, while digging into the assortment of food on her wooden plate.

"... All grown or caught right here in Daray," Leona said.

"Yeah!" I agreed. "It's fantastic! It's just so rich and full of flavour!"

"Well, I'm glad you're enjoying it," Leona smiled. Her attention was then drawn towards Ethan, sitting upright against the cavern wall with an empty plate. "Ethan, are you still hungry? I can take you outside and we can get some more food if you like?"

The change of Ethan's expression answered Leona's question. Once Leona and Ethan were beyond the cavern's opening, I realised that this was the perfect opportunity to ask Charlotte about whether she had any feelings for Ethan.

"Uh ... Charlotte," I called reluctantly.

"Yeah," she answered through a mouth full of food.

"You know when Ethan and I got home after we had been caught by Mr Law ... well, Sully."

"Yeah, Bee."

"I can't help but think that ... well ... the way you acted when you greeted Ethan ... it seemed that you..."

"Brianna Shield!" Charlotte's threw her plate down. "Are you trying to say that you think I like Ethan in that way?" Charlotte's face turned scarlet, but not from embarrassment. This was turning out to be much harder than I had anticipated it to be.

"Shush!"

"Were you trying to say that you think I like him?" Charlotte whispered this time.

"Well, yes," I admitted. "Come on, Charlotte! You have to admit that you acted like that! I mean, you were hesitant in hugging him and your face went all red!"

"I was hesitant and red in the face, because I didn't want him to think that I liked him! I didn't know how to show that I was glad that he was safe, without it seeming like I was so glad in that way!"

"Well, in that case, you better tell him or show him how you really feel, because he is under the impression that you..."

"No! He isn't, is he?"

"I'm afraid he is."

Charlotte and I were no longer alone; the opening of the cavern door put an end to our discussion. Ewan was the first to re-enter and was followed in by the rest of the group. Once everyone was comfortably seated around the fire, Ewan began to instruct us on how we would make our departure.

"All right, we need to plan our trip very carefully and have a couple of options up our sleeve if we intend to make it to Kael unharmed." There was no fear in Ewan's voice. It appeared that he had done this a number of times. "Keelty, Faolon, you will lead our party to warn us of any potential dangers ahead. Dougal, you will follow directly behind Keelty and Faolon for support." Keelty, Faolon and Dougal nodded in agreement. "Leona, you will have your bow at the ready and be behind Dougal. Behind Leona, will be you, Zephan, and you will be walking directly ahead of Ethan and Charlotte, to protect them. Rona, you will be behind them, protecting Brianna. Is that clear so far?"

Everyone nodded and Ewan continued.

"Very well, then. Quinn and I will be at the back of the party on our horses with our arrows and swords at the ready." Ewan then dedicated all of his attention to Leona and me. "Leona and Brianna, you are the only people here capable of understanding Keelty, Faolon and Dougal. Whatever they tell you, you must alert me and the others of it as quickly as possible. Do you understand?"

Leona and I nodded. Ewan's plan seemed logical, but I dreaded the possibility of considering what Plan B involved.

"If we are ambushed by Cillian's men, you, Zephan, must fly Ethan and Charlotte to Kael and get them there safely at any cost. Rona, you must fly Brianna to Kael with Zephan and the others. But, try to separate yourselves; that will make it much more difficult for Cillian to determine where you are heading. Make sure that you remain as low as you can within the forest or as high as you can, so you are not easily seen. Understood?"

"Yes," Rona answered.

"Understood entirely," Zephan affirmed.

"But, if we are ambushed," I queried, "what will happen to everyone else? You can't just fly away like we can?"

"We'll manage," Quinn answered. "We know the land like the back of our hand."

"Quinn's right, Brianna," Ewan assured me. "We will hold Cillian's men off, giving you a good chance to make it to your father safely."

"But, you're all putting your lives in danger for my sake!" I cried. "I don't want you to put you in another life-threatening position! You've already done so much!"

"I don't mean to put a lot of pressure on you, Brianna, but, a lot is at stake and we need you. You offer our cause more than you know. We need you safe." Ewan affirmed.

"You're not going to win here, Bee," Ethan said, as he gave my shoulder a reassuring pat.

"I know that now, but, I just ... I don't want to see people get hurt because of me."

Quinn raised himself from the floor and made his way to the cavern's opening and slid the stone wall aside. "It's almost dusk. We must move, quickly."

"Very well," Ewan agreed. "As soon as we are all beyond the cavern, take the positions we agreed on."

Quinn stood by the cavern opening and, as everyone made their way out, I was beginning to grow nervous. *What if we are ambushed? What if people get hurt?*

"It is a possibility," Quinn replied, despite that fact that I didn't ask him aloud! I didn't speak to him! Only Quinn and I remained in the cavern. Did he hear what I was thinking? "But, have some comfort in the fact that no one will be killed. Cillian won't risk bringing Morrigan back until he has you and the carrier."

My confused expression gave Quinn reason to say, "I understand what your brother was referring to earlier now."

"Is that an apology?" I blurted out, sounding rather smug. "...For doubting me?"

"If that's how you see it," he casually replied, which confused me even more. "You're nervous, aren't you?"

"Is it that obvious?"

"Well, it explains Zephan's explanation earlier. That's why I heard what you were thinking. Your strong nerves caused you to send your thoughts."

"Well, yes. I am nervous," I admitted.

"Try not to be. Being nervous makes one more vulnerable. All right?"

"Uh ... I'll do my best," I replied sarcastically.

"As I said, there won't be any killing, Brianna."

"But, that doesn't weigh out being seriously injured or captured, does it?"

"Hurry along, you two!" Leona cried from outside the cavern.

Quinn raised his arm, inviting me to leave first. I didn't smile or say thank you. I was still holding a grudge and I didn't want to give Quinn the satisfaction.

Once everyone was in place, Ewan gave his final instructions. "The entire trek takes a few hours. We shouldn't encounter any problems until we are situated directly between Tarmon and Cathal." Ewan climbed upon his sturdy, brown horse and paced around us for the remainder of his instructions. "By the time we reach that point, it should be dark enough for us to remain unseen and we'll only be an hour away from Kael. The dark will make it very tricky to see where we are going, but we don't want to draw attention to ourselves by using flames to guide us. So, Keelty, Faolon, Dougal, Leona, Zephan and Rona, we'll have to rely on your night vision. Your eyes will be our eyes." Ewan made his way to his position, nodded to Keelty and Faolon - their cue to begin leading us.

I couldn't recall a time when I had to remain silent for so long. There were many moments when I opened my mouth to speak, but then realised that I wasn't supposed to. It was unsettling and made me more nervous.

The forest was green and mystical; greatly resembling the ones I had read about in books. Apart from the faint, crunching sounds our feet made against the forest floor, there were few noises, which made Charlotte, Ethan and I far more unsettled than the others. After all, this was our first trek through an unfamiliar forest. Occasionally, faint sounds and the cracking of twigs would come from the nearby bushes; Quinn and Ewan would hold their bows at the ready immediately after hearing a sound.

After almost two hours of walking through narrow spaces amongst the moss covered trees, the forest revealed an opening. The trees were gradually becoming wider apart and the ground was worn. It appeared that it was a road greatly travelled, which made me assume that we had reached the part of Daray between Tarmon and Cathal.

Hesitantly, Ethan and Charlotte, only a few metres ahead, glanced back at me once they realised where we were. We shared the same expressions of fear, fear of what was about to happen. Having a gun pointed at me was enough to deal with for one day. Potentially, I was about to face something equally as frightening and unpredictable. *How will I cope?*

My heart was racing, and despite the cold, damp surroundings, I began to perspire. Every step seemed to be dragging on and on as if I was unconsciously dreading the possible outcomes. My body was quivering through fear and, as my body shook, the carrier lightly bounced against my chest. Rona sensed my fear and reassuringly placed her hand on my shoulder. If I didn't see her placing her hand on me, I was certain that I would have released a large gasp.

To try and calm myself down, I looked on ahead to read Keelty, Faolon and Dougal's body language. If anything bad was going to happen, I knew that they would be the first to react. Unlike our encounter with Sully on the cliff's edge, from what I could make out in the dark, Keelty's hair was not raised and she seemed relatively calm.

While watching Keelty, she turned her head around and looked directly at me, obviously knowing that I was staring at her.

"At this stage, we have nothing to worry about. If anything should happen, you will be safe and I will alert you immediately," Keelty thought. Rather than speaking back, I simply nodded.

As I was about to turn away, the reaction I was dreading to see came. The hair on Keelty, Faolon and Dougal's neck stood up. Each one of them turned to meet Leona's eyes, then mine.

"A number of people are approaching us from behind!" Faolon cried out, but for the others, it would have sounded like an anxious bark.

I hesitated with my required response, but Leona cried out immediately, "Behind us!"

"Move! Quickly!" Ewan urged.

Faolon set a speedy pace, with Dougal and Keelty following close behind. Within seconds of returning my gaze back to Leona, she was no longer in her true form. She had morphed into a large, sandy coloured four-legged creature, greatly resembling a lioness.

"Fly low with Ethan and Charlotte, Zephan, until it's safe to go above the forest!" Quinn cried, and Zephan did as Quinn instructed. Effortlessly, Zephan held Charlotte with one arm and Ethan with the other, flying only a few metres from the ground, but easily matching the pace of those ahead.

Immediately after Zephan received his instructions, Rona raised me up. My heart jumped! In the swiftness of being lifted, I felt as if I had left half of my body behind! When we passed where Leona had morphed, Rona lowered herself to the ground and quickly scooped up Leona's belongings.

Quinn and Ewan were only metres behind; their horses' hooves tapping out a staccato beat against the ground in their haste.

Whoosh!

A flaming arrow landed into the ground just ahead of Keelty and Faolon. The feathers of the arrow were purple. Morrigan's followers were after us.

"Keep going!" Ewan cried.

Rona turned around to make sense of who was behind us. As she turned around, I was able to make out images in the distance. Through the darkness of the fast approaching night, faint balls of light were drawing closer and closer towards us down the worn forest road. As the light drew closer, a repetitive noise grew louder and louder. Within seconds, the incoming sound overpowered Ewan and Quinn's horses. Rona turned back to look, while still trying to maintain a fast pace. But, a few short seconds later, Rona turned again. Hooded figures, concealed by black cloaks that appeared purple in the flames' light, were riding magnificent black stallions; their head dresses and saddles were coated with silver plating. The band of figures resembled an incoming arrow, with one hooded figure acting as the arrows tip.

The sight of the hooded figures made me think back to the Morrigan book. Not only had I come across them in the book, I had dreamed about them! In the same dream in which I had seen Quinn, they seized me!

Our party was struggling to match the pace of Cillian's men. The pursuers released more flaming arrows. The arrows seemed to be coming from all different directions and were only landing metres away from us!

"We must venture off the main road, Ewan!" Quinn insisted. "...For cover! We are no match for them! They have greater numbers than we have ever known them to have! We have no choice!"

"Zephan! Rona! Take them! NOW!" Ewan urged.

Zephan and Rona flew us up towards the tallest trees of the forest without delay. Before I lost direct vision, I managed to see the remaining members of our party leaving the open space of the forest and retreating into the trees, with the hooded figures close behind.

"What will happen to them?" I cried, but no one answered me. Zephan and Rona were far too occupied in taking us safely beyond the forest. As we broke through the leaves of the tallest trees of Daray, there was a faint image of a castle in the distance. Whether it was Tarmon or Cathal, I could not be sure, but I knew that we had almost reached Kael.

Now beyond the forest, I asked Rona of the potential whereabouts of the others. "Do you think they lost them? Will they still make it?"

"They know the forest well, Brianna."

"But what does that mean? Just tell me! Will they be alright?"

It took a while for Rona to answer, which aggravated me further. "They should lose them! They should!" Rona's tone was also fearful, but she was trying to remain optimistic.

As we flew above Daray's forest border, all I found myself dwelling on was the wellbeing and whereabouts of the others. Guilt consumed me; I was reminded of my parents, back home. We had been missing for a day! *What were they thinking? Would they believe the Morrigan book's story?* There was no way of truly knowing what they did or did not accept as fact. All I could do was hope that, somehow, they believed every word of our letter and knew that we had good reason for acting as we did.

Rona and Zephan began to drop. Their wings, once beating frantically, were now gliding us down towards the earth. The sky was almost completely consumed by the night and the colours of the ground were undetectable. As we landed, Rona did not release me immediately; her red eyes scanned the surrounding area, checking whether we were safe.

"All right," Rona said and nodded to Zephan. "Remain close. We are almost in the Kaelin people's territory and they don't like to be disturbed."

"So, keep well away from the water, unless we tell you otherwise," Zephan warned, "Or we might never see you again." Following Zephan's warning, Ethan and Charlotte inhaled deeply, mimicking my own fearful response. "Follow me. Rona will stand behind you three." Zephan began walking towards a nearby open space. The night sky made it murder to work out the surroundings, but it did not stop us from hearing the eerie noises from the nearby shrubs and swamp-like water dwellings.

The air was much cooler here. My body shuddered as we drew closer to the mist shrouded water. In my mind, I saw myself being dragged into the water by a strange, haunting figure. Considering Zephan's warning, it was hard to remove the image from my head. To draw my mind elsewhere, I tried to make conversation.

"Rona, is my father meeting us near here? Is there far to go?"

"Craig should be just beyond this pond." Rona's answer gave me great joy, until I realised what we would have to endure.

We had reached a very open area with a large body of water, stretching for what seemed like miles! In the open space, the moon was kind enough to provide us with some light. I hoped that this wasn't the pond Rona was referring to. "All you have to do is cross here and your father will be waiting on the other side."

Ethan, Charlotte and I shared disbelieving looks.

"That is *not* a pond!" Ethan exclaimed. "That's a *bloody* ocean! There is no way we are walking through that! Tell me you're flying us across!"

"I'm afraid neither I or Rona, or any Prislen or Lucian for that matter, can fly across."

"Why the hell not?" Ethan cried.

"Our clan's history with the Kaelin people is not a pretty one. It is complicated, but essentially our clan leaders disputed with one another and severed any ties. The Kaelins are where they are because centuries ago, some of the druids who didn't agree to Donelle and Cuchulainn's plan, only had here to reside. They chose to live solitary lives. Over the centuries, they have adapted rather well to water."

"That still doesn't explain why you can't fly us over though," Ethan pressed.

"The Kaelin people have vowed that any Prislen or Lucian who passes beyond this point shall never return home. None of us wanted to take that chance."

"But, how did Rona come past here to deliver the news that Brianna's father was aware of her arrival then?" Charlotte questioned.

"I took the longer journey," Rona explained. "Rather than returning to Daray through Kael, I flew around Tarmon and through the Bryan clan. It is a much longer journey, but Zephan and I have no other option."

"So, what is going to happen now?" I asked anxiously.

"Unfortunately, you'll have to venture through here alone. If we were successful in being undiscovered, the others would have been able to accompany you," Zephan answered.

"Why wasn't this possibility mentioned to us before?"

"We didn't want to make you fearful."

"But, Zephan, why didn't we just go through Bryan, then?"

"Humans are forbidden there, unless you are dying or dead. The Lucians have claimed most of this area, as well as parts of Daray."

"Then how did you get past? I thought you were both banished."

"With great difficulty, I assure you."

"Can't we just wait for the others?" Charlotte suggested.

"No. We need you to get to Crag as soon as possible. Crag should be a safe haven for you," Rona insisted.

"But, isn't there a chance that we won't make it past this point? The Kaelin people will harm us, won't they?" Ethan asked, clearly worried by what awaited us.

Zephan approached me before speaking again and he looked intently in my eyes. "The Kaelin people were once druids and vowed to not harm others. They were misled when Morrigan wanted to infiltrate Donelle's plan. Since then, they felt remorseful. After the destruction that occurred in Oran-Roy during her uprising, they went against Morrigan's cause. Remember, Brianna, the Kaelin people are capable of seeing things before they happen. If they see you and the others as people willing to fight against Morrigan's cause, they'll let you pass unharmed, but that might not stop them from tempting you."

Zephan's justification of why we had to continue still failed to ease our concerns. Rona sensed this and said, "Your father would not be waiting beyond Kael if he knew you weren't going to arrive. Let that calm your nerves."

"But, wasn't my father expecting everyone?"

"Zephan and I will make it to Crag by our usual means. The others will be able to pass through Kael. We'll most likely see you in Crag by tomorrow morning." Rona looked towards Zephan, suggesting that we should go on. "Brianna, the three of you must leave. Your father expects you."

"All right, we'll go. Please be safe."

"We will."

"Oh, I almost forgot!" Rona cried. "You mustn't fully submerge yourself into the water! But, be warned, you will be tempted to do so. Resist this temptation at all costs."

Immediately after their warning, Rona and Zephan made their way back towards Daray. Within a few short moments, Rona nearly blended in with the black of the night, escorted by Zephan's ghostly presence.

"Of course," I hushed to myself, "Don't you both remember from the book? The Kaelin people test those who pass through their waters."

"Yes, as they see the future, they tempt us to see what lies ahead," Charlotte added.

"We can't be tempted - all right?"

Both Charlotte and Ethan nodded.

"Well," Ethan sighed, "let's get this *bloody* trek over with." Ethan made his way towards the water, but I stopped him with my left arm across his chest.

"No, I'll go first," I insisted. Charlotte and Ethan displayed looks of concern for my safety.

The water was like ice and it seeped through my jeans, ventured beyond my ankles and eventually reached my waist.

Despite walking through the water, it remained still; there were no ripples. As we walked through the water, my toes were becoming numb and I couldn't stop my teeth from chattering!

"*Come. Come. Come. Don't you want to take a look? Come,*" an eerie voice echoed over the water.

"Did you both here that?" I quickly asked Ethan and Charlotte.

"Yeah, I heard it, Bee," Ethan nervously replied.

"Charlotte? Did you hear it too?"

"Yep, but I was hoping I hadn't," Charlotte answered, also sounding rather scared.

"*Don't you want to see? I'm sure you'll be happy. Come. Come. Come.*"

"Walk faster," I instructed. "Don't listen to it!"

"*Oh, don't listen to her! Just come on in and have a look. There is no harm in doing so! Come into the water. Come. Come. Come.*" The voice was soothing and almost hypnotic. I could now understand the temptation of which Rona had warned us.

As we walked faster through the cold water, ripples began to pass us, but our own movement hadn't formed them. I quickly glanced behind to check on the others. Just behind Charlotte, large, hollow yellow eyes peered from out of the water. The creatures had large, pointy ears and dark sea weed-like hair covering most of their pale ivory skin. The Kaelin people hadn't given up on us yet.

"Don't look back, guys," but of course, Ethan and Charlotte couldn't help themselves.

"*Crap!*" Ethan silently screamed.

"*Argh!*" Charlotte cried.

"*Come. Come. Don't be afraid. Don't you want to see all the good that will come to you? Come.*"

"Keep going!" I screamed.

"*Brianna Elsa.*" As the soothing voice called my name, a paralysing chill ran up my spine. But I kept moving. "*Don't be foolish. Don't you want to see what your parents in Ireland are thinking right now? Don't you want to know where your mother is ... where your brother is?*"

My legs stopped moving. In that moment, I questioned the warnings. *Should I risk the consequences involved, so that I can have knowledge of whether my parents believed us? Do I give in to the voice, to find out the whereabouts of my mother and brother?* As my mind contemplated the decision, the paralysing chill intensified; so did the voices.

"*We know your future, Brianna Elsa. Don't you want to see it? Don't you want to put a stop to a death? Don't you want to know the source behind the Morrigan book and who gave the carrier to you? You would be foolish if you denied us. Foolish.*"

"Are you tempting the others?"

"*No. They are not worthy of seeing what lies ahead. We only offer our visions to those strong of heart. But you are you are like us. You are of this land. It is you whom people have placed faith in, to destroy all that is left of Morrigan.*"

"Do I? Am I the one who destroys her?"

"*Come and have a peak.*"

"... And you can tell me how to stop a death!"

"*Yes.*"

"*Who?*" I pleaded in my head. "*Who* will die?"

"*Come below the water and you shall see.*"

Rona's warnings escaped me. It would be wrong of me to avoid preventing a death! There wasn't a fight in my judgement. I decided to plunge and nothing was convincing me otherwise. My body started to relax. I felt light, weightless and I wanted to lie down, so I gave in and allowed my body to fall.

Silence.

There was no splash. My body was stopped before hitting the water. Something was holding me up.

"Come on, Bee, we're almost there!" Ethan assured me.

"Stay strong!" Charlotte encouraged. Charlotte and Ethan, supporting one of my arms each, dragged me through the water until we reached land. Exhausted, mentally as well as physically, our bodies collapsed into the moist dirt by the water's edge. The voices had gone.

"I feel so weak," I barely managed to say.

"Come on, find your feet." Ethan pulled me up from out of the mud.

"Thanks, but, that's not what I meant." I turned back towards the water. The yellow eyes submerged and the ripples disappeared with them. "I let them tempt me ... I'm so ... I'm..."

"... Only human, after all," an unfamiliar deep voice spoke from a distance. It startled the three of us and we quickly stood tall.

Small lights flickered beyond the nearby trees and were gradually growing larger as the rustling noises intensified. Black silhouettes were appearing amongst the trees. One of the figures came and revealed himself. The light from the figures' staff exposed a fair man with iridescent blue eyes and short, rich blonde hair. The man's face was strong, with clear, distinctive features. He wasn't incredibly tall, but he was broad shouldered and appeared very athletic.

"Hello, Brianna." The man removed his bow and arrows from his back and let them rest on the ground. His gaze did not leave me. "I cannot tell you how long I have waited for this day to come."

The man standing before me was my father.

Chapter Thirteen

Lessons in Combat

"Craig Elsa?" I asked, to confirm that the man standing before me was indeed my father.

"Yes." He quickly responded. "Show me your left wrist, Brianna." As he spoke, Craig stepped towards me and pulled away the white sleeve covering his right wrist. The sleeve revealed a bow and arrow enclosed by a bold circle; the symbol of the Crag clan.

"Yes," I replied. "Just like my own," and I wiped away the mud from my left wrist to also reveal the symbol of Crag.

"I didn't really need to see your markings to know who you were, Brianna," Craig informed me. "You look just as your mother did when she was your age."

"Even the crazy hair?" Perhaps it was silly to talk about my hair in the very first discussion I would have with my father, but what does one say to a parent after being unaware of their existence for eighteen years?

"Yes, *even* the hair," Craig said, smiling as he spoke. "That's one of the things that attracted me to your mother..." As my father spoke of my mother again, his expression of contentment was overpowered by sorrow. His gaze left my face and he avoided looking at me directly. Seeing me was reminding him of everything that he had lost. In this awkward moment, I didn't know what to do and I couldn't find the words to express how I felt.

Hesitantly, I approached my father and stretched out my right arm so that my hand was able to reach his shoulder. As I touched his shoulder, his eyes immediately flicked back towards me and he met my glance again. Craig's eyes were watery, but he was withstanding the power of his emotions. He was holding back the tears, holding back all of the pain and emptiness he had felt for these eighteen years, which must have felt like an eternity to him. At least I was ignorant of all of this. I had no knowledge of these events, which allowed me to live free of any pain. Ignorance truly is bliss. In that moment, I found a likeness between my father and me; we both favoured hiding our feelings, so that we would be recognised as strong people. He and I associated tears and the showing of emotions as a weakness ... But is showing how you truly feel a flaw?

"I know that seeing me must be hard. Seeing me is just reminding you of what you lived without for so long and I am sorry for that, but..."

"I am not sorry that you are here," Craig quickly interrupted, shaking his head in disagreement at what I was saying. "I am ... overwhelmed with joy that you are finally here. I'm just sorry that I wasn't able to see you grow up, see you..."

"Don't be sorry," I enforced, "What happened was out of our control and I know that you did everything in your power to do what was best for your family." The emotions were bubbling up within me, too, and holding them back made my voice strained. "... And," I swallowed, trying to clear the emotional lump in my throat and looking down at my feet, "If you hadn't acted as you did, things would have been much worse."

Craig's right hand gently lifted my head, returning my focus to him. He wiped away a tear (that had managed to break through my tough barrier) with his thumb, which acted as a catalyst for more tears to seep from my eyes. Craig's hands tenderly brushed through my curly hair and he smiled.

"Just like your mother." Slowly, Craig ushered me into his arms. "Just like your mother's," he sighed again, while stroking my hair. As I rested my head against his chest, I allowed my arms to wrap themselves around his waist. In my mind, I had played out this event hundreds of times, but all of the imaginary scenarios could not compare to the reality that was now.

I let go of my father, deciding that it was time to introduce him to Ethan and Charlotte.

"So, Craig ... uh ... father ... I mean..."

"What would you like to call me?" Craig asked, understanding the awkwardness of the situation.

"The man who raised me, Roy Shield, well ... I call him Dad, so ... so ... would you *mind* if I called you father or even Craig ... for now ... until I..."

"That is fine."

"Oh," I quickly returned my attention back to Ethan and Charlotte, who were both waiting patiently. "Uh ... Craig, this is Ethan and this is Charlotte." As I introduced them, both Ethan and Charlotte stepped forward and offered their hand to greet my father. "Ethan is my brother and Charlotte is our very good friend."

"I'm very glad that Brianna didn't venture here without support. Thank you," Craig said while shaking Ethan and Charlotte's hand. "You have both helped her arrive safely."

"Well, we didn't do much," Ethan admitted. "It was mainly Brianna."

"Yeah," Charlotte added. "Brianna did everything."

"But, I couldn't have done it without them."

"Brianna," Craig's tone changed abruptly. "The others, are they on their way?"

"We had complications," I confessed. "We were seen by Cillian's men and Rona and Zephan separated us from the others, so that we would get here as quickly as possible."

"Rona and Zephan said that they would most probably arrive here in the early hours of the morning," Ethan said.

"Yes," Charlotte added, "They also expect the others to arrive here in the morning."

Craig turned to the men standing behind him and nodded, signalling the men to begin unpacking their carry bags and to set up camp. "Due to the circumstances, we will sleep here and wait for the others to arrive. Once they have been attended to, we'll make our way to the Oran-Roy clan." Craig signalled us to sit on a nearby fallen tree and he prepared a fire. "In the meantime, I'd like to hear a bit about you three."

For the next two hours, I shared everything with my father, from my life in Ireland through to the Morrigan book. Ethan and Charlotte described what they had witnessed and how they had experienced the gift I seemed to possess. Craig spoke with us about everything that had led him to this moment. He became very intrigued by how the three of us came to know of Oran-Roy through the Morrigan book.

" ... And you are *certain* that you don't know who the author is?" Craig queried.

"We did all that we could, but it appeared that the author used another name," Charlotte answered.

"It just doesn't make sense," Craig said, shaking his head in confusion. "No one can leave Oran-Roy *unless* they are the Carrier or know the Carrier. Only Zia and the King's before him had the means to leave Oran-Roy."

"Well, the book we've told you about, said that Zia assisted a man called Dallas Conlan to escape Oran-Roy," I explained.

"*Why?*" Craig continued to question.

"Dallas Conlan was of mixed blood too. The book said that his mother, Glynn, my mother's aunt, came to know of a man in Ireland and ... I guess you can assume what happened next."

"So that would make him the first mix blooded person after Morrigan?" Craig inferred. "Did the book go into detail about the circumstances surrounding Zia and Dallas?"

"Yes. Zia and Dallas were good friends. They eventually realised Dallas' true identity - that he was Glynn Kael's son, his cousin – and was being protected by the Darians. They were only young when Zia helped Dallas escape. Dallas feared that some people had discovered who he really was. This is also why we believe him to be the author, because he knows of Oran-Roy. Wait ... didn't Leona explain this?"

"If a Darian makes a promise, Brianna, they never break it," Craig explained. "Leona must have been asked not to divulge this and she obeyed."

"I understand."

"But, this Dallas, well ... if Dallas is indeed the author, he wrote of you before you were born, even before your mother and I met."

"Well, he is mixed. And the Morrigan book described him having dreams of the future. It makes sense that he would be the author."

"Yes, that explains why the book was written many years before what he wrote about had actually happened."

"Yes," I struggled to say through an unwelcome yawn, a yawn that reminded me just how much time had passed. It was almost midnight.

"You all must be exhausted," Craig assumed. "Why don't you try to sleep before the others arrive? I'll see to it that my men set up shelter for you here by the fire, so that you keep warm."

One of my father's men came and began arranging places for the three of us to sleep. Ethan and Charlotte decided to assist the man, which gave me the opportunity to speak to my father about the Kaelins.

"Uh ... father?" I nervously asked.

"Brianna," he answered.

"As ... as we crossed the Kaelin waters, the Kaelin people said things to me that ... that made me question so much. If it weren't for Ethan and Charlotte, I would have fallen into the water."

"Come with me," Craig said calmly. He lit his staff and directed me into the nearby woods just beside the water. "They tempted you?"

"Yes, and it makes me feel so..."

"You are not weak, Brianna," Craig quickly affirmed. "The Kaelin people tempt those that intimidate them or those who have a lot of questions that need to be answered or solved. They might see our future, but they do not make it happen."

"But, there was one thing they said that scares me."

"Do you want to share it with me?"

I didn't answer.

"Here is my first form of advice that I wish I was able to share with you years ago. You may tell me anything. Do not fear revealing anything to me. I'll be here to listen whenever you need me to."

After a few steps without talk, I plucked up the courage and consoled in my father for the first time.

"The ... the Kaelins asked me whether I ... whether I wanted to put a stop to a death. That's what made me let myself give in. I ... I couldn't ignore that!"

Craig stopped walking and held my arm. "Brianna, the Kaelins induce us to question things for which we stand. They sense that you are here to achieve things beyond what you know yourself to be capable of achieving. Even though they have warned you of a death, you cannot allow yourself to see what lies ahead. Too many people have wasted the good in their present lives to know of what may be in the future."

"I understand what you are saying, but what if the person they speak of is within our cause and, besides, a death means that Morrigan will return, doesn't it?"

"Morrigan needs to return at some point so that she will be removed permanently from..."

"But..."

"Brianna," Craig's tone deepened, "seeing what lies ahead destroys the now. We must have faith."

"What if it means Charlotte? Or Ethan or..." I started to panic.

"Brianna! Can you see what the Kaelins do now? They've put so much doubt in your mind that it makes you only consider the future! You can't let it consume you!"

I didn't respond. I was too frustrated to speak and I was fearful that if I opened my mouth I would cry. Craig sensed how I was feeling and moved his hand from my arm to my cheek.

"You're stubborn like your mother, too." His words managed to make me smile. "You're also strong like her. But, Brianna, if you are ever tempted by the Kaelins again, you must do what you can to close your mind. Do not allow them in. If you do that, they will see you as an equal and will leave you alone, as they have done with me."

"So, if you go into the water, you are not tempted?"

"No, they respect me for not giving in and it is important that you try to do the same."

"I will."

We turned around and began making our way back to camp.

" ... And Brianna," Craig said.

"Yes."

"I wouldn't mention this to your brother and friend."

"I wasn't planning to."

*

"Bee!" Someone was shaking me. "Bee! Wake up!" Ethan wouldn't leave me alone until my eyes were completely opened. As I wiped my weary eyes, I realised that it was the early hours of the morning. I forced myself up and turned towards the water, where I could hear a commotion of some sort. When my eyes came to the source of the sound, I saw what I did not wish to see.

My father was supporting a very limp Quinn. Quinn appeared to be unconscious, or so incredibly fatigued that he was unable to find his feet. His scar was no longer distinguishable on his ivory face, with blood trickling from a deep cut above his forehead. His shocking state caused my heart to race. The sound of my heart pulsated beyond my chest! I couldn't bear seeing Quinn as he was! He was in this state because of me! I dreaded laying my eyes upon the others.

Once Craig had a few of his men attending to Quinn, he raced back to the water's edge. Ethan, Charlotte and I followed.

"Is anyone else hurt?" Craig asked, extremely concerned.

"No," Ewan cried, rather out of breath. "No one is as badly injured as Quinn." As Ewan made his way out of the water, blood seeped slowly from his left sleeve, formed drops and fell to the water, like the first few drops of a storm, the blood eerily suspended in the water. Ewan could see that I was feeling guilty.

"He'll be alright, Brianna."

I said nothing, but took off my sweater and began tightening it around Ewan's wound.

"Apply some pressure." I didn't look at Ewan when I spoke.

"Brianna," he said again.

"What happened?" I blurted out, but my question was ignored. Keelty, Faolon and Leona, holding Dougal, were scrambling out of the water. Zephan and Rona were waiting on the bank to assist, having arrived sometime in the night, while we were sleeping. I breathed a sigh of relief when I could see that they were all fine.

"You're all okay? You're all right?" I asked impatiently.

"We're fine, Brianna," Leona answered. "How's Quinn doing, Ewan?"

"He's lost a lot of blood, but he'll be fine."

"So, uh ... Cillian's men didn't make things easy, did they?" Ethan said, trying to draw out the information he sensed I was anxious to hear.

"Quinn incurred his injury from a tree believe it or not."

"A tree!" Charlotte cried.

"Yes. It was incredibly dark and as we were riding as fast as we could through the narrow parts of the forest, Quinn hit his head on a very low protruding branch."

"So, you lost Cillian's men?" I asked.

"They stopped following us once we were comfortably in the forest. They wanted you, Brianna. Once they knew that you had escaped, they stopped pursuing us. We're of no use to them. But, you are the Carrier and Cillian needs you."

"That's why we needed you to arrive here as soon as possible," Zephan enforced.

" ... And I take it you've met your father," Rona pried.

I smiled and met my father's stare. "Yes. We've been well acquainted."

My father returned the smile.

*

"So, you're going to insist to Ewan and Quinn that they train us, Bee," Charlotte clarified, as we were preparing to sleep by the fire.

"I have to! We can't allow a repeat of the situation we just had. At least if the three of us were trained up a little, perhaps we could be of some assistance, rather than sitting back and having to be protected all the time."

"I agree with, Bee," Ethan announced, as he was arranging a spot to sleep by the fire.

"We weren't putting this up for a vote," I assured him.

"Yeah, I know that! But, I think you're right." Ethan casually slumped onto his sleeping mat, with his elbow against the ground to support his head. He removed his glasses before continuing. "Look, based on what your father and everyone else were saying today, it might be two months until we actually are in the Oran-Roy clan, because of the trek and all the planning involved. In that time, we could encounter loads of obstacles. So, if we have a few sword and archery skills up our sleeve, we'll be less of a worry for everyone."

"So, when are you going to ask them? Are you really sure about asking Quinn? I'd just ask Ewan," Charlotte suggested, now sitting comfortably on her sleeping mat. " ... Or, you could even ask your father to train us."

"I thought of that, but that's the last thing he needs, based on what he explained to us today, don't you think?"

"Why? I'm sure he'd be happy to..."

"But, Charlotte, he has to continuously attend to his men from Crag who serve him, as well as make plans so that all of these people are able to make it to Oran-Roy in one piece! The last thing he needs is a couple of teenagers nagging him to be trained. I don't want to become a burden to him after knowing him for only twenty-four hours."

"I don't think he'd see it like that, but I understand what you mean. I guess Quinn and Ewan then are ... *or*, just Ewan is the best person to ask."

"You're probably right, Quinn has..."

" ... A stick up his butt, or something to that effect," Ethan blurted out.

"Shush!" Charlotte and I harshly hushed Ethan.

"Well, he does! I don't know what the hell is wrong with him! But, he's got one hell of an attitude, or some sort of mood swing thing going on!"

"All right! We get it! Just keep your voice down!" I begged.

"Quiet as a mouse!" Ethan whispered, and then rolled over to try and sleep. " ... Night."

" ... Night."

The next morning, Leona kindly attended to Ethan, Charlotte and I, helping us to find some new and much needed clean clothes. Ethan was rather satisfied with his medieval looking white blouse, loose brown trousers and leathery brown boots that came just below his knees. Charlotte, too, was very taken by the emerald green material dress and quaint, black slip-on shoes she was offered to wear. Unfortunately, the women of Oran-Roy didn't seem to fashion shorts or pants, which resulted in me having to accept a blue long sleeved full length dress. The dress was beautiful, with a light blue satin-like belt for the waist, as well as light blue stitching bordering the buttons along the sleeves and the front of the dress. To put to rest the dread of wearing a dress, I insisted upon wearing my once white pair of converse shoes. Charlotte and Ethan were unable to refrain from giggling when they first saw how I looked.

"What?" I exclaimed, but they averted their eyes elsewhere. "I'm after comfort! Not style!" I tried to reinforce, but the giggling was contagious and I struggled to defend myself further.

"Anyway," I dragged out, trying to shake out the remaining chuckles I still had. "I've really got to speak to Ewan, especially now that I'm dressed for the occasion!" Still in a silly mood, I offered Charlotte and Ethan a curtsy before I left.

Making my way around the camp, I came to realise that Ewan was nowhere in sight. Asking my father's men didn't end the search; they all seemed to be unaware of Ewan's whereabouts and, for that matter, my father's, as well.

"So, you have absolutely no idea where they went?" I asked a large, broad shouldered man with long, black hair tied back in a ponytail.

"I'm sorry," the man replied in a deep voice.

"They're hunting, collecting food for the journey ahead, Brianna," Quinn answered, as he revealed himself, stepping out of the closest tent. Awkwardly, Quinn stood in front of me with his arms folded, waiting for me to say something.

After the uncomfortable moment of silence, I finally thought to say, "So, you're feeling better?"

"Much," he quickly answered, with his eyes not even looking at me directly.

"Look, I'm sorry that you got hurt! But you don't have to take that tone with me!" The man I had just questioned about Ewan and Craig's whereabouts sensed where the conversation was heading and walked away.

"Why do you always jump to the conclusion that I'm angry with you, Brianna?"

"Because you're ... you're..."

"What did you want to ask Ewan and your father? I'm sure I can be of some assistance." *He speaks to me rudely and then he offers me help! Ethan was right! This guy has more mood swings than anyone I've ever come across! Wait! Keep it together! If you get too emotional he'll probably be able to hear this!*

"It can wait," I quickly answered, trying to maintain my emotions and also averting my eyes away from his; I wanted him to know that I didn't appreciate being patronised.

"You seem just a little impatient. Are you sure it can wait?" Quinn's voice had a cunning edge. I didn't know whether he was being sarcastic or just plain rude!

"Fine!" I cried, gritting my teeth and meeting his eyes again. "Charlotte, Ethan and me would like ... actually, we're insisting that we are trained, or taught how to fight and protect ourselves, so that we are no longer a burden to protect."

"Well, you certainly know what you want."

"I knew I should have just waited until Ewan got back," I mumbled to myself and I started to walk away.

"You're going to need more than just Ewan to train you. After all, I am from Cathal - the clan *most* skilled with the sword."

I stopped walking and turned around to meet his eyes again. "All right then, Quinn. You can *assist* Ewan in training us."

"When do we begin?"

" ... How about this afternoon? Ewan should be back by then."

"Fine," he answered quickly and he began making his way back inside the tent. "I will inform him as soon as he arrives."

"Good." I responded tersely and walked away, still unable to find words to describe Quinn's personality. *I don't know what Leona meant when she referred to him as 'Quiet Quinn'. He's more quizzical than quiet!*

*

"We will begin with the sword, because it is most likely that you will encounter danger within close proximity," Ewan explained, as he paced along the line Ethan, Charlotte and I had formed. I felt as though we had just been recruited into the army.

Ewan and Quinn had decided to train us in a nearby clearing, heavily surrounded by forest. The location ensured that we would be undisturbed, free of danger and would avoid being the victims of humiliation resulting from our poor, or non-existent, skills.

"Quinn's clan are renowned for their sword fighting skills. But, before we demonstrate the skill of the sword, it is important that you become comfortable with the weight of the sword." Ewan stopped pacing and stood centrally. We were waiting for instruction, but Ewan seemed to be waiting for us. "Well then, pick them up!"

Feeling rather stupid, the three of us picked up the swords laid at our feet.

"Try to get familiar with the sword's weight. Swing it around *very* slowly and try to remain balanced when you do so. Spread out before you swing the swords, of course."

Ethan was standing upright first; the weight of the sword didn't seem to be an issue for him. Once comfortably holding the sword upwards, I appreciated how strong a Knight was required to be for battle. I quickly peered over to my right where Charlotte was, but she wasn't standing upright yet. The tip of her sword was still on the ground.

"I'll help lift it up with you," Ewan offered Charlotte, quickly realising that her small frame was struggling with the sword's weight. Ewan helped Charlotte raise the sword, so that her arms were above her head. Gradually, Ewan reduced the amount of assistance he was offering. When Ewan finally let go, the weight of the sword proved to be too great for Charlotte. The sword wavered backwards and its weight dragged Charlotte down to the floor. My first reaction was to giggle, but I stopped myself. As Charlotte found her feet again, she couldn't help but laugh, which made it safe for Ethan and me to join in. Quinn wasn't too impressed.

"Just get on with it!" Quinn groaned, raising his eyebrows and trying to look severe, but it wasn't enough to subdue the giggling. When Ewan and Quinn weren't watching, the three of us would exchange amusing looks and then find ourselves bottling up our laughter.

Over the next two weeks, Quinn and Ewan focussed on building up our arm strength. With no rest days in between training sessions, Charlotte, Ethan and I found ourselves crawling exhausted into bed shortly after the sun set!

Only when Quinn was satisfied, did our training sessions come to an end, with some sessions ending well after dark! Almost every morning the three of us would feel the effects of the training. Barely managing to lift ourselves up from bed was one of the side effects. Our arms would slump along the sides of our body – too tired to lift themselves up beyond our waists. However, we quickly learned that the more we complained about the workload Quinn was insisting upon, the harder the sessions would be. The rain didn't seem to be an issue for Ewan or Quinn; they didn't even consider postponing our sessions when the rain was torrential! They would simply say, *"rain doesn't stop a battle or the possibility of having to defend yourself!"*

On the final day of sword training, Quinn had Leona fight against the three of us individually. As uncoordinated as Ethan was when it came to sports, I was amazed by how skilled he was with the blade! After just two weeks of training, his arms and shoulders had changed and he was becoming noticeably toned. Occasionally,

Leona managed to claim Ethan's sword, but, for the most part, Ethan was able to maintain his ground.

Charlotte was still struggling with the weight of the sword, so Leona had an easy challenge before her and wasn't intimidated in the slightest. I'd hoped that Charlotte would do better in the bow and arrow training, but at least she was committed to the training whole-heartedly.

As for me, I couldn't deny that the strength and balance work we had done with Quinn had paid off. In just two weeks, I went from being almost incapable of holding a sword steadily, to putting up a reasonable challenge against Leona.

"It's in your blood," Leona would say, if I performed incredibly well, but, on most occasions, Leona would beat me hands down.

After two weeks in Oran-Roy, I was beginning to become accustomed to the way of life here. When I considered how well I fitted in, a surge of guilt flooded my thoughts. *What must Mam and Dad be thinking at home?* Considering the state Mam and Dad could potentially be in made my insides churn!

The bow and arrow training proved to be far less strenuous than handling a blade, but it required just as much, if not more, concentration. Quinn and Ewan began the training by showing us how to hold the bow correctly. Once they were satisfied, Quinn and Ewan created target boards and nailed them to the closest trees of the surrounding forest. After one week, none of us had yet managed to shoot a bullseye. Quinn and Ewan made it seem so effortless in their demonstrations! Nine times out of ten, both were able to hit their intended target. Yet, despite our poor aim, the distance and speed at which we released our arrows was exceeding Quinn and Ewan's expectations.

*

"I can't believe that we've been here for almost a month!" Ethan exclaimed.

"I know!" Charlotte agreed. "It's gone by *so* quickly!"

"It's the training Quinn and Ewan have you doing," Leona explained, "Time always seems to go by fast when you're busy and preoccupied with a lot of things."

"Hey, Leona," I asked, as I came to join everyone, "The entire time we've been here I've been wanting to ask you something."

" ... And what might that be?"

"What does it feel like when you change ... you know ... when you morph into an animal?"

Leona smiled before answering. "Well, it depends on the animal I'm changing into, really. If the animal is larger than me as I am now, it almost feels like a sudden bout of growing pains – my muscles seem to stretch. But, if I am becoming smaller than myself, my muscles contract and tighten."

"Is it painful?" Ethan queried.

"No. I've been doing it for so long that I don't even think about how it feels as I change."

"Brianna," Craig called, as he was approaching our gathering. "May I see you for a moment?"

I left my spot by Leona and followed my father into his tent. "What did you want to see me about?"

My father removed a white cloth from over the stone in front of where I had seated myself.

"It was Zia's. He gave this to your mother, but, I'm sure she would be most happy if you were to carry this." Craig picked up a silvery bow, placed it in my hands and began running his fingers along the bow's framing. "Vos es verus; Vos es putus of pectus pectoris; Vos es fortis; dare vestry donum tamen usquequaque subsist versus."

"Latin," I replied.

"Yes."

"I think that the Morrigan book made some mention of these words. What do they mean, though?"

"You are true; you are pure of heart; you are brave; share your gift, but always remain true."

"Ah, I remember now. These words are carved in the Oran-Roy tree, aren't they?"

"Yes. It's the creed that all mixed-bloods must fulfil. To fulfil it, they must use what they have been given for the good of the people."

"Will we be leaving for Oran-Roy soon?"

"This time tomorrow, we'll be beyond Crag."

"Well then," I stood up with the bow. "I better get some practise in."

"That would be wise," Craig said through a smile. "You're very eager to try it, aren't you?"

"I am."

"Off you go then, before the night is upon us."

As I left my father's tent, I quickly glanced over to where everyone was sitting and eating. Everyone appeared to be deep in conversation, so I decided to try the bow out by myself in the clearing.

When I had the arrow in place, I faced the target on the tree and tried to emulate the stance shown to us by Ewan. My right hand pulled back the arrow as far as the bow allowed.

I released the bow.

It missed the mark by inches.

"Come on, Bee, come on, Bee," I hushed to myself as I prepared another arrow. "Concentrate. Concentrate. Back straight like Ewan showed."

Crunch.

I twisted to face the bushes behind me and froze with the bow stretched at its maximum.

Crunch.

"Who's there?" I demanded.

No answer.

Not sure where the sound had come from, I slowly spun within the clearing; my arrow ready for release as I scanned the surrounding bushes.

Rustle.

I spun to meet the sound.

"Brianna!" Quinn cried with his hands raised above his head. The tip of my arrow was only metres away from his chest. I loosened the bow and lowered it to below my waist.

"Why were you sneaking up on me like that? I could have shot you!"

"Not using that technique," Quinn assured me, completely unfazed after just having an arrow pointed at him; his lack of fear making a mockery of my technique. "You have to concentrate more on your core for support ... your centre."

Without hesitation, Quinn approached me and raised my arms, placed his right hand below my ribs and his left hand on the centre of my back. As he touched me, I forgot to breathe. A shiver travelled down my body. Quinn gradually slid his left hand lower down my back and applied a small amount of pressure to correct my posture. As his right hand remained below my ribs, Quinn aligned his left arm with my own.

"Now," he softly spoke, his warm breath against the back of my neck, "keep your back arched as it is now, it will make it easier for you to align your chin with your left shoulder." Quinn's right hand found mine. "When you pull, your elbow should slide horizontally."

Quinn pulled the arrow with me. "Focus on the target," he instructed as he let me go. Stunned by Quinn's manner, I didn't move and kept my eyes focussed on the target.

I released the arrow.

It was almost a bullseye; my arrow only centimetres away from the mark.

I lowered the bow, which reminded me to breathe.

Slowly, I turned around to face Quinn. His eyes were still focussed on my arrow beside the target on the tree. "That ... uh ... that helped," I struggled to say, slightly out of breath. It might not have sounded like it, but I was thanking him for the assistance.

Quinn's eyes left the arrow and interlocked with mine. "That technique has never failed me." I guess that meant you're welcome. "Yes ... uh ... never failed me ..." his eyes flickered away as he stopped speaking.

I thought Quinn hadn't finished talking, so I waited, but he decided not to continue. After an awkward silence, I pulled my eyes from his and bent down to collect my arrows from the ground.

I didn't know what to make of Quinn and I didn't know what to make of my reaction to his touch. *Why did I react as I did? Why did Quinn's touch give me goosebumps? Wait! Stay calm and together or he'll probably hear this if your emotions are what allow others to hear you!*

With all of the arrows collected from the ground, I stood and proceeded to remove the remaining two arrows from the tree, but there was no need.

"Here," Quinn placed the two remaining arrows in my right hand.

"Thanks," I replied, avoiding eye contact. I could feel blood rushing towards my cheeks, so I quickly looked to my side, hoping that Quinn wouldn't notice. "Well, I'd better get back and show the others this bow Craig gave me."

"Yes," Quinn agreed, averting his eyes to the forest floor.

I said no more and walked back towards camp in a state of confusion. As I made my way through the trees back to camp, the only conclusion I could come to was that I just fulfilled a very 'stereotypical' moment most commonly seen in romantic films. *Wait! That doesn't mean that...? No! I refuse to believe that!*

I couldn't understand why I reacted in such a way to a person I struggled to understand! Don't you need to really like someone to react as I did?

Chapter Fourteen

Vos es Verus

… As Cuchulainn emerged from the base of the Oran-Roy tree, the voices of past heroes fell silent. His once green and amber clothes were now white…

- Excerpt from 'The Morrigan Book'

The journey to the Oran-Roy clan was quite a hike! After a day of trekking, we made camp just beyond the outskirts of Crag. I was disappointed that we didn't rest up in Crag; I wanted to see where my father had come from. Craig detected my disappointment when we journeyed passed the rocky hillside of his birthplace.

"Don't worry," my father said. "When things become more settled, I'll see to it that you'll see *everything* there is to see in Crag."

Over the course of the day's journey I avoided Quinn at all costs. I didn't want to face him after our 'run in' at the clearing. I was scared of realising that I could have been wrong about him. I didn't want to be hurt again and build up feelings for someone and then realise that all of the anticipation was for nothing. Besides, I was still confused, which made me feel insecure and I didn't want Quinn to see that. I couldn't decide how to feel and couldn't infer what brought this sudden change in Quinn. I still hadn't shared my 'run in' with Quinn with Charlotte and Ethan, but, after the evening meal, when everyone was preparing for the night ahead, the three of us were left alone by the fire. I was ready to share everything with Ethan and Charlotte, but it wasn't me who initiated the conversation.

"You've been a bit quiet today, Bee," Ethan expressed, once he felt that we were not in earshot. "... Something bothering you?"

I've always been somewhat of an open book with regards to my emotions; Ethan's suspicion confirmed that. "Ah ... actually, there is something."

"Spill!" Charlotte left the log she was sitting on, then came and sat directly in front of me, holding her hands beneath her chin, ready to listen to whatever I had to say.

"Well, remember yesterday afternoon ... when I showed you the bow Craig gave to me?"

"Yeah," they both answered.

"Well, before that, I was practising with the bow in the clearing." Pausing for merely three seconds aggravated Charlotte.

"And..."

"While I was practising, Quinn came."

"And..." Charlotte was again not satisfied.

"Quinn was ... was very ... really..."

"Really what?" Charlotte couldn't bear the wait; her impatience annoyed me, but I refrained from revealing that.

"He was really friendly, perhaps too friendly, to the point that it was unsettling."

Ethan's expression changed, quicker than the pace he searched through television channels. "What did he do?" As he spoke, Ethan stood up and became tense. "Did he do anything that made you feel uncomfortable?"

"No!" I quickly assured him. "Not uncomfortable like that!"

Ethan sighed and sat back down. "... Good because if he had, I was ready to beat the crap out of him; even though he is twice my size and has a little bit more muscle tone!"

"Your chivalry is very flattering, but I want to hear what Bee has to say!" Charlotte said, sarcastically. She then looked at me intensely, keenly waiting for what I was about to reveal. "So, what did he do?"

"Well, he scared me as he came out of the bushes and I could have shot him!"

"Yes and..." Charlotte was not very subtle in wanting me to get to the point.

"He came up to me and helped me hold the bow and arrow with his technique. After I tried to hit the target, it was ... sort of ...

an awkward moment. We both tried to avoid looking at each other and..."

"I knew it!" Charlotte cried, like she had just found the solution to the world's biggest problem.

"Knew what?" I asked unsure by what she meant.

"He likes you!"

My face went all red. "You really think so?"

"Well, I'm not an expert in this sort of thing, but he must like you! Ethan and I were speaking about it when you were walking with Craig this afternoon."

"What?" I said, rather shocked by what Charlotte just confessed.

"When you think about it, Quinn's..."

"Bee," Ethan interrupted Charlotte, his tone very serious. "Take it from me. You can tell if a fella really likes a girl if he starts out by being reserved, rude and all 'macho', or, if he does..." Ethan looked down into his lap.

"Or..." I invited him to continue.

"...Or, if a fella is really obliging and compliments almost everything that the girl he likes does." Ethan's eyes quickly flickered to Charlotte and then quickly retreated back to me. I tried to be subtle when I looked at Charlotte; she was avoiding making eye contact with Ethan. Sensing that both Charlotte and Ethan were now the ones uncomfortable in this conversation, I decided to move things along.

"So, Ethan, you think that because Quinn was rude to me, he likes me?"

"Yeah, that's what I just said!"

"But, why the sudden change? Why, out of the blue, was he nice to me yesterday?"

"You said you were alone in the clearing, yeah?"

"Yeah..."

"That's my point, Bee. You were alone and he decided to make a move." My face must have appeared puzzled, because Ethan felt the need to further justify his thoughts. "He's not going to chance making himself look like a fool in front of everyone! Quinn wanted to see how you'd react alone with him. Then, if it was the reaction he was hoping for, he wouldn't be afraid to be nice to you in front of everyone." *How on earth did Ethan know all this?*

"So," Charlotte said, "How did you react?"

"Uh, I ... I guess I was ... pleasant." Charlotte and Ethan sat silent and wide-eyed, still wanting me to divulge more information. "When ... when he touched me, I ... I got goosebumps. My face went all red."

"So that's why you've been avoiding him," Charlotte surmised.

"What do you mean?" I quickly replied.

"When your father told us to ride with someone for the difficult part of the trek along the edge of Crag, you were closest to

Quinn and without hesitating, you walked over to stand by Ewan so he would invite you to ride with him."

Embarrassed that I allowed my emotions to dictate my actions, my face turned red. I knew that Charlotte was right, but it was hard hearing the truth. "Was it that obvious? Do you think Quinn would ...?"

"... Know that you felt that way?" Charlotte finished asking for me. "Well, it's hard to say, but, I bet he knows that he has made a slight impression, which will make him feel optimistic." Rona and Zephan were making their way to us by the fire, ending our chat.

"I think it will be best if we all get an early night," Rona advised. "We'll be setting off early tomorrow morning."

"How long, until you think we'll arrive?" Ethan asked Zephan, as Zephan was stocking up the fire with more wood.

"If Craig's men hadn't collected more supplies and horses as we journeyed along Crag's border, I would say two to three weeks. But, now, it appears that we'll be in the Oran-Roy clan before the week's end." My heart leapt at Zephan's news. I was excited and nervous at the same time. In just one week, some of my questions would be answered!

When I went down to sleep that night, Quinn occupied my thoughts. Trying to drag my mind elsewhere was a difficult feat and sleep was appearing to be further and further out of my reach as I lay awake pondering.

*

"All right, everyone! Listen up! Listen up!" Craig announced as he sat tall on his amber horse, addressing the party. "Early this afternoon, we should reach the bridge crossing over the Rona River. Once we are beyond the crossing, we are within Oran-Roy clan borders. Where we are heading is sacred ground and we shall be safe there." Before continuing his address, Craig invited me to join him on his horse. "My daughter, Brianna, will be initiated once we arrive there, according to the traditions we uphold for all of the mixed bloods of Oran-Roy. Remain vigilant on the final leg of our journey and I thank you all for your service." Craig tightened his grip around the reigns, signalling me to put my arms around his waist. "Ya!" My father cried, as he led our party on the last leg of our journey towards the Oran-Roy clan.

After hours of riding, an ornate, silvery bridge emerged from the mist. As we were almost ready to cross the bridge, large leaves, with shimmery, silver edging, blew along the ground.

"The leaves of the Oran-Roy tree," Craig told me. "We're here, Brianna. Are you ready?"

Truthfully, I wasn't sure. Despite being here for over a month and knowing that this awaited me, I wasn't prepared. The Morrigan Book described the initiation of many future heroes of Oran-Roy. Contemplating all of the brave and heroic acts they had done before me made the pressure almost overwhelming. *What if*

I'm a failure? What if I contribute nothing? Craig sensed my uncertainty.

"It's alright to be afraid. We aren't meant to be ready for everything, Brianna, but, by doing it, we become ready. If everyone waited until they were *completely* ready, nothing would be accomplished, would it?" My father's wise words didn't calm me, but I tried to pretend that they did.

"Thanks," I said as Craig lowered me from his horse. Once I was safely on the ground, Craig remained on the horse. "You ... you aren't walking with me?"

"We'll walk on behind you."

"But, what ... what do I do when I..."

"You know as much as any of us here." That was comforting.

"But I thought you knew..."

"Not one of our party has been here before, Brianna. Because we are not mixed, we must be lead by one of mixed blood."

Before walking towards the bridge, I turned around to meet everyone's eyes. Ethan and Charlotte smiled and gave me a little 'thumbs up' signal. Leona, Zephan and Rona gave me a respectful nod. Keelty, Faolon and Dougal, gracefully bowed, lowering their heads to the ground. Ewan offered me a subtle smile, as well as a gentle nod to wish me well. The last pair of eyes I came across was Quinn's. Six days after Quinn's change in manner at the clearing, we still hadn't had a proper conversation with each other. Apart from the general *'Morning'* and awkward *'How are you?'* exchanges, we didn't share any words. Quinn's gaze differed from the others. It was a gaze of concern, like he cared for me greatly. When I finally managed to pull away my eyes from his, my heart decided to have a mind of its own. Nervous energy was bottling up inside me; the nerves too strong to suppress.

"I wonder what will happen."

"I can't believe I'm going to witness this!"

"I know she'll be okay."

"If only her mother were here to see this."

"I think she's nervous. She always looks like that when she is scared about something."

"I better tell her how I feel before she finds out by hearing my thoughts."

The thoughts of my family and friends devoured my ears! I couldn't distinguish the voices, but I had a suspicion of who said what.

When I turned to face the bridge, the voices stopped and the mist began to lift. The bridge creaked with my every step. Its railings were old tree trunks, with thick branches coiled around them. The thinner, coiling branches still bore leaves of the Oran-Roy tree. A black figure emerged from the lifting mist as I was almost across the bridge.

"Brianna Elsa," the approaching figure gently called. The voice was female; I assumed it was Donelle, an ancestor of mine.

"Donelle..."

Before answering, Donelle became completely visible; the mist no longer shielding her. She wore a black cloak with a hood that masked her face. No longer walking and now in full sight, Donelle's hands, covered by ornate, shimmery black gloves, lifted her hood. The hood unveiled long, toffee coloured, curly hair, framing a very pale, smooth face. Ruby red lips and a left brown eye and right green eye were striking against her fair complexion. A circle of flowers, resembling roses, rested upon her hair, with small, fluttering butterflies of many colours. The only word fit to describe Donelle's face was angelic.

"Follow me," she silently instructed, then turned around to face a long, stone stairway. In awe of what was about to happen, I wasn't able to move, but, once Donelle had gracefully travelled up a few steps, she turned around, silently inviting me to join her. The silent invitation seemed to convince my legs to move and I followed on. The stone steps were well imbedded into the smooth, green hillside. Venturing up the steps, a large object gradually came into focus, my sight fighting against the slow moving mist. As we continued our steady climb, I found myself walking under the large suspended branches of the Oran-Roy Tree.

As the mist began to lift, the afternoon sun's rays shimmered against the outline of the tree's leaves. As the light reflected against the silvery edges of the leaves, you could almost imagine the graceful sound that raindrops make when they hit glass. The tree created a shadow blanket over the entire hillside. Never before, had I seen a tree so large and beautiful, each branch abundant with thousands of leaves, reflecting thousands of silvery beams. Almost at the top of the hill, and at the heart of the tree, other figures in black cloaks like Donelle surrounded the stone path, each holding their hands together and bowing their heads. Their stance and peaceful countenance made me think of Ethan. *I bet he would say that these people looked like the Jedi's in Star Wars.*

When I walked past the other cloaked people, they followed on and walked directly behind me. Donelle finally stopped. We had reached the trunk of the tree. As the Morrigan book had described so well, the roots of the tree protruded from the earth and formed an arch under the body of the tree. Donelle proceeded on and walked down into the sacred space beneath the archway. I was finally here; I had finally reached the place where all the mixed blooded people of Oran-Roy were initiated. Above the archway, the words engraved on my bow - the words I had come to know from the Morrigan book - were carved deeply into the tree's bark.

Inside the archway, it was dark and there were more stone steps that guided me down to a body of water. The only way to reach the other side was by fully immersing, giving myself up to the cold water. I was about to leave behind all my insecurities. I was about to accept what was to come. I was about to be welcomed.

With the water now at my waist, I knew I had to submerge completely; the ground below me was too low for me to continue on foot. I took a deep breath, then gave in and dove into the chilly water. Below the water's surface, a young, male voice began to echo in and out of the surrounding space.

"Vos es verus. Vos es putus of pectus pectoris. Vos es fortis. Dare vestry donum tamen usquequaque subsist versus."

As my head broke the water's surface, the voice stopped. When I came into the light and left the archway, I realised that my dark green garments had turned white. My eyes quickly found Donelle, waiting patiently for me on another stone path. Her once black cloak and gloves were now white. I turned around to meet the other Druids that walked on behind me. Their black garments were similarly transformed. When I looked to meet Donelle, I realised that she wasn't wet, which made me quickly run my hands through my hair, then along my dress. I was dry. There was not a single drop of water on me!

"Brianna Elsa," Donelle softly announced, "you are ready to fulfil what has been entrusted to you. Before you achieve what lies before you, you will be guided by a past hero of Oran-Roy. When you entered the water, you were spoken to by Cuchulainn."

"Cuchulainn!" I cried. "He guided my parents and like you, is my ancestor."

"Yes, he is. He has been called again to serve you and to help you to fulfil that which only you can do."

"When will he come?"

"When he is needed most by you."

"And what is it that I must fulfil? Is it about Morrigan?"

"You will discover that for yourself, but, before you embark, one other will accompany you down to the shores of Breena. There is something you must receive there." Donelle raised her arm and invited me to join in sitting with her on a nearby stone. "Brianna, what do you believe you possess? What is your gift?"

"I ... it seems that I am able to send my thoughts to others and also hear their thoughts."

"That is true. But, in time, you will also come to possess something greater."

"So, in *some* time I'll come to know what that is."

"You will." Donelle looked down the hillside and saw everyone waiting for me. "Before you go to the shore, Brianna, I need to be certain that you understand the words spoken to you by Cuchulainn."

"You mean the words in Latin."

"Yes. Do you know what they mean for you?"

"Yes. My father reminded me that it means to remain true, to remain faithful and to not let my gift change what I know to be right."

"What your father speaks is true." Donelle smiled, before speaking again. "Remaining true and being faithful are powerful things." Donelle held my hands and looked into my eyes. "For many years I have been unable to use my gifts to service the needs of others." I quickly looked down at her gloved hands and realised to what she was referring. In the Morrigan book, Donelle was once capable of healing the sick, but, after Morrigan became aware of the love she and Cuchulainn had, she cursed her; her once healing hands, became hands that brought death. A tear seeped from her green eye. "I still have faith. Do not lose faith in those closest to you, Brianna." Donelle released my hands to wipe away her tears. "In time, we will speak again."

As I made my way down the stone steps, Donelle called my name again. "Brianna!"

I stopped and turned to face her. "Yes?"

"Please tell Cuchulainn vos es verus for me."

I smiled and was quickly drawn back to the Morrigan book. Vos es verus meant more than 'you are true' for Cuchulainn and Donelle. For them, it must have been like saying *I love you*; an alternative way of expressing how deeply they cared for one another.

"I will."

*

"So, she didn't say *anything* else to you? You didn't do *anything* else? I want *all* the details!" Charlotte cried oblivious to the fact that everyone was listening to our conversation.

"I've explained everything there is to explain," I stressed to her.

"Well," Craig said, "you mustn't wait any longer. You need to go down to the Breena shores as Donelle said." Craig looked amongst everyone, which seemed to give him an idea. "Quinn, accompany Brianna down to the shores. Your horse is the fastest and most reliable. If you leave now, you should be able to return here before sunset." *What is Craig thinking? Is he deliberately trying to get the two of us alone?*

"Uh ... why don't we *all* go?" *Was it too obvious that I was trying to avoid being alone with Quinn?* "I'm sure you'll all want to see what I'll be receiving."

"You heard that Donelle said *one* other, Brianna," Craig reinforced.

"Oh." The familiar feeling of blood rushing to my cheeks came. "Well ... uh ... shouldn't you come with me, father? Or, perhaps Zephan or Rona should fly me there?"

"Zephan and Rona are already searching for food along the river."

"Uh ... all right then." I wasn't in the position where I could hide my red face.

"Quinn's been to the Breena shores before. He's very familiar with the Breena clan." Craig was trying to convince me of his choice. He must have thought I didn't have much confidence in Quinn, but that wasn't the case.

"Well," I finally managed to pluck up the courage to face Quinn, who was avoiding me as he attended to his horse. "Let's go, Quinn." As I mentioned his name, his head quickly turned to face me.

"Very well," he replied awkwardly.

Quinn mounted his horse and then offered me his arm without looking at me directly. Grudgingly, I held his arm and allowed him to pull me up onto his horse. Charlotte offered me a look of, *'you'll be alright'*, in contrast with Ethan, who was trying not to laugh and most probably was thinking, *'sucked in!'* If only I was able to use my ability whenever I liked, because I would have been sharing a few stern words with him!

Quinn tightened his grip around the reigns and slowly rode down into the nearby woodland, which I assumed to be the borders of the Breena clan. No longer in sight and in earshot of our party, Quinn reverted back to the Quinn I encountered in the clearing six days ago.

"Hold onto me, Brianna. We'll be venturing down a large slope soon and you'll need to have a secure hold, so that you don't fall."

I slowly wrapped my arms around Quinn's waist. Once my hands were clenched together, Quinn removed his left hand from the reigns and placed it over my hands. His touch made me jump. The sensation I felt six days ago occurred again. I couldn't deny that the feeling was pleasant, but I didn't want to develop a liking for him if I didn't know how he truly felt. Never having been in a serious relationship before, I wasn't sure how to go about this. Do I make him bring everything to the table, so I know what to expect, or do I just go with it, without discussing anything, assuming that everything will reveal itself when the time is right? We remained silent for a few minutes, until I decided to break the silence. I had to know what he was thinking! If only the gift I had was able to come and go as I pleased!

"Quinn?"

"Yes," he replied, very casually, making me change what I had intended on asking him.

"How are you so familiar with Breena? Isn't it too dangerous to venture to clans beyond your own by yourself?"

"The entire time you have been here, as well as before you arrived, we have been travelling in a large group. A large group makes us more susceptible to danger as we're easily spotted..."

"I know that! But, we have safety in numbers at least. You didn't answer me, why do you know Breena so well?"

It took Quinn a few moments to collect his thoughts before answering. I patiently waited, not wanting to frustrate him to the point where he would refuse to answer me. "Many years ago, my ... my sister was taken from our home in Cathal."

"That ... that's terrible. Did you go after her in Breena?"

"I have searched everywhere. Breena is only one of the clans I have searched."

"It must have been dangerous," I assumed. "Is ... is that how you got your...?" Quinn sensed where this conversation was heading, so he ignored my question.

"Hold on!" He cried. I tightened my hold around Quinn's waist as he raced the horse down the sloping land. Through the surrounding trees, I was able to make out the setting sun's reflection on the sea. We were close.

"How much further?" I struggled to ask, bouncing up and down on the horses' back.

"A fair while," Quinn replied abruptly. He seemed too occupied in riding us safely down the steep slope to maintain a decent conversation, so I remained quiet.

After many silent minutes of making our way down the rugged hillside of Breena, an open field came into sight. Large rocks were scattered throughout the tall, thin grass of the field. As we approached the edge of the field, the coastline of Breena appeared, the ocean water crashing against the shore and churning up the fine, white sand. Quinn rode along the edge of the field until the hill began to slope down towards the shoreline. When we reached the sand, he stopped the horse and offered out his arm to help me down. He dismounted in a single smooth motion and then looked at me, expecting a response.

"So ..." I said rather awkwardly.

"We're here," Quinn informed me, despite me realising that already.

"Yes, funnily enough, I realised that."

"Well, where to from here?"

"I ..." *Why did he suddenly seem to think I had all the answers?* "I don't know!"

"Where did Donelle tell you to go?" he calmly asked.

"She ... she just said to come to the Breena shores."

"All right then." Quinn hung his cloak over his horses' saddle and removed his boots.

"Uh ... do we have to go into the water?" I sounded so incredibly stupid.

"We're walking along sand, Brianna. It's much easier to do that in bare feet."

"Right." I also removed my cloak and Converse sneakers to make the walk along the sand an easier one.

The sun was almost meeting the horizon. To pass the time away as we waited for whatever it was to which Donelle had referred, Quinn and I walked along the wet sand. Walking in silence was too uncomfortable to put up with, so I thought I'd initiate conversation. Besides, if Quinn liked me, I needed to learn more about him in some capacity.

"Quinn, you mentioned your sister earlier and I was wondering whether..."

"I don't want to speak of that now." He quickly brushed my effort aside.

"All right!" I raised my hands, surrendering that subject until he was ready to tell me. In that moment, I realised one key quality about Quinn. Provoking him only made it harder to hear what you wanted to hear - a very difficult thing for me to accept, being an incredibly impatient person.

"So..."

"I'm sorry about how I made you feel ... in the clearing, Brianna," Quinn quickly blurted out. I was taken aback by his comment.

"Uh ... are you referring to when you were rude and distant with me in front of everyone since I've been here, or when you caught me off guard when I was alone practising?" I was surprised with myself. In light of the nervous energy I was feeling, I didn't think I'd be capable of saying so much with such confidence. It seemed that I also surprised Quinn. He didn't expect me to respond as I did.

"Well, I ... I'm..."

"Because," I spoke over him, "I accept your apology for making me feel inadequate in front of everyone since I've been here, but, if you're apologising for helping me in the clearing ... there's no need to apologise." My voice lowered as I came to finish what I was saying. So far throughout this conversation, we gazed ahead along the Breena shore; our eyes never met.

"You mean ... you didn't mind how I helped you?" Quinn sounded bewildered.

"No," I quickly admitted. "To my distaste, I ... I think I actually ... enjoyed it." I looked over my left shoulder at the water, hoping that if Quinn did turn to face me, he wouldn't be able to see my red face.

"So, does that mean you ... do you ... do you like me, Brianna?" As mysterious and confusing as Quinn was, I was attracted to him. My feelings and the way I reacted justified that conclusion. I avoided him to avoid the risk of being hurt again, but now it was clear that the person I was fond of seemed to be fond of me. Despite this, I didn't want to be the first to admit attraction, in case I had greatly misjudged things.

"Do you like me?" I quickly asked, still not looking at Quinn directly.

Quinn was the braver one. "Ever since you arrived," he admitted.

So Ethan was right!

As my mind was racing back to replay all of our encounters, I remained silent. This worried Quinn and in case he felt that I didn't hear him the first time, he clarified his words.

"I ... I like you ... a lot, Brianna."

I decided to ease his nerves as a result of my hesitation. "Well, I ... I feel the same, Quinn." *Wow!*

Quinn's left hand clasped my right forearm, making me quickly turn to look up and face him. I was right, Quinn was the braver one; he made the effort to look first. "Well," he said, with a smile forming on his face.

"Well," I also smiled. "If we both feel as we do, we'll ... we should get to know each other a bit more. What do you say?"

Quinn didn't answer me. His attention was drawn away by a large wave crashing into the sand further along the shore. "Quickly!" he urged me, still holding my arm. We ran down to meet where the sound had come from, but the water was still. As the evening sun touched the ocean, the water along the shore retreated back to the ocean, like water being sucked down a drain. The shore was bare; almost as if the sand spooked the water. But suddenly, the crashing sound returned. The fleeing water was now a raging wave. The wave finally collapsed against the shore and something broke through the water.

A black stallion stood on its hind legs and released a triumphant cry. Effortlessly, the horse leapt amongst the tumultuous, white waves to find the shore. The stallion's eyes sought out Quinn and me along the shore. It gracefully galloped towards us; flicking up chunks of white sand as its hooves dug into the beach. The horse's wispy, black hair flew through the wind as it made its way toward us. As it came to a steady stop, the horse lowered its head. I went to pat it, but Quinn blocked me with his left arm.

"Careful," he warned me, but I knew that we were not in any danger. This wasn't a wild, untamed horse. This was Epona; the horse that was offered to Cuchulainn and, now, she was being given to me, to fulfil that of which I would come to know of in time.

"This is Epona, Quinn," I moved his arm aside and gently stroked Epona's cheek, then ran my fingers through her black mane. "She was Cuchulainn's horse and Donelle told me that Cuchulainn will be my guardian, when the time is right."

"*The* Cuchulainn!"

"Yes."

"Well, can you speak to Epona, like you can with Keelty and the others?"

"I don't think so. Epona's not from Daray. I can only speak to the animals born there." I continued to stroke Epona, still amazed by her impressive entrance. Quinn came closer to Epona and then stroked her smooth neck. Never before had I seen a horse with such power and grace. I was certain that Quinn would say the same.

"Brianna, there won't be much light soon. We should probably head back," Quinn advised.

"You're right." We turned around and headed back to the grassy hillside, where Quinn had left his horse. Loyally, Epona followed on closely behind me, just as Lulu or Tess would do back home. I felt comforted to know that she would be by my side, helping in whatever awaited me. After putting our shoes and cloaks back on, Quinn was about to mount his horse, but something made him hesitate.

"Do you want my saddle to ride Epona back?"

"Uh ... thank you, but, I have a feeling I'll be alright." I walked by Epona, ready to ride her, but something was stopping me. *I can see why Quinn offered me the saddle now. How on earth can I ride Epona if I can't get on her?* Whether Quinn heard my thoughts, or not, he knew what I was thinking, which explained why he crouched down and clasped his hands together. I stepped on his hands and held onto Epona's mane. Quinn raised me up, high enough so that I could comfortably reach Epona's back.

"Thanks," I said, looking down at Quinn.

Quinn smiled and then mounted his horse. "Well, would you like to lead the way now that you have a horse?"

"You know I don't know the way back. How 'bout we follow you?" Again, Quinn smiled. I think he was trying to be friendly, yet funny at the same time.

The sun, now slowly sinking below the horizon, made the ride back to the Oran-Roy clan a speedy one by necessity. Epona comfortably matched the pace of Quinn's horse, as we rode through the Breena woodlands. Holding onto Epona without a saddle, made the journey slightly uncomfortable, but not murder.

Even though I was without a reign to control her, Epona moved in accordance with what I thought or told her. Despite this, I still missed riding with a saddle and, as soon as I reached camp, a saddle was the first thing I would seek, even before the evening meal.

Suddenly, Quinn came to an abrupt stop and left his horse. "We're here." Quinn stood by Epona, waiting to assist me off her back. I liked his gentlemanly ways; all this chivalry made me feel like I had gone back in time. I swung my right leg over, so that both my legs were resting on Epona's left side. Quinn held out his arms and supported my waist. As I slid down Epona, I needed to place my hands on Quinn's shoulders. Slowly and very gracefully, I floated down to the ground. Everything seemed slower as I looked up into his green eyes. I was living a cliché!

Despite how much I was enjoying Quinn holding me, I wasn't ready for us to progress beyond this point. My arms fell from his shoulders and my eyes fell with them. "We better go and show everyone then."

I headed on forward and Epona trotted on behind me.

"Brianna!" Quinn cried, as he ran to catch up. "I'm sorry that I didn't answer your question about my sister and my ... my scar."

"It's alright. I just figured that you would tell me when the time was right."

"Good ... uh ... very well, then."

Together, we silently walked back to where Craig had said they would be setting up camp. This time, the silent walk wasn't awkward; rather, it was a comforting silence. I found myself just happy being in Quinn's presence, whether we shared words or not.

When we reached the place of our departure, no one was there! There were no signs of people having been here at all! Had something happened?

"Quinn! *Where* is everyone?" I cried, panicked and jumped to the worst conclusion, like I normally tended to do. I turned around, but no one was in sight! I raised my hands to my head, fearing the worst!

"Now, don't panic! I'm sure everyone is fine!"

"But where are they? What's happened? ... Where are they?"

Chapter Fifteen

Clashes & Celebrations

I ran up the stone steps leading up to the Oran-Roy tree, trying to see if I could get a better view of the surrounding area. When I felt high up enough, I turned around to scan the bottom of the hill. With the moon as my only source of light, I struggled to make out anything, apart from the silhouettes of the large overhanging trees circling the field and Quinn standing by the horses at the base of the hill.

Why isn't Quinn concerned? His lack of worry gave me an inkling that he wasn't being completely honest with me. This thought calmed me, so I continued to pursue it. Whether Quinn was, or wasn't hiding something from me, this possibility was keeping my mind from jumping to agonising conclusions.

Quickly making my way back down the stone steps, something caught my eye. A light flickered amongst a mass of shrubs beside the bridge over the Rona River.

"Quinn! Over there!" I cried, pointing in the direction of the wavering light, as I met him at the base of the hill.

"What?" He replied, raising his arms, trying to appear confused.

"Follow me."

Without delay, I pursued the light by the bridge at a rapid pace. As I ran, I could hear the hooves of Epona and Quinn's horse following close behind me. The mist in the near distance meant that I was close to the Rona River, but I still hadn't found the source of the light. Eventually, I came across large shrubs that bordered a small woodland dwelling. As I parted the leaves of the shrubs, the light revealed itself. The small parting I managed to make was not large enough for the horses to pass through, so Quinn left his horse and followed me into the dwelling.

"SURPRISE!"

Immediately, I was swarmed upon by all of the familiar people I had come to know over the past weeks in Oran-Roy. Joyous music was being played; traditional Celtic celebratory music filled the atmosphere, in the form of fiddles, pan flutes and drums. The centre of the dwelling had a roaring fire and the surrounding shrubs and trees were decorated with golden lanterns. Shocked, I almost fell back into the shrubs! Struggling to maintain my ground, Quinn, from behind, placed his hands on my shoulders and ushered me forward to meet the gathering of people. The bellowing 'surprise' confirmed my suspicion; Quinn had kept the secret well.

As Quinn steered me forward, I found Ethan and Charlotte's smiling faces amongst the crowd. Still bewildered by the surprise, I wasn't sure whether I was smiling at them or still looking shell-shocked. Continuing on through the mass of people, I recognised some of my father's men, as well as Rona, Zephan and Leona, all smiling and congratulating me. Quinn continued to urge me forward, but, when we reached the fire at the heart of the decorative dwelling, I found my father waiting for me. Quinn released my shoulders and joined Ewan, who was also standing by the fire. My father raised his arms. The music slowly faded and the people became quiet.

"My daughter, Brianna has been welcomed into Oran-Roy!" The crowd cheered as my father paused. The attention was very overwhelming.

"With her return, our cause has become stronger." Again, people responded by cheering. "So, tonight, we officially welcome you among us." Craig removed his sword from his side and raised it triumphantly. Rather than cheering, all those with swords followed my father. In this moment of silence, everything was justified. I was finally filling that empty place that had always existed in my heart. I knew who I was born to be.

Craig lowered his sword and met my eyes. "Welcome." Craig bowed his head and then knelt down. As those in the front lowered their heads and knelt down, the pattern continued. It was a domino effect and in only a few seconds, everyone before me was at their knees. Goosebumps arose along my skin and the cool night air wasn't responsible. When Craig returned to standing, he rested his hand over my right shoulder, brushed my curly hair aside from my face and kissed my forehead.

"Welcome home." The music erupted and the crowd burst into activity! A circle formed around the fire and people started to dance. "Well," Craig said, "I'm sure you have a lot to share with your friends. Go and celebrate!"

I did as my father said. All I wanted to do was find Ethan and Charlotte and take them to meet Epona, although that wasn't *all* I wanted to share with them.

*

"Wait! Say that again! I couldn't hear you over the music!" Charlotte cried, fighting against the tremendous noise of beating drums and overzealous singers.

"Come closer!" I suggested. Once she was sitting beside me, I continued. "What I said was that Quinn said he liked me."

"Oh my God! I knew it!"

"Shush! I don't want anyone to..."

"Who is going to hear us in all this commotion?" Charlotte had a valid point, but I couldn't help but be careful - it was in my nature.

Ethan, sitting on my other side wasn't surprised at all. "I told you so, didn't I, Bee?"

"Yeah, yeah," I casually brushed him aside.

"So," Charlotte begged, dying to hear more, "you're a couple? Is it an official thing?"

"Well, we ... we've admitted how we both feel, but ... but I suggested that we need to learn more about each other. So ... so I guess if he is truly genuine about his feelings, he'll tell me what he has failed to share with me so far."

"All right! All right! Enough of this! I want to ride Epona, Bee!" Ethan clearly had heard enough of this topic. "When are you going to let me ride her?"

"How's first thing tomorrow?"

Ethan didn't have the chance to answer, as we were joined by Leona, Ewan and Quinn, each holding an extra glass.

"I'm sure you're all in need of a drink!" Leona assumed, as she found a seat beside Ethan and offered him a glass.

"Thanks a million," Ethan didn't hesitate.

Ewan offered Charlotte his extra glass and Quinn offered me his.

"Thanks," Charlotte and I gladly welcomed the drinks. After a minute or so of awkward silence, despite the occasional slurping noises, Ewan decided to ease the tension.

"None of you have danced yet!"

"Well, there's a reason for that," I quickly answered.

"Why's that?"

"I'm not the dancing sort."

"... And what of Ethan and Charlotte. Are you two the *dancing sorts*?" Ewan's cheeky tone made all those present chuckle.

"I like dancing," Charlotte eventually managed to admit. "But, I'm afraid I'm the only one out of us three who does."

"In that case," Ewan placed his glass on the nearby stump and offered his arm to Charlotte, "Show me how *well* you dance." Charlotte's expression made it clear that she was keen to dance. I took her glass and encouraged her to go. Ethan wasn't too impressed by Charlotte's choice. Leona detected his sombre mood and very untraditionally, stood before Ethan and imitated Ewan, by offering him her arm.

"Dear, *kind*, sir, can I interest you in a dance? Show *me* how well *you* dance!" Leona's face was beaming. It seemed that her spontaneity and cheeky ways had an influence over Ethan.

"One can't hurt!" Ethan gave into Leona's charm and they made their way to the dancing circle formed around the fire.

After Ewan and Leona's offers, Quinn felt obliged to ask me, but I could tell he was only asking because he thought that I felt left out. Quinn was about to stand, but before he had the chance to speak I looked at him directly and said, "It's all right. I have a feeling that you hate to dance just as much as I do." As he sat back down, I continued. "Don't feel that you have to ask me just because the others were asked. It's okay, really."

"Well ... you assume correctly. I don't dance and don't think I *ever* will." This was the first time I saw Quinn laughing in a relaxed way. We were becoming comfortable around one another and I liked it.

"Tell me, Quinn, you knew all along that they were putting together this party, didn't you?"

Before answering, Quinn tried to refrain from smirking. "I did."

"Well, you're good at keeping something secret. I've never been good at hiding a secret or how I feel."

"I know." Quinn's certainty took me aback.

"How do you know?"

"I'm not saying that it's a bad thing, Brianna."

"Sorry, that came out wrong. I ... I didn't think you were making fun of me ... I just ... I'm shocked that you've picked that up. Is ... is it that obvious?"

"Well, what I have noticed is when you say something, but you feel differently, your eyes look down and you make an interesting expression. You..."

"What?" I laughed.

"You ... you slant your eyebrows and blink peculiarly. Your eyes seem to roll as you look down." Continuing laughing gave Quinn reason to further explain. "It's ... it's hard to describe, but I noticed that very soon after I met you." Quinn continued to look at me, waiting for me to respond, but I didn't know how to!

"I ... I don't know what to say!" I admitted while laughing.

"Well ... now that I've made you feel a little embarrassed, I give you my consent to return the favour."

"I ... I can't think of anything!"

Quinn had a sip of his drink and then casually replied through a sigh, "Ah, I must be perfect then."

"I like the funny Quinn," I admitted. "I know Leona calls you Quiet Quinn. But, now that I know you a little better, I can see that you're not quiet at all. You're funny and interesting." My compliment made Quinn look away. I had embarrassed him. "There! I did find something to embarrass you with!"

"What?" He casually replied, raising his hands in confusion.

"I just complimented you and you became bashful. You don't like it when people compliment you! You're humble and that is a very nice quality to have."

"Yes, I am very proud of my humility!" Quinn beamed.

"... And witty, too!" I added.

Again, following another compliment, Quinn acted as he did before, looking away and running his fingers through his hair. "See! You just did it again!"

Quinn laughed. "I ... I did, didn't I?"

"You did." I smiled.

While talking with Quinn, we were in own private world and I completely forgot about the others dancing! As I looked over to the fire, no one was there and I realised that the music had stopped. Everyone was preparing to sleep!

"I ... I didn't realise how late it was!" Quinn looked around the dwelling and seemed equally surprised.

"Yes, it is late," he agreed. "People must be wanting an early night in preparation for tomorrow." Quinn stood up, ready to leave.

"Wait, what's tomorrow?"

"Following tonight's celebration, we carry out a tournament in the morning."

"A tournament! What ever for?"

"It's just for fun, Brianna. It's a game we call *Diúracaim agus rithim.*"

"Which means?"

"Shoot and run."

"... Sounds pretty violent."

"No, no. Don't worry; you'll see what it is in the morning."

"So, you're competing in it?" Quinn was about to answer, but Ewan joined us and he answered on Quinn's behalf.

"Quinn is the current champion. I've come close a few times, but he *always* seems to win."

"Really?" I replied in a curious way.

"Well ... well I..."

"He's the best person I know at *Diúracaim agus rithim.* Which means..." Ewan yanked Quinn by the arm and made him walk away, "He needs his sleep, because he needs to defend his title."

"Uh, all right then," I said.

"... Night!" Ewan cried while stealing Quinn away.

Quinn looked back and smiled. I couldn't help but smile back.

As I lay down to sleep, fatigue didn't seem to set in. I was running high on adrenalin after the evening's festivities. In one day, I had been welcomed into Oran-Roy by Donelle, admitted my feelings to Quinn, he had done the same, received a horse from the ocean, been surprised by a celebration to officially welcome me and had a strange, yet, wonderful conversation with Quinn. Mulling over the wonderful experiences, guilt released its wrath upon me, spoiling any happiness I was feeling. *Mam and Dad must be going insane at home! Here I am having a wonderful time, discovering where I'm from and building new relationships while my parents are in turmoil!*

The uneasy thoughts brought on by the guilt, also made me consider the remaining agonising questions that were yet to be answered. *Was Ethan still interested in Charlotte? Why did I see Quinn in a dream before meeting him? Is my unknown ability seeing the future? Did the carrier and Morrigan book come to me from Dallas Conlan; the man we suspected to be Zia's friend residing in Ireland? What does the piece of parchment I received from Leona on the morning of my arrival in Oran-Roy mean; what is its purpose? Would I ever come to meet my brother, Brogan, and my mother, Keira, under Cillian's regime? Who were the Kaelin people referring to when they said that I could put a stop to a death?*

My mind wasn't switching off! There was too much to consider! There were too many things that I still needed to know! Despite not knowing a great deal and being unsatisfied by this, I decided to let the positives outweigh the negatives. I needed my sleep. To put my mind at ease, I recalled Quinn's chivalry and how he smiled at me. I remembered how he felt as he helped me off Epona. Through my imaginings, the tiredness managed to seep in and I fell asleep, greatly anticipating what awaited Quinn and me the next day.

*

"No! Don't wake her up! Maybe she had trouble sleeping! Just let her rest!"

"Charlotte! I know she wouldn't want to miss this and she would have a go at us if we let her sleep through it!"

Before opening my eyes, my morning was ushered in by Ethan and Charlotte's arguing. I decided to end their debate and meet them outside my tent.

"Don't worry," I said through a yawn. "I'm awake."

"Well then, you better get ready," Ethan advised.

"Why? What's the rush?"

"Bee, the tournament! It's starting in the next few minutes!"

"Oh yeah!" I hurried back into my tent and picked up the first pieces of clothing I could find, quickly got dressed, went by the fire and scoffed up some breakfast left for me by Charlotte, then made my way to the open ground at the base of hill near the Oran-Roy tree, where the tournament was meant to take place. Eventually, Ethan, Charlotte and I managed to find Ewan and Quinn in the crowd. At this stage, all we could see were two large, tall wooden stands. Each stand had a horizontal panel at the top, with ten or more ropes dangling from it.

"So," I said standing next to Quinn, trying to get his attention, "you'll have to explain the rules so I can follow."

"You see the thin ropes hanging from the beam of wood...?"

"Yeah..."

"Well, an apple will be hooked onto each rope. Now, look over to your right." Quinn pointed to a set of two markers on the ground. "See these two dirt markings...?"

"Yeah..."

"They indicate where each competitor starts and finishes. Behind each marker, you'll see a crate. The crate is for..."

"... The apples, I'm assuming."

"Yes."

"So, how does one get the apples into the crates?"

"Well, from one's horse, the competitor has to remain behind their marker and make the apples fall from the ropes. Now, they do this by shooting the ropes, so that the apple falls."

"What happens if you hit the apple?" I enquired.

"Well, you may get lucky, but, hitting the apples is normally messy ... you may have to pick up a lot of pieces!" Quinn was smugly amused.

"...Point taken. What happens when the apples fall?"

"Once the apples have fallen, the rider can retrieve them and place them into the crate. The competitor with the most apples in his crate..."

"... Or her crate."

Quinn rolled his eyes. "Then, in his, or her, crate, is the winner."

"That's it!" It didn't sound as spectacular and as grand as what I expected. When I heard the word tournament, my mind immediately thought of jousting and sword fighting!

"It's very complicated," Quinn assured me.

"How so?"

"There are a number of strategies to consider. Should you aim to have all the apples off first and then collect them to place in the crate, or do you collect them one at a time to ensure that you have more apples in the crate, rather than more apples on the ground?"

"All right, there is strategy involved," I admitted. "Well, when are you competing?"

"Well, there's no set order. Whoever's ready competes and those who are the best continue. But, in saying that, I still should go and prepare my horse and bows." Quinn turned around, making his way out of the crowd.

"Good luck, then!" Wishing him well made him turn around to face me again.

"Will you be cheering me on, Brianna?" He had a cheeky smirk on his face.

"That depends who you are competing against!"

He said no more, but left me with another smile.

*

"Do you think this is as exciting as soccer, Ethan?" I jokingly asked.

"Riveting," he replied in a very sarcastic tone.

"Oh, come on! It's pretty interesting!"

"It's all right, but nowhere near as exciting as the EPL."

Attending to bringing us some drinks, Charlotte finally returned, carefully making her way through the passionate crowd with the drinks in hand.

"Did I miss anything exciting?" Charlotte queried.

"Not really," I assured her, "but I think Quinn is competing again once they set up for the next one."

"So, then," Charlotte's tone was cheeky, "You'll be cheering him on again I suppose." She nudged my shoulder as she took a sip from her glass.

"Well, yeah." To avoid any more speculative comments about Quinn and me, I decided to make conversation with Ethan again. "You're not going to have a go, Ethan?"

"Are you serious? I'll make a moron out of myself! Besides, Quinn's beaten Ewan and half of your father's men! What makes you think that I want to look like a thick mot?"

"A *thick mot?* I'll take that as a no then."

The tournament horn blew again, which meant that the next competitors would be taking their places.

"Yeah, Quinn is up again! Look!" I cried, pointing at him making his way onto the designated field.

Quinn led his horse to the marker closest to our side of the crowd. He mounted his horse and carried out a final check over his bow and arrow; conducted in the same manner each time he competed. The other competitor was Kieran; one of my father's men from Crag. He was much bigger than Quinn and appeared very intimidating, but Quinn wasn't intimidated in the least! He seemed calm and together, trying to focus on the task ahead. My father, Craig, the timer and starter of the race, held a small hourglass in his left hand and a green cloth in his right hand, which he raised up, to signal the competitors, then lowered, to indicate the start of the race.

As Craig raised the green cloth in the air, the crowd drew silent, greatly anticipating the race ahead. Before the cloth was lowered, Quinn quickly scanned the crowd, trying to find me. For his previous races, he wasn't able to find me amongst the crowd. Searching for me, his face was serious. Over the past few weeks in Oran-Roy, I discovered that when Quinn was tense or sombre, the scar across his face became prominent, but when he was relaxed and content, his warm presence almost faded away the scar. As his eyes interlocked with mine, his expression changed. When he smiled, I no longer saw Quinn, the young man with the scar across his face, I saw Quinn, the young man I found myself being drawn to more and more each day.

Quinn returned his focus back to my father. Quinn and Kieran prepared an arrow for release. Craig felt that the players were ready, so he lowered his arm and threw the cloth to the ground. Quinn's arrow was released first and had successfully shot off an apple. Kieran's first attempt missed, but he succeeded with his second shot. After Quinn had made six apples fall, there was less than one minute to go. He charged his horse down his lane, slid across his horse, hooked his left foot onto the front of his saddle, allowing his body to hang off the side of the horse, quickly grasped the apples without even leaving the horse and then raced back to his marker, throwing the apples into the crate, while still some metres away. Kieran had only made three apples fall, but he knew that time was running out and he had no choice but to collect his few apples and place them in his crate. Throughout the race, I refrained from cheering. I was nervous for Quinn and the last thing I wanted to do was call out his name and distract him; although, amongst the music and cries coming from the crowd, he probably wouldn't have been able to hear me anyway.

"Twenty seconds to go!" Craig blared, which made Quinn pick up his pace drastically. Even though he had seven apples in the crate, four ahead of Kieran, for the time remaining, Quinn competed as though he was the losing player! The crowd, counting down the seconds, seemed to urge Quinn on! In those final seconds, Quinn shot his eighth apple, retrieved it and threw it into his crate from at least fifteen metres away! As his apple hit the rim of the crate and fell in, my father cried, "Time's up!" The crowd grew wild; cheering, screaming and chanting Gaelic songs with the help of Celtic pipes and flutes, fiddles and drums! It was a magnificent site! I couldn't recall a time when I had witnessed such a jovial crowd!

Once Quinn had left his horse, Craig approached him and raised his arm, declaring him the winner.

"Yes!" I cried, fist pumping the air.

"He was *so* good!" Charlotte commented.

"Yeah, he was okay," Ethan admitted in a very bitter tone.

"QU-INN! QU-INN! QU-INN! QU-INN!" The crowd chanted. Like his usual humble self, Quinn displayed a subtle smile and avoided looking up at the crowd. When the cheering gradually diminished, Craig began to address the crowd.

"Who will be our next competitor? Who believes that they have what it takes to defeat our champion?" The crowd hushed amongst themselves, but no one was coming forward. "Let's not be so cowardly! Who believes that they are capable? Come forward!" Unlike the previous challenges, the crowd was still. No one was coming forward.

"I could put my hand up," I thought to myself. *"Quinn's going to beat me anyway, but at least it would be fun, wouldn't it?"*

"I will," I silently announced, hidden within the crowd.

"Who said that?" Craig asked. Before answering, I passed Ethan my glass and checked his and Charlotte's expressions; both had their mouths wide open in shock.

"Bee!" Ethan hushed harshly to me. "He'll thrash you! Do you want to be embarrassed?"

"It's just for fun!" I insisted, but as I gently pushed past people, I began to grow nervous; the silence of the crowd made me feel uneasy, making me regret my decision. Finally free from the crowd and in the open space for all to see, I addressed my father. "I'll play against him." Even though my voice wasn't shaking, I was extremely nervous; this was one of the few times where my feelings were not so obvious. Members of the crowd chuckled amongst each other, probably making fun of me, which only made me think, *I'll show them!*

"Well," Craig said, "many of you would argue that I am biased; however, I would argue that this young lady has offered a challenge more convincingly than any other of our previous competitors." The laughs coming from the crowd very quickly turned into whispers, following my father's kind words. "We are celebrating her initiation as a hero after all, so, Brianna has every right to compete in this event, if she so desires."

When I turned to face Quinn, I was unsure what to make of his expression; he seemed confused and tense all at once. *Was he nervous, or just shocked by my challenge?*

"So, uh ... are you scared?" I jokingly asked him, trying to break the ice. Quinn's uncertainty made me feel anxious and I didn't know what to make of it.

Before answering, Quinn approached me and lowered his head to whisper into my ear. "Are you *sure* you want to do this?" His question angered me.

"You're just like those people who were making fun of me!"

"No, no! I'm just saying ..."

"No! All I wanted to do was to have a go! Is there anything wrong with that?"

Quinn remained silent.

"There's nothing wrong in having a go! I'm ... I'm not embarrassed! *Epona!*" I yelled as loud as I could, and then whistled after her. "Besides," I continued as I placed a saddle over Epona's back, "*You* were my trainer. Don't you want to see how the training paid off?"

Again, Quinn remained silent, but this time, he moved aside and raised his arms, surrendering. Now that it was obvious to the crowd that we would be competing, the small whispers and doubtful remarks became cheers and chants.

"What am I doing?" I thought to myself, as I mounted Epona. *"No! Don't doubt yourself! It's always good to have a go! Besides, what's the worst that can happen? I lose and Quinn remains champion.*

Craig took his place between the two lanes, ready to begin the race. As he raised the green cloth, I turned to my right to face Quinn and discovered that he had also turned to face me.

"May the best man ... sorry ... may the best person win?" *Was Quinn's stammer from nerves, or was he genuinely trying to be funny?*

I simply nodded rather than talking, fearful that my nerves, as well as my annoyance in Quinn, would come across if I spoke. I quickly returned my attention back to Craig, then realised that I didn't have my bow and arrows! I was about to dismount from Epona to retrieve them, when I was stopped by Ewan; he was standing beside Epona with my bow and a collection of arrows in hand.

"Thanks," I sounded out of breath and the race still hadn't begun!

"Don't be nervous, Brianna," Ewan kindly advised, "Have fun! Oh, and by the way, if you do beat him, don't let him live it down, all right?" I was certain that Ewan knew I would lose, but I appreciated his take on the situation. At least he didn't doubt me in an obvious manner!

I smiled. "Alright, but I don't think that will be the outcome."

With my heart pumping tumultuously, I was reminded to recall Ewan's advice – *don't be nervous*. Ewan was right! There was nothing to be nervous about! I was having fun and there was nothing wrong with me taking up a challenge I knew I was going to lose!

Our arrows ready for release, Craig lowered his arm and threw the green cloth to the ground! The race had begun. Quinn's first shot was successful, which confirmed that he wasn't going to go easy on me. It took me three attempts to successfully shoot a rope, but in that time, Quinn had made three apples fall! Surprisingly, my nerves seemed to leave me as I made my first apple fall! Preparing for my next shot, the advice Quinn gave me that day in the clearing came to me - *keep your back arched, it will make it easier for you to align your chin with your left shoulder. When you pull, your elbow should slide horizontally.* Another apple fell to the floor! Preparing my next arrow, I tried to glance over at Quinn without him noticing; he had only made one apple fall in the time I had made two apples fall! Quinn seemed flustered, which made me question, was he performing badly, or, was I outperforming him?

"One minute remaining!" Craig yelled. The crowd was roaring; their chants and screams a great deal louder than they were before!

"Come on, Bee! You've got nothing to lose! Give it all you've got!" I encouraged myself, as I stretched my bow, ready to release my next arrow. Again, my aim was perfect! Another apple met the ground, only giving me more confidence to crack on! Preparing my next arrow, I managed to peek over to Quinn's lane; there were still only four apples on the ground! But, for his next attempt, Quinn was successful and he now had five apples on the ground.

"Come on, Bee! Only three more and you're in front!"

A clean shot!

"Only two more apples, Bee!" I had never felt so competitive, which made me question, was I doing this to have fun, or, did I want to prove a point after being ridiculed?

"Thirty seconds to go!" Craig cried.

Preparing my next arrow, again, gave me the chance to glance over to Quinn's lane; there were still five apples on the ground. It then occurred to me, rather than attempting to make another two apples fall, I should only try for one more; that way, I would be certain of having five apples in the crate before time ran out!

I extended my bow and released my arrow. Another clean shot! Before the apple even made contact with the ground, I was already driving Epona down the lane. When I reached the apples, I thought about attempting Quinn's technique of not leaving your horse to reduce some time, but Quinn was still behind the marker of his lane. With that time to spare, I leapt off Epona, gathered the apples and held them within the first layer of my dress. I mounted Epona carefully, ensuring that I wouldn't lose any apples on my way up and charged Epona down the lane, passing Quinn riding up his own lane to retrieve his five apples.

"He may have the same number of apples, but, if I get there first, I'll probably win! There can't be much time left!"

Almost half way down the lane, the surrounding sounds amplified then quickly faded to an eerie *almost* silence. The noises coming from the crowd, while still audible, seemed distant and subdued, replaced by a more distinct set of voices that were competing to be heard, but one very familiar voice rose above the throng...

"I can't believe I'm going to lose! Why did I get distracted? I'm better than this! I don't want her to lose, but if I lose, what will they think of me? I'll be ridiculed! Perhaps she'll miss the crate! Just hurry up and you could still win!"

"Ten seconds remaining!"

Hearing Quinn's unsettling thoughts changed my intentions. Rushing past the crate, I hurriedly directed all five apples towards its mouth, in the sure knowledge that such a reckless release would cause at least one miss. Quinn raced past and released his five apples into his crate with an expertise honed through endless repetition.

"Times up!" Craig announced.

Two of my apples had escaped my crate as planned. With only three apples in my crate and five in Quinn's, he was the winner.

After quickly assessing the crates, Craig approached Quinn, now standing beside his horse, and raised his arm. The crowd's reaction was mixed; some were roaring and singing; others were stunned, with expressions of complete bafflement!

"She almost had him!"

"I can't believe I doubted her!"

"What a challenge that turned out to be!"

"If only she had taken more time!"

"Poor Quinn was almost beaten by a girl!"

With crowd members' thoughts rushing through my head, I wanted to escape and be surrounded by only silence. Walking to the quiet and abandoned dwelling, I questioned my actions.

You lost because you felt sorry for him! Admit it! If you had won, that would have made things really awkward! There's no way he'd want to be with you if you had beaten him! Besides, you know he's heaps better than you. It was probably a combination of being tired, as well as being shocked by your decision to compete that made him perform badly.

Finally alone, and in my tent within the camp, I tried to accept why I acted as I did.

"I felt sorry for him," I admitted out loud to myself.

Suddenly, a wave of tiredness swept over me; competing in the race, with the considerable build up of adrenalin that it produced, and hearing the thoughts of others, had worn me out. As I lay down, about to sleep, light engulfed my tent.

"You deliberately lost!" Quinn said through gritted teeth, standing at my tent's opening.

Shocked, I sat back up and tried to find my feet so I could argue my case. "How dare you burst into my tent unannounced? I could have been..."

"DON'T!" Quinn stepped into the tent, the flaps fell, making the tent as dim as it was before. "Why did you deliberately lose?" As Quinn forcefully questioned me, he pointed at me, like he was accusing me of committing a serious offence!

"Don't point at me like that!" Angry tears delicately seeped from my eyes, which only made me angrier. I didn't want Quinn to see me in such a weak state!

"Answer me then!" Quinn urged.

"For one second, could you stop being selfish and think about me for a minute here?"

Quinn was about to yell again, but restrained himself, then let out a frustrated sigh and frantically ran his fingers through his hair. Suspecting that the silence meant that Quinn was allowing me to talk, I quickly spoke, taking up the opportunity before he had chance to accuse me of anything else.

"I heard your thoughts, Quinn."

"You what?"

"I heard your thoughts!" I repeated much more forcefully. "So," I continued once I had calmed down, "I heard you thinking about how the others would judge you and ridicule you if you had lost. And I..."

"That doesn't..."

"I was being sympathetic for God's sake! Can't you see that I cared so much about you that I didn't want you to feel hurt?" More tears fell from my eyes as I realised how open I was with Quinn.

Quinn's forceful expression became one of regret and sympathy. "I'm ... I'm sorry. You're right. I'm being selfish."

"You are! Besides, the way I performed should be a compliment to you! You trained me, after all!" I cried out, then folded my arms and turned away from Quinn. He had made me so angry! I didn't want to speak to him like this! I couldn't face him in this state!

"You know," Quinn said in a light hearted tone, trying to make this situation seem a whole lot better, "It would have been better if you had just won. It's obvious to everyone that you deliberately lost, so you might as well have..."

"DON'T!" I yelled at Quinn just as he did to me a few moments earlier. "Don't!" I repeated, with my finger now pointing into his chest. After a long stare, I quickly turned away again and faced the back of my tent. I was hoping that he would leave at this point, giving me a chance to release a bucket of tears, so I could feel a little better, but he didn't. Quinn placed a hand on my left shoulder.

"Turn around please, Brianna."

I shrugged my shoulder, so that Quinn's hand would fall off.

Again, Quinn held my left shoulder. "*Please*, Brianna," he urged me again.

"I ... I have ... nothing ... I have nothing more ... I have nothing more to say to you," I barely managed to say, as I struggled to refrain from crying. I dreaded people seeing me cry!

"Well, *I* have something to say to you," Quinn said forcefully, but not angrily. His hand twisted me around, but I looked away as he tried to make me face him. "I've never been good with people, Brianna and I've never been good at saying ... at saying thank you or apologising. And I..."

"So, what are you trying to say? Are you apologising, or are you thanking me?"

"Both," Quinn quickly answered. "I want to apologise for the way I just acted and the conclusion I came to. I want to apologise for thinking of myself and not considering you and ... and

I ... I want to thank you for ... for making me realise that I ... that I can be happy again ... even ... even if I..."

"Can we finish this later?" The question was obviously rhetorical in nature. I still couldn't bring myself to face Quinn and I wiped away my tears.

"Certainly," Quinn quietly replied, accepting the futility of continuing. Still facing the back of my tent, I heard the flaps respond to his retreat. Quinn was gone.

Chapter Sixteen

Quinn's Tale

…*"Back again Cuchulainn?" Craig felt Cuchulainn's present as he was walking through Daray's border.*

"Do you know why, Craig?"

"Keira is with child."

"Yes and you should be happy. Don't allow stress to dampen this joyous time. I told you all will be well. It is meant to happen."…

- *Excerpt from 'The Morrigan Book'*

"Brianna! Are you alright?" Charlotte anxiously asked, gently waking me up.

"What time is it?" I queried.

"It's almost six o'clock, Bee! You've been asleep for hours!"

"Hours!"

"Yeah, when we…"

"You should have woken me!"

"Well, I was going to, but when we came here and realised where you were after the tournament, you seemed really out of it, so Ethan and I decided to let you rest."

As I sat up, I gathered my thoughts, trying to remember what happened before I nodded off.

I was arguing with Quinn and once he left, I was still upset. I must have cried myself to sleep...

"Brianna?" I must have been mulling over my thoughts for quite some time for Charlotte to have to remind me of her presence.

"Oh, yeah, uh ... sorry. I was just ... just trying to recall what happened before I went to sleep."

"Speaking of that, why did you disappear after your match? Ethan, myself and the others didn't get the chance to speak to you!"

"Oh, uh ... I ... I wasn't feeling great. I was really light-headed, but I'm okay now." My lack of eye contact with Charlotte didn't make my story convincing.

"I didn't see Quinn once he took off after the race either," Charlotte knew I wasn't being completely honest with her; her enquiring, suspicious tone made that very clear.

"Don't do that Charlotte!"

"What?"

"All right! All right! I'll tell you." I finally gave in.

"Good! I don't have to resort to interrogating you." Charlotte folded her legs and rested her elbows on her knees with her hands supporting her head, ready to listen to everything I had to share. "So," Charlotte encouraged me to begin. "What went down after the race? You're keeping me in suspense! I can't wait any..."

"Quinn came and found me, Charlotte."

"Well, I gathered that, but what..."

"He accused me of deliberately losing." I blurted out quickly.

"Did you? Did you deliberately lose?"

I nodded.

"But why, Bee?"

"I heard his thoughts, Charlotte!"

"What did he...?"

"He was really concerned about losing and what that would do to his reputation."

"So, because of that, you lost?"

"You make it sound like I'm an idiot!"

"No! No!" Charlotte quickly reassured me. "It's just, you didn't have to lose, Bee. The win was rightfully yours! But, I know your intentions were good." Charlotte placed her hand on my knee. "Your actions definitely prove that you have feelings for him. What you did was nice; it shows that you care for him."

"Well, he didn't seem to see it like that!"

"I bet he did after he realised what your intentions were."

"It doesn't matter whether he realised or not!" I brushed aside. "He was so rude to me! He really upset me!"

Charlotte stood up to leave the tent. "Well, I can tell you that he is beating himself up about whatever happened."

"What do you mean?"

Charlotte opened the tent flap. "Quinn hasn't been himself all afternoon. It's obvious that he regrets what happened."

"Good! He deserves to feel guilty!"

"Bee," Charlotte calmly spoke, "you can't hold a grudge forever. Don't you think he's suffered enough?"

"Wait! So you're on his side now?"

"I'm not on anybody's side. Just, give him a chance, okay?"

I didn't answer. I knew Charlotte's words were wise and true, but I wasn't in the mood to agree with her.

"Your dinner is out here when you're ready," Charlotte said, as she left me alone in the tent.

So, he's been beating himself up about it, has he? The angry thoughts were slightly alleviated.

Confused as to how I should act now, I remained in my tent and ran through a number of different scenarios in my head. First, I thought of Quinn coming to me with a bunch of flowers to apologise. Deciding that that would most likely not be the outcome, I continued to ponder.

"Maybe he'll give me the silent treatment for a while; we'll avoid each other at all costs. Then, the silence will drive him so mad he'll come and explain himself!" I thought to myself. But,

again, I wasn't satisfied and I came to the conclusion that creating potential outcomes in my head wasn't helping me at all!

Still sitting and contemplating in my tent, I found myself playing with the thinner of the two chains around my neck; the chain of the prayer box Ethan had given me for my birthday. Not wanting to leave the tent and to pass the time away, I decided to open the prayer box and remind myself of what I longed for. The last time I had read it was on the night of my birthday just over a month ago. I gently flicked the latch and removed the tiny scroll of paper from the box.

I want to be an author and help as many people as I can by sharing my story with them.

"And what a story it is so far!" I mumbled sarcastically to myself. I placed the small scrap of paper back into the box, pressed down the latch and let the box clang against the carrier chain as I released it.

Still having no desire to go outside, I decided to rest my head against my pillow and picture myself bravely confronting him. I was about to select some convincing words for my speech when my tent flaps moved.

"I know my dinner's out there. I'll be out there in a sec, Charlotte. I just ... I just want to clear my head a little bit more."

"Well, I'm *not* Charlotte, but that is precisely why I am here." The unfamiliar voice made me jump.

Now sitting upright, I found a handsome young man sitting on the chest that was storing my new clothes. His attire was simple; loose brown trousers, a white shirt and bare feet. The man's hair was wavy and fell beside his lightly bearded face. Looking closer, I realised that the man's eyes resembled my own; however, his right eye was blue and his left brown.

"*Cuchulainn?*" I asked.

"Yes, it is I," he calmly replied. "And I'm sure you know why I'm here, Brianna."

"Well, Donelle said that you would come, but, I'm not *entirely* sure why you're here," I admitted. "But, I know who you are and what you did."

"Many things are troubling you and I'm..."

"I'm the *only* one who can see and hear you, *right?*" I was still a little shocked.

"Yes, Brianna. I'm here to counsel you, as I did your mother and father in times of great doubt."

"Wait, are you telling me that you've come to help me out with what just happened between Quinn and me?"

"I'm afraid not," Cuchulainn chuckled. "Although," he added, "I am known to be of *some* assistance in that area." He smiled.

"Keira and Craig; my Mam and Dad," I inferred.

"Yes."

"So then," I dragged out rather awkwardly, allowing Cuchulainn to explain his reasons for being there. "You're here because..."

"It is important that I steer you in the right direction to help you use your gift, Brianna."

"And that is..."

"What you already know yourself to possess and something even greater."

"But, I'm guessing I won't know what that is tonight, right?" I had finally accepted that self-discovery was quite a popular theme in Oran-Roy.

"Yes, again," Cuchulainn laughed. Based on the descriptions of the 'mythical' Cuchulainn I had read about in books, I wouldn't have considered him to be funny; after all, humour was not normally associated with a famous mythical warrior, described as ranking alongside Gods and Goddesses. "Brianna," Cuchulainn's tone became serious, "you will have some trouble with what you possess."

"*Trouble?*" I said.

"Your ability is becoming prominent now and you *must* learn to control it. Find something or someone that grounds you, so that your ability to hear and send thoughts can be suppressed, otherwise..."

"I'll lose myself like Morrigan did."

"Not necessarily like Morrigan, Brianna." Mentioning Morrigan made Cuchulainn uneasy; after all, he and she did have a *very* interesting history. "But, if you let it consume you and dictate your actions, it will be difficult to fulfil what has to be done."

"So, will my ... will what I do come more often now?"

"Yes."

"So, *how* do I go about staying...?"

"Grounded?" Cuchulainn finished for me.

"Yeah."

"Find something or someone who helps you remain yourself; pure of heart and true."

"Hmm - the words on the Oran-Roy tree."

"Indeed."

"Donelle filled that role for you, didn't she?" I enquired.

"She did indeed." Cuchulainn looked down into his lap as I mentioned Donelle; he still loved her after all this time.

"Is it hard?"

His delayed answer made me feel that I had crossed a line.

"*Sorry* ... I just..."

"Don't apologise, Brianna. Ask me what you like." He met my gaze again. I was comfortable enough to continue.

"Is it hard, knowing that you *can't* see her, or be with her until you have finished what has been set for you?"

Cuchulainn sighed. "It is," he admitted. "But holding onto what we shared, for however short it was, helps me."

"*Oh*, that reminds me! Donelle wanted me to tell you, *you are true.*" Cuchulainn's face beamed as I spoke those three simple words. "Does it mean what I think it means?"

"It was *our* way of saying how much we cared for each other; it was how we said *I love you.*" I felt all warm and gushy inside. *How sweet is that?*

Unexpectedly, Cuchulainn's body began to fade into the thin beam of light within the tent.

"*Cuchulainn! What's...?*"

"I've said all that needs to be said for now, *although*," he smirked, "your friend's words were wise."

"*You too!*" I rolled my eyes.

Cuchulainn was now almost invisible.

"When will I speak to you again?" I quickly asked, just as his face had almost faded away.

"When you need me," he answered, as his body drifted away into the small, dim ray of light.

*

What or who can keep me grounded? How and when will I figure this out? As cool and as exciting as the whole 'self discovery' thing was, it was also frustrating. I didn't need more questions to add to my ever-growing list! But, since being in Oran-Roy, the list did nothing but grow! Tossing and turning, trying to get to sleep, I wasn't able to forget the words Quinn and I shared earlier that day. Minutes spent attempting to drag my mind towards greener pastures, failed; I wasn't tired, which I realised was as a result of sleeping during the day. As I turned over to my right side, thinking that a change of position might help me get comfortable enough to sleep, the light from the small fire in the campsite flickered against my tent, making interesting shapes as the gentle night breeze shifted the flames.

Adjusting my position didn't help me sleep and the dancing light from the fire had caught my attention.

"*Urgh!*" I grumbled, giving in and realising that I wasn't tired enough to sleep. I lifted up my sore body and exited my tent to sit by the fire. Watching the flames was relaxing; the way they moved in the calm breeze was hypnotic. Staring intently at the flickering flames, I pondered over Cuchulainn's words.

"*Who* keeps me grounded?" I whispered to myself. "*Who* makes me feel comfortable?"

Crack.

The noise of footsteps creeping over the forest floor brought me out of my trance. I turned around and found Quinn; the last person I wanted to see at that moment. As he came into the light, I decided to act as I did earlier and make him see that I was still disappointed in him. I returned my attention to the fire, remained silent and deliberately failed to acknowledge him.

"Can't sleep either?" he casually raised.

I didn't answer.

Quinn came and sat directly beside me with very little space between us. I adjusted my body and twisted slightly towards the left, avoiding any chance of eye contact.

"You're still angry with me," Quinn quickly inferred.

"Hmm," I replied in a miffed tone, playing the role of the typical 'disgruntled girl'. My behaviour made me recall Charlotte's advice, as well as Cuchulainn's confirmation. Even though I was known for holding grudges, I decided to listen to whatever Quinn had to say. After all, based on how he was acting, it was quite clear that he was regretful and wanted to make amends. Besides, I wanted what he and I shared to grow into something more. But, how could we become something more if I was unwilling to forgive him?

"Brianna, what you did for me today was one of the nicest things *anyone* has *ever* done for me. Instead of thanking you, I was rather selfish and thought of my ego above your kindness." Quinn's words extinguished the remaining flames of anger. I didn't answer him, hoping that he would continue to speak. He did. "I didn't consider how this would affect you. My behaviour today was unacceptable and for that I am *sincerely* sorry."

Finally, I decided to face Quinn and free him of worry. "Apology accepted," I said with a smile.

"Well," he continued, "I'd still like to make amends if I may, Brianna."

"You've done enough, Quinn. *I* should apologise now." I placed my hands over his; our knees were now touching. But, I still didn't have the strength to look him in the eye. "It took a lot of courage for you to apologise and I denied you of that opportunity earlier today and for that *I* am sorry."

"Thank you, Brianna, but I would still like to make it up to you. There ... there's somewhere I would like to take you."

"Is it quite close?" I keenly asked.

"Yes, rather close."

"When would you like to take me?"

"Well, since we're heading back to Crag in two days, tomorrow afternoon should be the best time."

"I would like that." I looked down at my hands over Quinn's and considered moving them away, but hesitated. "Where is this place you want to take me to?"

"It wouldn't be a surprise if I told you," he swiftly replied.

"So, it's a *surprise*, is it?"

"All that I will reveal is that it was once a place I used to call home."

"Can you tell me...?" A burst of cool raindrops suddenly falling from the sky cut me off. Within seconds, the light rain turned torrential.

"*Quick!*" Quinn cried out over the bucketing rain rebounding off nearby tents. When I realised that Quinn was guiding me towards shelter further away than my tent, I stopped him.

"*Wait! This way!*" I clenched Quinn's wrist and pulled him towards my tent. As we made it inside, the drumming sound of the rain hitting the nearby tents diminished, the rain becoming a light drizzle. I draped the opening flaps around the poles of the tent, so that the light from the fire and the lanterns could enter.

Following a moment of standing still, waiting for one another to speak, Quinn and I simultaneously sat down on the mat of my tent.

"You ... you wanted to ask me about..." Quinn reminded me, ending the uncomfortable silence.

"Oh yes! You mentioned your home and I was wandering whether, you..." I averted my gaze as I was about to ask Quinn to divulge his past, thinking that it might make my request seem a little less severe, "whether you were ready to ... do you think you could tell me about..."

"Myself?" His casual tone surprised me and drew my eyes back to his.

"Well, *yes* if ... if that's all right? I don't want to pressure you, but I feel that I should..."

"It's alright, Brianna," Quinn stopped me, raising his hand. "It's about time that I share everything with you."

Before divulging his past, Quinn looked down into his lap and fiddled with his hands, drew in a deep breath and then met my enquiring gaze.

"Where do I begin?" he asked through a sigh.

"Wherever you want to," I quickly answered.

"As you know already, I'm from Cathal. My father is second in line to rule over Cathal, but, that might change very soon, or perhaps it has already happened without me knowing."

"*Really?*" I blurted out. "But *how* would you be unaware of that? *Surely* you should have been informed!"

"Well, I'll explain that soon," Quinn calmly assured me.

"Sorry, sorry! I'll keep quiet and let you keep talking."

"My father, Cargon Logan, is one of two sons, with his older brother, Rafer Logan, the current ruler of Cathal. My mother, Enya, was a great artist and met my father through producing works of art for the Cathal Castle."

"*Was?*" I queried hesitantly.

"I only knew my mother for eleven years, Brianna."

"I'm ... I'm really sorry to hear that, Quinn."

"She died giving birth to my younger sister and my only sibling, Rowena."

"You have a sister?"

"Well ..." perhaps I had pushed Quinn too far. *Does his sister have anything to do with his scar? Is she still alive?* "Rowena has been missing for ... a great deal of time."

"I'm sorry." In that moment, sadness and deep sympathy overcame me. I couldn't begin to contemplate experiencing Quinn's set of circumstances!

Before speaking again, Quinn looked to the ground, cleared a lump in his throat and then raised his head to face me again. His eyes glistened with tears, but, like me, he tried to hold them back.

"Rowena was ... taken ... from our home almost four years ago."

"How terrible!"

"My father was threatened by Cillian."

"*Threatened?*"

"Yes. In whatever Cillian was and is still planning, he wanted my father's help, which would mean Cathal's support. My father rightly refused to help him, but Cillian said that his refusal would come at a price. After he threatened my father, I urged him to act! I *urged* him to investigate further and seek help from fellow clans if it was required. But, my *cowardly* father stood back and failed to act. I begged him to send Rowena and me away, just in case Cillian had intentions of harming either of us to punish my father, but he tried to reason with me and convince me that I was being overly cautious. He *ensured* me that we would be well protected if we remained in Cathal."

"So, you remained in Cathal?"

"We did. It was ... it was the *biggest* mistake I've ever made and one that I will regret forever - placing my trust in my father."

"Is ... is that when...?"

"Two days after Cillian's threat, two of his men came to abduct my sister in the night."

I silently shrieked!

"A noise came from her room. As I made my way down the corridor with my candle to check on her, I could hear Rowena tossing around in her bed. I thought that she was having a nightmare, so I decided to wake her up. When I reached her door, I saw one of Cillian's men attempting to take Rowena and escape through her window. Immediately, I charged towards the man, but ... but, I didn't realise that there was another man standing behind the door."

My hands were now over my mouth.

"He and I scuffled and my candle blew out as it fell to the floor. I ... I couldn't see well and then ... then all I remember was falling to the ground, clasping my ... my bloody face."

"Oh, Quinn!"

"The ... the man's blade is what caused ... caused this." Quinn ran his fingers along his scar.

"And ... and your sister was...?"

" ... Taken as I remained on the floor, like a ... like a coward!"

"*Quinn!* You were *not* a coward! You were hurt! How could you...?"

"*I ... I should have done more! If ... if only I had brought my sword! I knew Cillian had made a threat! I should have done more to protect...*"

"Stop!" I leant over to get closer to Quinn, placed my hands on his knees and looked directly into his green eyes. I finally realised what Ewan meant about Quinn. Quinn's past haunted him, not allowing him to be happy without experiencing guilt. "You did *everything* you could have! Blaming yourself won't help bring Rowena back!"

A single tear seeped from Quinn's eye. He quickly wiped it away, hoping that I didn't see it. "Speaking about this has eased my worries a little, Brianna." As he spoke, he rested his hands over mine.

"What you need to do, Quinn, is look to the future, because, assuming the worst when you *don't* know what has *really* happened is not a good use of your time." ... *Wise words, Brianna. Maybe you should practise what you preach!*

"You're right," Quinn admitted.

"Tell me, how come you're unsure whether your father is ruling Cathal or not?"

"I haven't been home since this happened, Brianna."

"You ran away?"

"Ewan and Leona helped me recover. Leona was able to help me see through my right eye again. They found me when I was leaving Cathal."

"Is that when you first met them?"

"Yes. Once they brought me back to full strength, I decided to search for my sister."

"Did you go after Cillian?"

"No. I ... I *almost* did, but Ewan advised me not to. He suggested that I remain with them and help their cause in the revolt against Cillian. Alone, I would have been putting myself in an unwinnable situation. But, alongside Ewan and Leona, we have formed the large party you've been with since you arrived. That's how your father's cause ended up joining with our own."

"So, you travelled throughout Oran-Roy?"

"Yes. We secretly travelled amongst the clans of Oran-Roy to unite the people, to try and remove Cillian's threat of bringing Morrigan back. Here and there we have made bonds and strong ties, but we've also come across people who could potentially ruin everything. It was a chance we had to take."

"I gather that your travels made you very familiar with Breena? That's why my father asked you to guide me there."

"Yes. I spent quite a lot of time there, but not only for our cause."

"What else?"

Quinn took a good few seconds to respond. "I ... I did some ... thinking there you could say, I guess." I sensed that Quinn didn't want to elaborate on that too much, so I decided to ask about another matter.

"So, what makes you think that your uncle might not be ruling Cathal?"

"I suspect that Cillian is using my father as a puppet, with my sister as the bargaining chip, ensuring that whatever he is planning in Tarmon has Cathal's support. So, perhaps my father has taken control now; I can't be sure."

"Well ... at least that means your sister is still alive ... right?"

"I ... I assume that and I certainly hope so, but there is no telling *how* she is or *where* she is." Quinn looked down into his lap, attempting to hide away his watery eyes. Every time he spoke of his sister, he constantly put himself down. Gently, I placed my hand beneath his chin and raised his head up, so that we were facing each other again.

"Thank you for being open with me. I ... I really appreciate it, Quinn. And now I..." I could feel blood rushing towards my cheeks, "now I feel that I know you. I've also come to learn why you were distant with me when I first met you."

"What do you mean?" he was curious.

"Well, I ... I don't want to sound *too* bold, but, you *did* say that you liked me since I arrived. Now I realise that you acted as you did because ... because you were scared of making a connection with me and losing it. I think that you were subconsciously pushing me away because you were scared that you could experience the same pain you felt when you lost your sister and mother. So, my judgement of you was unnecessarily harsh."

Quinn smiled and caressed the side of my face, delicately brushing my hair aside. "You *do* know me."

I smiled.

"So," Quinn said with enthusiasm, "now I think that it's *only* fair that *I* learn more about you and your life in Ireland. You explained it to Leona, Ewan and the others. Do you think you could share it with me now?"

"Of course."

Now, well into the night, I shared with Quinn anything I could recall about my life in Ireland. After describing my likes, dislikes, home life, hobbies, the traits of the twenty-first century world, my parents, Ethan and Charlotte, Michael and school, Quinn felt that I hadn't explained quite everything.

"Do you mind me asking if ... if you had any ... any previous ... courting, or, relationships in Ireland, Brianna?" Quinn's words were spoken slowly; he was treading lightly. But, rather than answering him straight away, I couldn't help but laugh at his use of the word *courting*!

"*Courting!*" I giggled. "Back home, we don't use that term anymore. People only used that term *years* ago!" When I realised that Quinn wasn't amused, I quickly composed myself. "So, I gather that term is still used here?"

"Yes. But, did you have...?"

"Oh, well, no ... not ... not really."

"Not really?" Quinn's confusion was asking me to elaborate.

"Well, I knew this one person who I wanted to have something with, and I ... well ... I had anticipated *too* much *too* soon with him and, in the end, when I realised that it wasn't going to eventuate, I was really hurt. But, it was me, not him. I ... I set myself up to fall." I would have thought that speaking about something such as this would have been terribly uncomfortable with Quinn, but it wasn't!

"So," I continued, "to *officially* answer your question, I haven't courted someone. Besides, I'm *only* eighteen. So, I'm not very ... not very experienced with this ... err ... this sort of thing." My cheeks were completely flushed now. *Was I ready for this yet?*

"My sister is your age," Quinn quickly said, realising that I was feeling a little awkward in continuing that subject.

"*Really?*"

"Yes."

"So, that would make you...?"

"Twenty – nine, yes."

"Oh." *I didn't realise he was eleven years older than me! Well, eleven years isn't so bad! What will Mam and Dad think though?*

"Has that surprised you?"

I wasn't going to lie. "Well, yeah, but, it ... it doesn't worry me ... I ... I just think that my parents back home would say I'm a little young at the moment, but, they'd be okay with it in a couple of years, I guess."

"Brianna, I don't want to make you feel uncomfortable and the last thing I want to do is ..." I knew where Quinn was going.

"It's alright, Quinn." For a short moment, we both scanned our eyes around the tent, allowing each other to surpass the uncomfortable questions. "So," I had to break the silence, "would you say that we are ... that we are ... courting?" My voice was extremely low; I seemed to become quiet when I was nervous.

"I ... I would say ... yes." My heart was racing at a million miles an hour, but, despite that, I was thoroughly enjoying the moment. *How old fashioned is this? It's very romantic! Who would imagine me, courting?*

"Well, I'd ... I'd like that." When I finished speaking, Quinn gently stroked my cheek and we became lost in each other's eyes. Many thoughts were going through my head. *Do I kiss him now? Is he waiting for me to lean in? What the hell do I do? I've never done this before!*

Quinn's face became mischievous and then he smiled. "Well, it would *also* be a first for me." *Damn! He heard my thoughts! He probably heard that too!*

"*Oh, sorry!*" I quickly apologised, raising my hands to my head. "I've ruined the ... err ... the moment haven't I?"

Again, Quinn smiled before responding. "No, you just made it a funny moment, that's all."

I was surprised by Quinn's reaction. Prior to this moment, I hadn't thought about how my ability would impact on a relationship. After all, if I wanted to, I could read his mind if I felt that he was untrustworthy. I then considered, would that make Quinn feel uneasy all the time, like he was under the spotlight on a stage whenever he was around me, unable to think anything without me knowing about it? *How is this going to work?* I needed to address this with Quinn immediately.

"Quinn, my ability won't be very *fair* on you unless I ... unless I manage to control it soon. I don't want it to hinder anything between us."

"Well," he casually said, "at this stage, it has done nothing but bring us closer together, wouldn't you agree?"

"Well, *because* I heard what you were thinking during the race, that's what caused the argument we had earlier."

"But, *I'd* argue that it has ... broken the ice, wouldn't you say?

I silently considered what Quinn was saying.

"I don't think we would have been able to sit here, as we are now, and comfortably speak about ourselves to one another, if we hadn't crossed that line today."

"That's true," I admitted. "But, Quinn, I'd understand if this became tough on you. I'll ... I'll do my best to keep my ability controlled, but if I don't..."

"You will. In time you'll be able to use it at your will." His understanding attitude calmed me.

"Thanks." Another issue then came to mind. "Quinn, I *know* that my Mam and Dad were not from the same clan and they were still able to have a relationship, but, would we be *frowned* upon because we aren't from the same clans?"

"Look at Rona and Zephan, Brianna."

"I just wanted to make sure."

"You are like no one I have ever met, Brianna." Quinn's compliment caught me off guard.

"I ... I feel the same of you, Quinn." After an extended period of complete silence, Quinn held my arms and guided me up, so that we both standing.

"I should let you rest now and I think it's stopped raining as well."

Quickly, I glanced over to the opening of my tent and realised that Quinn was right. So immersed in Quinn, I didn't even notice that the rain had stopped and I wasn't so sure that I'd be able to sleep with so much excitement running through me!

"Yes, well, thanks again, Quinn."

"Thank you." Quinn lowered his head, brushed my hair off my face and kissed my cheek. "I'll see you tomorrow." The hairs stood up on the back of my neck. It was a pleasant sensation.

Leaving the tent, Quinn bid me farewell with another smile.

"Oh!" I called out to Quinn, almost beyond the tent entrance. "Do you mind me asking why you performed poorly when I raced you?"

"Brianna, *you* performed well. Your performance was *very* admirable." He affirmed.

"Come on, Quinn," I laughed, "you *know* you were off your game. It's *very* flattering that you don't want to take anything away from my performance, but, *truly*, why did you perform badly? You could have beaten me in a heartbeat if you raced me as you did against Kieran and Ewan."

"Well," he said, with a cheeky expression, "I was blown away by you choosing to compete and..."

" ... *And* what?"

"And also by your ... beauty." *That was incredibly corny and sweet at the same time!*

"Well, I *have* made an impression," I said, also with a cheeky air.

"You certainly have," Quinn declared as he walked out of the light.

Lying down to sleep, the last thing my eyes saw was Quinn's shadow.

With my eyes shut, holding onto what they just saw, a pleasant calm fell over me. I couldn't recall a more interesting, honest and funny conversation than the one I just shared with Quinn. He made me feel so comfortable; I was able to be myself in his presence and not worry about what he would think of me. The only other people, who made me feel the same, were Ethan and Charlotte.

But, could Quinn be whom Cuchulainn was referring to?

Would Quinn help me remain true?

Chapter Seventeen

The Cave

"You must have had a very pleasant sleep," Craig inferred, after the bouncy way I had collected a hefty portion of breakfast from the fire. "I can see that the extra hours of sleep have made you very happy this morning, Brianna." Craig's light-hearted, yet suspicious tone and inquiring glance, which wasn't at all subtle, gave me reason to suspect that he knew what was responsible for my mood.

"Well," I spoke casually, attempting to sound like I had nothing to hide, "I was much drained after the tournament. The sleep has revitalised me, you could say." Despite being almost certain that my father knew Quinn to be responsible for my good mood, I didn't wish to discuss the circumstances with him just yet.

"*Hmm,*" Craig replied with an interesting smirk. He left the log he was sitting on and walked towards me. "Continue to sleep for as long as you did last night, Brianna; it has given you a new glow." Craig placed his hand on my shoulder, lowered his head and kissed my cheek, smiled and then left me alone by the late morning fire to finish my breakfast.

For the first time, I had just shared a 'coded' conversation with my father. Like a good night of sleep, Quinn had revitalised me. My father, without directly saying so, had just given Quinn and me his blessing. Would my parents at home feel the same way? That unpleasant, guilty sensation always seemed to return whenever I felt exuberant. But, very quickly in my mind, I came to the conclusion that worrying would be a wasteful task; I wasn't in Ireland and I wasn't in the position where I could confront my parents, so I decided to suppress the worry and deal with it when the time was right.

"Brianna!" Quinn's voice dragged me away from my ponderings. "I see you also slept in," he said, finding a space opposite me to sit.

"I did," I replied with a smile. "You haven't seen Charlotte and Ethan this morning, have you?"

"No, sorry. I haven't. Apart from just walking past your father, you are the first person I have seen or spoken to today."

When I finished my last bite, I decided to share my father's blessing with Quinn. "Quinn?"

"Yes."

"I just spoke with my father and he said that ... well, he didn't *actually* say so, but he *suggested* that he was okay with you and I ... together."

"I know," Quinn casually answered, in between biting into his bread slice, as if I was repeating a conversation we had already shared.

"Did he tell you when you just saw him now?" I questioned rather dumbfounded.

"No, Brianna." Quinn swallowed, placed his now empty plate on the nearby log, acting as a table, and then spoke again. "Just before the tournament began, I asked your father for permission to court you."

Things are really old fashioned around here!

"Oh, well ... that explains how he spoke to me this morning."

"I have great respect for you and your father, Brianna," Quinn further explained, "and I wanted to do things in the correct manner."

"I'm grateful for that." I smiled and again found myself captured by his emerald green eyes and warm expression. "So, *when* should I be ready for you to take me to this *secret* place?" I keenly asked.

"Well, your father intends to address everyone shortly and inform them about our departure and the ensuing events. So, after that would be a good time." Quinn also seemed excited, which made me look forward to the afternoon even more. It was nice to feel wanted, to know that someone who wasn't directly linked to you, as family is, wanted to spend time in your presence.

"Wonderful," I said, as I smiled my consent.

"Well, until then, I promised Ewan that I would help him hunt for the day's meals. So, I better go and find him."

"Yes, do that. I didn't get round to letting Ethan and Charlotte ride Epona yesterday, so I should probably see to that. I'll see you later." Apart from catching up with those closest to us, both Quinn and I were dying to divulge our evening discussion. As he would share our words with Ewan, I would be doing the same with Ethan and Charlotte.

With both of us now standing up ready to find the others, Quinn looked down at me and stroked my arm. "See you soon."

In return, I stroked his arm and looked up to meet his eyes and repeated, somewhat redundantly, "Yes, I'll see you later."

Feeling suddenly very much alone while on my way to seek out my dear friends, I filled the void of not being in Quinn's company with thoughts of the previous night and recollected the words we spoke to one another; visualising our discussion was as clear to me as if I were I watching a film.

"You're finally up!" Ethan's cry snapped me out of my thinking. "Couldn't sleep, could you?"

"Not exactly."

"Something happened with Quinn, didn't it?" Charlotte couldn't help herself.

I buried my neck into my now scrunched up shoulders and exhibited a hard to conceal grin.

"Tell me!" Charlotte agonisingly pleaded.

"Don't keep us in suspense, Bee!" Ethan cried out sarcastically in a high-pitched voice, waving his arms around, trying to impersonate Charlotte.

"All right! All right!" I tried to calm Charlotte down. "Come into my tent and I'll explain everything there."

"Wow! I still can't get over what you told us! What a crazy twenty-four hours, Bee!" Charlotte sighed as we walked back to the main campsite, after riding Epona.

"Yeah, riding Epona was pretty amazing stuff!" Again, Ethan was making fun of Charlotte's interest in my affairs.

"Well, things with Quinn might not interest you, Ethan! But, having Cuchulainn come to you, too, Bee! I'm beside myself!" Charlotte's keen, delightful interest in my dealings reminded me of just how fortunate I was to have such a supportive friend.

"I'm just pulling your leg, Charlotte!" Ethan felt the need to remind her. "I agree with you! What Bee has witnessed over the past day has been ... impressive."

"Thanks," I said to Ethan, raising my arm up and letting it rest along his shoulders for our stroll back to the camp.

When we had reached the base of the hill and were almost back at the camp, out of nowhere, Ethan began whistling the tune of 'The Mighty Quinn'. He then broke out into song.

"*Come on without! Come on within! You've not seen nothing like the mighty Quinn!*"

"I hadn't made that connection yet, Ethan!" I laughed. It took Ethan to bring up one of our Dad's favourite songs to associate it with Quinn. "I'll remember that now!"

Once we arrived at the campsite, people began congregating around my father, eagerly waiting his address.

As Craig raised his hands, silence fell amongst the crowd.

"Tomorrow morning we will make our way back to Crag." His voice was strong and captured all who were present; those who were muttering ceased. "In Crag, I and those near to me in command will deliberate on what our next step will be against Cillian's cause." People murmured amongst themselves, sharing their thoughts on what my father's next approach might be. "This is when we will need to be *most* vigilant!" The crowd cheered when Craig paused to catch his breath. "Cillian intends to bring ruin to Oran-Roy! We *cannot* let that happen! It is time that we *unite* Oran-Roy and its clans as it were before Morrigan's reign!" The crowd roared. "*Even* though most of us here have not been called to serve Oran-Roy, as my daughter has (many people within the crowd turned around to find me), we *all* serve a purpose to restore what has been destroyed. Mixed, or not mixed, we can help." Craig scanned the crowd and stopped when his eyes found me. The crowd fell silent. "Let us restore what made this land great." As the crowd applauded my father's final words, the hairs stood up on the nape of my neck; I was moved by the strength of the reception he had received.

With the address over, people began to disperse.

"Your Dad is *pretty good* at making speeches, Bee," Ethan commented.

"Yeah, he is," I agreed.

As I was about to walk into the campsite, I was stopped when I heard Ethan whistling 'The Mighty Quinn' tune. Sure enough, Quinn was coming to meet me.

"Have fun, Bee!" Charlotte encouraged.

I smiled and then looked at Ethan, to see what he would make of me leaving with Quinn.

"Yeah, have fun, Bee," he said with a slight smile. The older brother's protective instincts were still in gear.

I waved Ethan and Charlotte goodbye as I walked to meet Quinn halfway.

"Ready to go?" he asked.

"Yep; I'm ready to be surprised."

*

"How much further, Quinn? We've been walking for quite some time now. I don't see why we couldn't have stayed on the horse. And I can't stand not seeing where I'm going!"

"Not long, not long," Quinn insisted; he was holding my hands, guiding me down what I thought to be a hillside in a forest of some kind, based on the crunching, rustling noises I made as I walked. "Careful, now!" Quinn warned me. "There's a small step to descend. That's it," he said, once I had safely stepped down onto a hard surface. A salty smell filled my nostrils and the air was cool. *Was I near the ocean?*

"All right." Quinn's warm breath blew against my face as he reached around my head to remove the blindfold.

"I've been here before," I remarked, while watching the calm water stretch across the sand of the shoreline. "This is Breena, isn't it?"

"It is. This is where..."

"...We came to find Epona," I finished.

"Yes."

"*Well*, it ... it's not much of a surprise, Quinn," I said, trying not to sound too disappointed.

Quinn made a funny expression.

"*What?*"

"This *isn't* the surprise."

"Oh. *So* what's...?"

"We're standing above it."

My puzzled expression gave Quinn reason to elaborate.

"See this?" he said, crouching down then rubbing his hands along a groove among the rocks.

"Yes."

Quinn dug his fingers into the groove then dragged a flat stone over its neighbouring rock; a dark hole was exposed.

Quinn stood up, signalled towards the hole, inviting me to enter first. "After you," he encouraged, after his hand signal failed to convince me to cross the threshold.

"Err ... it's ... it's *pitch* black in there. *How* am I supposed to see where I'm going?"

"Feel your way down. Once you reach a certain point, there will be enough light for you to see." Quinn's confidence didn't alleviate my doubts.

"Can't *you* go first?" I sounded like a wimp!

With a heavy sigh, Quinn stood over the hole and gradually lowered his body in with his arms gently easing himself down. As his head vanished I panicked.

"*Quinn?*"

"It's all right, Brianna!" My tone gave Quinn reason to reassure me. "I'm almost down." The sound of Quinn's feet hitting the ground echoed out of the hole. He said something, but the echo that was produced drowned his words out. I assumed he was saying that it was safe for me to go down, but how exactly was I going to do that without comfortably seeing where I was going? Unlike him, I wasn't at all familiar with this.

Very slowly, I lowered my feet into the hole, with my arms gently guiding me down deeper into the darkness. When my feet met the first set of protruding rocks, my nerves eased a little. Comfortable that I was secure, I rested all of my weight on the stones and let go of the rim of the hole to lower myself even further down into the opening. With my head now completely below the breach of the crevice, I ran my hands along the narrow, stone wall surrounding me and prepared myself for finding the next set of stones. When my left foot slid off the stone it was resting on, my entire weight, being supported by one rock, proved too much. The rock gave in and I fell down with it. Neither the rock nor I, were a match for gravity.

Like a flimsy ragdoll, I bounced against the stone walls of the narrow hole. Trying to latch onto anything, my right side heaved into the wall, ripping my sleeve and grazing my arm against the cold, sharp rocks. Stones followed me down the hole and scratched my forehead and cheek as they met my face. There wasn't time to scream! There wasn't time to cry out in pain! All I tried to do was hold onto anything I possibly could!

Finally, the agonising fall ended. I landed over my right arm onto a hard, stone surface. Rocks continued to scatter down the passage and pierce my fragile skin. When the noise of rocks scattering against stone ended, a hot, unpleasant sensation consumed my right arm, but I had experienced much worse than this before. As painful as my right arm was, it didn't compare to the pain of the carrier symbol appearing on my right palm well over a month ago at school.

"*Brianna!*" Quinn's voice echoed and filled the cave. "*This is my fault! This is my fault!*" He mumbled to himself as he brushed off the remains of the rocks from the fall off my body. Quinn scooped me up and carried me towards a small amount of light further within the cave.

"Where are you hurt, Brianna? Where are you hurt?" I had never heard Quinn sound frazzled. *"Brianna! Where does it hurt?"* Quinn rested my back against a large rock found under a ray of light coming from a small breach in the sheltering stones above.

"Ah!" I winced when Quinn gently ran his fingers along my right wrist.

"I think your wrist is sprained; if not, it might be broken."

"I ... I didn't hear a crack," I struggled to say, trying to get my breath back after the adrenalin rush.

"Your arm is badly grazed," Quinn discovered, as he continued to examine my injuries. Without hesitation, Quinn ripped off the remains of my right sleeve and threw it aside. Then, he threw his cloak to the ground and ripped a large strip of material from the base of his shirt. He rushed towards a small, nearby puddle of water, dabbed the strip of material in it and then raced back to attend to my wound.

"Ah!" I painfully flinched when the cool water made contact with my arm.

"I'm sorry, Brianna, but I *have* to wash out the wound or it *won't* heal well."

"I know ... I know," I quickly replied, just wanting Quinn to get on with it so the pain would soon subside.

After a few painful dabs and a great deal of stinging, Quinn very carefully wrapped another strip of material from his shirt around my arm.

"I'm *so* sorry I made you come down here, Brianna," Quinn apologised over and over, as he was dabbing the cuts on my face, arms and shins.

"It's ... ah! It's not your fault, Quinn."

"Let me wrap your wrist up now." Quinn was avoiding directly looking at me; he felt terribly guilty.

"Ah!" I cried, while Quinn began wrapping a strip of my dress around my wrist.

Quinn gently turned my right arm around, so that my palm was facing up. Gracefully, he ran his fingers along the carrier symbol. "Did ... did it hurt when it made that mark?"

"Yeah," I quickly answered, "Heaps more than now. So don't feel bad. I know you're feeling guilty for taking me here, because I'm hurt, but you weren't to know that the stones would give way."

"No, Brianna, I did know that the first few sets of stone were weak. I told you before you came down, but, you mustn't have heard me. So, this is my fault. And now you're hurt due to my stupidity and..."

"Quinn?"

"... The only way out of here is waiting until the tide draws out in the morning."

"Quinn!" I said more forcefully this time, giving him no choice but to look at me directly. "It – was – an – accident. Okay?"

He didn't respond.

"Don't beat yourself up about it, all right?"

Again, he remained silent.

"Quinn!"

"All right," he gave in through a sigh.

"So, is this all the surprise was ... a dark cave?"

Quinn chuckled. "No! I'll show you, but are you all right to walk?"

"Just help me up and I should be."

Quinn supported my waist and hoisted me up from the cold floor then offered me his hand. "They'll be a few awkward steps, so, watch where you plant your feet." When I clasped onto his warm hand, that familiar, tingling sensation dispersed throughout my body.

As Quinn guided me further into the cave, I began to hear water trickling from the walls; it made a calming, pleasant sound.

"So, the tide is high at the moment?" I queried.

"Yes, I'm afraid that our only way to leave will be by swimming out of the other opening once the tide is lower in the morning."

"Do you think the others will worry?"

"I'm not sure."

"Well, at least they know I'm with you."

"That doesn't mean anything."

"Of course it does!" Quinn's humility angered me. "Just because you think that you failed to keep your sister safe doesn't mean that you can't protect me!"

Quinn stopped walking and turned to face me. "Are you always going to associate everything I do with that?"

"No, but I..."

"Let's just keep going," Quinn suggested and continued on walking. He was avoiding going back to that dark place in his life.

"I'm sorry," I urged myself to say after a period of deafening silence. Quinn stopped walking again.

"It's all right. I shouldn't have been angry with you, because you're ... right ... you're right about me ... again." There wasn't much light in the cave, but I still managed to see Quinn's rare smile.

After a few minutes of walking and enjoying my hand being held by Quinn's, we came into a breathtaking space; crevices in the above rocks let in beams of light that reflected off the shimmery, crystal, blue water. Moss adorned some of the stones and simple, leafy vines fell from some of the highest rocks.

"This is beautiful!" I said, blown away by the peaceful scene before me.

"This is where I stayed for quite some time after I left home." Quinn guided me closer towards the water and invited me to sit down on a large stone. "Being here, I was able to clear my head a little. I ... well, it's my favourite place to be and I wanted to share it with you."

I was speechless.

"I haven't shown this to anyone or told anyone of it before ... apart from you." Quinn rested his hand over my left hand, which drew my eyes away from the dazzling water.

Again, I struggled to articulate words. I was in a daze of complete happiness. Despite just falling down a dark hole and some injuries notwithstanding, the happiness seemed to be suppressing any pain I might otherwise have been experiencing. What Quinn was expressing and sharing made me feel special. Knowing that someone deeply cares for you makes you feel indescribably satisfied.

"Brianna?" I was so transfixed by the vulnerability of his words that I hadn't even got round to answering them.

"This has made me ... really, *really* happy, Quinn."

He breathed a sigh of relief when he realised that I was deeply touched.

"Not only is this place amazing, but, you bringing me here means a lot."

Quinn smiled. "I like that you are yourself with me, Brianna."

I was taken aback by Quinn's random comment.

"Because of my face and how I appear, many people act very cautiously around me and try to appear that they are looking at me and not my scar." My heart was melting. *Those stereotypical descriptions about how you feel when you're in love were true!* "You *see* me, Brianna. You look beyond my scar."

"That's because there is a great deal more to you than that scar."

'Humble' Quinn averted his gaze to the glistening water.

"So," Quinn was keen to avoid talking about himself, "How are you finding your ability?"

"Well, you saw firsthand last night that I'm *still* not able to control it."

"You'll be able to soon, though."

"Cuchulainn said that I will need to focus on someone or something that keeps me grounded and that that will help me manage it."

"*Cuchulainn?*" Quinn cried, obviously shocked by my words.

"Yeah, he..."

"Has *he* appeared to you?"

"Yeah, just after the ... err ... fiery words that we exchanged with one another yesterday."

"Wow," Quinn ran his fingers through his hair, quite intrigued by what I had revealed. "That must have been *quite* an experience."

"It was," I agreed. "He surprised me, though. He wasn't what I expected him to be."

"How so?" Quinn spoke very quickly; he was dying to find out more.

"Well, he was funny and witty. But, when I told him what Donelle wanted me to pass onto him, I felt so sorry for him and her."

"Well, they were separated by Morrigan. It must have been hard for both of them to go on without one another, especially in the circumstances in which they were placed." Quinn's expression revealed his curiosity. "What did you pass on that made you feel sorry for Cuchulainn?"

"All I said was *you are true*."

"...The words of the Oran-Roy tree."

"Yeah."

Quinn's expression was now confused. "So, after *years* apart, *that's* what she tells him?"

"For them it meant something else though ... it was their way of saying *I love you*." As I spoke those three simple words that revealed so much, I realised that I felt this way for Quinn. What I once felt for Logan was different; a crush and a type of excitement or anticipation. But, with Quinn, he was filling up an empty part of me and he embraced who I was. I may have only known him for two months, but Quinn was making me feel something so powerful; it was unlike any other feeling I had ever experienced! The only word fit for describing these feelings for Quinn was love.

"You're cold, aren't you?" Quinn observed my shivering.

"A little," I admitted.

"Here," he said as he removed his cloak. "I don't need it."
Once the heavy, black cloak had covered my shoulders, Quinn
pulled both sides of it so that it was completely around me.

"Thanks," I looked up to meet his eyes.

Quinn's left hand stroked my right cheek and then
gradually slid down below my chin, slightly raising my head. I
relaxed my eyes and could feel Quinn's warm breath against my
cold face. When I opened my eyes, his face was only a few inches
from mine. Our eyes now interlocked, Quinn tilted his head,
waiting for me to do the same. I moved my face slightly higher in
order to meet his, then closed my eyes and waited. Quinn's soft
hands held my face and then he kissed my lips. The soft noises
within the cave became distorted by the sound of my racing heart
echoing through my ears. With my eyes still closed, I continued to
kiss Quinn and my hands found his shoulders and then navigated
their way to the back of his head; my fingers racing through his
ebony hair. Any doubts evaporated in this moment. The kiss
dispersed all fear and all rational thought; it justified my feelings,
setting them free. *For a first kiss, this was something indeed!*

Whether he heard me or not, Quinn ended the kiss. As his
hand stroked my face, I opened my eyes.

"You are true ... Brianna," Quinn said, still holding my
face. Too blown away by the kiss, I was unable to express the same
love I had for him through Cuchulainn and Donelle's words, so I

leaned up, met his lips again and wrapped my arms around his neck. Quinn's cloak fell from my back, ending our second kiss. Rather quickly Quinn pulled it from the ground, wrapped it around me as he did before and pulled me towards him, to rest against his chest. As my head lay upon his chest, I could feel his heart beating just as fast as mine was.

"Quinn?"

"Hmm..."

"You've been *so* honest with me about everything and I think it's time that I share something with you that only my father knows about."

"And what's that?" he questioned as he played with my curly locks.

"The Kaelins said something to me that *really* concerns me."

Before answering, Quinn ushered me back to an upright position so that he could see my face. "What did they say?"

"Its ... well ... Craig didn't want me to tell anyone, but, it's eating me up inside and I feel that I should be honest with you."

"Go on."

"The Kaelins tempted me as we walked through their waters. They ... they asked me whether I ... whether I wanted to put a stop to a death."

Silence.

"Quinn?" I was desperate to receive an answer.

"I don't know what to say, Brianna," he admitted. "Are you feeling guilty that you didn't listen to them further?"

"Well, I know that you're not supposed to give in to them, because seeing the future isn't good, but, a *death*. I *should* have seen what I could have done to prevent one, don't you think?"

"Brianna," Quinn stopped me, "fate is fate and it is meant to remain unknown. Knowing what lies ahead is dangerous and it can change people. You mustn't..."

"But, Quinn! What if that person was you? What if it was Charlotte, Ethan, Ewan, Craig or any of the others? Because of me, they'll die!"

Very calmly, Quinn held my shoulders, ready to reason with me. "Don't be angry with yourself. Remember what you told me?"

"No."

"You told me not to feel guilty about Rowena. You said there was nothing I could do and that I did everything in my power. You must also..."

"But I chose not to act! You acted!"

"This is different, Brianna."

I decided to agree. "I know." I sighed and looked towards the floor.

"Can't you see that the Kaelins have placed this idea in your head to torment you and create doubt? It's doing terrible things to you. If you dwell on it too much, it will only make things worse."

"I know you're right."

"Well then, it seems that we've both been of good service to each other this afternoon."

I smiled. "We have." Suddenly, I reminded myself of something else that I wanted to share with Quinn.

"I have something else I want to tell you."

"Enlighten me."

"I know this is going to sound strange, but, after seeing Cuchulainn yesterday and hearing him mention that in time I will possess something greater, I was reminded of a dream I had before I came here."

"What was that?"

"Like I said, this is going to sound *completely* obscure, but I ... I dreamed of you."

"You..."

"I saw you ... in my dream."

Quinn didn't know what to make of this, which explained why he remained silent to let me explain further.

"You and I were being held by Cillian's men." I stopped myself; I didn't want to go into detail about the state he was in.

"*And...*" Quinn wanted more.

"Well, you were being..."

"*Being* what?" Quinn was attempting to drag out every detail.

"You were hurt," I finally revealed. "The Morrigan followers were hurting you."

"Well, it was *just* a dream, Brianna. Although, *how* could you possibly envision me before knowing me?"

"That's what I thought too. Do you think that eventually I'll be able to ...?"

"See the future?" Quinn finished for me.

"Yeah."

"That seems likely. You did see me before you met me, so, it must be possible."

"But, what did it mean? What if something...?"

Quinn could already see where I was going. "Again, I will tell you the same thing. Don't worry about what lies ahead. *All right?*" He smiled and lifted up my chin.

"All right," I grudgingly agreed.

With no other option than to remain in the cave until the tide lowered the following morning, Quinn and I laughed and shared stories with one another for hours. Like any discussions I had with Quinn, they all seemed to come to an end all too quickly. As the light seeping through the small gaps in the rocks above gradually diminished and cooler air found its way into the cave, we realised that night was upon us.

"Is there any way we can light a fire?" I queried. Quinn's cloak was unable to block out the entire cool, evening chill.

"I can try, but, with not enough open spaces in the cave, it would get very smoky in here. We also don't want to attract attention from unwanted foes."

"True." I said following a tiresome yawn.

"It seems that you are in need of catching up on some sleep," Quinn inferred.

"I must be."

"Well," Quinn patted his lap, "why don't you lie down and sleep? We have until the early hours of the morning to worry about leaving."

"I'll make your leg go numb if I lie on you!"

"Well, if that happens, I'll just have to throw you off then," Quinn joked through a grin. Again, Quinn patted his lap, inviting me to sleep. It didn't take me long at all to accept his offer.

Following another yawn I bid Quinn a, "Goodnight then," as my head rested against his thigh.

"Good night."

"And thanks for today."

"*Even* the sprained wrist, grazed arm and cuts and bruises?" He wittingly responded.

"Yes. *All* those things were worth enduring for this moment ... and ... kissing you." I must have been blushing.

"Well, *I've* loved every moment of being with you today, too."

"So have I."

And I fell asleep as Quinn brushed my hair aside and soothingly caressed my face.

Chapter Eighteen

Plan of Attack

"Are you *sure* the horses will still be there, Quinn?" I asked, while making my way onto the sand from the cool, sea water.

Rather than answering my question, Quinn, still behind me, splashed the cool, ocean water against my entire back.

"I'm *trying* to dry off!" I cried, but then, I decided to kindly return the favour, so I splashed Quinn. Attempting to avoid Quinn's second splash, I lost my balance and fell into the wet sand. While trying to return to my feet, a wave brought me down and I fell into the wet sand again.

"You look like you're in need of some assistance," Quinn laughed from behind. As he grasped my wrist to pull me out of the sand, another wave met the shoreline and tossed him down; he fell against the sand like a flimsy ragdoll.

Once I removed my head out of the sandy water, I very cheekily said, "*Who's* in need of the assistance now?"

As we hurriedly clambered out of the sand in an attempt to avoid being dragged down by another wave, we couldn't help but give in to bouts of uncontrollable laughter. My hands rested against my knees, which kept me from falling over. When the remaining chuckles finally faded and I eventually caught my breath, I stood upright and my eyes interlocked with Quinn's. He offered me his hand. I accepted and we walked along the wet sand in silence, admiring the new day ahead of us.

"How is your wrist, Brianna?" Quinn said after minutes of silence.

"Not bad; still tender, but not too bad."

"Brianna?"

"Yes?"

"Do ... do you miss your home?" Quinn's eyes hadn't left the shore.

"Well ... yes, but, not necessarily the way of life. It's ... it's Mam and Dad who I miss." I paused, offering Quinn a chance to comment, but he remained quiet, his way of silently requesting me to divulge some more. "... And the dogs. I just hope that Mam and Dad believe what we wrote in the letter, but I can't help but feel guilty knowing that they must be *so* worried not knowing our whereabouts."

"What did your letter say?"

"We tried to explain our reasons for leaving."

Quinn sighed, then rested his arm along my shoulders and warmly held my arm. "Don't feel guilty."

"But I do," I admitted. "Perhaps I should have just told them everything and then left."

"You had your reasons. They'll understand that when you return home safely."

Up until that moment, I hadn't considered how Quinn would feel about my ties to Ireland. Would he expect me to return home? But, what would that mean for us? Would he follow me there, or remain here? *Am I looking too far into the future? Wait! Concentrate. You don't want him to hear that! Remain grounded. Remember what Cuchulainn said!*

"You ... you didn't hear that, Quinn, did you?"

"Hear what?" He appeared confused; the reaction I was hoping for.

"Don't worry," I tried to quickly change the topic, "It's nothing." After an unsettling silence, I needed to talk. "Quinn, I was thinking..."

"Yes."

"Us ... we're ... we're sort of from different times, if you know what I mean."

He made a light chuckle. "We are."

"I feel as though I've pulled you out from a book."

Again, Quinn laughed.

"Are you making fun of me?"

"No," he quickly replied, still chuckling though.

"You're laughing!"

"It's because you're so ... so..."

"So..."

"Fascinating."

"How so?" I can't wait to hear this!

"You are unlike any girl I have ever met, Brianna." *Aw. That is truly the nicest thing anyone has ever said to me.* Quinn stopped walking and brought me to a graceful halt, then gently turned me towards him. Now looking up at him directly, he decided to continue. "I think you are the only person I can truly be myself around and ... and I ... I like myself, when I'm with you." Quinn's words made me recall what Cuchulainn had shared with me, *"Find something or someone that grounds you, so that your ability to hear and send thoughts can be suppressed."* There and then, I was certain that Quinn was that someone.

Completely entranced by his words and emerald eyes, I failed to respond.

"Brianna?" Quinn snapped me out of my trance.

My eyes flickered, and then focussed their gaze back up at Quinn's face. "Sorry, Quinn. I was just ... really blown away by what you just said. It's ... it's the nicest thing that someone has ever said to me ... ever."

We both smiled and continued to walk along the Breena shore, holding hands silently, perfectly happy just to be in each other's presence. Close to the border of the Breena woodlands, I thought about Mam and Dad again. *What would they think of Quinn?* Quinn noticed that something was troubling me.

"You're worried, aren't you?" He asked sympathetically.

"How could you tell?" I quickly questioned.

"You ... you did that funny facial expression when you try to hide something that is bothering you."

"And I thought I was the mind reader," I laughed.

"How are you coping with that, by the way?"

"...My hearing thoughts?"

"Yes."

"Honestly, I'm finding that when I'm..." I hesitated; I didn't know whether it was too soon to reveal how Quinn was helping me. *Would that put too much pressure on him?* I decided to be honest with him. "When I'm with you, Quinn, I'm myself and I'm comfortable. It has helped me control it, because I haven't really had to think about it."

"So, you haven't heard my thoughts last night and this morning?" Quinn suddenly sounded a little anxious.

"Uh ... no. It's ... it's not like it happens every waking moment, Quinn. Is ... is there something you're worried about?"

Quinn released a sigh of relief, which made me fear that he was failing to tell me something.

"Quinn?" I asked him again.

"Err ... no, no, no," he quickly attempted to brush aside his thoughts. But as he read my facial expression and saw past it, I did the same for him, and attributed his lack of eye contact with his keeping something from me. Very unsatisfied with his answer, I decided to question him further; I wasn't going to give up; it wasn't in my nature!

"Now you are the one hiding something!"

"Now, that's not fair," Quinn stopped walking, wanting to sort this out. "You never told me what was bothering you."

True. "Well, you asked me about another subject entirely."

"So, what was...?"

"Whoa!" I waved my arms, stopping Quinn, realising what he was doing. "Now don't go changing the subject so we avoid what you aren't telling me!"

Quinn didn't answer. He pressed on forward into the Breena woodlands. I grumbled and quickly followed on behind.

"Quinn!" His pace was deliberately fast. "If ... if you tell me what you're not saying, I'll do the same," I yelled from behind him, rather out of breath in account of clambering through the shrubs and forest floor after Quinn.

My proposition seemed fair, because Quinn stopped walking. As I stood beside him, he began to walk again, but at a calmer pace that was much easier for me to match.

"Brianna, I ... I'm not ... I'm not hiding something. It's just, I thought about..." Quinn's gaze didn't shift from the forest floor ahead. "Look, I ... I can't say!" Even with the little light that had made its way between the forest trees, I could still make out Quinn's reddening cheeks.

"It's alright," I assured him, "we have to be honest with each other, feeling as we do."

"Ah, the horses are just up ahead."

"Quinn!" I clenched his arm and made him stop walking. Against his wishes, he slowly turned around to face me, but he failed to look at me. I didn't need any more words to express what I wanted from Quinn; he knew that I wouldn't rest until he was completely truthful with me.

Before speaking, Quinn released an anxious sigh and ran his fingers through his hair; something he always did when he was unsure. "Look, I'm glad that you didn't hear my thoughts because ... because..."

I raised my eyebrows and stared at Quinn intently, silently urging him to go on.

Quinn continued on towards the horses to avoid eye contact with me as he answered. "There are some things a man just ... just thinks about when he ... when he ... kisses and ... holds the ... girl he lo ... really likes."

"Quinn!" I gasped.

"Well, you wanted me to be honest with you!" He openly admitted, while he adjusted the saddle on his horse.

Quinn was honest, but, a little too honest for my liking at this stage of our relationship, but, I had pressured him into revealing too much. How could I be angry with him for leaving some things to the imagination? After all, we weren't a 'normal' couple. If every woman in a relationship could potentially hear the thoughts of a man, wouldn't humanity cease to exist? How could I possibly hold this against Quinn? Everyone can think freely, in the comfort that no one else will know, but that was not the case for us. Would this lack of freedom drive Quinn away? Even though Quinn had seemed to help control my ability, would having the potential to delve into his thoughts threaten what we might have?

"Quinn, Quinn," I said, holding his arm and urging him to turn around. "I'm not angry with you. Don't ... don't be ashamed. You're entitled to think what you like in the comfort that no one else has to know." I ran my hand down his arm and held his hand. "Now I understand why you didn't want to say anything and I'm sorry that I pressured you."

"Brianna, I..."

"I understand if you don't ... don't," it pained me to say this, "want to ... be ... with me."

"Brianna, just..."

"How are you supposed to feel comfortable with me if there is the risk of me going into your head?" I might not have been crying, but I wanted to. I was afraid of the possibility of dealing with letting go; I feared that I had anticipated too much too soon, without considering matters more. "Please, please just tell me if this is going to be too hard for you! Because, if ... if I need to..."

"Brianna, Brianna!" Quinn held my shoulders. "Have you forgotten last night?"

I shook my head, worried that if I were to speak I would wail instead.

"I know that your ability will be a ... a challenge to deal with at times, but, we'll make it work. We will. I just felt ... well, embarrassed earlier and that is what has created this sudden doubt in your mind." Quinn's hands left my shoulders and then held my face. "I wasn't annoyed with you. You cannot deny the gift that has been given to you and I understand that."

"Cuchulainn was right," I confessed. "You do keep me grounded." Quinn humbly looked away. "You're too humble, you know."

Quinn laughed. "Don't you remember? I'm very proud of my humility."

Quinn supported my foot as I mounted Epona. "Be light on your wrist. Use your other hand for the next few days."

"Thanks."

"Now," he said once he was comfortably on his horse, "let's think of how we are going to reveal our set of circumstances to everyone."

*

"I was about to send out a search party," Craig said, with a very interesting expression, as Quinn and I reached the centre of the camp and mounted off our horses.

"So, you weren't worried?" I asked Craig, rather surprised by his reaction.

"No," he admitted. His eyes quickly flickered towards Quinn. "I knew that you would be in ... safe hands, Brianna. Although, Charlotte and Ethan were a little concerned about your whereabouts."

As their names were spoken, Charlotte and Ethan emerged from a nearby tent. Charlotte's face was beaming as she sprinted towards me, in contrast to Ethan's folded arms and slow stroll, with a very unimpressed look on his face.

"We thought something had happened to the two of you!" Charlotte cried. "I was really worried, but your father assured me that you were all right."

"I'll leave you all to catch up," Craig said and smiled as he walked away.

"So," Ethan grumbled, "Quinn and you were..." He wasn't at all impressed.

I was about to shout, *'What's with that attitude, Ethan?'* but before I had the chance, Quinn could see the anger bubbling up inside me, placed his hand on my shoulder and said, "We fell into a crevice when we were walking along the rocks at Breena. We had to wait for the tide to lower in order to have a means of leaving. Brianna needs to take it easy with her wrist too. She has a nasty sprain."

"It's nothing!" I insisted.

"Hmm. I see." Ethan wasn't buying Quinn's interpretation of our time together. "It must have been pretty cold down in that crevice, Bee." Ethan lowered his head and glared over the rim of his glasses right at me. Charlotte, trying to be subtle, elbowed Ethan's arm and gave him a very intimidating gawk. "But," he quickly changed his tone, "I'm glad to see that Quinn has brought you back safely."

"Your arm, Bee!" Charlotte cried as she noticed the strips of material wrapped around my arm.

"Charlotte! Please don't fret!"

"You're back!" Ewan happily cried, as he entered the clearing with a large bird of some kind over his shoulder, which I suspected was today's lunch.

"Perfect timing, Ewan," Quinn replied. "Could you do me a favour?"

Ewan placed the limp bird over a log by the fire and then came to stand by us. "Certainly." As Ewan answered Quinn's request, his eyes darted to my bandaged arm. "Brianna, you're hurt!"

"That's what I would like you to help me with, Ewan," Quinn explained. "I wanted to have a word with Ethan and Charlotte and was hoping that while I was doing so, you could re-bandage Brianna's injured arm."

"Err, yes. Yes, of course." Like Ewan, I was unsure what to make of Quinn's need to speak with Charlotte and Ethan alone.

"We won't be long, Brianna," Quinn advised me, as he stroked the side of my face.

Ethan and Charlotte, who were also puzzled and rather uncertain about Quinn's intentions, reluctantly followed him beyond the clearing and well into the surrounding forest.

Ewan looked at me and raised his arms in confusion, not knowing what to make of what we had both just witnessed.

"Don't ask me!" I warned him. "I know just as much as you know."

Ewan signalled for me to sit on the log by the fire. "Come and we'll talk as I attend to your arm."

"Ah!" I winced as Ewan removed the existing strips of cloth from my arm.

"Sorry, Brianna, this is going to sting a little," Ewan apologised.

"Don't worry," I insisted, "If I could endure swimming with my arm this way in salty sea water, this will be fine."

"You know, Brianna, I've never seen Quinn so happy," Ewan casually mentioned while gently dabbing my arm. Waiting for an answer, Ewan struggled to hide a smirk.

"If you wanted to ask about Quinn and me, you could have just asked rather than trying to ... ah!"

"Sorry!"

"It's okay."

"Well, you were saying, Brianna ..."

"You know, you're just as bad as Charlotte!"

Ewan remained silent, trying to make it seem that he wasn't intentionally prying, but I knew that he was just dying to hear my take on things before speaking with Quinn.

"Ewan, I know Quinn's spoken to you about us. If there's something you want to know, just ask."

He hesitated, trying to make it seem that he wasn't too desperate to hear what I had to share. "Well, since you offered," Ewan sighed, "I just wanted to say that you're the only person I've seen make such an impact on him."

"Really?"

"Oh, yes. Don't tell him I told you, but, almost every waking moment we've been alone, all he speaks of is you."

"Well," I didn't know how to respond. "That's nice to know ... I suppose."

"Quinn hasn't been this happy since before he lost Rowena." Ewan wrapped a final strip of clean cloth around my upper right arm and then clapped his hands together. "All done!"

"Thanks, that's much more comfortable now."

"So," Ewan sat opposite me and rested his elbows against his knees, interlocked his fingers and stared directly into my eyes, waiting for me to provide a detailed description of what Quinn and I had gotten up to.

"Geez, Ewan!" I rolled my eyes. "We've kissed! Happy now? Is that enough information to satisfy you?"

"Well I'm," he paused and then smiled, "I'm very happy for you both."

"You really are just as bad as Charlotte, Ewan."

Together we laughed and when our chuckles eased into sighs, Ewan brought the conversation back to Quinn. "What do you think he's speaking to them about?"

"Like I said, you know just as much as I do. But, don't worry, as soon as they get back, Charlotte will explode if she doesn't share with me what happened. And I'll be sure to let you know exactly what was said, if Quinn fails to do so."

"I'd appreciate that, Brianna. I'm ... intrigued by the effect you've had on my friend."

I smiled. "Don't mention it."

*

"I take it that you and Quinn had a nice evening," Leona cheekily raised, as she sat beside me following lunch.

"Ewan," I mumbled, shaking my head.

"He isn't very good at keeping secrets and I was *too* happy about it not to ask!"

In most circumstances, people feign enthusiasm, just to make you reveal everything, until they are satisfied, but, with Leona, she was genuinely keen; she sincerely cared for the wellbeing of her dear friend, Quinn. "You're happy for Quinn, like Ewan is, aren't you?" I asked.

"I am." She sighed. "It's nice to know that there is someone who can make him happy ... without trying *too* hard."

I smiled and my cheeks began to redden. "He's ... made me happy too."

Leona chuckled. "Hmm. You're blushing. I can also see how *he* has made you happy."

Not wanting to dwell on Quinn and me too much, I decided to ask Leona whether she was in, or ever had been in, a relationship. After all, Leona was ninety-eight years old; surely she would have learned something about intimate relationships in that time!

"Leona..."

"Yes?"

"I ... I don't want to pry ... but, have *you ever* been ... involved with someone?"

Leona was taken aback by my question.

"*Sorry*, Leona," I quickly apologised following her reaction. "I shouldn't have asked..."

"*No, no,*" she stopped me and waved her arms. "Brianna, I've *always* wanted to find someone who would care for me in that way. But, sadly, being Darian, there aren't many people I can ... well, settle down with. Remember, I'm almost one-hundred."

"There are no Darian men you know of who...?"

Leona laughed. "None!"

"None!" I repeated. "How can there be none?"

"It's not that," she quickly explained. "Most Darian people want to stay with Darians." She paused. "I don't want that."

"You mean you don't want to live as long as you do?"

"If a Darian is united with someone not of our race and clan, we no longer live a long life. You can't call yourself a Darian once you have made that choice."

Surprised by Leona's reason, I had to find out why she felt as she did. "Why don't you want to live as long as you're able to?"

"In my almost hundred years, Brianna, I have seen *too many* friends wither away, while I remain the same. It is *too* much of a burden saying goodbye to those who have just as much right to live as long as I am able to."

"So, you hope to find someone who is not Darian who will accept you?"

Leona nodded, but then became distracted and turned to face the outskirt of the forest behind us. "There are two people who *really* want to speak to you," Leona said, as left me on the log by the fire.

I stood up and walked to meet Ethan and Charlotte. For the first time in a long time, I didn't know how to greet them. I didn't know what Quinn had said or asked of them, which made me feel a little uneasy and hesitant in being the first one to speak. Luckily, Charlotte, being her usual extraverted self, broke the stifling silence.

"How's the arm?"

"Good, thanks," at this point, I still hadn't looked at Ethan, worried that he'd be in a foul mood.

"That's good," Charlotte quickly replied and looked to Ethan, hoping that he would soon enter the conversation.

"Oh, yeah," he coughed up. "It's good that it's on the mend."

"So..." I discovered that I was swaying from side to side; something I did when I was uncertain about what to do. "Let's go to my tent."

Ethan shrugged his shoulders, which was his way of accepting something while in a bad mood and Charlotte smiled and nodded. Ethan and Charlotte sat cross-legged and looked into their laps, twiddling their thumbs, unsure where to begin. Stubbornly, I remained silent, waiting for the silence to cave in on Charlotte and make her crack.

"Quinn is *really* nice, Brianna and his intentions are good," Charlotte spoke so quickly. I had to process her words before I answered.

"Is that what he spoke to you about?"

"Yes, but, *I* already knew that. It was someone else who needed convincing." Charlotte flicked her eyes over to Ethan, who was doing his best to try and avoid eye contact.

I folded my arms and looked straight up at Ethan. "Ethan?" My tone was stern; I needed him to know that I wanted a straight answer from him. "Ethan, look at me." Surprisingly, Ethan glanced up at me immediately. "Does this bother you?"

Ethan breathed out a frustrated sigh, which seemed to usher in his long awaited words. "He's a good fella, don't get me wrong! But, Bee, I just ... I just don't want you to get hurt!"

"Quinn won't..."

"Maybe not intentionally, but, Quinn is ... he's a few years older than you and I'm worried that you're going into this too fast!"

"Ethan, I'm..."

"Just be careful, Bee." Ethan's concern was sincere. "I ... Charlotte and I don't want you to get caught up in this so fast that you'll wind up regretting it, all right?"

I didn't know how to respond! Ethan's mentioning of his concerns wasn't the first time I had found myself doubting what Quinn and I had. Deep down, I knew that Quinn was genuine about me and I felt the same way, but perhaps I had entered into this *too* quickly. Perhaps that wasn't the case for how things happened in Oran-Roy, but, if we were in Ireland, I knew that my parents would advise me to take things much slower than how they had eventuated. Once again, that unpleasant, guilty feeling settled in the pit of my stomach. I was stuck in a compromising situation; never before had I been certain about my feelings for another person, but had I ventured into it too fast, without thinking things through?

"Look, I ... I see where you're coming from. Perhaps, I've gone into this too quickly, but I need you both to know that I have never felt like this about anyone before. When we get home, I'll cross that bridge with Mam and Dad when the time is right, but, for now, I need you both to trust that I'm in good hands."

Charlotte smiled. "I'm happy for you, Bee."

I faced Ethan, waiting for some kind of response. "He is a good fella, Bee. I just don't want to see you hurt. Just, take it slow." Ethan's words satisfied me, yet, at the same time, they made me fear what awaited me in Ireland.

A cool, strong wind lashed the tent sheets open, almost lifting the tent from its hooks. As I hopped up in shock and faced the opening, a familiar transparent face appeared.

"Guys go and meet Craig and everyone else at the heart of camp. I'll be there shortly."

Puzzled, Charlotte and Ethan left my tent, which gave me a chance to speak with Cuchulainn.

"You're in a much better way than when we last spoke, it seems," Cuchulainn jovially mentioned.

"Well, a great deal has happened since then," I agreed with him. "Speaking of the last time," I continued, "you said that you would counsel me when the time was right, *right?*"

"Yes," he calmly answered, as he took his seat on my large clothing chest.

"But, I ... I don't think I've noticed anything ... anything other than the abilities that I already know about, Cuchulainn."

"That is why I am here."

Still confused, and surprised by his sudden arrival, I continued to question him. "So, have I already done something, but I haven't noticed it?"

"Well, I guess that is a good way of putting it, although, you haven't really had much time to recognise it as of yet."

"So, it's happened recently then?"

"Within the last few minutes actually," Cuchulainn said through a slight chuckle.

"Wow ... you *are* fast!"

"I would have preferred you to discover it for yourself, Brianna, but time *is* of the essence and it is *most* important that you become aware of what you possess before you reach Crag."

Unsure how to respond, I sat back down and tried to recall anything peculiar that occurred within the last few minutes. Apart from the awkwardness felt by all three of us, I couldn't put a finger on anything that resulted from an ability I had. Cuchulainn was quick to recognise my lapse into thinking.

"Brianna, when you asked Ethan to look at you, did you detect anything strange?"

"Err ... *no*. I can't say I did." Obviously still confused, Cuchulainn further explained.

"In that moment, you felt *very* strongly about yourself and your feelings." Cuchulainn paused; providing me with the opportunity to catch on and discover what I had done, but, I continued to remain silent and looked up at Cuchulainn with a puzzled expression. "You asked your brother to look at you, Brianna. He did it immediately after your instruction."

"*Wait, wait!*" I said, shaking my head. "Are you *trying* to say that *I* made him do that?"

"Yes."

"*Whoa!* So, if ... are you saying that I can control someone's actions?"

"... Their thoughts, too."

Again, I was completely at a loss for words! Hearing and sending thoughts was enough to deal with and get used to, but now this!

"...Why the need for me to know so quickly, Cuchulainn?"

Cuchulainn stood up and began to fade into the light. "Learn to master this before you return to Crag. A great deal will be needed from you."

"But ... but, I still want to ask you about..."

"I've answered *all* that is needed for now." Cuchulainn's body dissolved into a thin ray of light, sneaking its way out of my tent.

He comes and tells me that I have the ability to control a person's thoughts and actions, yet he's only here for a few mere minutes!

Frustrated, confused and frazzled, I didn't know where to go from here. But, finally, after a few minutes of acclimatising to the recent news, an outrageous thought entered my mind.

If I can do as Cuchulainn said I can do, that would mean that I would be able to make my way into Tarmon! I could pass Cillian's men and make my way to Keira and Brogan!

Overwhelmed by what I had just discovered, I ran to the heart of our camp site and found Craig, Ewan, Leona, Rona, Zephan, Charlotte, Ethan and Quinn discussing the leaving arrangements.

"Brianna!" Quinn cried out, shocked by my undisguised zeal.

"I know what has to be done now," I assured everyone, while regaining my breath. "We now have a means of making it into Tarmon without much risk being involved."

"What do you mean?" Craig asked inquisitively.

"I think we have a plan of attack."

Chapter Nineteen

Brogan Elsa

...Craig joined Keira by the fire, nursing their newborn son. He stroked his son's smooth head and leaned in to kiss Keira on her cheek. Craig's stressful thoughts did not need to be voiced for Keira to know that something was troubling him.

"My love, Cuchulainn assured us we are safe here. The Darians will not let us down. Stop fretting!"

"My trust in Cuchulainn and the Darians is not what troubles me my love." Craig sighed, and headed towards concealed entrance of the cave. "What keeps me awake at night is not our son's deafening cries and not the fear of our dear friends betraying our trust. Your father is not a well man. It's only a matter of time until Cillian uses his death as a means of leaving Tarmon and revealing the truth of our son."...

- Excerpt from 'The Morrigan Book'

"Brianna, what's brought this on?" Craig asked, a little concerned by my sudden proposal.

"I finally know what other power I possess!"

"When did you discover this?" Quinn inquired.

"Just now, but, anyway..." I didn't want to explain the details of my recent discovery in that precise moment; I wanted to propose my plan so that I could finally be of some use. "I think that, as well as hearing and sending thoughts, I can control the thoughts and actions of others."

All present became wide-eyed. They looked around to see how this revelation had been received. Each felt reassured to see that everyone else's facial expressions were expressing the same doubts.

"Did this happen in the last five minutes?" Ethan doubtfully queried.

"Yeah!" I swiftly answered, wanting to return to explaining my plan. "Look, if I brush up on this and my other ability before we arrive in Crag, I'll be able to make it past Tarmon's defences and Cillian's men! I'll be able to get in contact with Brogan and, maybe, he'll be able to show me where Keira is! All we have to do is..." Simultaneously, Craig, Ewan and Quinn shook their heads in protest.

"It's too dangerous, Brianna!" Quinn warned me.

"He's right," Ewan agreed.

"Indeed. I am sure that you believe that you possess the abilities that you claim, but how can you know that you will have these abilities sufficiently mastered to ensure that they will not let you down when you face extreme pressure? Develop your abilities first." Craig followed.

"But, how are we supposed to get anything done?" I cried, raising my arms up and down with anger, frustrated at being met with cynicism. "You all said that my reappearance here meant something. So I'm telling you, you have to let me do this! You have to let me! Otherwise, there was no point in me returning, if we aren't going to use what I have to help restore Oran-Roy."

Again, everyone present read each other's faces to determine the consensus.

Leona smiled at me and stepped forward. "Brianna is right. If we can infiltrate Tarmon's borders and safely get Brianna within Cillian's quarters, where Brogan is most likely to be, and if she can master these new talents, we'll be able to find Keira and finally have access to Zia's writings."

Of course! The Morrigan book told of Zia passing on his writings to my mother close to when he died. But the book never said what was contained within his writings.

Excited by Leona's mention of Zia's writings, I met Charlotte and Ethan's beaming faces; like me, they could both recall what Leona had described from the Morrigan book.

"The book that we've told you about did mention Zia's writings, but it didn't say what they contained," Charlotte explained. "Leona, did Zia ever explain to you what was in his writings when he requested that you pass on that piece of parchment to Brianna?"

Leona shook her head. "I'm afraid he didn't."

"Keira is the only one who knows," Craig expressed. "Although, Cillian might have found the whereabouts of Zia's writings over the years and there is no telling how much he knows."

"So then," I said, intentionally redirecting the conversation back to the plan, "Is it settled? I will use my abilities to make it into Tarmon and then Cillian's headquarters, find Brogan and try to convince him to help me find Keira."

Silence.

"Well..." I couldn't wait any longer for an answer, so I decided not to and I put my ability to the test. I focussed on Quinn and tried to ignore everything and everyone around me.

"Her plan is sound, but it's far too risky! She'll need to be accompanied if everyone agrees to see this plan through. It's too risky though!"

I then focussed all of my attention on Zephan. He hadn't voiced his opinion yet and I was keen to hear what he had to say.

"Brianna speaks wisely. Her ability provides us with a means of infiltrating Cillian's bounds. Up until now, we haven't had an opportunity like this! We have to act!"

"Brianna!" Leona yelled. Too immersed in Quinn and Zephan's thoughts, I hadn't realised that I was being spoken to!

"Sorry, what did I miss?"

Craig stepped forward and reassuringly held my shoulders. "Brianna's right," Craig announced to everyone. "I believe that we must act and that Brianna is here to help us, but..." I released a frustrated sigh; the answer I awaited for was not looking promising. "... We can only see this through if you have mastered your new skills and if you allow us to prepare a safe and well-guarded means of passing you through Tarmon's border. You have four days to work on your control, or we'll just have to come up with an alternate plan."

I smiled and breathed a sigh of relief, which was in stark contrast with my earlier anxiety. "All right," I quickly agreed and then turned to face everyone else. "I know that since I have left Oran-Roy things have been extremely volatile and dangerous; you've had to live under a rock for so long that it's been difficult to take chances. But," I walked towards Ewan, who was standing beside Quinn and I patted his back, "When Charlotte, Ethan and I arrived here – thanks to Keelty, of course – Ewan and the rest of you took a chance in bringing the three of us to Crag. And now," I continued, "we're just taking another chance."

"... Another chance that could jeopardise too much, Brianna!" Quinn cried with his voice shaking with anxiety. "There's too much at stake!" Quinn turned around and paced towards the surrounding woods.

Without hesitating, Ewan turned to follow Quinn into the bushes, but I placed my hand on Ewan's shoulder and held him back. "No, Ewan, I'll go," I assured him and I went after Quinn.

Now well into the lush wood, with grey stones surfaced in moss and scattered leaves and overhung by enormous, overbearing oaks, I hurried in pursuit of Quinn, but he disappeared from sight for some time.

"*Quinn!*" I yelled, but only the frightened sparrows responded to my call, by fleeing the nearby trees. Continuing on through the wood, I eventually came across a sound. I stopped walking and tried to locate a loud and repetitive noise, but it was too difficult to trace, with other woodland sounds interfering. Frustrated, almost to the point of giving up and turning back to the camp, I remembered the skills I possessed. After taking a deep breath, I closed my eyes, pictured Quinn and attempted to shut out the background noise. Suddenly, my ears felt fuzzy, like the sensation of having water in your ears. I opened my eyes and could hear a troubled voice.

"I can't let her go through with this! She mustn't do this! There is too much at stake here! I don't ... I don't want her to ... she could get hurt!"

Finally, the worrying thoughts of Quinn gave away his whereabouts and brought me to him - drumming his palms into a tree trunk and knocking off its bark. After a powerful kick and a final swing at the tree, Quinn ferociously ran his fingers through his hair and then rested his hands against his thighs.

The timid touch of my hand against his back startled him. When Quinn realised it was me, he raised himself up and tried to appear as though he was free of worry. Like me, Quinn wasn't too good at concealing his inner thoughts and feelings.

Quinn cleared his throat and looked over my head. "You ... you heard all that ... didn't you?"

"Do you mean the thrashing of the tree or your troubled thoughts, Quinn?" Quinn didn't answer me; my humour had failed to fulfil its intended purpose. So, quickly, I cleared my throat to ready myself for persuading Quinn into believing that my plan was our only option. "Quinn, what do you want me to do?"

Quinn continued to stare over my head. His breathing was deep and rather rapid; he was holding back tears, but they were so desperately longing to be free.

"Quinn, what do you want me to ...?"

"I can't lose you!" Quinn blared, so loud that the birds nesting in all of the nearby trees were dispatched into the air. He clenched my shoulders before speaking again. "Don't you understand? You're ... you mean too much to me! How can I let you go into something as dangerous as this? How can I do that?"

He released my shoulders and leant against the tree he had been recently thrashing.

"You aren't letting me!" I tried to sound as reassuring as I could. "You aren't *letting me*, because I am *choosing* to do this, Quinn!"

Quinn breathed a heavy sigh of grief.

"This is about Rowena, isn't it?" I said rather bluntly.

"And what if it is?"

"Quinn, I thought we spoke about this! You can't let your regrets of the past prevent you from taking action!" I stormed towards Quinn and clasped his hands, then held them against my chest. "Look at me, Quinn." At first, he resisted. "Look at me, Quinn." Quinn could no longer choose to avert his eyes. As I had done with Ethan only minutes earlier, I had successfully controlled Quinn's actions and he had no choice but to follow my instructions. His luminous, green eyes fixated on mine. "You *must* trust me. If we don't put faith in anything, things will stay as they are and nothing will get done!" I raised my hand to meet his face. "I've never said this to you before, because I was afraid of how you might respond, but, I think you need to hear it now."

"What might that be?" Quinn queried. Delicately, I ran my fingers along his scar. Quinn closed his eyes as my fingers fell from his face.

"I like your scar, Quinn."

Quinn crinkled his eyebrows, unsure what to make of my comment.

"I like it because it reminds me of the sacrifice you were willing to make to save your sister." Quinn's head fell, but my hand caught his chin and raised his face back up again. "I know you're scared that something will happen to me, but, no good will come out of letting Cillian continue whatever he is doing. The longer we wait, the greater the chance of Cillian finding out how to control Morrigan and use her for his own personal gain. Things would have happened by now if he knew what to do, but my mother has obviously held her ground." Quinn started to shake his head. He opened his mouth, ready to speak, but I denied him of that right and continued. "There is a chance that Cillian could eventually track us down and claim the carrier if we sit back and do nothing, which could then lead to him raising Morrigan, but..."

"Exactly!" Quinn interrupted me. "Infiltrating Tarmon will only make that outcome more likely to eventuate!" Quinn held my shoulders with a stern grip. "Don't you see? To free Oran-Roy of Morrigan's curse for good, to have the clans united again, Morrigan will have to return in order to truly be destroyed. We cannot take that step until we know how to be truly rid of her! She is only bound, Brianna – not dead! If your plan falls through, Morrigan will return and we will have no means of knowing how we can remove her for good!"

"Exactly, Quinn! We have no knowledge of how to destroy her. That is why we must go to Tarmon!" I released an anguished sigh and then continued to justify myself. "My mother is the only person who knows what must be done once Morrigan is returned to power. Zia passed on his writings to her before his death. She is the key! Only the Carrier and the Druids of Oran-Roy can know the truth of how to annihilate Morrigan, but, in order for us to destroy her, as the existing Carrier, I must go to my mother in Tarmon and find out what has to be done."

Quinn remained silent, which gave me hope that he was finally seeing reason.

"Cillian most probably doesn't know what lies in Zia's writings, because, to this day, he hasn't committed murder – Morrigan hasn't returned. He will not bring about Morrigan's return unless he possesses the carrier and becomes aware of how to control her when she returns."

"But, Morrigan claimed that the one who released her would be rewarded. So, there's nothing stopping Cillian from..."

"Quinn, in all these years Cillian hasn't brought her back, why do you think that's the case? Cillian needs the carrier as an escape. If Morrigan overturns Oran-Roy, the carrier is his means of leaving. From that book I've told you about, it said that it was only rumoured that as Morrigan was being bound, she proclaimed that the one to kill in her name would be rewarded. Cillian isn't certain of that, Quinn. He won't take that chance until he has the knowledge contained in Zia's writings and the carrier."

Quinn sighed, slid down on the closest tree and sat against its trunk. I was surprised to see him smile and then pat the ground beside him, inviting me to sit beside him. As I sat down, Quinn looked down at my hands and fiddled with my fingers, then ran his hand along the carrier symbol on my right palm.

"You will go, whether I plead with you to stay or not..." Quinn sighed.

"You know me very well, Quinn."

Quinn raised his head and met my glance. "Well, then, seeing as though you are going to see this through, you must promise me one thing, Brianna."

"What's that?"

"I must escort you into Tarmon and accompany you until I feel that I can leave you."

"But, you'll feel the need to be watching me the entire time! Once I convince Brogan of..."

Quinn raised his eyebrows. "Brianna, promise me."

"Fine," I grumbled resignedly, then stood up and started walking back to camp.

"You know *me* very well, Brianna."

*

The four-day journey back to Crag involved training of another kind; rather than refining our swiftness with a blade and our shot on a target, I underwent hours of mind reading, sending thoughts and controlling others' actions and thoughts. Ethan, Charlotte, Quinn, Ewan and Leona were my main subjects; allowing me to enter their minds, send my thoughts to them and control their movements. By the third day of refining my ability, I couldn't help but make Ethan and Charlotte do silly things. Controlling Ethan into asking Quinn to dance and making Quinn accept his offer was amusing and too funny a moment to pass up. My subjects were not always thrilled with my results, but bore the situation manfully.

I struggled with controlling more than two people at a time. While making Leona and Charlotte run around in circles simultaneously, I tried to make Ewan join in, but wasn't able to manage this level of control. However, Craig was sufficiently impressed for our plan to proceed.

Following the evening of rest along Crag's border, beside Kael Creek where I had first come to meet my father, the morning was spent finalising our means of infiltrating Tarmon for that very night.

"Rona and Zephan," both nodded as Craig called upon them, "you will fly through Bryan and meet us just beyond the border of Tarmon's castle, on the Daray side."

"Agreed," Rona answered.

"Yes," Zephan affirmed.

"Good. Now, once the rest of us make it beyond Kael, Brianna, you will be accompanied by Ewan, Leona and Quinn into Tarmon to try and find Brogan." Ewan, Leona, Quinn and I nodded, confirming that we were fully aware of what we needed to do. "Do not forget what you must do as you enter Tarmon. Brianna, there will only be two to four guards on the side of the castle walls closest to the Daray forest. That is where the four of you will enter. Now, you three," Craig focussed on Ewan, Quinn and Leona, "Brianna will do her best to control two of the guards to let you pass, but, it is most important that if there are more than two guards, you silently put the others out of action. Understood?"

"Yes, Craig," Ewan and Leona answered, Quinn simply nodded.

"I don't know where Brogan will be, but, until Brianna finds him and controls him – if she has to resort to that – Quinn and Ewan, you must continue to accompany her. But, once Brianna is successful in communicating with or controlling Brogan to take her to Keira, you must both hide yourselves at the main entrance and remain there; if you were both to remain with Brianna and Brogan, it could potentially bring too much attention and more work for Brianna."

"Understood," Ewan affirmed Craig. Craig glanced across to seek Quinn's response and again, he nodded.

"Good," Craig clapped his hands together and then continued. "Leona, you will remain with Brianna and Brogan as a means of communicating back to Ewan and Quinn if Brianna encounters trouble."

"It will be an honour," Leona replied.

"Try to embody a small creature if you can."

"I'll do my best."

"Brianna," my eyes left Leona and returned to my father. "Before you leave Ewan and Quinn, it is extremely important that you leave the carrier with Quinn or Ewan; that way, if the worst were to happen and you were detained, you cannot be hurt as ... if..." Craig hesitated. This was a difficult matter for a father to speak of in relation to his daughter.

"If Cillian detains me, still being the Carrier will prevent him from killing me, because Oran-Roy would perish with the killing of the Carrier," I explained, saving my father from the words he did not wish to speak.

"Yes," he confirmed and then looked at Quinn and Ewan again. "Whoever holds the carrier must not wear it. I know you know this, but, you can only keep it in your possession, otherwise, wearing it would make you the Carrier."

Both Quinn and Ewan nodded, which eased my father's worries.

"All right then, Brianna," Craig's concerned, blue eyes looked at me sincerely, understanding that such a huge amount of pressure resided on me. "Do your best to retrieve your mother and make Brogan direct you all to the exit of the castle, where Ewan and Quinn will be in hiding."

"I will."

"Ewan and Quinn," Craig called upon them again, much more forcefully than he had done so before. "If Brianna is unable to get to you, Leona will inform you and then you will signal the rest of us waiting on the outskirts of Tarmon."

"How should we inform you?" Ewan asked.

"A flaming arrow would draw too much attention," Craig inferred.

"Perhaps I could inform you more surreptitiously," Leona suggested, raising her hand up hesitantly.

"Very good," Craig said. "Now, alongside with me will be Rona, Zephan, Keelty, Faolon, Dougal, Ethan and Charlotte." As Craig mentioned everyone's name, he met each one of their eyes. "We will remain hidden on the Daray side of Tarmon and only enter Tarmon if we are called on by Leona. If *too* many of us were to enter Tarmon, we'd create a distraction and it would ruin our chances of reaching Brogan and Keira."

All present nodded their heads and then looked around to read the expressions of those present. The silence was filled with unspoken doubts; no one felt comfortable to be the first to comment. For all present, the moment seemed surreal; for years my father and his party of supporters were in the dark and had no secure means of entering Tarmon. But, with my arrival and my ability, change was coming – a change that had been desired for so long. The yearning for change was like a bare and barren land craving rain after a long and agonising drought. Craig, Rona, Zephan, Leona, Keelty and Faolon, Dougal, Ewan and Quinn had been in a drought for so long and were longing to quench their thirst for progress, but now that it had finally dawned on them, they were almost too overcome to accept it.

After a few moments, the eyes of everyone present seemed to focus on me. It was clear that a great deal of responsibility was resting on my shoulders for the night ahead. If this plan did indeed fail, a lot was at stake. But, there was also so much to gain and it was this potentiality that urged me to act. Disturbed by the silence, I had to speak.

"We *will* be alright," I assured everyone, but I was especially directing my words to Quinn.

My father stood up and signalled for me to follow him into the neighbouring wood. "I just want to have a moment alone with Brianna," Craig informed everyone, then escorted me beyond the camp. "Brianna," Craig said as he held my shoulders, "a great burden has been placed on you. Please do *all* that you can, but the last thing we all want is for you to feel pressured beyond that with which you can cope." Craig breathed a concerning sigh. "I've already expressed to you how happy I am with you returning and I just want you to know that I love you and your mother loves you, no matter what happens."

"Thank you," I said as Craig hugged me.

"Brianna?"

"Yes?"

"Remember the words on the Oran-Roy tree and on your bow, on this night especially. Let them, as well as those closest to you, help you surpass the Kaelins' need to tempt you."

I gulped. *I forgot about walking through the Kaelin waters again!*

"Let Quinn walk with you, alright?" Craig advised me, as he brushed aside the hair from my face.

"That's probably best," I agreed with him. Up until that point in time, I don't think that I had truly considered what awaited me. As Craig and I walked back to camp, my nerves intensified with every step. So much was at stake, there was so much to lose and so much to gain.

"What will I be doing this time tomorrow?" I thought to myself. *"Will I be sitting with Brogan, Keira and Craig, embracing each other and making up for lost time? Will I be deliberating over our next plan of action, now that we have Zia's writings and information from my mother, or, will I be regretting ever formulating a plan... a plan that fell through?"*

*

"Brianna, you haven't eaten anything all day. You really must eat something. We're leaving any minute and you need to have some food in you!" Charlotte pleaded with me, but it was no use. No matter what words she employed to convince me, I would not eat; besides, if I were to eat, the nerves making my insides churn would have something to say about it.

Ethan agreed with Charlotte. "Yeah, Bee, it's not like you not to eat, even when you are nervous."

"I know, I know," I heavily sighed, "but, I'm feeling so uneasy that even if I were to eat, it wouldn't stay in my stomach, Ethan."

Ethan released a concerned sigh and sat beside me. Charlotte detected an Ethan pep talk coming along, so she too sat beside me.

"Bee," Ethan spoke in a worried tone, "Charlotte and I just wanted to wish you luck for tonight." I stopped fiddling with a loose thread from my trousers and looked up to meet Ethan's stare. I'd never seen him so concerned.

"Thanks," I replied, placing my hand over his and then doing the same for Charlotte. "You guys have been here for me all this time and I really appreciate it ... more than you know."

After an exchange of 'you're welcome' smiles, Charlotte had to get something off her chest. "Bee, no ... no matter what happens tonight, these past couple of months have been ... really great."

"Charlotte, you're speaking as though I'm going to die!" I cried.

"I'm sorry," Charlotte quickly apologised, "I'm just being my usual anxious self, but I just need you to know that."

"It's all right," I responded, "just promise me that you'll both be careful."

"We will," Ethan answered. "And don't worry, Bee, I'll keep Charlotte in line." Ethan formed a cheeky expression and slanted his eyes over to Charlotte, who was rolling her eyes.

"We're leaving now," Rona unexpectedly said behind us, which made the three of us stand up.

"... And we wanted to wish you well, Brianna," Zephan explained.

"Thank you," I replied.

Rona then stretched her arm out and rested it on my shoulder. "Vos es versus, Brianna."

Zephan also stretched out his arm and placed his hand on my other shoulder. "Vos es versus. Carry your spirit with you and those close to you, Brianna."

"I will," I silently replied, a little overcome with emotion.

As soon as they removed their hands from my shoulders, Rona and Zephan set off and very quickly, their slender bodies faded into the darkening twilight sky.

"It's time," I said, and nervously walked towards the edge of Kael creek, where everyone was awaiting my arrival. Before entering the icy water, Ethan and Charlotte offered me reassuring glances. I nodded, and then looked towards the water, quilted in a misty cloud.

"Brianna?" Quinn called as he held my quivering hand.

"Yeah?" I gulped.

"I will take you through." Not satisfied by my expression, Quinn felt the need to advise me. "You'll be all right, I'll keep you safe; just, remain strong."

I nodded and reluctantly stepped into the cold, murky water with Quinn holding my waist securely, yet tenderly. Keelty and Faolon, as well as Leona, with Dougal clinging onto her shoulders, were ahead of Quinn and me. Ethan and Charlotte followed closely behind us, with Craig and Ewan, carefully guiding Epona and the other horses through.

Waist deep in the freezing water, I discovered small pairs of yellow eyes peering over the water's surface only metres away from Quinn and me.

"Brianna Elsa."

I shuddered as a Kaelin eerily spoke my name. Quinn felt me tremble.

"Remember our time in the cave, Brianna?" Quinn asked, trying to take my mind away from the Kaelins' tempting ways.

"Yes," I smiled.

"What a shame that you don't want to know how to put a stop to the death of someone you care about."

"Keep talking to me, Quinn. *Please*," I urged him, petrified that I might grow weak and give in.

"Do you recall when you made me dance with Ethan?" Quinn chuckled. "It was incredibly embarrassing for me."

"A mere moment beneath the water's surface and you will know how to stop death!"

The voices were growing stronger.

"Brianna," Quinn reminded me of his presence, realising that the voices had not subsided. "Tell me about your dogs at home; tell me about your farm in Ireland."

"Uh, I ... my dogs, Lulu and Tess are ... are relatively big dogs and..."

"Come on! Sneak a mere peak Brianna!"

The voices were becoming frustrated by my refusal to submerge into their grasp.

"I walk them every day with Ethan and sometimes Charlotte ... down to ... to Blessington Lake."

"And what about that other place you told me about where you eat and drink often. What was it called?" Quinn's voice was overcome with worry.

"It's called *Madam and Miss Antique Shop* and ... and it's where Charlotte and I have a hot chocolate occasionally and..." I stopped talking – my body was no longer in the water. Distracted by Quinn's attempts to keep me from giving into the Kaelin's, I had left the water without even realising it! Shocked, I turned around to the lake. The yellow eyes narrowed and then submerged once more into the misty water.

"I ... I did it!" I cried out happily.

"You did!" Quinn pulled me in towards him, but when he realised that Ewan and Craig were leaving the water, he let me go and helped them with the horses.

"Here, Brianna," Ewan handed me Epona's reigns. I mounted Epona and droplets of water came flickering up at my face. After I wiped my face, I realised that Keelty and Faolon were having a good shake to dry off.

"Sorry, Brianna," Keelty apologised.

I smiled and then looked over to Leona who was trying to pull Dougal from her shoulders, but his claws were latched onto her leather vest.

"Not until the ground is dry!" Dougal demanded. "I won't walk on moist ground!"

Leona moaned. "Fine you fuss-pot!"

"Quickly," Craig advised and everyone responded immediately.

Within fifteen minutes, we were well within Darian territory and could clearly see Tarmon's castle, as well as hooded men, cloaked in deep purple cloth patrolling its border. The first time I came through here, in light of the dangerous circumstances we were in, I didn't get the chance to see the home clan of my mother.

Tarmon castle was enormous and composed of sharp, silvery stones. There were several towers, each with a grey tiled cone roof and a flag honouring the Tarmon clan symbol, the same as could be found on my right wrist. The castle was not fenced, but surrounded by tall, thin mossy-coated trees. Cillian's men were on horseback and continually circled the castle's boundary.

"Keelty, Faolon, is anyone closer to us than the men on patrol?" Ewan asked, which signalled Keelty and Faolon to lower their noses and sniff the forest floor.

"No," Keelty answered.

"But there were a few of Cillian's men here a few hours ago or so," Faolon added.

Ewan and everyone else looked to Leona and me to translate.

"No one is nearer than those guards on patrol," Leona translated, "But Faolon said that some of them were in this very spot a few hours ago."

"Good," Craig expressed, "that means that they're remaining closer to the outskirts of the castle for the night."

After a moment of silence, Craig met my worried expression; silently informing me that the moment had finally arrived.

I released an anxious sigh as I dismounted Epona and then attached my bow and set of arrows to the belt that ran diagonally across my chest and across my back. Quinn and Ewan, too, left their horses, prepared their bow, arrows and blade and then stood beside me, waiting for our final instructions.

"If our whereabouts are already known, like the previous times we have made attempts to infiltrate Tarmon, it will most likely be Brogan's doing, as there are no other mixed blooded people in Cillian's possession," Craig explained. "But, the sooner we find Brogan, the greater the chance we have of remaining undiscovered."

"Great! Some more pressure to ice the cake! That's all I need right now!" I thought to myself, but, given my nervous state, I had a feeling that at least Quinn and Ewan heard what I had thought to myself; their instant inquiring looks made me suspect that I had let slip.

"Leona?" Craig called.

"Yes?" She swiftly replied.

"Once you take care of the guards, you must morph into a smaller form immediately, understood?"

"I will," she assured my father.

Before leaving, I turned around to bid Charlotte and Ethan farewell. Instead, Charlotte pounced upon me and draped her arms across my shoulders, hugging me tightly. As she released me, our faces met and I discovered a tear trickling down her pale cheek. After Charlotte and I shared nods of best wishes, I was engulfed by Ethan's lanky arms and warmly embraced.

When Ethan let me go, I assured him and Charlotte, "I'll see you soon." They both nodded and then stood behind Keelty, Faolon and Dougal, who each lowered their heads, wishing me the best of luck. I thanked them by also nodding my head and then looked at Craig. Craig pulled me into his chest and held my head. The beating of his worrying heart made its way into my ears as I nestled against him.

"We are *all* with you on this night." Craig gently pushed me away and then I hurriedly left, without looking back at the remaining anxious faces, afraid that I would crack under the pressure and quit at the last minute.

Leona, Ewan, Quinn and me approached the castle ahead.

"We must act swiftly," Ewan advised us, "Remember what Craig said? Time is of the essence."

When we reached the bordering trees of the Darian forest, Ewan, who was leading us, lowered himself, so that he could peer through the shielding bushes. The three of us quickly followed and awaited Ewan's instruction.

"All right," he whispered, "Brianna, when those two guards come within ten steps from us, have them prevent the next pair of patrolling guards from seeing us."

I nodded my head. I didn't want to answer through speech, concerned that if I were to do so, I might shriek!

As Ewan had described, two of Cillian's men were drawing closer to the bush we were hiding behind. The black stallions trotted arrogantly and released aggressive breaths that were visible in the chilly, night air.

Almost past us, one of the men came to an abrupt halt. The second guard quickly followed and the volume of the stallions' breathing lowered. I closed my eyes and took a large breath. With my eyes still closed, I felt Quinn's hand upon my shoulder. Surprisingly, I wasn't startled by it; rather, Quinn's touch dispelled the nerves, allowing me to concentrate on the task at hand.

As I opened my eyes, I looked to the un-faced men and almost felt my body levitate up towards them. Quickly, I imagined what I wanted the men to do and, almost instantly, the images in my head were being acted out before me.

Both of the guards pulled hard on their reigns and raised their stallions' front legs from the earth. Each horse let out a roar and turned towards the next pair of guards, trotting around the nearby bend of the edge of the forest.

The guards, who were under my control, drew their swords and firmly held them at the other men's chests. Clearly confused and baffled by what to make of their fellow guards' manner, the other men were distracted enough for Leona to take care of them.

Within the blink of an eye, Leona's limbs ripped through her clothes and standing before us was a giant, cat-like creature. The creature stretched itself beyond the bush and charged at the uncontrolled guards. From metres away, Leona leapt up and forced the guards off their horses and firmly drove them into the ground, leaving them unconscious. The two standing guards were still under my control, but Quinn and Ewan mounted the horses and knocked them out with the handles of their blades. The guards fell limp from their horses and Leona chased the horses into the neighbouring forest.

"Nicely done, friend," Quinn said, as he returned his sword to his belt.

"Yes, same to you," Ewan agreed.

"Oh!" I cried, as a little red-breasted sparrow nestled against my neck. "Leona!"

The sparrow chirped and then fluttered to rest on the very tip of my shoulder.

"We really must go then, Brianna," Quinn kindly urged, but, as my eyes left the limp men on the floor, an idea popped into my head.

"Wait!" I cried. "Perhaps you should both take the men's cloaks, just in case you struggle to make it to the entrance."

Ewan and Quinn exchanged questionable looks, but then nodded.

"That's a sensible idea," Ewan commented, as he hurriedly removed the cloaks from the two nearest guards. "Let's move."

Close to where we left the motionless guards, there was a stone archway that held a wooden door. Ewan opened the door, peered inside and waved his arm, silently guaranteeing us that the coast was clear. The door revealed a narrow winding staircase, surrounded by stone walls. We tread lightly until we reached another door.

A flickering ray of light seeped beneath the door. People were talking.

"Cillian is wasting his time if you ask me," a man with an angry voice commented, as he poured something into a glass. "Keira has had her mouth shut for eighteen years! What makes him think that she'll give in now?"

"It's not that!" A younger male voice responded.

"Well, we'll continue this later," the older man casually brushed aside. "Here." The sound of keys echoed in the room. "See to it that you give these to Cillian once he returns from attending to those mix-blooded children."

Shocked by what I had just heard, I turned and met Ewan and Quinn's bewildered expressions.

The older man's leaving footsteps echoed down what seemed to be a stone hallway. Ewan gently patted my back and nodded, encouraging me to move.

My hand was shaking as it reached out for the gold, metal knob. About to grasp the handle, Quinn held my hand and we opened the door together. Of course, this door had a creak! The door was barely opened when the young man from inside the room stretched it the remaining way open. The young man was pale, thin and fair-haired and in a state of shock upon seeing our band. The man was about to scream, but Quinn thrashed the door against his face and he collapsed to the floor, holding his bleeding noise. Quinn dragged the young man up against the cold stone wall, while

Ewan had clasped his hands over his mouth. The young man was wide-eyed and in even greater shock; I actually felt sorry for him. But I couldn't allow for sympathy at a time like this.

"Take me to Brogan's quarters or wherever he happens to be this very moment and then escort these two men to the most unguarded exit of the castle!" I ordered the helpless man as I stared deeply into his eyes. His shocked face assumed a blank expression. "Take us to him so that we aren't seen by anyone!"

As the man relaxed, Quinn and Ewan loosened their hold and released him. Immediately, the young man opened the door, peered through and then turned to face us. "This way," he whispered and brought us into a wide hallway, with white and black tiled floors, smooth stone walls and an arched ceiling adorned with ornate, bronze chandeliers.

Before reaching the end of the corridor, the young man raised his arm, signalling us to go through the nearest door. Again, we found ourselves in another narrow binding stone staircase.

"Not long now," the young man advised.

The stairs led us to another door. The man, still well under my control, didn't hesitate in opening the door. This door revealed a large bedroom. To the left of where we were standing was a balcony; its glass doors were opened and the curtains beside it were rustling from the evening breeze. In front of us lay a large, four-poster bed with a blazing fire on the same wall beside it. On the bed, lay a sleeping young man.

"Is that Brogan?" I questioned with my thoughts.

The man, still under my power, thought *yes*, as my eyes remained fixed on the figure on the bed.

"Take Ewan and Quinn to the most unguarded entrance of the castle," I ordered the man and before retreating down the staircase, Ewan and Quinn nodded and smiled. Almost beyond the door, Quinn hesitated and then took one final glance at me before leaving me and Leona.

"The carrier, Brianna," Quinn reminded me with his thoughts.

"... Oh, yeah!" I removed the carrier from around my neck and placed it into Quinn's open palm. Before releasing the carrier completely, Quinn placed his left hand over mine.

"Vos es versus," he whispered almost inaudibly.

I smiled, released the carrier and then Quinn retreated down the stairs.

Now, without Quinn and Ewan at my disposal, a sense of vulnerability swept through me.

"All right," I sighed, as I walked ever so silently to the brother I had never known. *"Here goes, Leona."*

Without prior warning, Brogan morphed into a ravenous wolf and heaved me into the stone wall.

"Argh!" I painfully cried, as I crashed against the wall.

Before me, was a brown, hairy head of a wolf-like creature, with narrowing eyes and a snarling jaw, displaying white canines' dripping saliva.

"Brogan!" I screamed, terrified beyond belief. Then I raised my wrists, so that my markings were visible. I didn't want to resort to controlling him if I could help it. *"I'm your sister!"* I cried. *"I'm your sister!"*

Chapter Twenty

Backfire

The wolf slowly relaxed its jaw, concealing its terrifying teeth and then retreating to the other side of the bed. I struggled to return to my feet, but, once I did, Leona came back and nestled on my shoulder. Then, I saw the shadow of a wolf form into a human figure on the wall directly opposite me. A hand stretched out over the bed and hurriedly searched for the pants amongst the tangled up sheets. Once the hand had successfully navigated its way to the pants, it retreated back behind the bed. Only seconds later, a young, bare-chested man revealed himself from behind the bed.

Brogan's wavy, brown hair fell short of his shoulders; he was tall and lean, with incredibly defined muscles. When my eyes focussed on his face, I could see a younger version of our father, Craig. But, when I met Brogan's conflicted gaze, I almost felt as though I was looking into a mirror; like me, his right eye was brown and his left eye was blue.

Slowly, Brogan walked around the bed to me and when he came to a stop, he looked down and offered me his wrists. As I held them and raised them up higher, sure enough, I could clearly see the symbol of Tarmon and the symbol of Crag. When I lowered his arms, Brogan began to shake with fury. He paced to the other side of the room and ran his fingers through his hair. With each frustrated pace, he released sighs of worry.

No words were coming to me, for what words does one say to the brother they have never known? Where do you begin, explaining to a person that they have been living a lie their entire life?

Eventually, I coughed up the courage to end the uneasy moment.

"Brogan, I ... I *know* that this must be a shock, but ... but I need you to ... to calm down a little and listen to me for just a..."

"CALM DOWN!" Brogan cried. "HOW CAN I...?" Before he had chance to finish his words, I had clasped his left arm, silenced him and then lowered him to the ground.

"I need you to be quiet," I breathed. "Just as you have your own ability, I also have mine." Brogan was wide-eyed. "Based on what I just saw, you can take the form of animals. Well, I can hear and send thoughts, as well as control another's actions. I didn't want to have to control you, Brogan, but, if you refuse to be quiet, I can do much worse than silencing you. So, please," I raised him up from the ground, "remain calm and I won't have to resort to confining your every move and thought, all right?"

Brogan nodded and then sat down on the edge of his bed.

Unsure of what to do next, I reluctantly sat beside him.

"I didn't know I had a sister," Brogan said, looking down into his lap.

"I didn't know I had a brother until almost three months ago, so, I know how you feel."

Brogan sighed. "You coming here makes my head hurt."

"Sorry, but I..."

"I don't even know your name," Brogan quickly said.

"Oh, it's Brianna ... Brianna Elsa."

"Well, Brianna," Brogan left the bed and paced alongside me, "I suppose that you're going to tell me that everything that I have known for these twenty years has been a lie."

"Well, eighteen years."

Brogan had stopped pacing; he was waiting for an explanation.

"Look, I know what it's like to be suddenly confronted with new information, but please ... hear everything I am going to tell you."

Brogan returning to sitting beside me on the bed seemed to be his way of saying yes.

"You do know that Cillian is your uncle, yes?"

Brogan's expression changed. "No!"

"Well, he's our uncle, Brogan."

"My uncle?"

"Yes," I confirmed. "It was Cillian who was responsible for separating our family."

Brogan's hands held his fallen face. "... And what of our parents, then?" He questioned through gritted teeth.

"You mean that you've never known of Keira, our mother?"

"Keira is our mother?" Brogan clenched his knees. "Cillian told me that my mother died! He said that she was a poor Tarmon woman who served him here in the castle and that she fell in love with a man from Crag. He said that my father didn't want me after she died." Brogan left the bed and charged towards a tall table resting a tray of cutlery and cups. "He said that no one would help a mixed-blooded child!" The tray of cutlery crashed onto the stone floor and continued to rattle until each individual piece fell motionless.

"Brogan! I need you to remain calm!" I urged him.

"All this time, I thought that he had..." Brogan became silent and then returned to the bed under my control.

"I told you, I don't want to control you, but if you stay this loud, you leave me no choice!"

Brogan nodded and allowed me to further explain.

"Cillian is only interested in one thing; overthrowing our mother as Queen by claiming the carrier and releasing Morrigan's wrath for his own selfish needs."

Brogan sighed and wandered with his eyes until they found my hands. "You're the Carrier?" He questioned with disbelief, with his eyes drawn to my right palm.

"Yes."

He sighed. "How did it come to be in your...?"

"Brogan," I cut him off, "we don't have time for that now. What I need you to do is help me free Keira and claim Zia's writings. *Please* tell me that you know where they are?"

"Whether I know or not, you'll still see to it that I do, won't you?"

"Probably," I admitted.

"It is Brianna, isn't it?"

"Yes."

"Brianna, I ... up until this point, I have been comfortable with who I am, but, how can you expect me to suddenly change my way of thinking based on what a complete stranger is telling me?"

Leona's tiny beak pecked my ear; reminding me that we needed to hurry.

"We don't have time for this!" I grumbled and quickly found my feet. "That's it!" I clenched Brogan's wrist and forced him off from the bed. "This is hard to believe now, but you must trust me, Brogan!"

"Wait!" he pleaded. "Can't we just...?"

"No!" I cut him off. "Brogan," I heavily sighed, attempting to cover up my impatience with him, "consider if the situation was in reverse and you were in my position."

He nodded and scrunched his eyebrows – it appeared that he was genuinely attempting to fathom what I was saying.

"Wouldn't you want someone, who knew that you had been lied to for almost all of your life, to reveal the truth about everything?" I looked up to meet Brogan's insecure gaze, but his eyes were caught in a stare above my head. "Don't you want to look back at this moment, in years to come and realise how you accepted the reality of things and had enough courage to act and accept change?" Brogan's eyes were still fixated in a blank stare.

"Brogan?" I called upon him much more forcefully. "Don't ignore this. Don't make the mistake of continuing to live a lie." I reached up and gently lowered his chin, so that he had no choice but to look into my eyes. "Wouldn't you rather follow me and assist me of your own free will, rather than having me resort to controlling you?"

Brogan's eyes fell and looked down to the floor. His body became relaxed, so I freed his wrist and chin. "If I wasn't who I said I was, would I be giving you the choice to leave here freely?" I sighed. "We could have been on our way by now with me controlling you."

Before speaking, Brogan released a heavy sigh. "I find no flaw in your words, Brianna." As he spoke, Brogan gently clasped my wrists and brushed his fingers along my markings. "And, if Cillian is indeed the man you have painted him to be, then I have no choice but to believe the words of a sister." Brogan released my wrists and looked up to meet my stare. "I am choosing to join you

... freely, Brianna. So..." he breathed with an unexpected, subtle smile, waiting for me to advise him.

"So," I clasped my hands together, "we need to find Zia's writings, locate Keira and then meet my friends Quinn and Ewan down by the entrance we came through."

"All right," Brogan nodded and then paced across the room, reaching for his white long-sleeved shirt and deep green cloak from the chair by the window.

While he was dressing, I asked Brogan, "Do you know of Cillian's whereabouts this instant? As well as morphing into animals, are you capable of finding people or hearing people from a fair distance away?"

Brogan, now completely clothed, paced to the door to put on his knee high leather boots, bows and arrow, as well as his sword. "No ... to both questions," he quickly answered. "What made you think that I was capable of such things?"

My heart stopped. "So, you can't do anything else, other than morph into animals?"

"No," he answered again, coming to an upright position.

"Then I ... I don't understand how Cillian was aware of Craig's attempts to infiltrate Tarmon all these years!"

"I'm not sure that I understand what you..."

"All this time," I overpowered Brogan's words, "we assumed that you were capable of hearing people from a great distance away, because we thought you to be the only mixed-blooded person in Tarmon!" Leona pinched my ear. "Ouch! I know! I know! We have to get a move on! I know!" I assured the impatient, lively sparrow bouncing up and down on my shoulder. "But, Brogan, on my way up to your room, we heard men discussing mixed-blooded children. Are there more of us here? Are we no longer the only mixed-blooded people in Oran-Roy?"

Brogan appeared more confused than me. "Brianna, I haven't been informed of any other people like us."

All this time, not only had Brogan been subjected to a false understanding of his origins, Cillian had sheltered him from all of his schemes, taking comfort in knowing that should Brogan discover the truth, he would not be able to share the knowledge Cillian intended on keeping secret. *Why would Cillian deliberately neglect to include his 'adopted son' in his plans? Was he aware that Brogan would one day come to discover the truth? How was Cillian aware of Craig's attempted raids without using Brogan? Are those mixed-blooded children his tools, his weapons against us?* I needed more time with Brogan; I needed to know what he knew of Cillian's schemes and the Cillian he knew as 'father'. But, there wasn't time to raise these questions. We needed to find Zia's writings and we needed to free Keira.

"Brogan, there's so much I want to ask you, but there just isn't enough time!" I said rather anxiously. "The first thing we need to do is find Keira and Zia's writings. What should we do first?"

Before answering, Brogan slowly opened his wooden door and peered through the small space formed. He ushered me through the narrow opening and silently closed the door behind us.

The corridor was bare, long and narrow and composed of grey cobbled stone bricks. Bronze candleholders protruded from the corridor's stone walls, each holding droopy, waxy candles with a dim, flickering light.

"Brianna," Brogan whispered, as he scanned his eyes up and down the corridor, "I don't know what or where these writings of Zia's are, but, I do know where Keira is."

"Take us there first, then," I urged Brogan.

"This way..."

Brogan led us to a long, winding staircase at the end of the narrow corridor. "Tread lightly," he advised and I obeyed.

The corridor was cold and eerie with the candle flames moving ferociously from the night wind that was howling through the open arched window at the corridor's end. The sandstone steps were steep, with very little space to place your feet down comfortably. Scared of stumbling, my eyes did not leave the steps that awaited me and my hands did not leave the chilled, wrought iron railing.

"How much further?" I asked Brogan through thought.

Unaware that I had questioned him without speaking, Brogan whispered back, "Not long."

As we journeyed round the third turn of the staircase, a small ray of light escaped a narrow space beneath a wooden door, causing Brogan to turn around quickly. He raised his palm and then placed a finger over his mouth, urging me to remain still and quiet. Someone had just entered the room beyond the stone wall.

Without hesitation, Brogan opened the door and walked straight through the room's entrance.

"Ah, Dylan my friend," Brogan warmly greeted the man.

"Brogan!" a deep, husky voice cried. "I thought you were feeling too poorly to take on this patrol."

"I am suddenly back to full health, it seems," Brogan casually brushed aside. "Dylan," Brogan patted the man on the back, "You have taken my patrol for a few evenings now, but I'm finding myself ready to return to the routines of my day. I'll inform Cillian of your graciousness."

"Ah, well ... well I ... I suppose if you're back to full health Cillian wouldn't mind me letting you take the patrol again."

"Thank you, Dylan," Brogan said, while opening the other door to the room. "Have a good evening." Dylan's steps echoed loudly down another stone corridor. As his steps grew faint, Brogan ushered me into the room that was almost identical to the one Ewan, Quinn, Leona and I had entered when we first arrived in the castle.

"Don't you think it was a little suspicious that you needed him to leave immediately?" I asked.

"He's not the brightest guard we've been known to have," Brogan laughed.

"... So, where to from here, Brogan?"

"The corridor behind this door is where Cillian detains prisoners." Brogan carefully turned the rusty door handle and peered beyond the door. "Be weary, Brianna," Brogan cautioned, "If there are any other prisoners in there, other than Keira, some of them have been here for ... well ... longer than anyone should have to withstand conditions such as this."

"So ... are you suggesting that ...?"

"Some of their minds are ... they aren't who they once were."

"Brogan," I breathed as I clenched onto his left sleeve, "Tell me that Keira, our mother, isn't one of those people."

Brogan remained silent and averted his eyes to the stone floor.

"Tell me, Brogan!" I begged, as my eyes became glassy.

"Brianna," he sighed, "Up until now, I've known her to be a Tarmon commoner who made several attempts to remove Cillian from his place as King." Feeling guilty, Brogan ran his fingers ferociously through his wavy, brown hair. "Now that I know her to be my mother, I ... I realise why she has screamed out my name and called me her son, but I ... I thought her to be..."

"... Mad." I looked away and released Brogan's sleeve. "Take me to her please. I need to see her."

Once again, Brogan peered beyond the door and ushered me into the corridor. The coast was clear.

A horrid smell of mould and rotting food filled my nostrils as I left the small, stone chamber. Dripping water echoed down the long, damp and desolate tunnel. Walking deeper into the tunnel, a cool breeze made the hairs along my arms and neck stand. On both sides of the cobbled dungeon floor were small cells, with mere cracks in the walls as their only source of light for the poor souls who resided there.

"My mother couldn't possibly have been subjected to this throughout my life! She couldn't possibly have endured this!" Thoughts of worry churned in my stomach. *"If there is a hell, this must be close to it."*

As I walked further into the prison, I made sure to check every cell I passed, but they were all empty. I looked ahead to Brogan, but he had not stopped walking, so I continued to follow him, until I felt a tugging on my boot.

I looked down and couldn't control my reaction. *"Agh!"* My wail echoed through the entire dungeon. Three or more rats were at my feet.

"Brianna!" Brogan moaned.

"Is ... is someone there? Who ... who's there?" A disturbed, fearful female voice cried from a cell almost at the end of the tunnel. "Don't hurt me ... don't hurt me ... please!"

My gentle steps turned into a deadly run. When I reached the final cell, I found a thin and manky figure futilely shielding herself from harm in the corner of the cell. She was shaking uncontrollably. Overcome with the prospect of this person being my mother, I held my breath to withhold the tears.

"It's ... it's all right," I assured the woman. "Please don't be afraid ... we're here to help you." I offered my right hand between the thick, wrought iron bars of the cell. Out of the dim light, a pale arm reached my hand. Then, a second arm came into sight. The pale, cold hands held mine tightly and then a face appeared before me, framed by two of the cell bars.

The first things to capture my attention were two rich brown eyes, which almost appeared red in contrast with her white skin. The pale face was bordered by clumps of long, curly hair that had become matted in a few places. Again, it was almost like looking into a mirror. I could see myself reflected in this woman. But, as I continued to be transfixed by the amber eyes, I was troubled; the sadness and loss in the eyes engulfed my soul.

"Keira," I struggled to say, while restraining my tears, "I'm ... I'm Brianna."

Suddenly, the pale, haggard face was transfigured with untold relief and an extreme happiness. Keira's cold hands reached beyond the cell towards me and began to stroke my face and hair frantically.

"My ... my Brianna! I ... I knew one day you'd come!"

"I'm here," I assured my helpless mother. "I'm here," I said, but this time tears accompanied my words.

Repeatedly, Keira ran her frail fingers through the untidy hair that I had inherited from her. She was wide-eyed, in complete bewilderment that her long awaited daughter had finally found her.

Words escaped me; I was simultaneously overcome with fear and excitement.

"Mother," I finally managed to say, "Thank you." Tears welled in my eyes and gradually trickled down my flushed cheeks. "You ... you saved my life all those years ago and ... and it's cost you so much!"

Keira shook her head. "No, no," she repeated, looking down to the dungeon floor. "Nothing is too great for a mother to sacrifice for the life of her child." Keira raised her head and met my eyes once more. As she gazed in awe at me, my goal of releasing my mother from this hell fuelled into a raging fire of vengeance.

"I'm going to get you out of here right now," I assured my mother.

"But, Brianna," Brogan whispered harshly, "what of the writings you seek?"

"Zia's writings?" Keira questioned.

"Yes," I said, returning to face her, "We thought you might know where they are within the castle."

"I do, but take caution," Keira warned us in a severe tone, "If they fall into the hands of Cillian, Morrigan will surely return under his hand. You cannot let it happen! You cannot let it happen!" Keira began to shake and gradually her legs grew weak and she slid down against the stone wall.

"Keira!" I cried, stretching my arms towards her as far as the iron bars would allow me. "Are you all right?"

"Go!" She pleaded, waving her hands. "You must take the book and leave! They might know you're here!" To where had the woman I had just been speaking to vanished?

"Where is it?" Brogan said, crouching beside me.

"It is where only worthy mixed-blooded heroes may tread."

Brogan and I exchanged confusing looks.

"Where is this place?" Brogan asked again.

Keira snapped. A spark ignited inside her and began a blazing fire. "MY SON WHO IGNORED ME FOR THESE YEARS KNOWS!" Keira launched up at Brogan and pressed herself against the bars. "MY SON WHO SPENT HIS DAYS ALONE IN THE SANCTUARY HE WAS FORBIDDEN TO TREAD KNOWS!"

Shocked, Brogan fell backwards, quickly found his feet and stormed down the dungeon corridor.

"Brogan!" I stood up and cried.

"I know where it is!" He yelled before retreating down the stairs.

"Leona," I offered the little red sparrow my hand, "Follow him. Once he has the writings, alert Quinn and Ewan to meet us back up here, to free Keira."

Leona didn't respond and remained nestled on my palm.

"Go!" I ordered her, but still, the stubborn red sparrow didn't budge. "I know this isn't exactly what we planned, but we have to act quickly! Please just do as I say! I can't just leave my mother alone like this! She can't think we're going to leave her here!"

I could almost see Leona breathe a sigh of, *'if you say so!'*, and she grudgingly fluttered her way down the tunnel in search of Brogan.

With Leona now out of sight, I turned to again face Keira in her cell. No longer in an uncontrollable rage, Keira was holding her head and rocking backwards and forwards muttering words muffled by tears.

An unpleasant strain constricted my chest.

"Her mind is gone," I admitted to myself. "This would destroy my father."

"What have I done?" Keira wailed, now lying face down in the dirt of the cell floor. "They'll catch you, Brianna! You must go now!" Keira pressed up against the bars and pulled my hands up to her chest; clinging onto them as if it were the last time she would hold me. "They know you're here! They know you're here!" Her streaming tears left paths along her dusty face.

"I'm not leaving you!" I assured her, clenching her hands. "I won't leave you!"

CREAK.

An eerie sound dispersed down the dungeon.

"Agh!" Keira released my hands and fell to the floor shielding her ears, wailing. "Go now! GO NOW! GO NOW!"

BANG.

"Brianna," Keira calmly breathed, "they are here."

"Who?" I anxiously whispered as I found my feet.

"Go before they take you!"

Unconsciously, I started to walk backwards. With each small step the fear of uncertainty intensified. With adrenalin raging through my veins, all I could here was my terrified heart beating and draining my ears of any exterior sounds.

The dungeon door opened, but with little light, I could not see what awaited me. With no other way out and with no light to see who or what was seeking me, I was powerless. I needed to see who or what lied before me in order to control them.

Vulnerable and fearful, I crouched down and reached into the cell of my mother and clasped her hands.

"Don't worry!" I fearfully reassured her. "I'll be all right! I'll be..."

"ARGH!" Keira's scream faded as the whole world seemed to fade away and darkness consumed me.

Chapter Twenty-One

Interrogation

...Cillian's men assembled before him at the Tarmon gates.

"We have been delayed for too long!" The cloaked men cheered Cillian's words. "It is time to claim the carrier device as our own, execute our plan, build our army's strength and return back to the land of our ancestors! We will claim back what is ours! We will re-claim Ireland!"

The heavy sound of hooves beating against the earth made the trees tremble. The land feared the fate of their once peaceful dwelling. A flight of black crows followed the band of Morrigan followers...

- Excerpt from 'The Morrigan Book'

I moaned, as I regained consciousness and opened my eyes. Despite my eyes being open, I couldn't make sense of where I was. I was in complete darkness, entirely unaware of whom or what put me here.

I tried raising my arms, but thick ropes, that felt like they were made up of tiny, needle-like pincers, were bound tightly around my wrists.

I winced. Struggling against the rope only seemed to make it angry; the sharp ends of its individual fragments were breaking into my skin and drawing blood. I didn't need light to realise that.

I tried raising my feet from the ground; again, it was hopeless. Trying to stretch my ankles apart only resulted in pain.

My painful scream echoed in the eternal, empty pool of darkness. Once again, needle-like points drew warm blood from my cold body. I was truly helpless; like a lone soldier surrounded by the enemy, or a bird, with a broken wing, spiralling to its death – there was no way of escaping.

Coming to that depressing conclusion, my breathing became rapid, my mouth went dry and my forehead began producing small droplets of perspiration. After everything we had been through, was this what it was all going to come to?

Out of desperation I cried, "Quinn!"

The silence shattered my final feeling of hope.

"Quinn!" I wailed, with tears now accompanying my calls.

"It *seems* you are alone, Brianna." A fearsome, loathing voice whispered in my right ear – sending goosebumps down that entire side of my body. I gasped.

The devilish voice became silent and a burst of light erupted behind me; ahead of me a stone wall painted the silhouettes of large men, distorted by the flickering flames. Too afraid to meet the face of the voice, I remained still, continuing to face forward to cover up my fear.

"Who are you?" I demanded.

Footsteps lingered behind me and then stopped abruptly.

"I would have thought that I wasn't in need of an introduction!"

The shadows were no longer still as they were chuckling at the man's 'witty' remark.

"I *asked* you a question," I reminded all present, cutting the unsettling laughter.

"Ah, yes. Well, our last meeting was eighteen years ago." The voice slowly worked its way around me, until a figure in a deep black coat, which shimmered purple in the flame's light, crouched down before me and slowly removed the hood shielding his face. The man's amber eyes greatly resembled my own. His long and fierce face was hidden beneath an untidy, short and bristly brown beard with wisps of grey throughout it. His hair was short and wavy. I felt as though I was seeing a much older Ewan.

The features confirmed the conclusion I had come to when I first heard the voice speak. I was in the clutches of Cillian, father to my noble cousin, Ewan and *my* uncle. Despite the physical resemblance, Ewan bore nothing in common with the man he once called his father.

"Well," I tried to sound brave, even though my insides were churning in a way they had never done before! "Greetings!" If I showed Cillian weakness, I knew it would only empower him and I had no desire to give him any semblance of satisfaction. The image of my feeble, distraught mother was fuelling my brave stance. "Do I call you uncle, or ... is traitor and swine a more appropriate term of address for..."

My words were cut off by a firm slap across my right cheek, slinging my face across over my left shoulder, causing the chair, to which I was bound, to heave onto the cold, jagged stone floor. When my body finally stilled, a warm, agonising sensation spread across my face.

"I'm not here to play games." Cillian was no longer playful in tone. Effortlessly, he raised the chair I was attached to with a fluid movement of his foot. I rocked side to side until he grasped the chair arms and stared into my eyes. I wanted to shut my eyes and take myself somewhere else. I wanted to be laughing with Ethan and Charlotte in the barn late into the night. I wanted to be in a warm embrace with Mam and Dad back home. I wanted to be surrounded by all the new people I had come to love so quickly during my time in Oran-Roy. I wanted Quinn; I needed Quinn.

"Wait until ... wait until they see what you've done to me!" Repressing tears of fear and tears of pain, made speaking difficult. But I couldn't show any weakness! I couldn't let him win!

Cillian casually waved his arm, brushing my warning aside and started to pace the width of the cell.

"Quinn will kill you when he … when he sees me like this! He'll be here. He'll save me!"

Cillian lunged towards me, clenched my right hand and breathed, "Not if you are *already* dead." Cillian twisted my wrist, so that the carrier symbol was as plain as day. "Once I am the Carrier, you will no longer be of any use to us, but first," Cillian began walking another slow, intimidating circle around me, "you *will* tell us where it is, or who currently possesses the carrier."

"Or?" I spat.

"I don't think I need to inform you of what will happen if you fail to do that."

"I *will* stop you!" I assured Cillian.

"What makes you seem *so* sure?" He replied in a condescending tone that only fuelled my anger.

"I believe I can ... and I will."

"You are powerless when it comes to those who are dear to you, Brianna."

Cillian's threatening undertone took my mind back to the Kaelin's warning. Was this what they meant by putting a stop to a death?

As Cillian paced behind me, it suddenly dawned on me that I was not helpless; I was not powerless. With Cillian returning into my sight, I didn't hesitate to act.

Against his will, Cillian's constricting hands engulfed his neck. Gasping for air, Cillian was now helpless and powerless. Watching his attempts to breathe empowered me in a sickening way; I didn't want to admit it, but I enjoyed seeing him suffer.

"AH!" A hooded man belted a plank of wood across my knees without warning. Blood was drawn; I could feel it seeping from the gash. "AHHHH!" I wailed as the pain dispersed down through my legs. I scrunched my eyes, trying to hold back another cry of torture. Tears trickled from my eyes and ran down my face. Cillian had fallen to the stone floor coughing and gasping for air.

"Try ... try that again and ... and the consequences will be more severe!" Cillian warned while struggling to gain his breath. "There are ten men behind you! More than enough to undo anyone you put under your control!"

How did he know of my struggles to attempt more than three people at a time? How could he have come to know that about me?

"AHHHHHH!" I wailed once more, the pain too strong to keep inside. Crying was my only remedy to the pain. It was a small distraction that relieved the pain only minimally. I welcomed the tears.

Cillian regained his feet and clasped my chin. I had no choice but to look into those hollow, empty eyes warped by selfishness.

"WHERE IS IT, BRIANNA?" Cillian shouted into my face, making me shut my eyes and jolt my head back. "WHERE IS IT?" Cillian repeated, as my tears and cries failed to meet his demands.

"I … I … I don't know … know where..."

Cillian's boot met the wood between my legs on the chair, and then forced it upward, letting gravity do his work, flinging me down towards the stone floor under its unthinking compulsion.

My crying was beyond control now. My plan to refrain from showing fear had failed. It was hopeless.

"No!" Cillian bellowed at one of his men about to raise me from the ground. "She'll remain there until we have what we need!" The man quickly backed away, leaving me against the moist surface of the cell floor.

Feeling as though my life was dwindling away, like a candlewick struggling to drain the last drops of wax to fuel its flame, a sudden spark of adrenalin spread throughout my body - a final dose of adrenalin before my body's end.

"What do you hope to gain from this?"

Though my head was heaved into the stone floor, I could still sense the shock my outburst left on those in the cell.

"Bringing Morrigan back will only bring destruction! She won't reward you, you gouger! You just can't stand the thought that your sister, a woman, was chosen to lead over you!"

"STOP IT!" Cillian kicked the base of the chair, flipping it over, with the chair's back now against the floor. "You know nothing!"

My vision was beginning to fade. I was about to fall into a spell of darkness, but the sudden sensation of being raised from the ground prevented me from slipping into the dark.

CRASH!

A commotion further down the tunnel stopped Cillian's hand in its tracks alongside my already swollen cheek.

"Go!" Cillian instructed his guards. "GO! She won't be going anywhere! See to that noise! NOW!" he bellowed, when some failed to respond immediately, pointing the guards to the cell door.

As the blurry hooded figures stormed out into the black corridor, my neck no longer had the strength to support my head, with my head becoming limp and eventually resting atop my left shoulder. The cracks in the stone wall were fusing together and growing dim, slowly fading into nothing but a featureless shade of black.

"You will be fine," a calming voice assured me as everything became black. "Vos es verus," Cuchulainn's voice hushed in my ear.

*

"This is the song I was telling you about!" I interrupted Quinn, as the song, which reminded me of us, was being played.

"What's it called?" Quinn questioned with great interest.

"You Made Me Love You," I said, blushing and turning to face the floor. "It's sung by Nat King Cole. He's my favourite singer – you wouldn't have heard something like this before in Oran-Roy." When he failed to reply immediately, I felt incredibly embarrassed and I eased from Quinn's embrace. I moved towards my iPod, to skip the song.

"Brianna!" Quinn reached out his hand to my arm and yanked me down into his lap, back by the base of my bed, just after I skipped the song. "Don't be embarrassed, I want to hear it!" He chuckled.

"I wasn't embarrassed!" I lied, still trying to shield away my reddening cheeks.

"You are!"

"Well," I admitted, "you didn't respond how I thought you would immediately, so that made me question sharing it with you."

"Well, I was contemplating whether you were stating the title of a song or making a statement of intent! Play it, please."

Feeling as though my cheeks had returned to their usual colour, I faced Quinn, who was fashioning a very wide-eyed patronising expression.

"You're making fun of me!" I laughed, giving Quinn as much as a heave as I could to the shoulder.

"Please," Quinn became serious, "Just play it. I want to hear it."

"Fine."

I left the floor to play the song. Still feeling a little awkward, I remained at my desk chair, held my head up with my arms leaning against the desk, pretending to be listening to the track intently.

It had been a while since I had heard this song, but listening to it again allowed me to recall why it reminded me of Quinn and resonated with our story. Hypnotised by the words, I closed my eyes and had forgotten that I was not alone. Quinn's hand on my shoulder made me jump.

"How does one dance to a song such as this?" he said, with an unusual smirk across his face.

"I thought you didn't like dancing!"

"It's not that I don't like it," Quinn confessed. "I just feel more comfortable dancing when we don't have an audience."

Boy, we are terribly similar. Charlotte will die when I divulge this to her!

"Well," I got up from the chair and placed Quinn's hand on my waist and then held his remaining hand. "Like this," I showed him.

Slowly, Quinn began to sway me in time with the music. After a few chuckles and small jigs, our eyes interlocked. I then closed my eyes and rested my head against his shoulder.

When the song finished, my favourite song, 'The Very Thought of You', would be the next track.

"This is my favourite one," I revealed, while still swaying, despite the pause between songs. Quinn didn't answer, but brought his head down towards mine, gently nestling against his chest.

"Hmm." I sensed him smiling.

"What..?" I begged, smiling as I stopped swaying to meet his expression.

"These words I can attest to."

"Really?" I said, unable to refrain from smiling.

"Really."

"So," I sighed as I returned to swaying. "I'm not so good at the dancing thing, but my taste in music is pretty good. Wouldn't you agree?"

"Hmm," Quinn breathed, as he drew me closer towards him.

*

"She's in here! Get her before more guards are summoned."

"I'll get her and we'll meet you by the edge of the forest. Epona will be waiting," a familiar, comforting voice instructed. "Leona! Make sure that Brianna and I will have a clear passage out of the castle."

The sound of hastened footsteps finally reached me.

"Brianna! Brianna!" Warm hands rubbing my icy cold cheeks made me open my eyes. Slowly, the blurred figure before me morphed into Quinn.

I tried to speak, but was too overwhelmed with the relief of being found to produce words of any kind! Quinn sensed my urge, but insisted that I remain silent.

"It's all right!" He assured me, trying to embody a calm presence, but I knew he was trying to prevent me from worrying. The sight of my appearance must have been horrendous. "Don't try to speak. I'm going to get you out of here!"

As Quinn carefully slit the ropes binding my arms and legs, I felt as though my voice had returned.

"You – you shouldn't be here," I breathed, my voice raspy. "They want – they want the carrier..."

Quinn rested his finger over my lips.

"Brianna, I just want to get you as far away from here as possible. This wasn't what we planned."

The ropes fell to the floor. As I looked down, I witnessed their effect on my body. Red indentations and the remains of blood, drawn from my knees, had coated my ankles and feet. While Quinn was ripping part of his coat to seal my wounds, I tried to stand up, but failed and fell to the floor.

Quinn lunged to catch me, but was too late.

"I want to kill them! I'd give anything to take her place! I'm going to kill them!" Quinn's raging thoughts were louder than spoken words. Seeing me like this was his form of torture.

"Ah," I let out another wail of pain.

"I know, I know," Quinn stroked my forehead and then began attending to my lingering wounds. "All right," Quinn breathed as he began to lift me from the cold surface.

"Let me try to stand!" I cried out stubbornly.

Supporting my waist, Quinn raised me up, but my weight was too great of a burden to carry in my current state. Out of frustration, I moaned painfully. Tears fell to the floor.

"I'm carrying you," Quinn insisted and swept me off the floor, holding me like an injured child. I closed my eyes when my head nestled into his chest; his heart was racing. My body bounced up and down as Quinn ran through the castle. I didn't want to open my eyes. I wanted to return to my dream. I almost longed for sleep, or, was it death; a time-out from my suffering. My thoughts must have been sent to Quinn, because he felt the need to say repeatedly, "You're not going anywhere! Stay with me, Brianna!"

Drifting in and out of consciousness, I was unable to keep track of where Quinn was taking me, but, when a cool breeze raised my hair, I realised that we were outside of the castle. Awakened by the cold wind, I looked up and discovered that we were in the Daray woods. The pale light of the moon breached through the spaces between the forest trees leaves – our only source of light.

Suddenly, Quinn came to an abrupt stop, my body no longer bouncing, but still in Quinn's warm embrace.

A warm breath of air coated my face and then I heard a rumbling sound, begging me to open my eyes again. As they opened, my eyes viewed Epona, her ebony coat glimmering in the moon's light.

"Brianna," Quinn gently supported me in a standing position, "Take this and Epona will return you to Crag." Quinn returned the carrier to me, placing it around my neck. "I'll see to it that the others are on their way back safely."

"I'm not leaving without you!" I implored him. "You could get hurt!"

Quinn was not seeking my approval – he was ordering me to leave. I had no say. With the little strength I had, I could not resist Quinn raising me up to rest on Epona's saddle.

"Quinn, I..."

"Brianna," Quinn held my hands and looked up to meet my fretting gaze, "I will see you again. I will."

I didn't know how to respond. I didn't even want to consider the prospect of never seeing Quinn again!

Quinn reached up to my chin and stroked it, saying, "I love you."

"I..."

"Go!" Quinn slapped Epona's back and she stormed off, preventing me from saying what I had felt for so long.

What if I never get the chance to say that? What if Quinn is the person the Kaelins foretold about?

"ARGH!" A painful cry from behind us made me pull on Epona's reigns instantly. Despite the pain it caused my wrists, my desire to return to Quinn overpowered the pain.

"We're going back!" I breathed, tightening my grip around the reigns and disobeying Quinn's orders. With every leap Epona took, my body begged me to stop; my knees felt as though they were splitting open and my wrists and ankles burned as if hot pieces of coal were bouncing on and of my skin.

Returning to the small clearing that we had just departed, a body was struggling to lift itself from the ground; an arrow was protruding from the man's left shoulder.

"Quinn!" I screamed, as I pulled on Epona's reigns.

"No!" he cried. "Turn around! Go!"

Small flames encircled me, as hooded figures on black stallions were drawing in. Within seconds, we were surrounded with no way out. Epona screamed cries of desperation.

"Epona!" I tried to calm her down, but it was no use. Epona raised her front legs and kicked them in the air, attempting to defend me against the approaching threat.

Ropes were flung around Epona's legs and raised them from the ground, causing my body to fly backwards into the nearest tree.

CRACK!

The tree branch snapping, as my body made contact with the tree, was not the only source of the sickening sound.

Epona was restrained; her screams deafening!

Raising my head from the forest floor, I realised that I had experienced this before, but not through having lived it, but through having dreamt it. When I met Quinn's fearful gaze, something within me made me leap up from the ground towards him, but I was soon stopped. Two hooded figures launched themselves at my shoulders and heaved me back into the tree I had just crashed into.

An awful sensation was consuming my left side. Like in the dream, an agonising pain was emanating from my ribs.

Directly opposite me, Quinn had his knees embedded in the forest floor, with his arms restrained by two other hooded men.

"I love you too, Quinn."

I sensed that he had received my thoughts, through a faint smile amongst my fear and his pain. The arrow still remained in Quinn's shoulder; blood was spreading across his white shirt.

Directly behind Quinn, another dark figure began to emerge from the surrounding bush. When it reached Quinn it stopped and reached down for the arrow.

"AHHHHHH!" Quinn cried, as the figure pressed the arrow deeper into his body.

"I told you that if you failed to tell me where the carrier was that there would be consequences, didn't I?" Cillian's face emerged from the darkness.

"So," Cillian strode through the clearing and stood before me. "Let's try this again. Where is the carrier?"

My eyes quickly averted to Quinn. He shook his head, not wanting me to surrender the carrier under any circumstances.

"Still refusing to tell me?" Cillian paced back to Quinn. "One last time, Brianna," Cillian warned as he clasped his fingers around the arrow through Quinn's shoulder. "Where is it?"

"AH!"

Cillian drove the arrow further into Quinn.

"Don't give it to them!" Quinn urged me through his thoughts. *"Don't!"*

Chapter Twenty-Two

Sacrifice

…"If one murderous drop of blood is spilt, I shall return!"
Morrigan vowed as the druids of Oran-Roy bound her evil spirit to
her bow and last remaining arrow.

As her spirit became trapped, her lifeless, cold body fell
towards the damp ground. The white skin turned black and split
into hundreds of black clumps. The clumps slowly morphed into
crows and gradually took flight, fleeing away from Breena's border.

Morrigan's bow and arrow remained in a number of
pieces…

- *Excerpt from 'The Morrigan Book'*

"STOP IT!" I cried. "Stop it! If it's me you want, punish
me! Not him!"

Cillian signalled for the men to release Quinn; his
weakened body collapsed to the forest floor.

"Well," Cillian spread out his arms, "where is it then?"

"It's … it's…"

"I've never been a patient man, Brianna," Cillian sighed, rubbing his eyes in annoyance. "Just tell me where the carrier is and you and your friend shall be free to leave."

"It's not that simple," I spat.

"Argh!" Quinn moaned after being kicked in the chest.

"All right! All right!" I yelled. "I ... I..."

"Don't tell them!" Quinn urged me through telepathy once more.

"I ... I'll tell you once you ... once you try to convince me why you are in ... in such dire need of it." The only plan I had was stalling until Leona, Ewan and the others would hopefully locate us with reinforcements. I was hoping that Cillian would be a boastful man; after all, most evil schemers love to explain their cause for the preservation of their ego.

"If you insist," Cillian breathed as he removed a small club, with sharp blades protruding at the round top from his belt, letting it fall to the floor before Quinn. This was his subtle way of warning what was to come. "I'm not just in need of it, as you plainly put it, Brianna. I deserve it!" Cillian gritted his teeth; his scrunched up face was now only inches from mine.

"My mother was chosen," I replied with great stern. "Zia chose her for obvious reasons ..."

"He was wrong!" Cillian bellowed, so loudly that it echoed beyond the clearing, causing birds in the nearby trees to flee into the night sky. It was difficult to maintain focus, my body felt like it was falling apart! Every limb was in agony! But I needed to be strong, mentally. If there was ever a time to test the theory of mind over matter, this was the time to do it.

"You just want to be the Carrier for power! Prestige!" I blared. "You think that Morrigan will reward you if you bring her back!" I laughed. "She won't reward you!"

My words drove deeply into Cillian. I was targeting his weakness and felt that I had almost hit bullseye. "You're unaware of her creed - her prophecy!" A vein was throbbing out of Cillian's forehead. It was clear that I was getting to him. I had to keep this up for Quinn's sake!

"Just because you are the Carrier, it doesn't mean that she'll obey you! You're not mixed-blooded like her - like I am and my brother! But that's beside the point! She killed anyone who stood in her way of ruling! You would be standing in her way! If people were so sure that she would reward them, blood would have already been spilt through murder by now!"

"Brianna, Brianna," Cillian patted my cheek and continued to be condescending. A sudden, chilling calmness fell over him. The vein in his head was no longer visible. My recent feelings of satisfaction were suddenly diminished. "You really have no idea, do you?"

I didn't answer; Cillian was so immersed in convincing me of his beliefs, which is why I allowed him to crack on as I hung onto the hope that Quinn and I would soon be found.

"Morrigan only destroyed those who were against her cause. But yes, people, like you, who were against her cause, were also taken care of."

"So, you are supporting a monster who only stood for the destruction of human life then?"

"Morrigan had grand ideas and a grand vision for Oran-Roy," Cillian thrust his fist into the air, inviting his followers to bellow cheers of praise. "If she was not stopped by the Druids, Morrigan would have become the Carrier and enabled the Oran-Roy people to return back to Ireland and take control of what was stolen; what was taken away from them! With her, I can lead us back there to reclaim what was stolen! Ireland is rightfully ours!"

"Morrigan didn't just intend to claim back the former homeland of the Oran-Roy people!" I responded angrily. Cillian's reasoning was incredibly distorted! I could never understand how someone could support such an evil cause! "Morrigan wanted to slaughter innocent people and teach people like her to abuse their gifts to serve their own needs instead of the needs of the powerless! Besides, the Ireland I have lived in for the past eighteen years is not as it was all those years ago! The world beyond Oran-Roy is a completely different place! They have no idea this place even exists!"

Cillian turned towards Quinn, which made my heart stop. "Brianna, in this moment, you are the only safe person in Oran-Roy. The Druids will not let their Carrier die." Cillian continued to stare at Quinn as he paced by the sharp club on the floor, taunting me. Fearing what was to come was almost as bad as the physical pain. Awful images of Quinn being beaten by the club played through my head like a never-ending role of film. I had to stop it! I couldn't risk the possibility of Quinn seeing that! I couldn't let that outcome eventuate! I had to draw Cillian's attention back to me.

"The Druids won't save you from Morrigan, even if you are the Carrier," I breathed with distain. As I had hoped, Cillian's attention left Quinn and returned to me. He held his arms behind his back and casually walked towards me across the damp clearing. His slow, intimidating stroll sent chills through my body. Before his uneasy stride came to a stop, tiny cold droplets of water fell against my face and trickled down my cheeks; the weather paired well with the atmosphere of the evening.

"They have no choice but to do so." Cillian continued to speak as a rustling noise drew my attention to the bushes bordering the clearing. The men, who were not occupied in restraining Quinn and I, did not hesitate in raising their bows ready for release. When a hooded figure emerged from the shrubs, the followers lowered their bows and looked to Cillian. I focussed more and more on the small fraction of the face beneath the hood and almost breathed a sigh of relief as I recognised that sturdy chin.

"Ewan! Ewan is here!" I assured Quinn through thought. *"Taking the Morrigan follower's coat came in handy!"*

My eyes didn't leave Ewan, but as I continued to stare, I realised that he was not alone. Ewan lowered his head and signalled to his right; another tall, hooded figure was beside him and together, they were supporting a limp Brogan. I couldn't contain my surprise! Was Ewan with one of Cillian's men, pretending to assist him with Brogan, or was the other hooded figure from our cause and a means of escape from Cillian's clutches?

"Ewan, who is with you and is Brogan really unconscious?"

Ewan didn't flinch as my thoughts were heard by him and he quickly answered, *"Zephan is here beside me and Brogan is unconscious. Guards found him once he left the hall of heroes. We took care of them. Do exactly what we tell you, Brianna."* Ewan seemed worried. *"Someone knew that we would be coming here for Zia's writings and for your mother tonight. We don't know how, or who, but it's the only thing that explains why we have been so unsuccessful."*

"Ah," Cillian clasped his hands together in a sickening, sadistic manner as Ewan and Zephan released Brogan to the wet forest floor. "You would think the boy would have more respect for the man who took him in and cared for him his whole life!" Cillian looked to his followers for a unanimous supportive response. While Cillian was enjoying the attention, then attending to Brogan, I had a chance to communicate with Ewan again.

"What are you three planning?"

"Brianna," Zephan responded this time, Ewan was turning Brogan's body over for Cillian to examine, *"You need to control as many guards as you can when we instruct you to. You need to have them injure Cillian, which will cause the other guards to ambush. That will give us an opportunity to leave."*

"I can only control three people at best, Zephan!"

"That should still create enough of a distraction for us to leave."

"When do you want me to do this?"

"When you receive the signal from Leona. She and the others are taking much longer than we expected and I don't know why."

"Are more of Cillian's men holding them up?"

"No, Brianna." Zephan's tone amplified my worry. *"It's much worse."*

"Worse? What could be worse than...?"

Communicating with Zephan was interrupted by another hooded figure entering the clearing.

"Leona?" I questioned the unknown being, as it leant over and examined Brogan.

"No," the smooth voice replied. *"It's Rona, Brianna. Once Leona arrives, we will be able to leave here safely."*

"Is everyone alright? Ethan, Charlotte, Craig and ..."

"As far as I know, yes."

I breathed a sigh of relief, which wasn't as subtle as I intended it to be. Cillian's menacing eyes darted towards me, then looked to either side of my head. His followers, still firmly holding my arms, released me. Freeing my arms came as a shock and my weight dragged me face down into the damp earth.

As I raised my head, black boots were only a few inches from my face. My eyes ran up the figure and stopped as they met Cillian's sinister grin.

"Search her for the carrier," Cillian ordered the men, "While I search Brogan." Quinn raised his head and found my watering eyes; I was fearful of what was to come. How was this all going to end when the carrier would reside in Cillian's hands? Quinn's anticipating expression amplified my nerves; he feared what the men were going to do to me. His fearful reaction intensified my own.

My eyes did not leave Quinn's as the men grasped my shoulders and raised me from the ground. Painfully, Quinn attempted to raise himself up, but as soon as he placed pressure on his left shoulder, he cried out in pain and collapsed back into the floor.

"No!" I cried, as one of Cillian's men kicked Quinn in the ribs. "He can barely…!" My words were cut short as the men twisted my body around, heaving my back into the moist ground.

"Argh!" I wailed and curled up towards the pain beating in my ribs. With every breath, the pain grew; consuming my chest like an uncontrollable forest fire. The larger of the two men knelt beside my body, clenched my wrists, and then leaned over me, digging my arms to the forest floor, making it easier for the other man to search me for the carrier. The other faceless man looked down towards my chest; the carrier's chain must have been visible. I tried to resist the man's hold of me, but it was no use. As the other man lowered himself towards me, I considered kicking my feet into his face, but as they barely left the ground, the pain within my ribs and knees intensified.

The man's concealed hands grasped the collar of my shirt. My heart, racing at a million miles an hour, pounded out all the surrounding sounds of the Daray forest.

I gasped as my shirt was ripped open; the carrier was now exposed for all to see. Even though I could not see the face of the man searching me, I sensed a twinkle in his eye as he stroked the carrier, wishing he could claim it as his own prize. As he raised himself up from the ground, his hands did not leave the carrier, still chained to my neck.

"ARGH!" The carrier chain's latch opened and was stripped from around my neck. When my wrists were finally freed, I twisted my body, so that my chest was now facing the damp earth. It seemed as though Cillian's followers felt no need to hold me back in my current physical state.

Raising my head from the very familiar damp surface, I saw Cillian, crouching over Brogan's body, while a concealed Ewan, Zephan and Rona continued to look on.

"What's he searching him for?" I asked the others telepathically.

"Zia's writings," Rona answered. *"But, don't fear, Brianna, he won't find them with Brogan."*

"Where are they?"

"Ewan has them."

"Brianna?" Ewan remained ever so still as he called upon me.

"Yes."

"I know this appears that we are at a disadvantage, but as soon as Leona arrives, remember to do exactly what we have told you."

"All right." I replied, without conviction, which made Ewan concerned.

"Are you in too much pain to do as we discussed?"

I wanted to answer *yes*, but how could I? My pain could not be compared to Quinn's current state, the anxiety of Mam and Dad back home and Keira's hell. If I allowed this pain to stand in the way of helping my family and friends, all I would be leading them into would be more intensified pain. I couldn't allow myself to live with the feeling of regret, thinking that I could have done more! I wasn't going to allow Cillian and his followers to destroy what Zia and people like Donelle and Cuchulainn stood for.

"Brianna?" Ewan was waiting for my response.

"No. The pain won't stop me. As soon as I hear word from Leona, I will do as you ask."

Ewan and I ended our discussion just as Cillian gave up searching Brogan for Zia's writings.

"ARGH!" Cillian blared in Brogan's face, then clenched on to the damp earth beneath his feet and threw it into the air as he raised himself up. "Where is it if it is not with him?" Cillian demanded an explanation from the three newest arrivals in the clearing, whom he thought to be his followers.

"We saw him leaving the passage with the writings in his possession my ..." Zephan's words were overpowered by another tantrum from Cillian.

"Then where are they?" Cillian paced alongside Brogan's body, running his fingers through his hair, anxious to hear the whereabouts of his father's writings. It was satisfying seeing him in a doubtful state of mind. But, unexpectedly, Cillian's manner and expression changed as though he had made an astonishing recollection. Once again, the protruding vein from Cillian's forehead faded away, causing that uneasy feeling to return to the pit of my stomach.

"Brianna," a familiar voice whispered. I wasn't sure whether the voice was in my head or being said aloud, but it eased my new nerves.

"Leona?" I asked, desperately longing to hear her voice again.

"Do what was discussed now."

Without hesitating, I closed my eyes. Flashes of the memories I had recently formed from my time here in Oran-Roy raced through my mind, as if I was channel surfing. Memories of arriving on the Oran-Roy bird and meeting my new friends began to draw me away from any of the physical pain I was experiencing.

I then recalled meeting my father for the first time, learning combat under Ewan and Quinn's guidance, being initiated by the druids of Oran-Roy and coming to the realisation that I had developed feelings for Quinn. As Cuchulainn advised me, I considered who and what had made me true. It was these experiences and the people I had come to know on this journey that made me realise who I was and what I was capable of achieving.

I continued to channel all of the beloved experiences and relationships formed here in Oran-Roy when I opened my eyes, ready to use my abilities to see an end to all this chaos.

Three of the followers, closest to Quinn, left Quinn's body and strode over to Cillian under my control. But, when they reached Cillian, something caused them to stop. Cillian raised his hand before the three followers, and then turned his attention to me, barely managing to hold myself up against the nearest tree.

"What's going on?" Ewan asked me in a baffled tone through thought.

"I ... I don't know!" My heart was racing. Why weren't they responding to my control? *"They're not doing what I'm controlling them to do!"*

"Something isn't right!" Zephan insisted. *"Is Leona even here yet?"*

"I heard her voice!" I explained. *"She was behind me! She told me to act!"*

Cillian quickly drew his gaze from me to Ewan, still masked beneath the deep, purple cloak.

Cillian's manner intensified my nerves. Quickly, I closed my eyes, attempting to block out the surrounding sounds in order to hear Cillian's thoughts.

"Your plan has failed you, Brianna." My spine tingled as Cillian's eyes made contact with mine, precisely as I heard his thoughts.

"He knows!" I warned the others. *"He knows!"*

"NO!" I screamed at the top of my lungs as Cillian's hand stripped Ewan's cloak. Ewan fell to his knees, trying to resist Cillian's pull, but he was no match for Cillian and Ewan's face was revealed before his father's followers.

Immediately, following Ewan's unveiling, weighted nets were tossed over Zephan and Rona as their feet barely left the forest floor. Again, I concentrated on the guards, this time those closest to Rona and Zephan, and attempted to make them remove the nets. They remained still. No matter how much I concentrated, nothing I did was working! Had my ability been suppressed? What was going on?

Two guards dug their spears into either side of Ewan's neck. One of the guards had pressed so hard that blood was trickling from the spear point's indentation.

I didn't know what to say or how to respond! There was nothing I could do if my ability to control was not working! I tried to stand upright by using the tree to pull my body up, but I quickly slid down the tree's side, with my back against its trunk in a completely hopeless position. Silent tears fell from my eyes. I couldn't fathom how Cillian knew our plan! I wasn't certain whether he was capable of stopping the control I had over the guards, or if someone was helping him! Feeling as though I was in the most dangerous, vulnerable position of my life, I turned to Quinn.

"Leona?" Quinn asked in thought.

I shook my head. *"She spoke to me. I heard her voice but she isn't here! This is my fault!"*

"No! Perhaps it wasn't her! Perhaps there is more to this! Maybe someone is helping Cillian!"

"Ewan said the same thing when they arrived here."

"Ah!" Cillian happily cried as he removed a small and rather tatty brown book from Ewan's shirt. "I never understood you, son."

"I can say the same about you, Cillian," Ewan replied with such confidence; his bravery slightly lifting my spirits.

Insulted by Ewan's remark and not referring to him as 'father', Cillian rolled his eyes and gave the guards a subtle cue to lower their spears. Without warning, Cillian thrashed Ewan face into the ground by his hair.

"How could you not have faith in your father's cause and choose to associate yourself with these fools?" Cillian spat at the ground beside Ewan's body. The two guards raised Ewan up, digging his knees into the ground and holding his head back by his hair. His face was smeared with mud, but the now heavy rain began leaving trails across the smudged dirt masking Ewan's swelling cheek. "What I am doing is reclaiming what is ours! And me being the Carrier will help us reclaim it!"

Everything fell silent for one, brief moment, then, very calmly, Ewan replied, "Whatever my mother saw in you was either a lie, or has been completely consumed by your hate." Ewan returned the favour and spat at Cillian's feet and continued to stare into his father's hollow eyes.

Cillian rubbed his eyes and then mumbled, "Hold him up beside the girl." Ewan tried to resist the guards as they dragged him across the clearing and then positioned him beside me against the tree.

Cillian signalled the guard closest to me. Reluctantly, the guard obeyed and dropped the carrier into Cillian's hand. The possibility we all dreaded was about to occur before our eyes. With an incredibly jovial, arrogant expression, Cillian tucked Zia's book into his belt and smiled as he placed the carrier's chain around his neck.

As the carrier fell against Cillian's chest, a cool sensation tingled through my right palm. I raised my palm up before my eyes and saw the black carrier symbol slowly fading away into my skin. The sensation was not painful; it felt as though someone had poured some cool water over my hand. As each black pigment grew fainter and fainter, Cillian's pain grew.

"ARGH!" Cillian collapsed into the forest floor, clasping his right palm in utter agony and contorting his body in strange ways from the pain. The veins in his arms and neck thickened and throbbed. Despite my dire predicament, I still enjoyed seeing him in pain after all the horrid acts he had committed. I only wished the circumstances were different.

When the burning sensation consuming Cillian's palm came to an abrupt end, he lifted himself up from the ground, raised his palm and waved it for all his followers to see. Cillian paced around the clearing and laughed, so pleased that he had finally received the very thing he had longed for his entire existence. As my eyes followed Cillian around the clearing, my gaze remained with Quinn as Cillian paced alongside him. Quinn's eyes were barely open. His head was lolling up and down, as he struggled to maintain consciousness.

"Quinn!" I cried, which had no effect on him. "Stay awake!"

Ewan realised the reason behind my cries.

"Quinn!" He also cried. "Don't you dare close your eyes! Quinn!"

Our yelling was useless; Quinn's head eventually fell against the floor.

"No!" I screamed. "Ewan! He could die! He's lost too much blood!"

"We wouldn't want that, would we?" Cillian was beaming as he positioned himself in the centre of the clearing.

"Make the guard by Zephan and Rona slip them his dagger!" Ewan demanded through thought.

"It might not work like before!"

"Try!"

While Cillian had men examine Quinn, I attempted to do as Ewan had told me, but once again, the guard failed to act under my control.

"He's alive," one of the followers advised Cillian.

"Good, good. We wouldn't want to welcome Morrigan back *just* yet." Cillian signalled for one of his followers to hand him a bow and arrow that was resting against a large, nearby stone. As Cillian began preparing the bow, anger fuelled within me that was indescribable.

"That's my bow!" I cried. A fiery pit of fury was boiling up within me, ready to erupt at any moment.

"Yes, you're quite right. You're very observant, Brianna; a trait quite common within our family." The followers chuckled sinisterly. Cillian's banter was sickening.

"Brianna! Try again or I'll have to do something else that will end all this!" Ewan begged me.

Rather than looking at the guard, I continued to stare at Cillian with a forceful, threatening stare while controlling the guard to drop his dagger beside the netting covering Zephan and Rona. I had no idea whether controlling the guard was successful this time. The only way of knowing would be if Zephan and Rona would soon be free.

"How ironic that the end of you will be by your *own* weapon," Cillian chuckled in a casual manner as he prepared one of my silver arrows on my engraved bow, presented to me by my father, Craig. Overwhelmed by Quinn's state and the prospect of having an arrow pierce my skin, words escaped me! Everything I had aimed to achieve in Oran-Roy was going to come to a brutal end! Many people were now going to suffer as a result of what I had failed to accomplish.

"What an awful way for me to be remembered!" I thought to myself, but Ewan's response told me that my thoughts were not only heard by me.

"Don't think that, Brianna!" He assured me. *"Without you, we would still be living here like hermits, achieving nothing and just avoiding trouble! You started this! You gave us the opportunity to fight back and aim for a united Oran-Roy again! And for that, I'm sure I wouldn't be alone in saying this ... I thank you."*

Ewan's words brought tears to my eyes. I turned to my right and looked up to meet his face. "I'm so grateful that I have come to know you."

"Me also," Ewan replied whole-heartedly, with glassy eyes.

"Shut them up!" Cillian blared without removing his eyes from my bow. As Cillian had ordered, the nearest two guards slapped my face and then Ewan's. Water seeped from my swollen eyes.

"Think of what this will mean!" Ewan made one last attempt to reason with his twisted father. "How do you think the rest of Oran-Roy is going to react when they discover that you have been forming a mixed-blooded army behind their backs, just for your own gain?"

I finally understood what those guards were referring to earlier that night. It was finally starting to make sense.

"So, that's what the guard was speaking about when you, Quinn, Leona and I were making our way into the castle!"

"Yes." Ewan answered my thoughts. *"That's why the others are delayed."*

"They'll be overjoyed in knowing that someone finally decided to act and reclaim what was stolen from us!" Cillian threw my bow into the ground and stormed to Ewan. "Soon enough, son," he whispered in an unusually, terrifying calmly manner into Ewan's ear, close enough for me to hear, "You'll realise which side you should have chosen."

"No," Ewan firmly assured his father, "I have chosen wisely. You will live to regret your choices."

Cillian firmly grasped Ewan's jaw. "You are no son of mine."

"One of the most honourable things I ever did was leaving you, Cillian." Ewan's voice did not waver; he showed no fear facing his father. "I pity you, Cillian."

Ewan's final words aroused a wrath of hate within Cillian. Cillian released Ewan's jaw and paced back to my bow, now resting in the centre of the clearing.

"Now that I possess the secrets of my *beloved* father," Cillian patted Zia's journal tucked securely in his belt, "And the carrier, I can offer Morrigan a return where she and I will take my army and conquer the land of our ancestors that is rightfully ours."

"Cillian!" I yelled in annoyance. "Ireland, today, is full of innocent people who are completely ignorant as to what happened between Oran-Roy and Ireland centuries ago! Besides," I continued to stall, "How can you be so confident in Morrigan when you had to claim the carrier and Zia's writings before you would see her return?"

Cillian ignored me as he raised my bow and aimed the arrow for my chest.

"Hold her firmly against the tree so she cannot move," Cillian ordered the guards, already firmly holding my forearms behind my back.

"Are Rona and Zephan able to reach the dagger?" Ewan asked out of desperation.

"Zephan! Rona!" I quickly asked them through thought. *"Did the guard release the dagger? Can you set yourselves free?"*

"The ropes are almost cut, Brianna!" Zephan assured me, giving me one last hope that we would soon be free.

I turned to Ewan, nodded my head and offered him a final, reassuring smile, my way of saying that this should all be over soon. Ewan also smiled and then bravely turned towards his father, preparing himself for what was to come.

"What a way to return a hero?" Cillian closed his left eye, raised the bow and stretched it, preparing to release the arrow. "…By killing the person who was going to stand in her way."

With the guard's tight hold, I could barely turn my head over to Zephan and Rona. If they failed to free themselves from the netting in time, if Leona and the others did not arrive any second, my life would end and Morrigan's reign would begin again. In a final act of desperation, I lowered my head and looked directly at Cillian, blocking out everything but us. I visualised him lowering the bow and then tossing it to the ground. Despite being successful in helping Zephan and Rona free themselves with the guard's dagger, my recent vision failed to play out before me.

As I read Ewan's thoughts, I knew that he felt as though he had failed me and I sensed Ewan's struggle to free himself from the guards' hold. Repeatedly, he turned to Rona and Zephan, hoping for a miracle, but they were still trapped.

As I faced death, I recalled everything that made life worth living all within one mere second. Whoever said that having your entire life flash before you just before you die was a cliché was mistaken. I can assure you, it happens within the span of taking your final breath. I closed my eyes, wanting to live my final moment visualising me in Quinn's loving embrace.

The sound of the arrow being released drummed through my ears as Quinn and I were holding each other. Almost exactly as I heard the sound, something slid across the front of my chest. When I opened my eyes, Ewan was standing directly in front of me. Then, as if everything was happening in slow motion, Ewan's knees buckled and he fell to the floor. The silver arrow, intended for me, was protruding from his chest.

"No!" I screamed, as I tried to lower myself down to Ewan. I wailed and continued to struggle against the guards' hold. My eyes did not leave Ewan, as the guards dragged me towards the centre of the clearing. A puddle of blood was spreading beneath Ewan and beyond his arms, which now lay lifelessly alongside his body. His eyes flickered one last time as he vainly tried to raise his head. I heard him make a final effort to gulp some air, but his eyes closed and his head fell.

An enormous tearing noise drew my eyes away from Ewan's dead body. The guard dragging me towards the centre of the clearing released me, his attention diverted to Zephan's white wings breaking through a hole he had formed in the netting. As Zephan and Rona propelled themselves from the netting, a cold, eerie wind swept through the clearing; the haunting wind whistled through the forest trees.

The cool wind suddenly turned hostile! Everyone within the clearing was hurled to the ground; even the trees were bowing down and surrendering to the irresistible wind. Bodies were strewn all over the forest floor, waiting for the wind to ease.

Fighting the forceful wind, I managed to raise my head from the dirt and found Cillian, also powerless to the wind, lying against the earth with the silvery carrier device and Zia's writings a tantalizing arm's length distance from him. I thought about crawling towards them, but while the wind was this strong, how could I possibly manage to move, with so little remaining strength and frustrated by the injuries I had recently sustained? I tried to meet Zephan's gaze and urge him to reach for the carrier before it too would succumb to the wind's pull, which was dragging the writings further and further away each nerve-racking glance I took.

"ZEPHAN!" I didn't even hear myself cry; the frenetic wind silenced me.

With no one to hear me, no one able to defy the wind's brutal strength, I stared at the carrier hoping for a miracle before it escaped my sight. I closed my eyes, gritted my teeth and buried my head into the ground. My hands clenched the damp dirt as I imagined the carrier effortlessly moving along the forest floor and finding its way into my open hand.

I raised my head from the damp ground and continued to stare at the carrier. A gust of wind had collected dirt and small stones from the forest floor, sweeping them across the clearing. I buried my head in my arms, shielding my eyes from the incoming debris. When the wind eased, I looked up to find the carrier no longer beside Cillian. My heart sank.

"I looked away for no more than a few seconds and it's blown off somewhere!"

A faint shimmery light darted to my right, pulling me out of my grief. My eyes were upon the carrier, rolling across the moon-lit path, determined to reach my right palm and be united with its Tarmon guide once more. The cool touch of the carrier upon my icy skin created an inner spark of hope. My comfort was short lived and overpowered by the darkening display overpowering the moon's former tranquil splendour.

Small masses of black were now beginning to merge above the clearing. Deafening squawks and cries were growing louder and louder as a mass of black swallowed up the clearing.

My eyes struggled to maintain focus. I began wavering in and out of consciousness.

Amongst the chaos, I was yanked into the air by a vice-like grip that clasped my wrist.

"The writings," I murmured, "Zia's…"

While being lifter higher and higher into the cool night sky, I managed to look down upon the black mass now spiralling over Ewan's body and realised the true nature of the haunting darkness.

The last thing my eyes saw that night was a mass of crows reuniting to form Morrigan.

Chapter Twenty-Three

Counsel

...Donelle fell beside her dying love. As her pale skin met Cuchulainn's arm, his skin turned black. She was powerless, cursed and not ready to accept a life without Cuchulainn.

"NO!" she yelled with streams of tears.
Her welling eyes met Morrigan's stark stare.

"Now you will know what it is like to feel unloved and hated for what you can do."

Morrigan's body dispersed into a swarm of crows, making their way towards the Tarmon castle...

- Excerpt from 'The Morrigan Book'

"...How about Donelle, Ethan?"

"Donelle won't be able to help Quinn, Charlotte! Remember?"

"Well, we have no other choice but to take him to Ireland with us where he can get medical attention, Zephan. Ethan and I can get the two of them there via the Oran-Roy bird."

"Charlotte's right. Brianna got the carrier back so we can take the bird back home. We'll have to take Brianna and Quinn there for help."

"Go then! You'll be much safer there."

"But what about all of you? When should we bring them back, Zephan? What about … Ewan's …"

"…When they have returned to full strength. Now go! Summon the bird. Quickly! Keep the writings and all of us will be safely harboured in Breena, in the Druids safe hands until you return. I'll inform Craig. Now go!"

*

"She'll be okay, won't she?"

"Don't panic, Charlotte, the doctor said that she'll be just fine."

"But, she's been like this for over a day now! I'm worried, Ethan!"

"Don't worry! Besides, she might be able to hear what you're saying and Bee hates people worrying; it only makes her more anxious and she doesn't need that right now!"

*

"Just … just look at her! She's … she's not fine, Roy! She's not!"

"Tara, you need to calm down! The doctors said that she'll be okay! Stay with her and I'll bring you up a coffee, all right?"

"Okay..."

*

Beep. Beep. Beep. Beep.

An incredibly annoying tone gradually amplified its way into my ears, followed by yet another annoying sound; Ethan's snoring.

I opened my eyes, only to see another blanket of darkness; making me doubt whether I had even opened my eyes. I twisted my body towards the repetitive beeping noise that seemed to be projecting from an area above the right-hand side of my head, but I stopped half way.

"Argh!" I moaned, responding to the throbbing, stabbing pain in my side. Almost immediately after my painful cry, light engulfed the room.

My eyes flickered, trying to grow accustomed to the sudden flash of light.

"Bee! You're awake!" Ethan cried out and grasped my right hand before I could even make out his appearance. Once the splotches of yellow light faded away, a battered up version of my brother was revealed to be sitting beside me.

"What … what happened …. to your …?" With every breath, my chest practically winced in pain.

"Don't worry about me! This is nothing!"

Nothing! Ethan's left eye looked more like a ripened plumb than an eye socket! And his left cheek was so swollen it was almost swallowing his eye! If he could see me, amongst the newly formed Himalayas on his face, it was a miracle!

"Although," he chuckled, "I am a sight for *sore eyes*, don't you think?"

"Very funny," I sighed, rolling my eyes. "Wait!" I begged Ethan to stop laughing. How could I sit here, laughing after recent events? Everything came flooding back in an instant! My cousin died saving me! I watched Morrigan being formed! I watched Quinn sink into an abyss of unconsciousness! Nothing was funny! *Why I am laughing? Why the hell am I laughing?*

These flashbacks overpowered any happy feeling I had left within me, making me want to be sick! The excruciating pain consuming my knees, face and ribs was temporarily forgotten! The pit of my stomach contorted, my breathing became heavy and raspy, as though a piece of paper was being repeatedly scrunched up in the back of my throat! I couldn't breathe!

"Where is…? Is Quinn…?"

"Bee! Calm down!" Ethan clasped my forearms, avoiding the bandages on my wrists, and tried to make contact with my eyes, which were flicking back and forth between the white wall directly opposite me and the pastel blue sheets over my legs.

"Bee! Bee!" Ethan released my arms and darted for the corridor. "Nurse! We need help in here! She can't breathe!"

*

I opened my eyes to a sea of light gushing in through the nearby window. The pain I had felt earlier didn't seem as severe. Perhaps the nurse had increased my pain medication.

My ears began to channel in all of the surrounding sounds; the first of these was a muffling, wheezing sound that seemed to be coming from me – it was a breathing apparatus.

I coughed into the apparatus, fogging it up. No longer in need of it, I pulled it from my face and let it fall beside my bed. A clanging sound echoed from the mask hitting the metal framing of the bed, which was very quickly followed by hastened footsteps growing increasingly louder from the corridor.

When the footsteps stopped, I turned to face the doorway and was overwhelmed with joy.

"Oh! My poor darling!" Mam raced through the room and tenderly embraced me. I started to raise my arms to hug her back, but a stabbing pain in my wrists ordered my arms to lower themselves back to the bed.

"I'm so sorry I … I left without…" My words were drowned by relieved tears.

"It's okay, it's all right!" Mam stroked my hair, reassuring me that no harm could come to me now. "You're okay, that's the main thing. That's the … the main thing."

"Thank God!" A comforting and familiarly low voice rejoiced.

"Dad!" Mam let me go. Dad raced over to the other side of my bed.

"We've heard you've had a *very* interesting few months," Dad sighed, as we let go of one another.

"Hmm," I replied sheepishly, sinking back into my bed. "I … I *really* wanted to tell you, but … but I wasn't sure how you'd …"

"We always knew you'd end up on an unimaginable adventure, Brianna," Dad chuckled, "but next time, we'd like fair warning."

"School!" I suddenly thought. "What did you tell the school about us being…?"

Dad raised his hand and eased my worry. "It was all taken care of, my love. I have connections. Let's just say that your principal will be intrigued to find out how your volunteering program in South Africa went."

I forced a smile.

"So, you know what's happened though? Where we were and why?" That sickening, guilty feeling was beginning to simmer in my gut again. But, Mam and Dad's calm expressions seemed to suppress the unsettling feeling. To my surprise, both Mam and Dad nodded their heads and smiled. "You're … you're not mad at us? At *me?*"

"Well," Mam glanced over at Dad and then back to me. "I *can't* lie. Initially, I was worried sick and …"

"Initially!" Dad chuckled. "You know your mother, Brianna."

"Roy!" Mam rolled her eyes. "Although," she looked down and began fiddling with the loose threading on the blue quilt, "I have lost a bit of weight from stress. That's the *only* good thing that came out of not having you and Ethan at home."

"Is that a thank you?" I asked in a cheeky tone, but very quickly reverted back to a sombre mood, trying to convince myself that I couldn't be happy after recent events.

Mam and Dad sensed the shift in my mood and immediately recognised why I felt as I did.

"Brianna," Dad's heavy hand over my thigh pulled me from the dreaded thoughts. "Ethan and Charlotte told us *everything*, right after you were admitted here and given the all clear."

"*Everything?*"

"Everything," Mam assured me.

"I'm sorry I didn't tell you. We thought of leaving the book, but we knew we would need it to…"

Dad held my chin and made me stop talking. "We understand why you acted as you did."

"And we were a little annoyed and concerned that …"

"What your mother is trying to say is that we realise you had good reason for acting as you did. And, we were surprised to come to know of … of where you're from and your 'abilities'…"

"They told you what I am capable of and … who I'm … uh … who I met in…?"

"Yes." Dad replied as he glanced over to Mam, who was once again fiddling with the loose threads of the quilt. They knew that I was referring to Quinn. It appeared that Mam wasn't so impressed by my relationship with Quinn. What pieces of information were Ethan and Charlotte forced into divulging? Quinn!

"I need to see Quinn, Dad! I need to see him!" I threw the thin sheets off me and tried to slide off the bed, but was stopped when I saw metal braces clasped around my knees. "What the hell?"

"The doctor said that you'll be fine, Brianna," Mam tried to calm me down, but I could tell by her tone that the sight of my knees was disturbing her just as much as it was disturbing me. "You had some small fractures in your knee caps. He said that it looks more serious than what it actually is!" The assurance wasn't helping. "The braces prevent you from moving them. They need to remain straight. You also fractured a rib, Brianna. Get up nice and slow when you have to."

"How … how long am I going to be like this for?"

"He said that the braces can come off after a week or two, depending on your progress and then you can have some guards on that will allow for more movement."

"But … how can I do anything like this? I … I need to get back to … for Ewan's …"

"Brianna!" Dad's stern voice put a stop to my concerns. "You *need* to get yourself right before you go back to Ora … Oran …"

"Oran-Roy, Dad."

"Yes."

"Take me to Quinn, *please* Dad!" I begged him. "A wheelchair, being carried there, I *really* don't care how you do it. I just *need* to see him!" After a few exchanged looks, Mam and Dad both nodded. My desperate pleas were successful.

"I'll just ask the nurse, Brianna," Mam advised me, as Dad opened up a wheelchair that had been propped up against a set of drawers beneath the window.

Within a minute, a nurse came into the room, closely followed by Mam, confirming that I was going to see Quinn.

"We'll have to keep your legs straight, love," the nurse explained, while holding my legs up as Dad raised me from the bed and carefully sat me in the wheelchair. "This raise will keep them straight while you're in the chair."

"Thanks."

The pale blue hospital corridor felt like a never ending tunnel in a nightmare. Uncomfortable thoughts of Quinn's state haunted me down the sterile corridor. *He might look different. What if he doesn't remember me? He lost so much blood! Who knows if he'll be okay?*

I was grateful for the sudden jolt in the wheelchair, even though it was just for the merest moment. It drew me away from fearing the worst, allowing me to have a moment of relief.

"I'll warn you, love," the Nurse said in a mournful tone, ending my sudden relief, "He's not in the best of ways."

My breathing became shallow; I was trying to hold back the tears. I was preparing myself for something terrible. I didn't know whether I could cope. No matter the assurance or help from those closest to me, nothing could prepare me for what I was about to see. Despite dreading what awaited me and not knowing how to respond, I put all my fears aside. As Cuchulainn had advised me, I remembered who made me see myself, who made me true. It was my turn to be the strong one now; for Quinn's sake I had to be.

"We'll wait in your room, love," Mam warmly held my shoulder.

"Take all the time you need," Dad stroked my hair and bent down to kiss my forehead.

"Okay," I barely managed to say, struggling to refrain from tearing up.

Just as Mam and Dad's footsteps faded away, blending in with the surrounding white noise of the hospital, the nurse wheeled me through the doorway. Before I had the courage to look, a chilling beeping noise sent shivers down my spine. It wasn't until the wheelchair stopped beside the bed that I had built up enough strength to raise my head and look at Quinn.

Automatically, my hands covered my open mouth in shock. Quinn was a tangled up mess of wires and tubes! The largest tube, coming from his mouth, was connected to a machine; Quinn wasn't breathing on his own. When I looked beyond the coils of tubes, I struggled to find his signature scar amongst the recent cuts and swelling consuming his face. Bandages were wrapped around almost every limb of his body!

"Is … is he … is he in pain?" I begged to know. My tears could no longer be stopped and my heavy breaths brought pain back to the left side of my chest.

The nurse didn't answer me immediately.

"IS – HE – IN – ANY – PAIN?" I cried so loudly that people beyond the doorway, having a very involved discussion, became quiet.

"He's … he's in a coma, love." The nurse patted my shoulder. "I'll let you spend some time with him."

As the nurse left the room, I heard the door close behind her.

"Quinn!" I wailed, with tears streaming down my swollen face. "Don't you dare leave me!" Amongst the wires and tubes, giving Quinn life, I found his left hand and clenched it tightly. "I'm here and I'm not going anywhere! Just like when you found me! Stay with me! Stay with me!"

My head plunged into the bed by Quinn's left arm; the thin white sheet over him soaking up my tears. When my eyes could no longer produce any tears, I raised my head and wiped away the remaining droplets of water from my puffy cheeks.

"I know you can hear me, Quinn." I lifted Quinn's arm, still holding his hand tightly, and rested it against my face. "I ... I haven't come this far to lose you, Quinn." After the tumultuous journey I had been on with Ethan and Charlotte, as well as the many people I came to know along the way, I wasn't going to let it end this way. "You're going to be okay, Quinn," I assured him, as if he were awake, completely aware of my presence and sitting before me.

"Well," I was becoming more composed now and decided that moping around Quinn was not going to improve the situation. And if he could indeed hear what I was saying, why not relive our recent fond memories? "Remember when we first met?" I chuckled. "You were so ... so strange with me. But, you took me by surprise when I was practising my aim in the clearing. I ... I didn't know what to make of it!"

Gently, I returned Quinn's arm back against the bed, still holding onto his hand. "Ha!" I laughed. "I'll never forget when I deliberately lost the tournament so you wouldn't be embarrassed! You were so mad at me! At the time, I was just ... just so incredibly disappointed in you, but ... but now all I can do is laugh about it!"

"Hmm," I sighed, suddenly becoming a little lost for words. "It … it feels really strange just sitting here talking to you, but … but not receiving a reply."

I loosened my grip on Quinn's hand and slid my hands back into my lap, fiddling with my hospital gown. "So," I continued, but now looking down into my lap, "I really need you to come out of this, Quinn. Not just for my sake, but … but for your sister's and all your friends. We need you and won't be able to achieve what we need to without you."

"I couldn't agree more." Ethan's voice pulled my attention from my lap to the now open door. So immersed with Quinn, I didn't even hear the door open.

"We're glad to see you up and about!" Charlotte was beaming! Unlike Ethan, her face appeared to be scratch and bruise free.

"Well, in a manner of speaking," Ethan quickly added and then raced from the door, pulled up a chair and sat beside me.

"You know what I mean, Bee," Charlotte said, as she hugged me gently, afraid that she might cause me to incur further injury - which would probably be impossible with her small frame, anyway.

Charlotte also pulled up a chair and sat beside me in the remaining space, then reassuringly held my hand as it rested in my lap. "How're you holding up, Bee?" Charlotte's eyes flickered from Quinn to me.

"I … uh … I guess … as well as I can be," I quickly replied, slumping over and almost sinking my head into my lap, avoiding eye contact.

"He's going to pull through," Ethan's touch startled me. "The doctors said that he lost a lot of blood and incurred a pretty nasty bump to the head amongst all the commotion."

"I bet they wanted to know how we both ended up in such a mess," I assumed.

"We were pretty quick on our feet coming up with an explanation." Ethan seemed so proud of himself. He folded his arms across his chest, arched his back and beamed as though the Queen had just knighted him.

"But," Charlotte felt that she wasn't being credited for her efforts and quickly ended Ethan's fame, "Ethan is conveniently forgetting that I was the one who came up with what to say."

When Ethan and Charlotte realised that their efforts to humour me were not working, the three of us found ourselves sitting in a deafening silence; each of us wanted to say something, but it seemed that our unanimous silence said all that we needed to say – it spoke of loss, empathy, disbelief and a longing to somehow wind back the clock and reverse the events that had brought us to this moment.

Ethan cut through the silence. "Are you able to hear Quinn's thoughts when he's like this, Bee?" This sudden notion of Ethan's triggered sparks in my brain! If I could indeed hear

Quinn's thoughts, while in a coma, was there a possibility that I could help him pull out of it?

"I ... I never thought of that ... but, I guess I could try. Oh, wait." I suddenly recalled my inability to control people that dreadful night that I never wanted to be reminded of ever again. "Were you filled in on what happened with Cillian and ..." I couldn't say his name again, it would remind me of how I failed and that he was gone.

"Yeah, Bee," Charlotte placed her hand on my arm. "Zephan and Rona gave us a ...Oh! Before I forget!" Charlotte removed a small old looking notebook from her pants pocket. "Zephan asked us to hold onto Zia's writings until we returned."

"How on earth did he get the book? It was blowing away!"

"While Zephan grabbed you, Rona took advantage of the confusion and managed to take the book."

"*Thank God*," I sighed. Wanting to get back to hearing what else Charlotte and Ethan were told, I asked, "So what else did you hear from Zephan and Rona?"

"They gave us a brief recount of ... of what happened." Charlotte hesitated on almost every word, fearing that she might reignite what I had tried to put out of my mind.

"So you're aware that I wasn't able to control anyone effectively and ... that Cillian was fully aware of ... of what I was trying to do?"

"Hmm," Ethan nodded. "But, did you consider that perhaps someone was inhibiting what you were trying to do?"

"I did, yeah. Ewan thought…" Saying his name dissolved any remaining words into thin air.

"It's okay, Bee." Charlotte gave Ethan a nasty look, insisting that he stop pressuring me into reliving recent events.

"Anyway," I needed to drag my thoughts elsewhere, "How come Ethan is unrecognisable and your face and body seems to be untouched?" I patted Charlotte's dainty arm.

Charlotte rolled her eyes. "Ethan made me promise to stay out of harm's way. He said that my small frame wouldn't be able to cope with anything. But," Charlotte continued, "Ethan didn't listen to Craig's instructions to remain under Keelty's protection. No! He had to follow Craig and his men."

"I couldn't just sit back and do nothing!" Ethan spread his arms, trying to defend his actions. "I had to check out who we were dealing with, so I …"

"Wait," I stopped Ethan, "Are you talking about the mix-blooded children?"

"Yeah!" Ethan answered. "Apparently, Cillian secretly merged two clans, under the rest of Oran-Roy's noses, and has formed an army of people like you!"

"We heard it mentioned when Brogan and I were trying to free my …" Brogan! "Did you see Brogan? Was he alright?"

"Rona was looking after him when we were leaving. She said that he would be okay. They'll be hiding in Breena where it'll be safe. No one can come to harm in Breena with the Druids, remember?" Charlotte advised me.

"At least that's some good news," I mumbled, while rubbing my droopy eyes.

"Bee," Charlotte stroked my hair, "You're exhausted. You need to sleep."

"I've been asleep for almost a day, Charlotte. It's the last thing I need." Once again, I clasped onto Quinn's hand, hoping for a miracle. "What I need is to be here, with Quinn."

"Well, why not give hearing Quinn's thoughts a go, Bee?" Ethan encouraged.

"Ethan!" Charlotte was being rather overprotective. "She's been through too much!"

"No, no," I assured Charlotte, shaking my head from side to side, "It might put me at ease if I can hear that he's okay."

"But you're …"

"Charlotte!" I breathed. "It will be okay." Like an insecure child who had just been sent to the corner, Charlotte dropped her head, sunk into her chair, folded her arms and pretended not to be bothered.

My grip around Quinn's hand tightened. Looking upon his battered face, I slowly closed my eyes, picturing him and only him in my mind. Surrounding sounds quickly became muffled, as if I had submerged myself into water.

"Your father was doing what he thought was right at the time, Quinn."

A solemn female voice sent me spiralling down a dark hole. Before I saw Quinn, I heard his voice respond to the woman.

"If he had done things differently, Rowena would still be with me, mother!" Hearing Quinn's voice allowed me to visualise him, which in turn, painted the scene he was in.

Quinn was only wearing brown pants; it had appeared as though he had just come from a swim. He was lying against a rock, protruding from a cave wall – the cave that he had taken me to where we had shared our kiss.

"Sometimes we can never understand why things are as they are," Quinn's mother counselled him. *"But, you cannot let this strain you and your father's relationship! It won't help you find Rowena!"* Finally, Quinn's mother came into sight. She was a tall, slender woman, with long wavy locks of black hair that glimmered red when it came in contact with the sunrays seeping through the cracks in the rocks sheltering above. Her face was warm and genuine, as though she wouldn't hesitate to welcome a complete stranger into her arms. I could clearly see Quinn's face in hers.

"You know I'm right, son," Quinn's mother sat beside him against the rock.

"Hmm," he reluctantly agreed.

"It's not too late to fix things with your father."

"I'm not sure of that."

His mother released a heavy sigh. *"You need to, Quinn. Your father is a good man who had a moment of indecision that cost him a great deal."*

Quinn was trying desperately to disregard his mother's words, but I could see them sinking in.

"Don't cause your father to lose both of his children. If you work with him, he might gain you both back."

Quinn held his legs up to his chest and rested his chin upon his knees. *"I know you're right,"* he sighed. *"I'm ... I'm just ... just so ..."*

"...Angry with him?"

"Yes."

"Forgiving him might relieve that anger."

"I miss you." Quinn turned around and faced his mother.

"You shouldn't have to. I'm with you always." His mother opened her arms. Quinn rested his head over her shoulder. *"By the way,"* his mother's tone becoming playful as she freed Quinn from her arms, *"I like Brianna. She reminds me of myself at that age. Worship the ground she walks on, son, but not just because she is Tarmon's princess."*

"I'd love for you to meet her," Quinn smiled. *"She's stubborn, like you and just as ..."* Quinn's voice suddenly grew

faint. He and his mother blended in with the dark cave. A sharp pain ran through my forehead, thumping through my skull and dragging me out of Quinn's mind. When I opened my eyes I found myself in Quinn's hospital room, with his helpless body still lying before me and my hand still tightly clutched around his. The pain had thankfully subsided.

"Whoa." I shook my head and repeatedly opened and closed my eyes, adjusting to the light of the room.

"What did you hear?" Ethan couldn't wait for an answer.

"It seemed as though it hurt you, Brianna," Charlotte was still concerned. "Ethan!" she yelled, "I told you not to encourage her to do it!"

"I ... I didn't just hear Quinn's thoughts," I explained, "I saw what he was ... well, I think it was a dream. I felt as though I was sitting in the same scene he was."

"I'd kill to be able to do that!" Ethan was like a five-year-old boy in a young man's body.

Charlotte gave Ethan an unimpressed look. "Never mind that, what did you see?"

"Well, at first I heard a woman's voice. But, once I heard Quinn's, I pictured him and could picture everything he was seeing!"

"Where was he? Who was with him?" Ethan begged to know.

"He was … he was talking with his mother … in the cave he took me to. It's where we … well," I could feel the blood slowly rushing to my cheeks, "it was a place where his mother used to go to a lot."

"And…" Charlotte waved her hands demanding more.

"He was himself. Just speaking with his mother about his father, sister and …"

"You," Ethan said for me.

"Yeah," I blushed.

"Well," Ethan leaped up from his chair and stretched – his fingertips almost hitting the ceiling, "I'm in need of a meal. Charlotte, let's go grab something to eat."

"Brianna would want us to …"

"Charlotte," Ethan widened his eyes and looked over the rim of his glasses, "let's go and get some food."

"Oh, right," finally taking the hint, Charlotte hopped out of the chair and proceeded to the door. "I better meet my parents back in the cafeteria, anyway. I need to work on earning their trust back."

"Oh you'll be right!" Ethan's eyes rolled. "Want anything from the cafeteria, Bee?"

"Uh … actually, a packet of crisps would be really nice. I think I've forgotten what they taste like."

"Coming right up!" Ethan hurried along Charlotte into the corridor and closed the door behind him, leaving me alone with Quinn.

"Just you and me again," I sighed, stroking Quinn's arm. "Oh," I yawned, "Come to think of it, I do need sleep." As quietly as I could, I tried to lower the metal railing on Quinn's bed, but quickly realised that a loud noise brought on by a little more force wouldn't wake Quinn up. Finally, the screechy bed rail fell beside the bed, allowing me to rest my head by Quinn's arm.

My eyes, growing heavy, shut tightly, blocking out the blaring light. About to slip into a deep sleep, a tight sensation around my hand sent an uncontrollable rush of adrenalin through my veins.

My head sprung up from the thin mattress. I rubbed my eyes with my free hand and then focussed on my left hand holding Quinn's.

"Please tell me you did what I think you just did and that I wasn't dreaming?"

My eyes flickered back and forth between Quinn's face and his left hand.

"Come on, come on," I said over and over to myself. And as I had hoped for, as I wanted more than anything else in the world in that moment, Quinn's fingers tingled in my jittery hand.

Chapter Twenty-Four

'Let go'

Three months later …

"You know there is still so much of Oran-Roy to see, Brianna! You really haven't seen much of it at all."

I knew what Quinn was doing, so I decided to do my best to ignore him, pretending that I was too caught up in my own imaginings to answer.

"Brianna?" Quinn breathed, gently running his fingers through my hair. We were seated beneath my favourite oak tree, on the cliff where I had first ridden the Oran-Roy bird, admiring the crimson sky heralding the burgeoning night.

"Hmm," I sighed, closing my eyes and nestling up against Quinn's chest.

"We have to go back soon. We … we can't delay it anymore."

"I told Mam that we'd be back by dark. We've still got another fifteen minutes or so."

"I know you know that's not what I meant."

Quinn was hesitant in reminding me of what he knew, and what I was doing my best to ignore, but he also knew what was truly best for me, even when I couldn't face it myself.

Part of me wanted to go back and see my father and new friends. I wanted to solve the missing pieces to the puzzle, be brave and face what I feared. But, at the same time, going back to Oran-Roy would only remind me of the damage I had left behind – the problems that I had ultimately caused and fled from. Despite these doubts, I knew Quinn spoke the truth and no matter how long I chose to ignore reality, I would have to confront it eventually. I couldn't dodge the coming wave; I had to endure its tosses and turns, wait for the motion to subside and break through it to find comfort in calmer waters. The hardest step was to let go, allowing my body to fall into the rushing waters, with the confidence to endure its challenges and triumph.

I sighed and sat back up, holding my knees against my chest and looking out towards the sky. "I know you're right, but..."

"...But! There is no reason why we should still be here. They're waiting for us in Breena. We need to go back and show them what we have learned from Zia's writings if we are to stop Morrigan."

"Well," I was trying to delay the inevitable, aware of how this would annoy Quinn, but, at the same time, hoping that it would put his concerns to rest, "My Mam and Dad have just gotten used to Ethan and I being back. I'm almost finished my final year of school and I ..."

"Brianna!" Quinn's firm hold on my shoulder forced me to turn around and face him. "You and I have recovered and we are therefore well enough to travel back. Well, actually, we could have gone back a week or more ago."

"Yes, but ..."

"You cannot delay this!" Quinn was frustrated by my constant dismissal. "It's only going to get worse if you disregard what you know has to be done!"

I knew Quinn was right. Lost for words, I stood up and began pacing towards the house.

"Stop!" Quinn firmly clasped my wrist, jolting my senses. He yanked my arm, making me turn around and face him, but I chose to stare at the ground. "This is not the Brianna I know! This isn't the Brianna I ... I fell in love with!"

I folded my arms in a stubborn manner and continued to protest by staring at the ground and biting my lip.

"The Brianna I couldn't help but love was brave, charismatic and looked fear straight in the eye and she was ready to face what she had to!" Quinn sighed and lowered his head. "Look at me," Quinn softly spoke and gently raised my chin.

Our eyes met, and no matter how desperately I wanted to turn around and run away from Quinn's words, his eyes had a hypnotic hold over me and I couldn't turn away.

"I hate seeing you in this state, just like you hated me being in a coma. It is destroying me seeing you torture yourself over something that we had no control over!" Quinn's hand left my chin and slid up towards my cheek. "Huh," he laughed and brushed his hand across his face and hair over his forehead, "This is just like when you were telling me to not feel guilty over my sister."

"The ... the roles have reversed," I managed to give Quinn the smallest hint of a smile.

"Exactly!" he laughed. "What you saw in my mind has relieved my doubts, Brianna. Speaking with my mother has ... inspired me to carry on! So, you see? You ... you need to let go, Brianna. It was you who taught me the wisdom that I am passing onto you now!"

My eyes closed as Quinn lowered his head down against mine.

"Do you understand? You must let go. If not for yourself, do it for those who care about you."

I nodded and quickly wiped away an unexpected tear running down my cheek.

Quinn held my head and looked down into my eyes. "I will not watch you carry this burden anymore." Quinn wiped away the trickles of tears with his thumbs. "My friend, Ewan, would not want you to carry this grief with you."

My trickling tears turned into a raging stream. "I know."

Quinn pulled me into his chest and didn't release me from his comforting hold until I had stopped whimpering.

"I've become such a cry baby since I met you!" I laughed, which pleased Quinn. "I never used to be like this!"

"I'm sure I can't take all the credit for that," he wittingly replied. "Well, then," Quinn held my hand and began walking back towards the house. "Let's tell everyone that we are leaving."

"When?"

"Tomorrow afternoon."

"Oh, and Quinn?"

"Yes?"

"I saw my Mam and Dad come and have a 'chat' with you while you were in the stables the other night and ..."

"And..."

"They ... they didn't give you a hard time, did they?"

Quinn smiled. "They still have a few concerns. I told them of my intentions for you and they said that they were a little concerned about ... about how we became so close so quickly."

"What were their other concerns?"

"Don't worry about that for now."

"Quinn!"

"You'll have to speak to them, Brianna. I did all I could."

"Then why am I still worried about this?"

"You really need to work on keeping your thoughts to yourself – literally."

"I'm tempted to read your thoughts now … but, it wouldn't be right. Some … some sort of moral principle is holding me back from doing so."

"Well, it's good that you can't always rely on it at this stage. Let's keep it that way then," Quinn chuckled, but I felt as though his chuckle was in an effort to prevent me from worrying about yet another issue.

*

"Brianna! Hop under the umbrella! I don't want you getting sick from being wet in the cold air!"

"Mam!" I moaned. "I can't hold an umbrella while I'm on the bird! I'm going to get wet anyway!"

"Don't fret, love," Dad chuckled at Tara's protective pleas.

"Yeah! Brianna's got a point, Mam," Ethan agreed, as he too began walking without any protection from the light drizzle. "Charlotte! Really?" Ethan cried, humoured by Charlotte's attempts to remain dry for as long as possible, with her flimsy umbrella struggling to remain steady against the bellowing wind.

"What?" Charlotte yelled over the calling whistles of the wind.

"You call that an umbrella?" Ethan chuckled. "Besides, it's not bucketing down. It's the wind you should be worried about."

"Uh … let me help you, Charlotte," Quinn offered, taking Charlotte's pack of unnecessary knick knacks she managed to do without for almost four months in Oran-Roy.

"Thank you, Quinn," Charlotte gave Ethan a very unimpressed look. Ethan mumbled under his breath, pretending that he was not the least bit concerned, when, more than likely, he was probably telling himself off for missing yet another opportunity to impress Charlotte.

As I ventured just beyond the large oak, which Quinn had come to call his favourite space during his short time in Ireland, I turned to find my parents and companions all anticipating the arrival of the Oran-Roy bird in their own way.

Like a temperamental bird, tidying up her delicate feathers, Mam was fiddling with some loose threads on her grey cardigan; distracting herself from the thought of having to part with Ethan and myself once again and with the uncertainty of our return. Dad, however, remained calm; standing with his large hands buried in his deep coat pockets, just waiting in anticipation of what he was about to witness.

When my eyes met Charlotte's, she sighed and offered me a smile of amazement, sharing her disbelief at how we had come to find ourselves in such an inconceivable moment. Charlotte's awe ignited memories that sent shockwaves through my mind. The events of many months flickered through my mind.

Receiving the Morrigan book, and coming to discover it to be far more than a mere piece of fiction, initiated a series of inextricable events that had unfolded towards this moment, in this place, before those most dear to me.

Along the way, most of my questions, questions pleading for answers, had been quickly resolved, only to be replaced by still deeper gnawings. I came to learn who I was and where I had come from, why I had unique markings on my wrists and two different coloured eyes. I discovered an unimaginable latent talent I possessed and how it would serve me well, but at times work against me. The whereabouts of my biological parents became clear and I formed new ties with people and creatures of my homeland. One of my newly formed ties was severed. As the Kaelins had foretold, a death was upon us. When Ewan was killed, a small fragment of me died with him. Perhaps, when I find peace in what happened that surreal night, then that lost, small fragment of my soul will return to me, but, for the time being, it seemed that no words, no kindness or understanding towards me, could tend my wound.

I still had unanswered questions, gnawing away at my soul. Like a parasite sucking the life out of its host, doubts would lay dormant and then suddenly eat away at me when I failed to satisfy the need to know *why*. I was still unaware of who wrote the Morrigan book and how the carrier came to be in my possession. There was an unsettling feeling that someone was behind these events; were we pawns on a chess board, being unconsciously directed to fulfil a destiny of someone else's choosing? Is it Dallas Conlan? Who is he? Where is he? Is he still alive?

After experiencing what I had seen in a dream months earlier, was I also capable of seeing the future? With the return of Morrigan, the answers to her downfall remained in the safe hands of our friends, waiting for our return to the Oran-Roy clan of Breena. Would Zia's writings contain all the answers that we seek?

Opening the carrier and summoning the Oran-Roy bird was my next step toward quelling my remaining qualms. My hands began to shake nervously, hindering the opening of the latch to the carrier. As the emerald face popped up, the serene, melodic tune began to play, summoning for the Oran-Roy bird. When I finally looked up, I found Ethan, Charlotte and Quinn farewelling my parents.

My slow walk towards them was agonising. I had dreaded saying goodbye to Tara and Roy since I had returned home. It was too painful, considering when I would see them next, or if I would see them again. I had faced the notion of a difficult, long and tumultuous journey ahead, but never accepted how Tara and Roy would not be a part of what I now needed to fulfil in Oran-Roy.

Like a defenceless ship in search of that light on the shore in an evening storm at sea, Tara and Roy were a guiding light. They had shown me the way home and the way to happiness up until this moment; they had kept me safe. Now it was time to venture beyond this home and seek out a new light in the pursuits that Oran-Roy had waiting for me.

"You ... you be safe now!" Dad raised my chin, so that my eyes could align with his.

I nodded.

"This is ... uh..." I couldn't recall a time I had seen Dad so lost for words! "We're incredibly proud of you and your brother, Brianna." Dad held my shoulders. "Hold onto what's important to you, no matter what happens. Just be safe and look after one another."

My eyes were becoming glassy. Once again, I nodded, then buried my head into Dad's chest and wrapped my arms around his waist. Dad stroked my hair until a tap on my right shoulder forced me to turn around.

"I'm not very good at saying goodbye, love," Mam spread her arms, inviting me in for one final embrace.

"I'll miss you too, Mam," a small tear fell down my cheek as Tara's arms pulled me into her chest.

"Be safe, my love," Mam's quivering hands patted my hair repeatedly. "Just be safe. May God be with you all."

Without warning, a powerful stream of air forced us to the ground, like an incoming wave. Finding our feet again, we turned to the cliff's edge.

The Oran-Roy bird's emerald green feathers shimmered in the setting sun's rays. Its wings beat the air with surprising grace, contradicting its enormous presence. With the rush of air pushing us into the ground from the Oran-Roy bird, as well as the chilling wind off the ocean that caused us to cringe, it seemed as though a higher authority was urging us to move on. It didn't take us long to follow through on the hint and we quickly gathered up our carry bags and headed straight for the bird.

Quinn and Ethan remained by the bird's side and carefully hoisted Charlotte and myself upon its smooth back. Charlotte and I latched onto the feathers as tightly as we could, as Quinn and Ethan positioned themselves directly behind us.

Whoosh!

The sudden rush of air raised us from the earth; I felt as though my body was still on the ground.

As we were gradually being raised higher and higher into the twilight sky, finally making our way to the coast of Breena, I attempted to find Mam and Dad between the flapping of the bird's wings. I offered them a final farewell with a cautious wave of my right hand.

Nestled up side by side, like two penguins trying to keep warm, Tara and Roy waved me and my friends an agonising goodbye as they gradually diminished into nothing more than small specks against a carpet of green.

*

"It's almost time," Donelle said, as she joined me by the base of the Oran-Roy tree, watching the sun make its journey over the distant horizon to christen the new day.

"I'm *never* going to be ready for this. I … I thought I could do this … but I … I can't. I'm *not* ready for …"

"…Saying goodbye?" Donelle reassured me, gently resting her white-gloved hand upon my own. "No one is *ever* ready for something as great as this, Brianna." Donelle raised her hand from mine and began fiddling with her golden brown locks of hair. "Hmmm," she sighed, "I *never* had the opportunity to say goodbye to Cuchulainn." Donelle stood up, glanced towards the rising sun and then back down to me. "Ewan needs to know that you are at peace with his act, Brianna, otherwise, he might decide to remain here and not be led by the Arawn pack into the next world."

Donelle reached down, clasped my hands and invited me to stand. "Let him know that *you* want him to have peace."

"I *know* you're right. I just can't help thinking that if I had handled things differently, perhaps this wouldn't have …"

Donelle shook her head. "Even mixed-bloods, gifted with skills unfathomable to most, are incapable of knowing what *might* have been." Donelle released my hands and began walking down the stone steps at the foot of the tree. "Ewan would not want you to endure a life of regret, when he chose to sacrifice his own life for the purpose of saving yours." Donelle continued on down the stone steps and left me to ponder her profound words.

A latch in my brain had finally been opened! My body fell against the trunk of the tree and slid down it until I reached the damp earth.

"I've been so selfish!" I repeated over and over in my head, burying my head in my hands. *"Ewan saved my life and here I am forgetting the fact that without his act I wouldn't be here!"*

"Argh!" I gritted my teeth and clenched the moist ground, ripping a chunk of the earth and throwing it over the cliff edge. *"Once again, Brianna, you've neglected to look at the bigger picture!"*

"You *really* need to work on keeping your thoughts to yourself, Brianna." Quinn's sudden presence made me leap up from the floor. Once over the shock, I faced the sun, now beaming well over the horizon, and folded my arms.

Quinn's arms came from behind me and held my tense, folded arms. His touch still seemed to send me into a lapse of surreal contentment; no matter how well you try, words cannot truly capture how overwhelming and powerful a loving embrace is for the soul. I closed my eyes and let my head lean back against his strong chest; his warm breath now blowing against the right side of my neck.

"You don't need to say anything, Quinn," I explained through thoughts, feeling as though he wanted to offer me some final words of encouragement to face saying goodbye. *"You, just being here, right now, is all I need."*

Quinn released me, turned me around and held my hand. When our eyes met, he smiled and began leading me away from the sun and down the steps to Ewan.

*

The blanket of mist covering the valley of the Oran-Roy clan and the cool, icy droplets of water falling so effortlessly from the sombre sky, were indicative of the emotions of all whom stood by Ewan's body, veiled by a white cloth. The sun was no longer visible – all warmth and happiness had left this place. In this moment, no sun existed for me. It was going to take some time before a sun would breach my horizon and warm my soul. Quinn's warm embrace, refusing to release me, Charlotte and Ethan's presence at my side, as well as Craig, Zephan and Rona's nods of support amongst the crowd farewelling Ewan, were slowly encouraging my sun to rise and triumph over the tumultuous perils it must face, returning some long-anticipated warmth to my life.

To my surprise, I had no tears – my eyes had been drained.

"Brianna." I flinched! Very quickly, I looked around, immediately realising that no one was looking at me. *"Who had said that?"* A cool air blew at my neck, an awful chilling sensation made my entire right side tingle, encouraging Quinn to hold me tighter. He looked down to meet my eyes and offered me a sincere expression of worry.

I nodded, assuring him that I was fine.

"I am not hearing voices now!" I assured myself. *"Not now!"*

Unexpectedly, the druids of Oran-Roy, led by Donelle, hidden beneath long, green, velvety robes, began processing down the stone steps from the base of the Oran-Roy tree. Gradually they emerged one by one from a curtain of mist at the base of the hill amidst the large congregation of people. Their sudden procession, as well as the melodic, solemn hymn they began to hum, which sent a peaceful echo through the valley, distracted me from the voice I had thought I heard call my name.

At the base of Ewan's veiled body, rested a woven basket, filled with stones. As Donelle made a pathway through the mass of people, she removed her hood with her gloved hands and, when she reached the basket beside Ewan, she stopped and looked upon the congregation to address them.

"Please offer Ewan a stone, allowing him to be escorted from this place, to a greater place, where he will find true peace." Donelle reached into the basket, clasped a small stone, then, with such grace and reverence, paced towards Ewan's veiled head, and laid the stone by him. "Lui ar sa síocháin, Ewan."

"It means, *rest in peace*," Quinn whispered in my ear.

After Donelle had offered a stone to Ewan, the other druids began to sing a familiar melody – The Carrier's Song.

You have the will to seek me
But do not fear me
I come to you as a passage of peace
I come to you as a means of peace

Whenever you call I shall come
For I am the Carrier that will always come
I will always return you home
I will always return you home

Just call me and sing my song
And whenever you hear my call
Whenever you feel my presence
Know I shall never abandon you

For I am the Carrier
I am the Carrier
For I am the carrier that brings you home
I am the Carrier

I am true

The peaceful tune ricocheted throughout the valley, sending chills up my spine as more and more people began to join in. After the tune had come to an end, the druids, as well as other members of the congregation gathered and began to repeat the melody, but this time in Gaelic. As the song continued, people began leaving their places to offer up Ewan a stone of peace for the next world.

"Brianna."

Quinn, still holding me, felt me jolt as I heard the voice I was doing my best to ignore.

"*What is it?*" he whispered into my ear, with great concern.

"I ... *uh* ..." I left Quinn's embrace and looked around me, but could not find anyone looking at me! All I could see were people forming circles around Ewan's body, preparing to offer him up a stone. My breathing was growing rapid and my heart wanted to break out of my chest!

Frantically, I brushed passed Quinn and beyond the few members of the congregation behind us and looked into the nearby trees of the Breena woods, bordering Oran-Roy.

"Why is she going over there?" I heard Charlotte cry out from beyond the forests' edge.

"*Brianna.*"

The voice seemed louder this time, and sent me further into the Breena woods, so keen to find the source of the voice that the forest sounds were drowned out by my thumping heart. As I parted the shrubs and flicked away prickly branches, no sound followed. The leaves failed to respond to me.

"*Brianna.*"

I gasped and turned to face the voice directly behind me. All I saw was a measly, old shrub. Its leaves had turned golden in colour and had become crispy with age.

"*Come.*" The voice called, from behind the shrub.

Too alarmed to speak, or to ask the voice who he was and lost in my need for answers, I didn't question what I was about to do. I didn't hesitate. The thirst of putting my confusion to rest made me unconsciously part the crumbling shrub, venture through it and come face to face with what was awaiting me on the other side.

As I rushed through the decaying remnants of the shrub, its old, thin branches, with dagger-like edges, pierced my skin. Too immersed in what awaited me, I chose not to acknowledge the pain of my newly formed cuts and I pressed on. Almost completely free of the shrub, my foot became wedged between two coiling branches. With as much force as I could possibly conjure, I attempted to heave out my foot.

CRACK!

My heave was successful, but resulted in me falling through the remaining set of crisp leaves and diving face first into the damp earth on the other side of the shrub. I raised my head, flicked the hair from my eyes and turned to face the shrub before leaving the ground.

A gentle breeze swept through the tiny forest opening and as the breeze danced through the remaining leaves of the shrub, the crimson leaves opened out and turned an emerald green. Shocked and weary, I scurried away from the shrub, with my back against the damp soil, like a crab avoiding being swept up by the tide.

"Brianna." Cuchulainn sighed.

The slight hint of humour in his voice put my fears to rest; I quickly leapt from the earth and turned to face my guardian.

"The *whole* time it was you?" I rolled my eyes, realising that there was no need for my worry.

But, to my surprise Cuchulainn said nothing.

"It … it *wasn't* you?" I asked.

Cuchulainn simply shook his head, smiled and then began walking out of the clearing and into the forest.

"But…?"

Cuchulainn stopped just before reaching the nearby shrubs; he turned and smiled at me as the clearing became illuminated. With the sudden rush of light, Cuchulainn was almost invisible – his body blending in with the white light. Small rays of light managed to make their way through the gaps of the trees circling the clearing; with great surprise, the leaves within the clearing began to flap, resembling butterflies, but, there was no wind! I couldn't hear the whistling calls of the breeze or feel its gentle, cool touch against my face. How were the leaves moving without wind?

Branch by branch, leaves began falling from the trees in pairs – gracefully spiralling down towards the ground and forming a spiral in the clearing's centre. The small tornado of flapping leaves rose from the earth – the wind so powerful, it was difficult to remain on my feet.

Bright light dispersed between the rushes of the spiralling leaves – so bright I found myself shielding my eyes. Then, the noise stopped, begging me to lower my arms; to take a curious peek of what had become of the lively leaves.

I lowered my arms, reluctantly opened my eyes and, while adjusting to the now dim light engulfing the dwelling, a luminous figure, shrouded in the once swirling leaves, emerged before me. Taken aback, I took a few steps towards the clearing's edge, but my eyes could not leave the floating figure, too transfixed and too desperate to learn the identity of the being before me.

Finally, the fixated hold the figure had over me subsided. Quickly, I turned to Cuchulainn, urging him to offer me words of wisdom – something to inform me of the purpose behind this phenomenal sight! But, all he did was to offer me a smile and a simple gesture towards the luminous, leafy figure.

Meeting the floating figure's warm expression, extreme contentment consumed my chest – unlocking regret's overbearing hold over me – I found lightness from within, an ability to breathe with such ease!

"*Ewan!*" I whispered, as relieved tears fell from my eyes and trickled across my flushed cheeks.

Ewan's spirit smiled, nodded, but then shook his head; the glowing leaves guided his luminous body down towards me. His white hand reached for my face, then held my chin. His left hand, which felt joyously warm against my cheek, wiped away a falling tear. His warm hands then held my face; his head fell and rested down against mine. A warm sensation swelled down my left side, as Ewan's right hand found my heart.

Overcome with warmth and a surreal sensation of peace, I closed my eyes; the burden of remorse, hatred and fear I had carried with me for far too long was leaving me. Ewan's warmth dispersed throughout my entire body, consuming the painful parasite of regret. Ewan was begging me to let go – to use the gift of his life to persevere and fulfil the task ahead.

Becoming cool again, I opened my eyes to find Ewan fading away into the leaves and into the forest dwelling's dim light. But something was forcing him to resist the pull of the light. I offered Ewan a smile of thanks, a promise that I would remember his sacrifice and choose to live. Now satisfied with the warmth and peace within my soul, Ewan smiled. The leaves moulded into a pack of dogs – the Arawn pack – while the hazy silhouettes of the Prislens gathered in the distance, waiting to guide Ewan into the next world.

A final burst of light poured in through the trees, engulfing the clearing and, as it grew faint and left the clearing dim, the Arawn pack, Cuchulainn and Ewan journeyed away, guided by the healing warmth of the light.

*

One week later ...

"I thought I would find you here," I cried, excited to find Quinn in the clearing where Ewan had come to me. "I finally realised that I can achieve what I put in this prayer box Ethan gave me."

"What's that?" Quinn left the floor to greet me.

"I've always had a love of stories and writing," I explained, while fiddling with the now enclosed prayer box dangling from my neck alongside the carrier chain. "I'm going to write about us, this place. I have a need to share what's happened here, but in a way that conceals this place. A way that ..."

"I understand," Quinn smiled.

I gently ran my hand up Quinn's arm, sensing that he was troubled. "Are you all right? I think you've had your head buried in Zia's writings."

"It's not the writings," Quinn sighed, as I leant against him and held his arm. "It's mostly just being here ... It's *my* way of feeling closer to him ... to Ewan."

"I only wish that you were here with me ... when he came to me..." I sighed.

"...No," Quinn quickly breathed and then turned to face me. "Ewan needed your guilt relieved. I'm glad he appeared to you. Even in Oran-Roy, Brianna, a place full of occurrences beyond most peoples' reckoning, what you experienced was very special indeed." Quinn held my hand and we left the clearing, on our way to celebrate Brogan's initiation into Oran-Roy.

"Hold onto that moment," Quinn whispered, then lowered his head and brushed aside my hair to kiss my cheek as we were heading on out of the Breena woods to fetch our horses.

"The main reason I'm thankful for Ewan appearing to me, is ... well ... *aside* from relieving me of my guilt, I feel like ... I have more hope and more ... faith and reason to do what still needs to be done."

"Before I had a look, your father was studying Zia's writings more closely this morning and ..."

"...Anything new?" I spoke over Quinn, eager to hear if there had been any more breakthroughs.

"Sadly ... no, but, Ethan and Charlotte had a good look too and ..."

"But, his writings are mostly related to Oran-Roy. When we looked at it back in Ireland there wasn't much we knew, other than the photos of Zia at famous locations. There wouldn't be much myself or Ethan and Charlotte would be able to ..."

"...Ah!" Quinn interjected. "Don't dismiss your friends so easily!" Quinn chuckled.

"Wait ... they found something? A lead? What?" I was very lucky that Quinn could tolerate my impatience.

"Well, Ethan seemed to think that some of the answers to what may have happened to Morrigan's possessions may be related to those photos."

"Whoa!" I grabbed Quinn's arm just as we had reached horses. "Ethan believes that some of the writings lead to places outside Oran-Roy?"

"Yes!" Quinn laughed. "Brianna, we really must …"

"Wait! How didn't I consider this before?"

"Brianna we're …"

"Zia had the Carrier! So, Ethan could be right! Perhaps Zia used it to place Morrigan's …"

"Brianna!" Quinn clasped onto my wrist, snapping me out of my newly formed fixation and thoughts. "Brogan's ceremony! We really must go!" He chuckled, finding humour in my excitement over my recent discovery. Then, without consulting me, Quinn picked me up in order to ride Epona to rush back for Brogan's initiation.

"Hey!" I laughed, as Quinn released me upon Epona's back.

"We are in a hurry!" Quinn chuckled again, while mounting his horse.

"Just for that …" I cried and pulled back on Epona's reigns, ploughing her on through the remainder of the Breena woods. "I'll race you back! And the loser …"

"…Has to clean the other's armour!" Quinn cried out jovially, as he galloped on passed me.

"You're on!" I cried, heaving Epona up the steep slope, catching Quinn and his horse with every stride.

Epilogue

Only the Beginning

"Ms Shield, can you tell us how you formed the story? Where did the initial ideas stem from?" A rather plump, fair-haired woman asked from the front row of reporters.

"Well, it was only when I was seventeen or eighteen, when I found a strong love for writing and literature. That was when I considered writing my own story."

"Yes, but what inspired this particular story?"

The camera flashes and immense array of people stretching out their microphones towards me upon the small platform suddenly overwhelmed me, delaying my answer. For the first time, it truly dawned on me that I had achieved my goal. I was a writer and now a published author. Before returning my attention back to the reporters, awaiting my responses, I raised my hand up to the small, intricate box, dangling from a chain around my neck that I had received from Ethan eleven years ago.

"It's happened." I said to myself. *"I did it."*

"Ms Shield?" The fair-haired, plump reporter called impatiently, as though she was offended by my delayed response; a journalist's subtle way of reminding me of their question.

"Oh, yes … well, when I was eighteen I received a book titled 'Morrigan', which you're all aware of, and I just couldn't put it down! I was disappointed to realise that the story ended there! So, I decided to dabble with the story in my own way. My parents were fans of the novel when they were young and that's why I was named after one of the characters in 'Morrigan'."

A young, tall, bearded reported, over towards the left hand side of the mass of people, questioned me. "Is that why you have the tattoos on your wrists? … Because you were such an admirer of the 'Morrigan' story and you wanted to emulate the characters?"

"Yes," I lied. *If only they knew…*"I thought that it was a nice way for me to acknowledge the world the anonymous author created, as well as the characters."

A small, petite woman with glasses, wearing a pinstriped suit, squeezed her way to the front line of reporters and asked, "Were you able to track the author down? Was the name used by the author able to provide you with any leads?"

Before answering, I removed my red glasses and placed them on the podium. "Unfortunately, all of the detective work I did was unsuccessful." *Another lie!* "Uh, next question please …"

I still wasn't used to this!

"How does it feel to have your first novel as an international best seller?" I wasn't sure who asked this question, but I answered.

"Uh, I … I don't think it has really sunk in as of yet, but I'm *extremely* appreciative of everyone who has assisted me in publishing it."

After the initial questions, journalists were now beginning to speak over the top of one-another. I then realised that I had to select one person when that happened. "Ah, yes," I signalled to a brunet woman with short, curly hair.

"The names used within your story are names of *real* people within your life, correct?"

"Yes, that's true," I quickly replied, trying to satisfy the mass of reporters.

I quickly turned towards my publicist, over to my right and she gave me a subtle nod and looked over the rim of her glasses. Her way of advising me to take only one more question; she liked to keep the press on their toes.

"Uh, only one more question, please."

"Ms Shield! Ms Shield!"

"Is it true that…?"

"Was it…?"

"Are you…?"

The questions were moulding into one eruption of sound! Amongst the chaos, I decided to tune in on some of the internal questions.

"Where are you currently residing after this sudden fame?"

"Are you and your family accustomed to all this attention yet?"

It turned out that they were not at all that different to ones being screamed at me.

"Yes, uh ... you please," I signalled for a bald man close to the back of the reporters, ending the mayhem.

"Thank you, Ms Shield. Are you planning on continuing with the 'Oran-Roy' book series? You did leave the book open for a continuing story! Will we be seeing more books in the near future? Is this only the beginning of more stories to come?"

"Well," I sighed, "I can answer yes to all of those questions." The reporters were almost crawling onto the stage, trying to drag out more! "I'm intending on continuing the story of Brianna and ... well, yes ... this ... I guess you could say that this is only the beginning for Brianna."

A Chronology of Oran-Roy

- *Darren unlocks the Magic of Daghdha*
- *The Oran-Roy Bird transports Darren's people to Oran-Roy*
- *The Oran-Roy clans are formed*
- *Darren weds Glynn and rules over Oran-Roy*
- *Darren and Glynn have a daughter, Donelle*
- *Half-blood children exhibit rare gifts*
- *The Druids are commissioned in Breena*
- *The Hall of Heroes is erected*
- *Delaney unleashes the Morrigan Beast*
- *Cuchulainn and Donelle wed and flee to Ireland*
- *Keith is born*
- *Darren presents Donelle with the carrier*
- *Delano rules over Oran-Roy and captures the mixed-bloods*
- *Donelle and the Druids prepare Keith to rule as a Tarmon King*
- *Morrigan ensures the demise of the remaining mixed-bloods*
- *Morrigan curses Donelle and kills Cuchulainn*

- *The Druids bind Morrigan*
- *Keith is King of Oran-Roy*
- *Mixed-bloods return*
- *Zia is crowned King*
- *A mix-blooded child takes refuge in Ireland*

THE CARRIER